SWEET TEA REVENGE

SWEET TEA REVENGE

Tea Shop Mystery #14

LAURA CHILDS

BERKLEY PRIME CRIME, NEW YORK

THE BERKLEY PUBLISHING GROUP
Published by the Penguin Group
Penguin Group (USA) Inc.
375 Hudson Street, New York, New York 10014, USA

USA / Canada / UK / Ireland / Australia / New Zealand / India / South Africa / China

Penguin Books Ltd., Registered Offices: 80 Strand, London WC2R 0RL, England
For more information about the Penguin Group, visit penguin.com.

This book is an original publication of The Berkley Publishing Group

Berkley Prime Crime hardcover ISBN: 978-0-425-25288-8

An application to register this book for cataloging has been
submitted to the Library of Congress.

FIRST EDITION: March 2013

PRINTED IN THE UNITED STATES OF AMERICA

10   9   8   7   6   5   4   3   2   1

Cover illustraion by Stephanie Henderson.
Cover design by Lesley Worrell.

ACKNOWLEDGMENTS

Heartfelt thanks to Sam, Tom, Amanda, Bob, Jennie, Dan, and all the fine folks at Berkley Prime Crime who handle design, publicity, copywriting, bookstore sales, and gift sales. A special shout-out to all tea lovers, tea shop owners, bookstore folk, librarians, reviewers, magazine writers, websites, radio stations, and bloggers who have enjoyed the adventures of the Indigo Tea Shop gang and who help me keep it going. Thank you, thank you, thank you!

And to you, dear readers, I promise many more books to come.

SWEET TEA REVENGE

1

Rain slashed against stained-glass windows and thunder shook the rafters as Theodosia Browning hurried up the back staircase of Ravencrest Inn. Her long, peach-colored bridesmaid's dress swished about her ankles as she balanced a giant box of flowers that had just been delivered to the inn's back door. It was the second Saturday in June, the morning of her friend Delaine Dish's wedding. Normally, Charleston, South Carolina, was awash in sunshine and steamy heat this time of year. But today, this day of all days, a nasty squall had blown in from the Atlantic, parked itself over the city, and turned everything into a soggy morass. Including, unfortunately, the bride's temper.

Theodosia reached the top step and stumbled, almost catching her heel in the hem of her dress. Then she quickly righted herself.

"Delaine!" she called breathlessly. "Your flowers have arrived."

Delaine Dish rushed out into the dark hallway and threw up her arms in a gesture of sheer panic. "Finally! And, can you believe it, the power's gone out twice already!"

"I know, I know," said Theodosia, trying to minimize the problem. "They lit candles downstairs for the guests. So all the parlors look quite dreamy and atmospheric." She hustled past Delaine, carrying the cumbersome box into the suite of rooms that Delaine was using for her dressing room. The groom, Dougan Granville, was cloistered in his own suite of rooms down the long, dark corridor.

"How does my bouquet look?" asked a jittery Delaine, as Theodosia carefully opened the box.

"Hang on a minute." Theodosia was practically as nervous as Delaine. All the bouquets had been ordered from Floradora, a florist she had recommended and often counted on to create distinctive centerpieces for her own Indigo Tea Shop over on Church Street.

"So many delays," worried Delaine, as another flash of lightning strobed, giving the room the flickering, jittering look of an old-time black-and-white movie. "My guests must be getting restless."

"Not to worry," said Theodosia. "Last I looked, Drayton and Haley were serving peach and ginger tea accompanied by miniature cream scones. So your guests were happy as clams." She lifted the bridal bouquet, a lovely arrangement of orchids, tea roses, and Queen Anne's lace, from its tissue paper wrapping and handed it to Delaine. "Here you go. And it's perfect."

"It is, isn't it," said Delaine, smiling as she accepted the bouquet. She stepped over to a full-length mirror and peered into its murky depths. "How do I look?"

"Beautiful," said Theodosia. And she meant it. She and Delaine had had their differences over the years, but today Delaine looked positively radiant. Her ivory, strapless ball gown–style wedding dress, with its delicate ruched bodice, served to highlight her dark hair and extraordinary coloring and set off her thin figure perfectly.

Delaine stretched a hand out to Theodosia. "Come over here, you."

Theodosia joined Delaine at the mirror and stared at her own reflection in the pitted glass. With masses of curly auburn hair to contend with, Theodosia sometimes projected the aura of a Renaissance woman captured in portrait by Raphael or even Botticelli. She had a smooth peaches-and-cream complexion and intense blue eyes, and she often wore the slightly bemused look of a self-sufficient woman—a woman who, in her midthirties, had found herself to be a successful entrepreneur, possessed a fair amount of life experiences, and had hooked up with a nice boyfriend to boot. So life was good.

Delaine patted her dark, upswept hair and her eyes glittered. She was a successful business owner, too, with her upscale Cotton Duck boutique. But she was of a predatory nature, always on the prowl for the next new experience or thrill. Theodosia, on the other hand, had found contentment. Her tea shop was cozy, charming, and always stuffed to the rafters with good friends and guests. And Drayton and Haley, her two dear friends, worked alongside her.

Delaine turned from the mirror and shrugged. Her nerves were starting to fizz again and she could barely stand still. She whirled one way, then the other, and asked, "Have you seen my sister? Where on earth is Nadine?"

"I know," said Theodosia. "She's late." Then again, Nadine was perpetually late.

"That woman would be late to her own funeral!" Delaine spat out.

There was a *clump-clump* from out in the hallway, and then an overly chirpy cry of, "Here I am!" Nadine charged into the room, looking damp, self-absorbed, and not one bit apologetic. "Sorry to be late," she chortled. "But did you know Bay Street was actually flooded? My cabdriver had to detour for *miles*!"

Delaine's mouth fell open as she stared in horror at her sister, who was practically a spitting image of her, if not a couple of pounds heavier. Nadine brushed drops of rain from her khaki trench coat as she struggled with the handle of a pink paisley umbrella.

"Close that umbrella!" Delaine cried.

Nadine stopped fussing, frowned distractedly, then stared down at the damp, half-open umbrella that was clutched in her hands. "What's wrong now?" she asked.

"Don't you know it's bad luck!" cried Delaine. "You *never* open an umbrella in the house." Delaine was a big believer in signs, portents, and superstitions.

"Sorry," Nadine mumbled. Then added, in a more acerbic tone, "But in case you hadn't noticed, it's raining buckets outside!"

"I noticed," said Delaine, gritting her teeth. "Really, do you think I *planned* for bad weather? Do you think I called the National Weather Service and asked for the *precise* day on which we were going to have a deluge of biblical proportions?"

Nadine stiffened as she struggled with her umbrella. "You don't have to be so snippy!"

"Whatever," said Delaine, turning away from her.

Not wanting to get dragged into a sister-versus-sister fight, Theodosia continued to unpack the five smaller bouquets made up of tea roses and chamomile. These, too, were perfectly composed. Dainty and fragrant and frothy with blooms.

"Maybe you could take these bouquets into the next room," Theodosia suggested to Nadine. "And give them to the other bridesmaids."

"I suppose," sighed Nadine, whose nose was still out of joint.

When she was finally alone with Delaine, Theodosia said, "Okay, what else do you need?" She was finding maid-of-honor duties to be more trouble than she'd ever imagined. Good thing it would all be over in a matter of hours.

Delaine did a little pirouette, letting her enormous skirt billow out around her. Then she peered into the mirror again. "I really look okay?"

"Gorgeous," said Theodosia, trying to stifle a yawn. She'd been up late, helping to decorate and arrange seating in the downstairs Fireplace Room.

"I do feel we could have used a touch more planning," said Delaine.

"It is what it is," said Theodosia. "You had such a short engagement." *Like about four weeks.*

"Which is why I had to settle for this place," said Delaine, her mouth suddenly downcast.

"It's lovely," said Theodosia. Truth be told, Ravencrest Inn, with its old-world cypress paneling, narrow hallways, and looming presence in the Historic District, was dark and a trifle shabby. The rooms were claustrophobic and furnished with mismatched pieces, and the plumbing clanked noisily. But Delaine had pushed everything ahead at warp speed so she could hastily tie the knot with one of Charleston's top attorneys. It was your basic Southern shotgun wedding without the baby.

"Did you see this place even has a widow's walk?" said Delaine.

"Which makes it quaint," said Theodosia.

"It's a dump," replied Delaine.

"But this is a pretty room," said Theodosia, trying to find one small spark of joy. Delaine was flitting about the room like a crazed hummingbird: dipping, sipping, constantly in motion.

"You think?" said Delaine. She pointed to a shelf of antique dolls that stared blankly out at them. "Look at that. Another silly collection."

"I find it interesting," said Theodosia, "that every room has been themed with a different collection. Teapots, dolls, angels, leather-bound books, you name it."

"But you know how I feel about dolls in particular," said Delaine, tapping her foot.

"I really *don't* know," said Theodosia. *But I have a feeling you're going to tell me.*

"They're horribly creepy," said Delaine. "With their glassy little eyes and puckered rubber faces. And, look." She pointed a pink-enameled finger at the offending shelf. "There's even a bride doll swathed in ghastly, frayed lace. Makes me think of *Bride of Chucky* or something nasty like that."

"This is not what you should be fretting about on your wedding day," said Theodosia, determined to stay upbeat. "Come on over here and let's pin your veil on."

Delaine ghosted across the room. "You know, I had a fight with Dougan this morning."

Theodosia gathered up a long veil of French lace and held it a few inches above Delaine's swirl of dark hair. "That's probably normal. Frayed nerves and all that."

"Don't you want to know what it was about?" asked Delaine.

Theodosia knew when she was being goaded. "Not really." She centered the veil, then set it carefully on Delaine's head and gently spread the sides of the veil over her bare shoulders.

"Dougan wants to cut the honeymoon short," said Delaine. "Because of work. We screamed and hollered; I'm quite sure everyone here heard us."

Theodosia picked up Delaine's bouquet and shoved it into her friend's twitching hands. "Time to get you married."

Could I be any chirpier? she wondered. *Could I be in any more of a hurry to jump-start this wedding?* "Let's get you and your lovely bridesmaids lined up at the top of the staircase so we can do any and all final adjustments. Then you, my dear, shall make the world's grandest entrance in front of your guests."

The lights flickered once again and thunder crackled as five bridesmaids, one maid of honor, and a nervous bride gathered at the top of the stairs.

"Remember," Theodosia told the bridesmaid at the front of the pack, a distant cousin of Delaine's who was supposed to lead the procession. "As soon as you hear that first note of music . . ."

Swish, swish, chuff. Someone was hurrying up the back staircase. They all turned, en masse, silk and lace rustling, to look.

It was Drayton Conneley, Theodosia's tea expert and dear friend. Dressed in a slim, European-cut tuxedo with a plaid cummerbund, Drayton's patrician face was drawn and slightly flushed beneath his mane of gray hair. Despite his normally quiet reserve, his eyes were crinkled with worry.

Theodosia hastened over to meet him. "What's wrong?" she whispered.

Drayton put a hand to his chest to still his beating heart. He was edging into his high sixties and not used to bounding up two flights of stairs like a crazed gazelle. "We have a problem."

"No lights?" asked Theodosia.

"No groom," said Drayton.

"Typical." Delaine's voice floated out behind them. "He's probably holed up in his room texting away. Dealing with some important client or political bigwig." She sighed deeply. "That's my Dougan. Always puts his work first."

Before Delaine could get any snappier, Theodosia said, "I'll take care of this. I'll go get him."

"Please," said Delaine, in an arch tone.

"Thank you," said Drayton, turning on his heels and disappearing back downstairs.

Theodosia flew down the narrow hallway to Dougan Granville's room. Interestingly enough, Granville was her next-door neighbor. Her home, her quaint Hansel and Gretel–style cottage in the heart of the Historic District, had once been part of his larger, more grand estate.

She rapped on the door of Granville's suite. "Dougan, it's time," she called out. Theodosia knew he was a hard-driving attorney who was probably working right up until the last millisecond.

Nothing. No movement, no answer.

Theodosia leaned forward and put an ear to the door. Maybe he was . . . slightly indisposed? Could it be that he really was a nervous bridegroom?

"Dougan? Mr. Granville? It's Theodosia. We're all waiting for you."

Still nothing.

Wondering what protocol she should observe for something like this, Theodosia hesitated for a few moments, then decided it didn't much matter. Guests were waiting; it was time to get moving. She gripped the doorknob and turned it, then pushed the door open a good six inches.

"Dougan," she called again, trying to inject a little humor in her voice. "We have an impatient bride who's waiting for her handsome groom."

There was no sound, save the monotonous drumming of rain on the roof and the gurgling of water as it rushed through the downspouts.

Theodosia pushed the door all the way open and stepped across the threshold.

"Dougan?"

The room was completely dark and ominously quiet.

Straight ahead, she could just make out a faint outline of heavy velvet draperies pulled across a bay window.

Did Granville fall asleep? He must have. Wow, this is one relaxed guy on his wedding day.

Shadows capered on the walls as she stepped past a looming wardrobe and pieces of furniture. The room had a strange electrical smell, as if an outside transformer had exploded. Theodosia tiptoed across the carpet, her silk mules whispering softly. When she reached the foot of the bed, she stared. A tiny bedside lamp shone a small circle of warmth on a battered bedside table, but there was no one lying on the bed. Nothing had creased the dusty pink coverlet.

What on earth?

Flustered, nervous now that they might have a runaway groom on their hands, Theodosia fumbled with the curtains and ripped them open. Lightning flashed outside, a sharp blade cutting through a wall of purple-black clouds.

Still, this is better. A little more light.

Just as Theodosia turned, something caught her eye. A fleeting image that she couldn't quite process but one that unnerved her anyway. She slowly retraced her footsteps. Back to the sitting room area that had been in total darkness, as thunder boomed like kettle drums in some unholy symphony.

That was when she saw him.

Dougan Granville was sprawled on a brocade fainting couch. His eyes were squeezed shut; his head had fallen forward until his chin rested heavily on his chest. On the small glass table in front of him was an empty glassine envelope and a scatter of white powder.

Theodosia tiptoed closer, her heart hammering in her chest, her brain shouting screams of protest. An unwanted shot of adrenaline sparked by surprise and fear had sent her blood pressure zooming. Still, she was mesmerized, hypnotized, at what she was seeing.

Was Granville just stoned? Or . . . something worse?

Theodosia moved closer and stretched out a tentative hand. The very tips of her fingers brushed the pulse point of his neck. Granville felt ice cold and lifeless. There was no pulse, no respiration.

Revulsion and fear rose up inside her like sulfurous magma from a roiling volcano. Theodosia understood, logically and viscerally, that Granville hadn't just fainted on this fainting couch like genteel ladies of old.

This man was seriously, catastrophically, dead.

2

Brilliant light strobed over Theodosia's right shoulder. Startled, she whirled around. Bill Glass, the sneaky, greasy publisher of the *Shooting Star* gossip tabloid, was standing there, hunched forward as he eagerly snapped photos!

Theodosia threw up an arm in startled protest. "Stop that! Stop it immediately!"

Glass, as local paparazzi, couldn't care less. "Relax, baby," he snarled. "This is pure gold. This is the kind of shot a guy like me dreams about."

Angered at his insensitivity, Theodosia got physical with him. She thrust out both hands and shoved Glass so hard he lost his balance and bounced against the door frame.

"Take it easy," cautioned Glass. "You're gonna break my camera!"

"Are you not hearing me?" Theodosia hissed. "Get out of here immediately!"

Glass retreated one step but raised his camera. "Don't

you get it? I'm *supposed* to be here. I was hired to take pictures. I was promised an exclusive!"

"Maybe on the wedding," said Theodosia. "But certainly not on someone's *death*!"

Bill Glass scrunched his face into a look of keen interest. "Is he dead? Are you sure about that?" He was a brusque-looking man with slicked-back hair and olive skin. Today, instead of his de rigueur khaki photo journalist vest he wore a wrinkled sharkskin suit, his one concession to the occasion.

Startled, Theodosia turned to stare at Dougan Granville again. "I *think* he's dead."

Glass pulled out his cell phone and waggled it at her. "Then maybe I should call 911?"

"Do that," said Theodosia, finally facing the fact they had a genuine emergency on their hands. "While I . . ." She didn't want to finish her sentence. She didn't want to finish her thought. Because she knew it was going to be up to her to deal with Delaine.

I'm going to tell Delaine what? That her husband tooted up on cocaine and overdosed?

Bad idea. Because as damning as the evidence looked, maybe that wasn't what had really happened.

Maybe.

As soon as Glass finished his call, Theodosia grabbed him by the lapels and shook him with all her strength. "Don't you dare take one more photo," she ordered. "Stay right here, close the door, and do not let a single living soul inside this room until the police and paramedics arrive." She shot him a warning gaze. "Do you hear me? Can you do that?"

"Bet your life, sweetheart," said Glass. He seemed almost amused by her anger and fury.

"And don't you dare take another photo."

"Yeah, yeah." He waved a hand at her.

"I'm going to go talk to the bride," said Theodosia, steeling herself, wishing this odious task hadn't landed on her shoulders.

"Are you gonna tell her the groom OD'd?" asked Glass.

"I . . . I'm going to tell her the wedding's off," said Theodosia.

"Then you'd better tell all those swells that are sitting downstairs to go on home."

"No," said Theodosia, sighing deeply. "I can't do that. They might be witnesses." She took another deep breath. "Or, worse yet, suspects."

Delaine was disbelieving, verging on hysterical. She stared wide-eyed at Theodosia. "It must be one of the groomsmen you saw!"

Theodosia shook her head. This was the second time she'd gone through her story. Delaine was having a horrible time processing the grisly news. Theodosia stood in the doorway, conveniently blocking Delaine's exit, while Delaine sat on the edge of the bed. Her hands worked furiously, twisting her four-carat yellow diamond engagement ring until her finger was red and raw.

"I simply don't believe you," said Delaine, as her sister continued to tip-tap at the closed door like an annoying woodpecker and the rest of the bridesmaids buzzed around outside. "I have to go see for myself!"

"No, you don't want to do that," said Theodosia. "Not until the police and paramedics arrive."

Delaine leaned forward and grasped Theodosia's hands. "Are you telling me there's hope? Oh, please say there is!"

"No, there are just, um, extenuating circumstances."

Delaine rolled her eyes. "You keep talking in circles, Theo, but what are you really *saying*?"

"You have to trust me," said Theodosia. "We have to wait until the police and paramedics arrive. Let them minister to him. Then you can go see him."

"You keep saying that!" complained Delaine. "And it's really quite maddening!" She fought to rip her veil off, but it was clipped in securely. "In fact, you're driving me crazy!"

Theodosia grabbed a bottle of mineral water that was sitting on a side table, twisted off the cap, and handed it to Delaine. "Here. Have a sip of water. Try to calm down."

"I'm trying," said Delaine. "Believe me, I'm trying." She jiggled the bottle back and forth and said, in a little-girl voice, "Are there any cold ones?"

"Maybe," said Theodosia, moving toward the mini bar.

That was Delaine's cue to bound to her feet and rush for the door. Flinging it wide open, she pushed her way through the cluster of anxious bridesmaids that hovered like gnats. Then, wedding gown and silk veil billowing out behind her, one high heel flying off her foot, she flew down the hallway.

"Delaine!" Theodosia shouted, sprinting after her. "Wait! Please don't go in there!"

Delaine was fast, but Theodosia was faster. Her years of jogging in White Point Gardens with her dog, Earl Grey, had paid off. She managed to grab the tail end of Delaine's veil just as she was ten feet from Granville's room. Grasping yards of imported French tulle, Theodosia reeled Delaine in like a prize marlin.

"Stop it! You're hurting me!" cried Delaine, clapping a hand to the back of her head.

"You stop!" Theodosia ordered. Then she carefully adjusted her tone. After all, this was a decorous moment. "Please, honey, you don't want to see him right now."

"But I *have* to see him!" shrilled Delaine.

At which point Bill Glass casually opened the door to see what all the commotion was about, and Delaine slipped into the room.

"Now you've done it!" said Theodosia, flapping a hand at Glass. "Thanks for nothing."

"What?" said Glass, feigning innocence.

"Aiyeeee!" came Delaine's tortured, high-pitched scream.

"How was I supposed to know she was gonna rush in there like that?" said Glass. He had two cameras slung around his neck and was about to light a cigarette.

Theodosia grabbed the cigarette from his mouth. "Don't do that. Show a little respect, will you?" She slammed around the corner and into Granville's room.

Delaine had found her fiancé, all right. In fact, she'd managed to collapse on the fainting couch right next to Granville. Her entire body was slumped against his lifeless one as she buried her face in her hands and wept uncontrollably.

Ten minutes later, the room became a veritable rugby scrum. Two uniformed officers arrived along with a pair of paramedics, a clattering metal gurney, and all manner of lifesaving equipment. Frank and Sarah Rattling, the owners of Ravencrest Inn, had also rushed upstairs and now hovered nearby.

But as much as the paramedics shocked Granville's heart with their portable defibrillator and pumped in liters of oxygen, as much as Delaine prayed and begged, it was simply no use. Granville was beyond the pale.

Relegated now to standing in the hallway, peeking in at the commotion, Theodosia fretted. With drugs so obviously involved, quite possibly cocaine, she knew it was only a matter of time before a police detective would be called to the scene.

A sudden tap on her shoulder startled Theodosia and caused her to flinch and whirl about nervously.

But it was Drayton who stared down at her with sad, gray eyes. He was accompanied by Charles Horton, Granville's stepson, a chunky fellow in his early thirties with a pink scrubbed face, brush-cut blond hair, and a flash of gold Rolex.

"How is he?" Drayton asked.

"Has there been any response?" asked Horton. A few minutes earlier, Theodosia had cued both Drayton and Horton in on all the trouble.

Theodosia shook her head. "Nothing at all." She jerked her chin toward the paramedics. "And they've been working on him nonstop. Pretty much tried everything. Chest compressions, shocking him, giving him a syringe of some kind of thrombolytic drug."

"Then he's a goner," said Drayton, while Horton just stared in horror.

"I'm afraid he was from the moment I found him," said Theodosia. She glanced into the room again where the paramedics were still working, then murmured, "Awful. Just awful."

"If you ask me," Drayton said in a low voice, as Horton slipped into the room, "this wedding, this marriage, was snake-bit from the very beginning."

"I don't know," said Theodosia, because she really didn't. "They seemed very sincere."

"Perhaps," said Drayton. "Perhaps I shouldn't judge."

"What's going on downstairs?" asked Theodosia. "None of the guests have left yet, have they?"

"No," said Drayton. "They're all milling about, looking unhappy and slightly uncomfortable. Fact is, they haven't been told about Granville yet. I merely explained to them that there'd been an extraordinary delay due to ill health."

"That's not going to hold them for very long," said Theodosia. There were dozens of bigwigs downstairs. True to form, Delaine had invited as many politicos, society people, and nouveau riche as she could possibly cram into a single room. Which made for a fairly lethal and paranoid gathering.

Drayton edged toward the doorway to peer in. "Was it really cocaine?" he asked. "Is that what killed him?"

"Apparently," said Theodosia. "At least I think so." The paramedics had transferred Granville to a gurney now and were about to roll him out head first. Delaine clutched pathetically at the arms of their blue jumpsuits, imploring the paramedics to keep working, begging them to try just one more lifesaving measure.

"We've tried everything humanly possible," said one of the paramedics. The name tag on his jacket read *J. Evans*. His youthful face was grim as he rolled the gurney forward.

"There must be *something*!" begged Delaine.

Theodosia stared down at Granville as they humped the front wheels of the gurney across the threshold and out into the hallway. His head bobbled loosely from the jolt, and the skin on his face looked dry and flaky, like ancient parchment. There was a faint scatter of white dust under one nostril. Granville was utterly lifeless and ghostly pale. Except . . . Theodosia bent forward, then did a sort of double take. Except for a pinprick smear of something dark on the flat white pillow they'd slipped under his head.

Blood?

Inhaling softly, Theodosia considered this and quickly deliberated. Then she held up a hand and said in a voice that was eerily calm, "There's one more thing you need to do."

Evans looked up at her sharply, a question on his face, and said, "What's that?"

"An autopsy," said Theodosia. "Take a look at this man's head. He may have been snorting coke, but I think somebody also hit him on the back of his head."

"They *what*?" said Delaine. She released her grasp on the paramedic and stared at Theodosia. Her lips puckered in amazement, her eyes were the size of saucers.

"There's blood," said Theodosia, pointing. "On the back

of his head. Like somebody might have clobbered him with something."

Evans quickly slid the gurney back into the room. "Let me take a look at that," he said. He didn't doubt her, but he did want to see for himself. His latex-gloved hands lifted Granville's head and rotated it slowly. "Hmm, there is a little nick." He paused. "Actually, not that small. Just difficult to see through all his hair."

"Easy to miss," said Theodosia. They'd been so busy working on his heart and respiration, they hadn't had time for a full examination.

"Wait a minute," Delaine said in a hushed tone. "Are you saying that Dougan was *murdered*? That someone hit him on the head?"

"This could change everything," said Evans.

Now Drayton got into the act. "But what could have struck him so hard that he was mortally injured?"

Theodosia gazed at the glass table with the glassine envelope and the white powder. She raised her eyes and looked at the love seat. Not much love there. Then she studied the built-in wooden shelves directly behind the love seat. Her eyes flicked across a row of heavy, globe-shaped glass paperweights. There was dark red glass, clear glass with purple swirls, and milky white glass with spatters of red, like confetti. All were softball-sized and potentially deadly, especially if brought down hard on someone's skull in a swift, deadly arc and wielded by a person intent on murder.

Suddenly, her mind still clicking in analytic mode, Theodosia realized that, in this line of perfectly arranged paperweights, one was decidedly missing.

"The paperweight," said Theodosia. "Find the missing paperweight and maybe you'll find the murder weapon."

"Murder weapon?" a gruff voice thundered from behind her. "Who said anything about murder?"

3

Detective Burt Tidwell loomed in the doorway like an enormous incarnation of Tweedledee (or Tweedledum). To say the man was overweight would be polite. His jowls sloshed; the vest of his suit strained across the bulk of his weather balloon–sized belly. The pop of a single button could be lethal to anyone in its way. His suit was sloppy and his cop shoes lacked polish. Yet his dark eyes shone with intensity. Tidwell headed the Robbery-Homicide Division of the Charleston Police Department and had a reputation for being taciturn, brilliant, and fearless. The officers who worked for him were either cowed or enormously respectful. Truth be known, the ones who worked directly under him would probably trek across hot coals if he barked the order.

"Detective Tidwell," said Theodosia. "Imagine seeing you here." She thought it unusual that a departmental head would answer a routine call like this. Then again, maybe he was here because it was Saturday. Or because he'd been specifically requested. Or maybe because Tidwell had no life at all.

Tidwell stepped into the room, his keen eyes probing and absorbing the crime scene in about five seconds flat. Then he leaned down and peered thoughtfully at Dougan Granville, who lay stiffening on his gurney. "Wrongful death," were Tidwell's only muttered words.

"Well, we know that!" said Delaine, staring at him with anger and concern. "What I want to know is, what are you going to *do* about it?"

"Why don't we begin by having everyone exit the room," said Tidwell.

"Are you serious?" said Delaine. "But I'm . . . I'm the bride!"

"And I'm in charge," said Tidwell. He made a shooing gesture. "Out. Everyone." When one of the EMTs put his hand on the rail of the gurney to push that out, too, he said, "No, leave him. He's fine just as he is."

Everyone shuffled through the doorway, heads turned and glancing back, leaving Tidwell in their wake.

"There seems to be . . ." began Theodosia, who had hung in the doorway.

"Please," said Tidwell.

"Cocaine," finished Theodosia.

Tidwell swung about to face her. "You've had it analyzed in a laboratory?"

"Obviously not," said Theodosia.

"Then kindly refrain from any comments or hasty conclusions," said Tidwell.

Theodosia folded her arms. She wasn't unfamiliar with how Tidwell operated. She'd encountered the man before in certain other cases. His modus operandi seemed to be to intimidate, anger, then analyze. Not exactly a warm, fuzzy way to operate. On the other hand, Theodosia had to admit that Tidwell was really quite brilliant. Most people who encountered him were initially fooled by his bulk and apparent buffoonery. But Tidwell was a former FBI agent who had single-handedly tracked down serial killers, forgery rings, and drug traffickers. Thus Theodosia had developed an enormous respect for him.

After Tidwell had sniffed and snooped for a few minutes, he turned toward Theodosia, who still hung in the doorway, and said, "You were saying when I first arrived? Something about a paperweight?"

This was Theodosia's cue. "Because of the apparent head wound."

"On the deceased," said Tidwell.

"Yes," said Theodosia. "And there seems to be a paperweight missing from the collection."

Tidwell turned toward the shelf full of paperweights. "Possibly." He studied the collection as rain continued to pound monotonously on the roof and the lights faltered and blinked again. Then he said, "There are guests downstairs."

"Almost fifty," said Theodosia.

"They must be detained," said Tidwell. He made a small gesture and two uniformed officers darted toward him. "Please make a suitable announcement to the guests, then record their names, addresses, and phone numbers."

"I do have a guest list," said Delaine. She'd crept back to hang at the doorway, too.

"Like I said," said Tidwell, nodding at his officers. Once the two uniformed officers had taken off, Tidwell stood in the doorway looking out into the hallway and addressed the rest of them. "Has anyone checked the nearby rooms?"

Frank Rattling stepped forward and cleared his throat. He was skinny with lank hair slicked back against a prominent skull. "Not yet. Do you think we should?"

"You're the innkeeper?" asked Tidwell.

"I am," Rattling nodded, while his wife, Sarah, stood nervously by. "We have only one other room occupied in this particular wing. The guest is a fellow by the name of Chapin."

"Which room was Mr. Chapin in?" Theodosia asked. She knew she was insinuating herself into the investigation but didn't much care. She'd discovered Granville, after all. So in her mind that made her an integral part of all this.

"The room next to this one," said Rattling. "Room three-fourteen."

"Has anyone checked that room?" asked Tidwell.

"No one's checked anything," said Theodosia. *Or even thought to check adjoining rooms.*

Frank Rattling marched a few steps down the hall, managing to look both flustered and officious. He rapped his knuckles against the door of 314. "Hello?" he called out loudly. "Anybody in there?"

"Open the door," said Tidwell.

"We don't like to intrude upon our guests," said Sarah. She was a pale woman with watery eyes who wore her dark hair pulled back in a low bun.

"Open it now," Tidwell ordered.

Rattling pulled an old-fashioned ring of keys out of his jacket pocket, searched through them, and finally found the one he wanted. He knocked again, then inserted the key in the lock and turned it. The door slowly swung open with a loud creak as several pairs of eyes followed its progress.

When no one called out from the bed or bathroom, Rattling took one tentative step into the room. "Hello? Mr. Chapin?"

"He's not there," said Theodosia. For some reason, she knew he wouldn't be.

"No luggage," said Frank Rattling, looking around. "No personal items, either."

"But his room is rented for two more days," said Sarah Rattling, looking puzzled.

"I'd say this Chapin fellow has checked out," said Tidwell.

"Unofficially, anyway," added Theodosia.

While the officers worked the crowd downstairs, Tidwell set about questioning all the people who were congregated on the third floor. By the time he questioned Theodosia, Bill Glass, the stepson Charles Horton, and several bridesmaids, and finally got to Delaine, she was overwrought, angry, and frustrated.

"This was to be your wedding day?" Tidwell asked. He leaned against a dresser, jotting notes in a black spiral notebook. Delaine was scrunched on the bed surrounded by crumpled tissues. Because of her jangled and overwrought nerves, Theodosia had been allowed to remain with her.

"*Excuse* me?" said a tearful Delaine. "Do you think I sit around in an eight-thousand-dollar ball gown just for the sheer joy of it?"

"Just answer the question," said Tidwell.

"Please," Theodosia said to Delaine. "Just try to cooperate."

"I *am* cooperating," Delaine muttered through clenched teeth.

"And when was the last time you spoke with Mr. Granville?" asked Tidwell.

"I don't know," said Delaine. She glanced at Theodosia. "Maybe an hour and a half before you found him?"

"I think that's about right," said Theodosia.

Tidwell jotted another note. "And that was when the two of you were heard arguing?"

Delaine frowned. "Not really arguing. More of a . . . disagreement."

"Not to put too fine a point on it, Miss Dish," said Tidwell, "but those are generally one and the same."

"Let me rephrase my answer, then," said Delaine. "Dougan and I were having a discussion."

Tidwell's furry eyebrows rose in twin arcs. "Concerning?"

"About . . . our honeymoon," said Delaine. "Dougan wanted to, um, alter the timetable slightly."

"How so?" asked Tidwell.

Delaine frowned. "Um . . ."

"He wanted to cut it short?" said Tidwell.

Delaine shrugged. "We discussed that possibility, yes."

Tidwell snapped his notebook closed. "Is it not true, Miss Dish, that the two of you were engaged in a shouting match? A rather heated conversation that was overheard by any number of people?"

Delaine's hand fluttered to her chest as she fought to project an air of supreme innocence. "I don't believe that's true at all."

"Several witnesses reported hearing a terrible argument," said Tidwell.

"Who said that?" Delaine snarled. "Was it Horton, his stepson?"

"Excuse me," said Theodosia, interrupting. "I think I see the direction this conversation is headed, and it's really quite unnecessary. I was with Delaine pretty much the entire morning."

"With her every second?" said Tidwell. One side of his mouth ticked upward.

Theodosia squinted as she recalled her morning. "Well, I did run down to check on the guests. Then I had to grab a couple pots of tea from the kitchen. Oh, and then the flowers were delivered to the back door."

"So not every second," said Tidwell.

"I suppose . . . no," said Theodosia.

"What else were you arguing about?" Tidwell asked. "And please answer honestly, because I assure you I've amassed quite a bit of information in questioning other witnesses."

Now Delaine looked embarrassed. "Just teensy little things."

"Such as an old girlfriend?"

"Well . . . that might have come up," said Delaine.

"I was told you became extremely agitated when you learned Mr. Granville's former girlfriend was a guest downstairs."

"Simone Asher!" Delaine blurted out. "He invited her without even consulting me! Can you imagine such a thing?"

"I'm sure it was quite upsetting," said Tidwell.

"It certainly was," said Delaine, fidgeting with the edge of her veil.

"Enough that you wanted to call off the wedding?" asked Tidwell.

Delaine stared at him with increasing hostility.

"Were you so upset that you wanted to do bodily harm to Mr. Granville?"

"No, of course not!" cried Delaine. "I wouldn't hurt Dougan; I loved him!"

Tidwell rose to his feet. "Please do remain in your room, Miss Dish, while I send up our crime-scene technicians."

"Why on earth!" sputtered Delaine.

"Fingerprints?" asked Theodosia.

Tidwell nodded.

"I am not a criminal!" Delaine shouted.

But Tidwell just nodded politely.

Theodosia stood outside the door of room 313, watching a uniformed officer string black-and-yellow crime-scene tape. *POLICE LINE*, it screamed. *DO NOT CROSS!* How could a day that was supposed to be filled with prayers and flowers and celebration end in such a fiasco? she wondered. It seemed unimaginable.

And now Tidwell was making motions that seemed to suggest Delaine was a prime suspect. Of course, that couldn't be further from the truth. Delaine might have railed at Granville this morning, might have screamed like a banshee over their honeymoon plans, but she certainly hadn't murdered him. Theodosia knew that the one thing that Delaine desired above all else, the one thing she couldn't magically conjure or buy for any amount of money, was to put the title *Mrs.* in front of her name.

And now her chance at that had been shattered. Yes, Granville's death was tragic, simply tragic.

Theodosia hunched her shoulders and turned to leave. Time to go home, she decided. Time to take off this silly bridesmaid's dress. To go downstairs and confab with Drayton and Haley, her tea shop cohorts. Get a hug and a kiss from her boyfriend, Max. Try to salvage something good out of this day.

Only someone had suddenly loomed in her way. "What?" she said, raising a hand, feeling a little threatened. Then she saw it was Bill Glass. He stood in the hallway, cameras still slung around his neck, looking disheveled and a little on edge.

"What are you doing here?" Theodosia asked. "Still angling to get that million-dollar shot?"

Glass shook his head. Like her, he'd lingered long after the body had been wheeled out, seemingly pondering the crime scene. "No, but this pretty much confirms what I've heard all along."

Theodosia turned toward him. "Confirms what? What are you talking about?"

"That this place is unlucky," said Glass. He flapped a hand. "Get a load of Granville's room number."

Theodosia glanced at the door. "Three-thirteen," she said tiredly. "So what?"

"You don't know?" said Glass.

"Know what?" Really, Glass could be awfully tedious.

Glass's brows pinched together and he looked suddenly somber. "You didn't know this place is supposed to be haunted?"

4

"It hardly feels like we've had any weekend at all," sighed Drayton. It was Monday morning and the Indigo Tea Shop wasn't yet open for business. He and Theodosia were seated at a small table next to the stone fireplace. Haley, their youthful chef and baker extraordinaire, had just ferried out a plate of scones, fresh from the oven. Though the atmosphere was cheery, the three of them were not.

"We've barely had any downtime," Theodosia agreed. "Between the wedding fiasco on Saturday and being debriefed by various investigators yesterday, our real lives were completely obliterated."

"But just think how Delaine feels," said Haley. She rarely had a soft spot in her heart for Delaine, but today she'd done a complete about-face and was really quite sympathetic.

"She feels awful," said Theodosia.

"Seriously now," said Drayton. "Do you think Delaine ever really loved Granville?" He plucked a scone from Haley's serving plate and placed it on his own smaller plate.

"She always struck me as being pretty much of a serial dater."

"She loved him," said Theodosia. "As much as Delaine could love anyone."

"Except for her cats," said Haley, pushing stick-straight blond hair behind her ears. "Dominic and Domino. Her two Siamese. I think she loves them more."

"You're probably right," said Theodosia. Delaine was a pain and a gossip and a little bit crazy, but when it came to small animals she was an absolute saint. She took in strays, bottle-fed abandoned raccoons, and braked for turtles, snappers as well as painted. Delaine had even spearheaded a major fund drive last year to finance a special cat and kitten wing at the Loving Paws Animal Shelter.

"Delaine was awfully desperate to get married," Drayton said as he split his scone in half and dropped on a frothy dollop of Devonshire cream.

"Desperate to find love," added Haley.

"Since their engagement," said Drayton, "poor Dougan Granville struck me as someone who'd suddenly awoken to find himself caught in a leg trap."

Theodosia considered their words. Yes, Delaine's rush to the altar had been like watching a NASCAR race: lots of torque, muscle, and speed. And, yes, maybe she had been a little desperate to find true love. But who doesn't want love? To experience the thrill and heart-thumping happiness that it brings? Wanting to love someone, to be in love, was certainly nothing she could hold against Delaine.

"Now what's Delaine going to do?" Haley wondered.

"She'll be in mourning for a decorous period of time," said Drayton. "And then she'll find herself another boy-friend." He popped a bite of scone into his mouth and peered at Theodosia. "Don't you think?"

"Probably," said Theodosia. But what else was Delaine supposed to do? Shuffle around in an ankle-length black hopsack dress and light candles under the moonlight? Mourn her lost fiancé until the end of time? Hardly. Life goes on. Albeit at a somewhat slower pace when one resided in Charleston.

"Have you spoken to Delaine?" asked Haley.

Drayton raised his eyebrows at Theodosia. "I'm pretty sure that question was directed at you."

"Yes," said Theodosia. "She called me last night."

"How was she holding up?" asked Drayton. He really did have a spot of sympathy for Delaine. But he was the stiff-upper-lip type who prided himself on displaying the minimum allowable amount of emotion.

"She's miserable and angry and sad," said Theodosia. "And absolutely furious at Tidwell."

"Is Delaine really a suspect?" asked Haley.

"I think we're all suspects," said Drayton.

"Anyway," said Theodosia, "if there's a very weak bright spot in all of this, it's that Delaine has finally accepted Granville's death."

"She's dealing with the harsh reality," said Drayton. "Processing it."

"Poor Delaine," Haley said again. "I really do feel sorry for her."

"My sympathy also lies with Detective Tidwell," said Drayton. "Even though he questioned a number of people, there isn't much to go on. If Granville's death was, in fact, a murder."

Haley looked puzzled. "I thought you guys said somebody conked him on the head with one of those fat glass paperweights."

"Could have been an accident," said Drayton. "He could have been, um, imbibing in his drug of choice and the paperweight rolled off and hit him."

Could it really? Theodosia wondered. Did heavy glass

paperweights just levitate off the shelf of their own accord? And then strike someone's cranium with such brute force that his brain was mortally compromised? No, she thought not. It had to be murder. The big question was, who was the mysterious killer who had insinuated his way into Granville's room?

Could it have been the mysterious guest in room 314? Or had there been a secret enemy among the downstairs wedding guests? Someone who'd sneaked up the back stairs and dealt that deadly blow? Or was it someone else? Theodosia knew it could be someone from Granville's not-so-distant past who wanted to settle a score. An angry, unhappy client perhaps, or someone involved with DG Stogies, his cigar store venture.

But cocaine was involved, Theodosia mused. So it must have started out as a druggie rendezvous. From the looks of things, Granville had sat down with someone for a chummy, prewedding toot of coke. Of course, the presence of cocaine seemed to add an extra element of danger. But who in Granville's or Delaine's inner circle might have been—or still was—a drug user? Or, worse yet, a drug dealer?

"Tell me about the cocaine," said Haley, almost as if she'd been reading Theodosia's mind.

"It was spilled on the table," said Drayton. "And there was white powder under Granville's nose."

"Wow," said Haley. "That's crazy weird." She thought for a moment. "That tells me Granville wasn't straight at all. He was kind of out there. A doper."

"Obviously," said Drayton, rolling his eyes.

"Maybe he got the coke from his stepson," said Haley. "What's the guy's name again?"

"Charles Horton," said Theodosia.

"That's awfully harsh, Haley," said Drayton. "Considering you don't even know Horton."

"I met him," said Haley. "And he seemed a little hinky."

"You think everyone over the age of twenty-five is hinky," said Drayton.

"Not quite," said Haley. "You guys are okay. But if you ask me, Tidwell ought to put Horton on his suspect list."

"Maybe," said Theodosia. But on a scale of one to ten, Horton seemed more like a one. Or maybe a two.

Drayton lifted the lid off a Brown Betty teapot and peered in. "This Darjeeling is probably steeped by now." He lifted the teapot and poured a stream of hot, steaming liquid into Theodosia's cup. Then he filled a cup for Haley and for himself. "A first flush from the Kumai Tea Estate."

"Tasty," said Haley, taking a quick sip.

"What's really excellent are these scones," said Drayton. "This is a new recipe, correct?"

"Peach scones," said Haley. "One of my granny's secret receipts."

"So the departed specter of the Parker clan still looms large in our midst," smiled Drayton.

Which suddenly reminded Theodosia of Bill Glass's final words to her. That Ravencrest Inn was haunted.

She thought of mentioning it to Drayton and Haley, then chased that thought clean out of her head. This wasn't the time to bring up such things as ghosts and goblins. Even here in the Carolina low country where ghostly legends prevailed and graveyards were roundly held to be inhabited by restless spirits.

The three of them sat in quiet repose for a few more minutes, sipping tea, talking. Then, as if an unspoken signal had been given, they began to prepare for their morning guests.

Drayton lit tiny white tea candles and laid out crisp white napkins, while Theodosia placed a tapestry of mismatched teacups and saucers on all the tables. Sugar bowls were filled, tea cozies laid out. Their reassuring morning ritual.

This, of course, was what it was all about. This was what brought Theodosia true happiness and contentment. Never once did she regret leaving the chew-'em-up, spit-'em-out world of marketing to run her beautiful little Indigo Tea Shop. In fact, being a tea entrepreneur was her dream come true. Her floor-to-ceiling cupboards were filled with the world's most exotic teas: delicately fruited Nilgiris, malty Assams, rich dark oolongs. Her tea shop itself, a former carriage house, sported pegged wood floors that had recently been given a red tea wash, as well as battered hickory tables, brick walls, leaded-glass windows, and a tiny fireplace. Of course, the place was crammed with items for sale, too. Vintage teapots lovingly scouted at local auctions, handmade tea cozies, tea towels, jars of Devonshire cream and DuBose Bees Honey, candles, wicker baskets, and cut-glass bowls all sat on shelves or were tucked into wooden cupboards. The walls were decorated with antique prints and grapevine wreaths she'd made and decorated.

When they were finally, perfectly ready, Drayton went to the front door and pulled back the white lace curtain. "Brace yourselves," he announced as he unlatched the door. "We've got Monday-morning customers."

But it wasn't the usual assortment of shopkeepers and neighbors who tumbled in this morning, eager for their morning cuppa and fresh-baked scones. Instead, it was two young men in their late twenties, blond surfer types dressed in jeans, T-shirts, and tennis shoes, and toting a video camera and various other pieces of electronic equipment.

"Gentlemen," said Drayton, looking a little nonplussed. "Table for two?"

The young man with the camera glanced around, noticed Theodosia standing next to a highboy, and came charging through the shop, dodging tables left and right. "You're Theodosia Browning?" he asked. "Right?"

Theodosia gave a slight nod. "Yes. May I help you?"

The man touched a hand to his chest and said, "I'm Jed Beckman, and this is my brother, Tim. We're ghost hunters!"

"We can't help you," Drayton snapped. "There are no ghosts here. But if you'd care to look at our take-out menu . . ." He grabbed a menu from the counter and thrust it toward them. "We can package up anything you like, especially since you fellows seem to be in a rush."

Eyes fixed firmly on Theodosia, Jed Beckman unfurled the front page of the *Charleston Post and Courier* and held it up for her to see. "Begging your pardon, ma'am, but it says here that you were the one who discovered the body of Mr. Douglas Granville in a room at the Ravencrest Inn?"

"I'm afraid so," said Theodosia. "But that's old news and completely out of my hands. The police have already launched an investigation."

"Because there was obviously foul play," Drayton added. "Now about your take-out order . . ." He disapproved of the two men's casual dress, and he disapproved of their questions. Basically, Drayton just disapproved.

"I don't know if you've paid much attention to the rumors," said Jed. "But Ravencrest Inn is supposed to be haunted."

"I really don't know anything about that," said Theodosia, stumbling over her words a little. "Perhaps you're thinking of the Unitarian Church Graveyard or the Old City Jail? I know there are nightly ghost tours to those particular sites."

"Really, *historic* tours," cut in Drayton, as four women pushed their way into the tea shop and gazed at him expectantly.

"Maybe you two should sit down so we can talk privately," Theodosia suggested to Jed and Tim. Lord knows, she didn't need her customers to overhear any talk about ghosts. This was a tea shop, after all. A genteel oasis of calm.

Not the fortune-telling room at Madame Viola's Voodoo Emporium.

"Thank you, ma'am," said Tim, as he and Jed settled at a nearby table. "And we'd like some tea if you've got it."

"We have an entire repertoire," said Theodosia. "What would you prefer? A nice English breakfast tea? Or perhaps an Earl Grey or Nilgiri?"

"I've only ever had tea bags," said Jed. "And Chinese restaurant tea. So anything you choose will probably be great."

"And perhaps a scone to go along with your tea?" asked Theodosia.

Both boys nodded, so Theodosia scurried off.

"What are you *doing*?" Drayton hissed to her at the counter. "You're encouraging them in their folly."

Theodosia grabbed two floral teacups with matching saucers and placed them on a silver tray. "I didn't tell you about this before because I thought it was just a silly story. But after everyone left on Saturday, after the police strung up the crime-scene tape and everything, Bill Glass told me that Ravencrest Inn was haunted."

"He was pulling your leg," said Drayton.

"Actually, he seemed rather serious. And you know Glass; he's *never* serious."

"There are no ghosts," said Drayton, as he measured out scoops of jasmine tea into a blue-and-white Chinese teapot. "They simply don't exist."

"Oh, really," said Theodosia. "What about the glowing orbs you encountered a couple of years back? The ones you saw hovering along Gateway Walk?"

Drayton pursed his lips. "That was different. That incident took place in a very ancient cemetery. On land where our forebears fought and died."

"So you're telling me those were legitimate ghosts while the ones at Ravencrest Inn are just posers?" For some reason, the notion amused her.

Drayton waved an index finger back and forth. "Trust me, entertaining a troupe of amateur ghost hunters can come to no good. It can only turn into a circus and cause more pain for Delaine."

But would it really? Theodosia wondered. Because, of all the people she knew, of all the people who *believed*, Delaine was strangely amenable to ghosts and spirits from the great beyond.

They were unbelievably busy then for the next twenty minutes. Theodosia greeted and seated guests while Drayton worked the front counter, brewing multiple pots of tea. Finally, when things settled down a bit, Theodosia turned her attention back to the ghost hunters.

"Is this a nonprofit venture on your part?" Theodosia asked. "A hobby?"

"It started out that way," said Jed. "But now our goal is to produce a reality show called *Southern Hauntings.*"

"Aren't there enough paranormal shows on TV already?" asked Theodosia. You could barely channel-surf without seeing a gaggle of ghost hunters pawing their way through some old prison or rundown mansion.

"We don't think so," said Tim. "There's really a huge demand for ghosts and the paranormal, and we think we bring a fresh perspective."

"How so?" asked Theodosia.

"Besides the obvious Southern angle," said Jed, "the other TV shows concern themselves with trying to contact ghosts of people who died years and years ago."

"Okay," said Theodosia, not exactly liking where this conversation seemed to be headed.

"But we want to make contact with new ghosts, recent ghosts," said Jed.

"A-ha," said Theodosia, though she did not share their enthusiasm.

"You see," explained Tim, "contacting the spirit world is a little like trying to establish a radio signal. Unfortunately, the longer a person has been dead, the weaker that signal is. What we want to do is try to contact the more recently departed."

"Because they emit a stronger signal," said Theodosia. She couldn't believe she was playing along with this.

"That's exactly right," said Tim.

"Here's the thing," said Jed. "We'd like you to go with us."

"Back to Ravencrest Inn," said Theodosia, suddenly not relishing the idea at all. "But that would require obtaining permission from the owners."

"We'll get it," said Tim. "We can be very persuasive."

"Everybody and his brother wants to be on a reality show these days," offered Jed.

"If you go in," said Theodosia, "you'll find that the place isn't all that large. So you certainly don't need me to function as any sort of guide."

"We were thinking of you more as a spirit guide," said Jed.

Theodosia leaned back in her chair. "Oh, dear."

"Because you were near him," said Jed. "When he died."

"And you found him," said Tim.

"And that's important?" said Theodosia.

"It is to us," said Tim.

"Let me noodle around your invitation," said Theodosia. She wanted to let them down gently. They were obviously well intentioned, but this really wasn't something she wanted to participate in, let alone help facilitate.

Tim leaned forward, a question on his face. "Tell me, Miss Browning, when you first walked into that room, before you knew the man was dead, did you feel anything? Was there anything strange in the air?"

Theodosia thought about the electrical pulse she'd picked up on immediately. A strange anxious feeling that had tickled her nerves, as if a transformer had just exploded. A feeling that something wasn't quite right, a sort of . . . low, menacing vibration.

"No," she said. "I didn't feel anything at all."

5

As always, Haley was a marvel in a kitchen that was roughly the size of a postage stamp. In her white smock and tall chef's hat that looked like an overblown mushroom on her head, she whirled and twirled her luncheon ballet: plucking a pan of bubbling pepper jack cheese quiche from the oven, giving her wild rice soup a quick stir, tasting her vinaigrette and adding a pinch more tarragon.

"Are the ghost busters gone?" asked Haley. She gave a mischievous smile. "Did they vanish into thin air?"

Theodosia, who'd been setting out white luncheon plates like she was dealing out a deck of playing cards, said, "How on earth did you know about them?"

"Drayton told me," said Haley. "Last time he buzzed through here. Though he seemed awfully put off by the whole thing."

"The intrepid Beckman brothers have their heart set on tiptoeing through Ravencrest Inn," said Theodosia.

Haley nodded. "Kids just want to have fun."

"Actually, it's a little more complicated than that," said Theodosia. "They also want to try to make contact with Dougan Granville's spirit."

Haley smiled. "They think maybe he's malingering over there on the other side?"

"Something like that, yes," said Theodosia.

"Then maybe he is," said Haley.

"Probably he isn't." Probably, Theodosia decided, Granville rested in the arms of the Lord now. At least she hoped he did.

"I bet Delaine wouldn't mind if they tried to contact her dear departed fiancé," said Haley. "She might even *like* the idea."

"Drayton thinks that any sort of ghost-hunting nonsense would just cause Delaine more heartbreak," said Theodosia. "He's of the firm belief that we should just leave it alone."

"Drayton thinks what?" asked Drayton, as he suddenly appeared in the doorway.

"Theodosia was just telling me about the ghost hunters," said Haley, as she plucked a Meyer lemon from a large bowl of lemons, grabbed a paring knife, and quickly created a small mound of lemon zest.

"Such silly fellows," said Drayton. "They're under the illusion they can contact an actual spirit and then record it using a camera or some sort of tape recorder."

"More like a digital recorder," said Haley. "Tape went out, oh, I don't know, maybe with disco music and shoulder pads the size of pillows?"

"I have no idea what you're mumbling about," said Drayton. He was a confirmed Luddite who basically abhorred technology. He scorned digital cameras and didn't even own a cell phone.

"I bet you still play vinyl records," said Haley.

"Naturally," said Drayton. His brows rose slightly as he

adjusted his bow tie. "Some things simply cannot be improved upon."

"Haley," said Theodosia, eager to put an end to the ghost-hunting issue, "why don't you run through our menu for today?"

That stopped Haley in her tracks. She loved nothing better than to tick off her luncheon offerings and her tasty repertoire of baked goods. "Oh. Well. Our savories include quiche, wild rice soup, tea-simmered chicken breasts, and tomato and cream cheese tea sandwiches."

"And for sweets?" Drayton prompted.

"That would be ginger scones and chocolate mint bars," said Haley.

"Excellent," said Drayton. He gave a perfunctory smile, then said, "I believe I shall brew pots of Assam and Indian spice tea. Those teas should make for excellent luncheon pairings."

"Go for it," said Haley, as Drayton disappeared.

Haley grabbed a soup ladle, frowned, and said, "Oh, rats." She stepped around the counter quickly, looking distracted, and said, "I forgot to tell Drayton about my apple crumbles. She rushed out the kitchen door and called after him, "And there's apple crumbles, plus we've still got apricot scones left, too." Hurrying back into the kitchen, she dusted her hands together and said, "Okay. So we're pretty much set for lunch."

"Anything I can do to help?" asked Theodosia. Haley was a martinet in the kitchen, secretive of her ingredients and recipes, wanting to control every single aspect. So she rarely asked for assistance. Yet Theodosia always offered. It was simply good manners.

Haley picked up a wooden spoon and gestured at her. "If you ask me, I think you should seriously consider accepting that ghost-hunting invitation."

"You think so?"

"Yup."

"Like Drayton, I worry that any sort of foray back to Ravencrest Inn might cause Delaine more pain."

"Why don't you let her decide?" said Haley.

"You mean ask Delaine?"

"Sure," said Haley. "In case you didn't know, she's sitting out there in the tea room."

Delaine looked tired but composed. She sat at a window table, gazing out onto Church Street where red-and-yellow horse-drawn jitneys lumbered past laden with tourists, and late-morning traffic was forced to blip around St. Phillip's Church where it stuck solidly out into the middle of Church Street. Hence the name Church Street.

Seated across from Delaine was a woman Theodosia didn't recognize. She was fairly young, maybe late twenties, with a pleasant expression, cool-looking narrow silver-blue glasses, and a cap of attractive brown curls. She wore a crisp khaki business suit that had a bit of a military snap to it.

Theodosia slipped past the velvet celadon green curtain that separated the tea shop from the back of the shop and threaded her way to Delaine's table.

"Delaine?" Theodosia's voice conveyed the fact that she was surprised to see her. "How are you doing?"

Delaine offered a sad smile. "Hanging in there."

"I'm surprised to see you here," said Theodosia.

"Where else would I go?" said Delaine.

Gee, I don't know, Theodosia thought. *Maybe a meeting with a funeral director? Or a minister?*

Delaine flipped a hand toward the woman sitting across from her. "Theo, I'd like you to meet Millie. Millie Grant."

Millie threw Theodosia a warm smile. "I'm Mr. Granville's secretary," she explained.

"Oh," said Theodosia. "How very nice to meet you. Considering the, um, circumstances."

Millie nodded and seemed to blink back tears. "It's been hard on all of us."

Theodosia glanced around and saw that Drayton had things under control for the moment, so she sat down with them.

"Where's Nadine . . . is she still in town?" Theodosia asked Delaine. Nadine was a divorcée from New York. But, to Delaine's great consternation, she seemed to be spending more and more time in Charleston. Theodosia figured Nadine was biding her time until she could move in permanently with Delaine, and thus be a permanent source of discord.

"Some help she's been in all of this," said Delaine, making a dismissive gesture. "She's either crying herself silly or dashing out the door."

"Well, if you need help with anything, I'll do whatever I can," said Theodosia. "Please don't hesitate to ask."

Delaine's eyes suddenly shone brightly with tears. "Thank you, Theo. I *do* need your help. After being interrogated and browbeaten by Detective Tidwell, I'm extremely upset!"

"If you'd like me to speak to him," said Theodosia, "just say the word."

Delaine reached across the table and gripped Theodosia's hand. "Theo, I need more than *talk*. I need action!"

"What did you have in mind?" asked Theodosia. "You need some help planning a memorial service or . . . ?"

Delaine did a double take, popping her eyes wide open and dropping her lower jaw. "Are you serious?" she screeched. "I want you to do what you *always* do. Snoop around, ask questions, figure things out! Help clear my good name!"

"You're saying you want me to investigate?" said Theodosia.

"Yes! Of course!" Delaine gave a quick glance around.

"Did I just walk into a parallel universe or something? That's what you're *good* at!"

"Not really," said Theodosia.

"You are!" said Delaine. "You've figured out crimes before!" She tapped an index finger against her head. "So we need to put your smarts to work on this!"

"But who exactly would I investigate?" asked Theodosia, knowing she was treading on eggshells.

"Simone, of course!" spat out Delaine. "Dougan's skanky ex-girlfriend. Really, Theo, the woman hates me. No, let me rephrase that, she *despises* me!"

"I somehow doubt that," said Theodosia.

But Delaine thought otherwise. "It *had* to be Simone who gave Dougan the drugs. She knew he'd had a minor flirtation with them a couple of years ago."

Theodosia tried to get a word in. "But why would she . . . ?"

"Simone was obviously trying to appeal to Dougan at a weak moment," said Delaine. "She was trying to get him high and then change his mind about marrying me!"

"Delaine, be reasonable," said Theodosia. "If Simone still had feelings for Dougan, she certainly wouldn't have *murdered* him."

"You don't know her like I do," said Delaine. "She's extremely cold and conniving. She probably figured that if she couldn't have him, then neither could I!"

Theodosia had to admit there was a small kernel of twisted logic there. Somewhere.

"Okay," said Theodosia. "If it'll make you feel any better, I'll pay a visit to Simone." *For about two minutes. Just to say that I did and satisfy Delaine's craving to snoop.* "Where exactly would I find her?"

Delaine fumbled in her Prada bag and pulled out a slip of paper. "Here. I wrote it all down for you. Simone owns a vintage shop by the name of Archangel. It's over on King Street."

"Near all the antique dealers," Theodosia murmured, as Drayton suddenly appeared at their table. His tray held a pitcher of sweet tea along with three tall, frosted glasses.

"My special Honey Hibiscus Sweet Tea," said Drayton. "Egyptian chamomile tea blended with hibiscus blossoms, rose hips, and a touch of honey." He nodded solemnly at Delaine. "I do hope you're feeling some better."

"Some," said Delaine.

"And hello to you," Drayton said to Millie.

"This is Dougan's secretary," said Delaine.

"Millie," said Millie, nodding.

"Lovely to meet you," said Drayton. "My sincere sympathies to you, too."

"Thank you," said Millie, as Drayton moved off.

Theodosia poured out glasses of sweet tea for all of them. When she handed a glass to Millie, the girl gave a little shiver and said, "I never met a real-life investigator before."

"Well, I'm not one," said Theodosia.

But Millie was not to be dissuaded. "Delaine was bragging to me earlier about how smart you are. How good you are at finding clues and figuring things out."

"Sometimes I get lucky," said Theodosia.

"Well, it sure is nice to have you on our side," Millie continued. "Especially after . . ." Her voice faded as she gazed sorrowfully at Delaine.

"What?" said Theodosia. "Did something happen?" Tidwell again?

Delaine sniffled, then dug into her bag for a tissue. "There was another nasty scene this morning," she whispered.

"What?" said Theodosia. What she really meant was, *Now what?*

Millie turned toward Theodosia with sorrowful eyes. "When Delaine showed up at Granville and Grumley, I'm afraid she was given a rather cool reception."

"Seriously?" said Theodosia. Delaine was treated rudely at her fiancé's law firm? Her *dead* fiancé's law firm? Shouldn't they have been bend-over-backward nice to her?

Millie nodded. "To be honest, they were perfectly awful."

Theodosia stared at Delaine. "Who was awful to you?"

"Pretty much everyone," sniffed Delaine. "Although Allan Grumley, Dougan's partner, was the worst."

"His *partner*?" said Theodosia. She found this totally bizarre, especially since Granville and Grumley had been known all over Charleston for being a hotshot team of lawyers, the kind of gunslinging attorneys that could intimidate and negotiate with the best of them. Her assumption had always been that the two men were arrogant, freewheeling, and extremely like-minded. That they got along famously.

"I was totally shocked," said Delaine. She sniffed again and daubed at her eyes with a hanky.

"Why did you even go there?" asked Theodosia.

"Just to obtain some paperwork," said Delaine. "But who knew I'd be met with such fierce resistance? Except, of course, for Millie. She was the one saving grace."

Millie reached across the table and patted Delaine's hand. "You know I'll always be there for you."

"I know you will, sweetie," said Delaine. "You were devoted to Dougan and don't think I don't appreciate it."

"Thank you," said Millie. Now she looked like she was ready to cry.

Her eyes going hard, Delaine gazed across her sweet tea at Theodosia. "I want revenge," she hissed. "Sweet revenge. My life's been ruined and the one man who loved me despite all my foibles is *dead*!" She took a gulp of sweet tea. "He loved me unconditionally and didn't think it was one bit odd that I talked to cats."

"Of course, he didn't," said Theodosia. *Women are considered odd only when they collect dozens of cats.*

"I know it's asking a lot of you, Theo," said Delaine, "but will you *please* go with me to Granville and Grumley tomorrow afternoon? Will you be my advocate? My ally?"

"Why do you even have to go there?" asked Theodosia.

"There are papers and things she needs to see," said Millie.

"Can't you take care of those things?" Theodosia asked Millie. "Run interference for her?"

Millie snorted. "Me? Are you kidding? I'm just a lowly secretary. Not even on par with a paralegal. Nobody there listens to me."

"Please, Theo?" said Delaine. "We need you. *I* need you."

"Of course, I'll go with you," said Theodosia. She hated the fact that Delaine had been treated badly. Rude behavior and taking advantage of people when they were hurting were two things that radically ruffled her feathers.

"The thing is," said Delaine, "I really don't trust Allan Grumley."

"Maybe he's still in shock, too," said Theodosia. "Maybe he's trying to figure out how the firm can move ahead and he's just crazed with worry." She figured there had to be a legitimate reason for Grumley's bad behavior, if that was what it really had been.

"And I'm not so sure about Charles Horton, either," Delaine added.

"The stepson?" said Theodosia. "Why on earth would you be suspicious of him?"

"I find it *très* strange that Horton suddenly came crawling out of the woodwork once our wedding was announced," said Delaine. "And that he suddenly wanted to go to work for Granville and Grumley."

"But Horton's a lawyer," said Theodosia. "So it really does make sense. And I'm guessing he probably wanted to reconnect with his stepfather after all these years. Maybe a happy event like a wedding just made for perfect, feel-good timing. I mean, Horton did live with his stepfather when he was younger, didn't he?"

"I suppose he did," said Delaine. "For a few years, anyway."

"Horton's mother was Granville's second wife?" Theodosia asked.

Delaine nodded.

"How many times had Granville been married?"

Delaine looked thoughtful. "Two that I know of. Maybe three." She blinked, looked up, and said, "Hello, Haley."

Haley gave an eager smile. "I brought you guys some fresh-baked scones and honey butter."

Delaine gave Haley's tray a listless glance. "I'm not very hungry."

"Try a bite," said Theodosia. "These scones are one of Haley's premier recipes."

Haley placed a scone on everyone's plate, then continued to stand at their table, throwing meaningful glances at Theodosia.

"Thank you, Haley," said Theodosia. She couldn't figure out why Haley was still hovering. Usually, she darted right back to her kitchen, like a little mouse to its hidey-hole.

Haley cleared her throat self-consciously and said, "Theo, you should tell her."

Delaine lifted her head and stared tiredly at Haley. "Excuse me?"

"Thank you for your input, Haley." Now Theodosia's voice carried a warning tone.

"Because I think she'll be okay with it," Haley continued.

"Now is not the time," said Theodosia.

Delaine's perfectly waxed brows knit together. "Now *is* the time," she said, sounding vexed. "Pray tell, why are you two making goo-goo eyes at each other? What little secret are you trying to keep from me?"

"Something pretty important," said Haley.

"The thing is," Theodosia said with reluctance, "we had a strange pair of visitors this morning."

"Two young men who claim to be ghost hunters," said Haley. "Jed and Tim Beckman."

"What does this have to do with anything?" asked Delaine, as Haley suddenly retreated, leaving Theodosia by her lonesome to sputter out some sort of explanation.

"They stopped by because they're filming a documentary on Southern ghosts," said Theodosia. She figured *documentary* sounded much more palatable than *reality show*. "And . . . well . . . they intend to explore Ravencrest Inn."

Delaine's eyes got wide and her every muscle seemed to tense. "What?" she said in a low whisper. "What did you just say?"

6

Oh, dear, now I have to go into the whole thing with her, Theodosia thought to herself. "Okay, Delaine, here's the thing. The Beckman brothers came across an obscure legend that says Ravencrest Inn may be haunted." She took another gulp of tea. "And they feel they have a better chance of contacting the spirit world since . . ." She paused. "Well, because . . ."

"Because Dougan died there," said Delaine. Her voice was hoarse, her eyes pinpricks of intensity.

Theodosia swallowed hard. Delaine had a way of tossing harsh realities out on the table. "Well, yes."

"And what exactly do these ghost hunters wish to do?" asked Delaine. "How do they intend to contact the spirit world?"

"I imagine they'll want to go inside room three-thirteen," Theodosia said with some hesitation. "They'll probably want to use infrared film and magnetometers and such to see if they can, um, make contact."

Delaine peered at Theodosia. "That's it?" She tapped manicured fingers on the table as if she were considering something. "I get the feeling there's something you're not telling me."

"They asked me to accompany them," said Theodosia. There, she'd said it. She'd laid out the whole foolish scheme. Indiana Jones and the Haunted House. Now Delaine could feel free to shed a few more tears and act highly offended, or toss the whole thing off as a stupid would-be parlor trick.

Instead, Delaine leaned forward and said, "I think it's a wonderful idea."

"You do?" Theodosia was stunned. Maybe Delaine hadn't heard her correctly. Sure, that had to be it. Delaine was still in deep, dark shock and not absorbing the full impact of her words.

"The only thing I ask," Delaine continued, "is that I go along!"

The rest of lunch was crazy busy. Theodosia ferried luncheon plates while Drayton brewed pot after pot of tea. Then one table requested a tea tasting of three different Japanese green teas, so Drayton had to pull down his tins of Sencha, Gyokuro, and Bancha and tend to that.

As lunchtime morphed into afternoon tea time, Theodosia was able to relax a little bit. The pace grew slower, their guests a little less harried and demanding. Mostly, the folks who came in for afternoon tea were looking for a genteel respite in the middle of their day. They wanted to slowly sip a cup of oolong or Lapsang souchong and savor their scones and jam.

Still, the phone continued to ring off the hook, and Theodosia found herself booking two tea parties and, depending on the bid she came up with, a catering gig for the Charleston Opera Society.

"That's it," said Theodosia, leaning over the counter as Drayton measured out scoops of Formosan oolong, "I'm not taking any more calls."

So, of course, the phone shrilled yet again.

Sighing, Theodosia picked up the receiver and said, "Indigo Tea Shop. How may I help?"

"Theo?" came a rich, baritone voice.

"Max!" said Theodosia. Note to all: This was one call she definitely wanted to take. In fact, she could just picture Max sitting in his office at the museum, feet up on his desk, looking more like a grad student than the PR director. Tall and thin, with a tousle of dark hair, he had an olive complexion and generally wore a slightly sardonic grin. Theodosia had decided that you needed a good sense of humor in that job just to deal with all the donors and docents.

"How are you holding up?" asked Max.

"Doing okay." Theodosia and Max had talked at length over the weekend about the wedding debacle and Granville's strange death. They'd turned it over and over, offering up a few suppositions, but had come to no firm conclusion. Now, Max was going to stop by for dinner tonight. "You're still coming tonight, right?"

"Wouldn't miss it," said Max. He'd been one of the wedding guests in the downstairs parlor who'd been kept in the dark, both literally and figuratively.

"Come around seven," Theodosia urged. "That'll give me time to take Earl Grey for a good run and fix us something wonderful to eat."

"I wouldn't mind one of your designer pizzas. Hint, hint."

"Any one in particular?" Theodosia loved to create interesting pizza combinations such as gorgonzola, figs, and caramelized onions. Or chanterelles with Burrata cheese.

"Why don't you surprise me?" said Max.

* * *

When the clock struck three and just a few tea room guests lingered, Theodosia ran into her office and trundled out two boxes of T-Bath products. This was her own proprietary line of tea-infused lotions and potions that were soothing, cruelty-free, and blended to her exact specifications. Much to her delight, the T-Bath products also sold like hotcakes in her shop, online, and at a few Charleston boutiques. Green Tea Lotion was her biggest seller, but White Tea Bath Oil and Green Tea Feet Treat were holding their own. And her two newest T-bath offerings, Ginger and Chamomile Facial Mist and Lemon Verbena Hand Lotion, were finding a following, too.

Just when Theodosia was sprawled cross-legged on the floor, with jars and bottles spilled out all around her, just as she was composing a new arrangement on her display shelves, Detective Tidwell came lumbering in.

She saw his heavy-duty cop shoes trudge toward her, saw his billowing trouser legs. Then Tidwell came to a halt and his booming voice called out, "Is that you down there?"

"It's me," said Theodosia. Her head popped up between two tables like a manic gopher. "You caught me restocking shelves."

"And a fine job you're doing," said Tidwell.

Theodosia pulled herself to her feet, dusted herself off, and gazed at Tidwell. "Tea?" He'd been coming in regularly for a couple of years now and she'd finally turned him into a tea drinker. Not quite a tea connoisseur yet, but Tidwell showed promise and she was infinitely patient.

"Please," said Tidwell, who had already deposited his bulk in a creaking captain's chair. "And a sweet treat if you have it."

"I'm sure we can scrape up a few crumbs," Theodosia

told him. She nodded to Drayton, who was already fixing a pot for Tidwell, then flew into the kitchen and grabbed a ginger scone and a mint bar.

When Theodosia set his tea and dessert in front of him, she said, "That's a tippy Yunnan tea."

"Interesting," said Tidwell. He lifted the lid of the teapot, gave a sniff. "Mmm, slightly spicy. Must it steep for another minute?"

"I think it's probably ready right now."

"Excellent," said Tidwell, as he lifted the teapot and poured a stream of golden liquor into his teacup. Then he glanced up and said, "Well, have you begun your investigation yet?"

"I wouldn't do that," said Theodosia. She tried to project what she thought was an air of sincerity.

Tidwell wasn't fooled. He let loose a belly laugh that caused his entire body to jiggle like a mound of shrimp in aspic. "Of course, you would," he growled. "And probably have. I'm positive the irascible Delaine Dish has already pleaded her case, playing the wounded victim and venting her deepest, darkest suspicions. She's probably come to you on bended knee, begging you to investigate whomever she sees as her suspect du jour." Tidwell took a sip of tea, lifting his pinkie finger as he did so. "Delicious."

"She did ask me to take a look at Simone Asher," Theodosia admitted. Why not tell Tidwell? What did she have to lose?

"Simone of Archangel," said Tidwell. "Mr. Granville's most recent ex-girlfriend. The one he spurned in favor of Miss Dish." He gathered up his cloth napkin and gently patted his lips.

"When you put it that way, it sounds like Simone really is a suspect," said Theodosia. She stared directly at Tidwell and, when he didn't answer, said, "Is she?"

Tidwell shook his enormous head. "Doubtful. Although she was questioned at length."

"What about Delaine? You questioned her at length, too. You don't really believe she's the killer, do you?"

"It doesn't matter what I think," said Tidwell. "It's where the clues lead and the evidence piles up." He picked up a silver butter knife, cut his scone in half, then applied an enormous pat of butter.

"And where have the clues led so far? *Are* there any clues?"

"That information is strictly confidential," said Tidwell, chewing as he answered.

"You can confide in me," said Theodosia. "After all, I was there. I'm a star witness."

Tidwell guffawed. "You were an unlucky passerby." He helped himself to another bite.

"I'm sure you've interviewed many of the wedding guests by now?"

Tidwell made a noncommittal grunt.

"What about Granville's business partner?" Theodosia asked. When Tidwell's left eye twitched oh-so-slightly, she knew she'd struck gold. "Ho, you *are* looking at him. At . . ." For some reason she couldn't dredge up the man's name.

"Grumley," supplied Tidwell. "Allan Grumley."

"Right. But what I'd like to know is *why* you'd take a hard look at him? I've always been under the impression that Granville and Grumley was an incredibly successful law firm. That the two partners functioned extremely well together. They certainly got enough publicity to bear that out."

"To all outward appearances, yes, they seemed like an unstoppable force. But when individual staffers were questioned, there appeared to be . . . let's just call it seeds of unrest."

"What kind of unrest?" asked Theodosia. She wondered

if this internal unrest had accounted for Delaine's poor treatment this morning.

"That I cannot divulge," said Tidwell.

"Are you taking a careful look at Granville's stepson, Charles Horton?"

Tidwell nodded. "I am."

"And?"

"He appears to be an amiable chap," said Tidwell. "I've found nothing out of the ordinary. Certainly nothing to suspect him of foul play."

Theodosia was beginning to feel frustrated. "Have you figured out who was in the room next to Granville? The mysterious Mr. Chapin?"

Tidwell hesitated for a moment. "No."

"What about the missing paperweight?" Theodosia asked.

"Nothing yet," said Tidwell.

Theodosia furrowed her brow.

"What?" said Tidwell.

"Don't you find it interesting?" said Theodosia.

"Find what interesting?"

"That the killer didn't bring a murder weapon with him," said Theodosia. "No gun, no knife, no rope. He used whatever was at hand."

"What you're saying is the murder wasn't premeditated," said Tidwell.

Theodosia tilted her head, considering this. "I guess I am. So that means the killer didn't start out with an intent to kill. He acted rashly, in the heat of the moment."

"It's certainly possible," said Tidwell.

"Then it had to have been a wedding guest," said Theodosia. "Unless someone else sneaked into the building."

Tidwell looked smug. "See, you are investigating."

Theodosia almost lost it. "Well, *somebody* has to!" she blurted out.

*   *   *

"I'm taking off!" Haley called. She popped out from between the velvet curtains, looking a little harried. She wore a T-shirt and jeans and had a colorful raffia book bag slung over one shoulder.

"Drayton's gone already?" asked Theodosia. She was just rinsing out a teapot. It was four thirty and their customers had long since departed.

"He's off to prep for his Heritage Society lecture tonight," said Haley. "Something about Carolina coast shipwrecks. Or maybe it's on lighthouse architecture."

"Trust Drayton to pick a slightly academic subject," said Theodosia.

"Our boy's a real smarty," said Haley.

"But you're off to class, too," she observed.

"Just a night school class," said Haley.

"What is it this time?" Theodosia asked. Haley vacillated between business, English, marketing, and art history. Probably, once she finished taking classes, she'd have enough credits for two master's degrees and a PhD.

"Mass communications," said Haley. "But I'm taking it mostly for fun."

"Then have fun," said Theodosia. After seeing Haley off, she did a quick check of the front counter, snatching up a tin of Dimbulla tea that had somehow lost its lid. *Can't have that happen*, Theodosia thought to herself. Heat, moisture, and light were the enemies of tea, and Charleston gladly offered all three of those in abundance.

"There it is," said Theodosia, spotting the lid behind a stack of shiny indigo blue take-out bags. She grabbed the silver lid and popped it on, just as someone pounded on the front door.

"Can't they read our sign?" she wondered aloud. "Don't they know we're closed for the day?"

But the pounding continued, a cacophony that built to an annoying din.

Stepping to the front door, Theodosia swept the curtain aside, ready to act out her slightly apologetic *We're closed* pantomime. But when she saw Charles Horton standing there, she undid the latch and pulled open the door.

"Charles," she said, wondering what he was doing here.

"I was afraid I'd missed you!" cried Horton. He had a loud braying voice that came across a little too high volume, a little too hearty, and echoed through the deserted tea shop.

"I was just leaving," Theodosia told him.

Horton took a presumptuous step inside. "Then I promise I won't take up much of your time."

"Okay," said Theodosia. She wasn't thrilled, but she knew she had to be cordial. If only for Delaine's sake.

"I know you're one of Delaine's dearest friends," Horton began.

Theodosia gave an imperceptible nod. "We're friends, yes."

"The thing is, Delaine and I seem to have gotten off on the wrong foot."

"Really?" said Theodosia, trying to show a modicum of surprise. Of course, they'd gotten off on the wrong foot. Horton had popped up a few weeks prior to the wedding and suddenly insinuated himself into his stepfather's life. And into his law firm. Which had left Delaine feeling a tad worried and suspicious. And could you really blame her?

"I think Delaine initially saw me as a rival for my stepfather's affection," said Horton.

"I don't know about that."

"And now I have the strangest feeling that Delaine thinks I had something to do with his death!" Horton said in a rush.

Theodosia wasn't sure how to answer this. Or even how to react.

Horton touched a hand to his chest and pulled his face

into a look of supreme anguish. "Me. I'm just as appalled by this terrible murder as anyone."

"Delaine is under a good deal of stress," said Theodosia. "I'm sure, in time . . ."

"Which is why I'm here to ask a favor of you," Horton blurted out. "Even though I really don't know you and am probably imposing like crazy."

"What exactly are you talking about?" asked Theodosia.

"I'd be grateful if you'd run interference for me," said Horton.

Theodosia focused a level gaze on him. "Run interference."

"Delaine isn't thinking straight," said Horton, twisting his face. "She's angry and bitter and scared right now. I know for a fact that her sister is giving her little if any support and . . ."

"And let me guess," Theodosia cut in. "You want to be there for Delaine. You want to offer a shoulder to cry on, so to speak."

"Exactly!" said Horton.

"Only the two of you are estranged."

"The thing is," said Horton, "we're practically family. At least we *would* have been had this marriage taken place." He held up a hand. "Look, all I'm asking is that you talk to Delaine. I know she listens to you, thinks the world of you if you really want to know the truth. Just try to convey the fact that I'm a good guy. That I'm willing to help her any way I can."

"Okay, I'll talk to her," said Theodosia. *But I don't know if I can convince her. Because I'm not totally convinced myself.*

Horton beamed. "You know what? You're a peach!" He opened his arms wide and enveloped Theodosia in a clumsy hug. He tried to deliver a peck on her cheek, but Theodosia turned her head so he got an ear instead.

"I'll run this by her," Theodosia promised, as she wriggled out of Horton's grasp. "Next time I see her."

7

With the surging Atlantic as a backdrop, Theodosia and Earl Grey jogged along a narrow beach littered with broken oyster shells, then sprinted up a short path into White Point Gardens.

This was the tip of Charleston's Battery. The place where rogue pirates had been hanged, where British cannons had bombarded the city during the Revolutionary War, and where old Civil War cannons still stood like sentinels. Edging the park was a row of elegant mansions. Here, fanciful Victorian homes stood shoulder-to-shoulder with Federal, Italianate, Gothic Revival, and Georgian-style homes. And like so many buildings in the romantic city once known as Charles Town, these homes were painted in a soft French palette: alabaster white, pale pink, pastel blue, and soft gray.

As Theodosia and her dog pounded across the grass, winds from the Atlantic caressed them, stirring up ions and intoxicating sips of sea air.

"Have you had enough?" Theodosia asked Earl Grey, as they bounced across East Bay Street and headed down a narrow cobblestone alley. "Did you blow out the carbon?"

Earl Grey tossed his head and strode easily alongside Theodosia. He was a Dalbrador, half Dalmatian, half Labrador. She had found him as a pup, huddled and miserable, a poor lost stray, hiding from the rain in the alley behind the Indigo Tea Shop. She had taken him in, warmed him, fed him, and been instantly captivated. Earl Grey, so named because of his slightly dappled coat, had been her constant companion ever since. On a lark, they'd started therapy dog training together. But almost immediately they began to take their mission very seriously. Now, Theodosia and Earl Grey visited hospitals and retirement homes where Earl Grey brought smiles and laughter to folks who were sometimes facing grim circumstances.

Theodosia swung open her back gate and cut across her small backyard. She'd done some more planting last month, and her once-scraggly garden was beginning to look a little more lush and verdant. Peeking into the tiny fish pond, she saw a half-dozen goldfish hovering in the crystal-clear water. Happily, they were still there. Last year she'd had trouble with a neighborhood raccoon who'd used her fish pond as his own personal sushi bar. This year the fish seemed to be holding their own. And thank goodness for that. Theodosia hated the thought of the poor little creatures being helplessly gobbled!

They ducked in the back door and went straight through the kitchen. Even though Theodosia had lived in her home for almost six months, she still hadn't done anything about the ugly kitchen cupboards. Still, the rest of the house more than made up for it.

In the living room, she knelt down and built a small fire. Even though the afternoon had been pleasant and warm, the evening was starting to feel cool. As she touched a match to the pile of kindling, Theodosia hoped there wasn't another storm cell lurking out there over the Atlantic. The storm on Saturday, the day of Delaine's wedding, had been quite enough. Some of the palmetto trees on her street still looked like they'd been blown inside out.

As red and blue flames snapped and danced off the walls of beveled cypress, the living room turned instantly cozy.

I love this place, Theodosia told herself. *I did the right thing in buying it.*

True, the money had been a stretch, but all the scrimping and saving had been worth it. For now, this perfect little cottage with the charming name of Hazelhurst was her pride and joy.

And what a cottage it was! The exterior was adorable and semi-quirky—a classic Tudor-style cottage that was asymmetrical in design with rough cedar tiles that replicated a thatched roof. The front of the cottage featured arched doors, cross gables, and a small turret. Lush tendrils of ivy curled their way up the walls.

Her small entrance foyer featured a brick floor, hunter green walls, and antique brass sconces. The living room had a beamed ceiling and polished wood floor. Chintz and damask furniture, a blue-and-gold Aubusson carpet, an antique highboy, and tasteful oil paintings added a finishing touch.

A log popped loudly and Earl Grey glanced at her.

"You're right," said Theodosia. "I have to get moving. I need to take a quick shower and start supper."

Earl Grey continued to stare at her with limpid brown eyes.

Theodosia reached out and stroked his sleek head. "Yes, he's coming over tonight. But please don't monopolize him too much, okay? Give me a chance once in a while."

Earl Grey thumped his tail with enthusiasm. But he wasn't making any promises.

* * *

Twenty minutes later, tendrils of hair still slightly damp on the back of her neck, Theodosia was in her kitchen peeling and deveining shrimp. Strains of Adele's "Rolling in the Deep" played on the CD player and Earl Grey was cozied on his dog bed in the corner of the kitchen, his bright eyes watching her every move.

Theodosia whipped up her pizza dough first, using King Arthur flour that Haley had ordered for her. Then she sliced an enormous heirloom tomato and arranged the juicy red slices on two plates, along with bunches of fresh basil. Just before she served the tomatoes, she'd drizzle on a nice mixture of olive oil and balsamic vinegar.

The pizza toppings made for easy prep work. She sizzled a dozen fresh shrimp, sliced black olives and red onion, and grated a mound of fresh Parmesan. Once the pizza dough was rolled out, she spooned on pesto sauce, then added the toppings.

Then she grabbed a bottle of Rubicon Cabernet Sauvignon and pulled the cork.

So what else? Ah, gotta set the table.

Theodosia placed two woven placemats on her kitchen table; set out knives, forks, and plates; then added a pair of wrought-iron candlesticks with twisted white candles.

And just when her kitchen was steamy and aromatic with top notes of basil, shrimp, and onion, Max knocked on the back door. As always, his timing was perfect.

Theodosia wasn't sure who was happier to see him, herself or Earl Grey. The dog danced and pranced his way around the kitchen, toenails clicking and ticking like castanets. But, of course, she was the one who got a wonderful bear hug along with a long, lingering kiss.

When the heavy breathing had concluded, for now,

anyway, Theodosia turned back to her dinner. Wine was poured, the tomatoes dressed, the pizza checked on.

"I love it when you make with the magic," said Max, lounging against the counter, sipping his glass of wine. His hair looked more tousled than usual tonight, and his face wore a satisfied grin.

"You're referring to my cooking?" Theodosia waved a hand. "This isn't much. In fact, it's downright easy."

"No, no, everything you do is pure alchemy," said Max. "You throw together bits of shrimp or pork, add fresh vegetables and a wonderful sauce and, presto-chango, dinner suddenly appears. Only it's not just dinner, it's a fanciful *creation*!"

"Really," said Theodosia. "It's just a simple pizza tonight. Per your request."

"But the cool thing is, you made it from scratch."

"Everything I learned about food chemistry and cooking I learned from Haley," said Theodosia. And it was true. Haley had taught her about the five basic tastes: sweet, bitter, sour, salty, and umami. And that baking generally relied on exact measurements, while cooking could be a lot more laissez-faire.

"Why do I somehow doubt that?" asked Max. "Why do I think you were born with a love and a knack for preparing great food. That you probably had a set of play dishes and one of those toy stoves when you were, like, two."

"You know," said Theodosia, as she peeked into the oven, "this is exactly what I'm in dire need of. Flattery and sweet talk. Definitely helps take my mind off Delaine."

"Has she been haunting you?" asked Max.

"Endlessly," said Theodosia, chuckling to herself at his choice of words. Lots of talk about hauntings lately. She opened the oven door and peered in. "Say, this pizza is going to be ready in about two more minutes."

"I take it Delaine stopped by today? At the tea shop?"

"She and a very nice woman named Millie Grant, who turned out to be Granville's secretary."

"But Delaine was bugging you."

"Oh, yeah. She wants me to look into things . . . you know."

"And you're undecided."

Theodosia shrugged. "I guess."

"Did you ask her about the cocaine?"

"She says she's never tried it in her life," said Theodosia.

"And you believe her?"

"I do," said Theodosia. "Delaine on cocaine would be like a Formula One car going three hundred miles an hour."

"What about Granville?"

"She said maybe, in the past. But not anymore."

"Clearly she was mistaken," said Max. He took a sip of wine and added, "Cocaine is basically God's way of telling you you have too much money."

"Oh, you," said Theodosia.

Max set his glass on the counter and opened his arms. Which was Theodosia's cue to toss her pot holder aside and help herself to another kiss and a hug.

"Really," she said. "You've been great about this." And he had. Max had been sympathetic and solicitous to her all weekend. In fact, he'd dropped by last night, on his way to a donor's dinner, to offer comfort and kisses.

"That pizza's not going to catch fire in there, is it?" Max asked, suddenly worried about his dinner.

No, Theodosia thought. *But I might.*

Theodosia waited until she'd served Max a second slice of pizza and poured another half glass of wine. Then she said, "How do you feel about ghosts?"

Max had been feeding Earl Grey a tidbit of golden crust.

When he heard her question, he paused and looked slightly bemused. "Is this a theoretical question, or have you heard chains rattling in your attic?"

"I don't have an attic," said Theodosia. "Just a crawl space. And I'm asking your opinion because I don't know if ghosts are whimsical entities or if there's the possibility they really do exist."

"Uh-oh," said Max. "Sounds like the beginning of an existential ectoplasm discussion."

"It's not funny," said Theodosia. "I really want your opinion on this."

Max squinted across the table at her. "Why do I have the feeling this somehow relates to Mr. Granville's recent passing?"

"Because it does," said Theodosia.

"In that case, you better give me some context. Fill me in a little more so I can better answer your question."

So Theodosia told Max about how Bill Glass, with complete sincerity, had told her that Ravencrest Inn was reputedly haunted. And then she explained to him how two amateur ghost hunters, surprise, surprise, had suddenly come galloping into her tea shop this morning.

"Ghost hunters," said Max. He looked skeptical.

"Yes, but fairly legitimate ones," said Theodosia. "The Beckman brothers are producing a reality show. Something called *Southern Hauntings*."

"Of course, they are," said Max. "Which makes them perfectly legitimate. And they want to rope you in . . . how? To conduct some sort of interview?"

"Actually, it goes a little beyond that," said Theodosia. "The brothers are determined to get permission from the Rattlings to actually go inside Ravencrest Inn and—"

"Do what?" Max cut in. Suddenly, he didn't look happy. Suddenly, he wasn't all that interested in another bite of pizza.

"I suppose they want to use an infrared video camera," said Theodosia. "To record any possible images or sounds."

"Eh," said Max. "You mean like a séance? Or fooling around with a Ouija board?"

"Nothing that spooky," said Theodosia. "The way they explained everything, it was more scientific."

"Right," said Max. "And what else are the Bothersome Beckman Boys up to?" He sensed there was something else she wasn't telling him.

"They asked me to go with them," said Theodosia. There, she'd spelled it all out. Now he could sit back and enjoy an insanely good laugh.

But he didn't. He remained quite serious.

"Run that by me again," said Max. "*Why* exactly were you invited to join the party?"

Theodosia drew a deep breath. This was the tricky part: making her explanation sound plausible. "Because I was the person closest to Granville when he died. As the ghost hunters explained it to me, I was nearest to him when his spirit left his body."

"Of course," Max said smoothly. "Now it's all crystal clear to me." He cocked his head to one side and assumed a serious expression. "Actually, the person closest to Granville when he died was the man who murdered him."

"I suppose you're right," said Theodosia. "I never thought of it like that."

"Well, maybe you should. Because this isn't something you should fool around with. You'd be treading on a murder investigation."

"But I'm not hunting for a murderer," said Theodosia. "It's more like, um, a parlor trick."

"But what if the murderer is still around? What if there's something in that guest room that he's still after?" Max stared at her with utter seriousness. "What if you stumble on something that impacts the investigation?"

"Okay," Theodosia said slowly. "You could have a point."

Then, like a storm that had suddenly blown itself out, Max's face broke into a grin. "Theo, are you kidding me? You want to go on a ghost-hunting expedition? That's what kids do at summer camp. They send their bunkmates out on a snipe hunt and toss in a ghost hunt for good measure." He was rolling now. "You drape a bedsheet over your head and scare the poop out of the little kids."

"When you put it that way . . . it does sound a little foolish."

"Because it *is* foolish," said Max.

"Still," said Theodosia, "Charleston is supposed to be one of the most haunted cities in America. Right up there with New Orleans."

"Come on," said Max. "You don't really believe in ghosts and witches and haunts, do you?"

Theodosia had to think about that. She'd been born and bred in the low country where tales of headless horsemen, pirate ghosts, and dead Confederate soldiers were everyday legends. Where kids were admonished to watch out for boo hags when they ventured out at night.

"You know," she finally told him, "I'm not entirely sure."

8

Theodosia strolled down King Street, enjoying the warm weather and bountiful sunshine that had finally been bestowed upon Charleston. Tall redbrick buildings with narrow white shutters caught the sun's rays and bounced them back at her, making her feel warm and relaxed. Palm trees bobbed their shaggy heads as gentle sea breezes ruffled their fronds.

Outside Gold Nugget Antiques, Theodosia pulled out her cell phone and called the Indigo Tea Shop. Drayton picked up on the first ring.

"Where are you?" he asked in a brusque tone. It was unusual for her not to be there helping with their morning setup.

"I'm basking in the sun on King Street," said Theodosia.

"Why are you not here slaving away with Haley and me?"

"Because Delaine asked me to have a little chat with Simone Asher, Granville's former girlfriend. And her shop is in this part of town."

"I take it Delaine believes that hard-hearted Simone is the one who murdered Dougan Granville?" said Drayton.

"Something like that, yes."

"I met Simone the day of the wedding," said Drayton. "She seemed a lot more interested in getting photographed for *Shooting Star* than she was in Granville. So trust me when I say she probably had nothing to do with it. This is just one of Delaine's strange delusions coupled with some sort of revenge fantasy."

"You're probably right. And even though your diagnosis is right out of Psych 101, I'm going to indulge Delaine's paranoia anyway."

"You say this ex-girlfriend owns an antique shop?" asked Drayton.

"Vintage shop," said Theodosia.

"Well, if you should happen to come across a Royale Garden Amari Chintz teapot, kindly grab it for me, will you? Mine has a nasty chip on the spout."

"I'll keep an eye out," Theodosia promised.

Archangel turned out to be both glamorous and lovely. The shop was a small jewel box of a space with whitewashed walls, Oriental carpets on a polished wood floor, and a twinkling crystal chandelier overhead. The walls were decorated with vintage shawls and fans, and there were racks packed tightly with vintage gowns and dresses. Small glass cases with pinpoint spotlights were filled with treasures that included antique cameos, Bakelite bracelets, gold compacts from the thirties and forties, elegant rings, and screwback earrings. Theodosia even spotted what she thought might be a genuine Verdura cuff. Amazing!

"Can I help you?" Simone Asher looked up from a small round display table where she was arranging a pair of hotpink Schiaparelli shoes, a black silk evening bag encrusted with rhinestones, a pair of gloves, a bottle of My Sin perfume, and a strand of pearls.

"Those are gorgeous pearls," said Theodosia. They were a dreamy pistachio-green color with an amazing luster.

"Tahitians," said Simone. "Natural, not cultured." She picked up the choker-length strand and fingered them like worry beads. "From the twenties. Back when pearls were truly matched for perfection." She smiled tightly and added, "You're Theodosia, aren't you? Delaine's friend." She straightened up and smoothed the white silk sheath dress she was wearing.

"That's right," said Theodosia. She took her time studying Simone, since she'd never observed the woman in her natural habitat before. She'd caught glimpses of Simone here and there, dashing through shops and restaurants. And she'd seen her at Ravencrest Inn this past Saturday. But she'd never carried on an actual conversation with her. Now Theodosia saw that Simone was everything Delaine had raged about. The woman was tall, thin, leggy, and a sun-kissed blond. Simone was probably in her late thirties but could easily pass for a few years younger. She had the polished air of a fashion model who'd come to the end of her career in front of the camera but had easily segued into another line of work where her beauty and fashion know-how would serve her well. Basically, Simone had an attractiveness quotient that most women would kill for.

"Are you a fan of vintage pieces?" Simone asked. Her languid way of speaking, a soft, melodic drawl, corresponded perfectly to the sensuous way she moved.

"I am," said Theodosia. She pointed at a black taffeta ankle-length dress draped on a mannequin. "Especially when we're talking about a dress as gorgeous at that one."

Simone smiled in agreement. "Lovely, isn't it? That's a nineteen fifty-one Christian Dior dress. What was termed *The New Look.*"

"And I love the skirt you have on display in your front window. The ankle-length pale green?"

"That one's a Balmain," said Simone. "A rather rare piece at that."

"Lovely," breathed Theodosia. And it was. That was the thing about fashion: Whether it was vintage or au courant, if a piece was beautifully designed and constructed, it just worked. Theodosia knew that if she paired a silk tank top with that long Balmain skirt, she could skip off to the opera and look stunning. Well, perhaps not *stunning*, but she knew she'd look awfully darned good.

"We have more recent items, too," said Simone, indicating the racks of clothing that were packed into her small shop. "A few Yves Saint Laurent pieces from the early seventies that are in surprisingly top-notch condition. And some Claude Montana and Versace from the mid-eighties." She pushed a hank of blond hair off her face and said, in her soft drawl, "Let me guess. Delaine thinks I murdered Dougan."

Theodosia wasn't prepared for such a straightforward statement.

Simone seemed to savor Theodosia's sudden discomfort for a moment or two. Then she said, "Let me save you some time. I've already been questioned at length by two different detectives. The fact of the matter is, I was there. At the wedding." She smirked. "I was an invited guest at the oh-so-swanky Ravencrest Inn. But did I creep up the back stairs and murder poor Dougan? Hardly."

"Do you know how he was killed?"

"I understand it was a lethal blow to the head."

"How do you feel about that?" asked Theodosia.

"Sad. Heartbroken, of course." But Simone didn't appear sad or heartbroken. Mostly she just looked bored with their conversation.

Theodosia decided to put her manners aside and play a

little hardball. "When you and Granville were together, did the two of you do a lot of coke?"

"Coke?" said Simone. "As in cocaine?" She fought to arrange her lovely face into an expression of stunned amazement. "No, of course not. Never in a million years! I don't do drugs, I don't even like to take aspirin." She shook her head, as if a swarm of hornets had suddenly attacked her. "Why would you even *ask* such a thing?"

"I didn't mean to offend you," said Theodosia, as she glanced around the shop. "Really, it was just an innocent question."

"I certainly hope so," said an indignant Simone. "Because I wouldn't want you thinking that I—"

"What's that?" Theodosia asked, interrupting her. She pointed at a small wicker stand tucked behind a rack of colorful clothing.

"Vintage Pucci dresses."

"No, behind them," said Theodosia. If her eyes weren't deceiving her, she was pretty sure the shelf held a small collection of glass paperweights.

Simone took a step forward. "Oh. Some vintage opera glasses and a couple of paperweights."

"Paperweights," Theodosia repeated.

"Yes," said Simone. "Interesting enough, they're what's left of a collection I sold to the people who own Ravencrest Inn."

Theodosia was utterly floored. "You realize, Simone, that Granville was probably struck on the head by a glass paperweight."

Simone threw her hands in the air. "For goodness' sake, now you really *are* accusing me of murder."

"You're the one who said it, not me."

Simone's face turned lobster-red and her eyes narrowed to Kabuki mask slits. She balled her hands into fists and leaned forward until she was just inches from Theodosia, invading her personal space. "Don't play games with me!" she snarled.

Theodosia fought to maintain a neutral tone. "And don't you play games with me!"

"I think," said Simone, taking a step back, "that you'd better leave."

And I think, Theodosia told herself, as she fled out the door, *that you've got a nasty temper.*

Theodosia parked her Jeep in the narrow brick alley behind the Indigo Tea Shop, buzzed through the back door into her office, and dropped her bag on top of her perpetually messy desk. Then she flew into the tea room to find it practically filled with customers. Though Drayton appeared to be more harried than usual, he relaxed visibly once he spotted Theodosia.

"There you are," said Drayton. "Thank goodness."

"Sorry to be late," said Theodosia. She slipped a long black Parisian waiter's apron over her head and tied it in back. "I see we're busy already."

"Now that the sunshine and warm weather have moved in, everyone seems to be out in full force! We've had tourists, neighbors, and tea clubs clamoring for tables. We might even have to put our wrought-iron tables and chairs out on the sidewalk."

"Good," said Theodosia. "I'm glad we're busy." She didn't fret unduly about business or about the tea shop being profitable. But the specter of a slowed economy was always in the back of her mind. For some reason, maybe it was their dedicated customer base or the fact that they worked weekends and evenings catering teas, the Indigo Tea Shop continued to hum along rather nicely. And Theodosia, with her business and marketing background, knew that the difference between making a living and making a profit was vast indeed. And her beloved little tea shop, knock on wood, continued to churn out a profit.

Drayton pulled a floral Spode teapot off the shelf, swished it out with warm water, and added three scoops of Yunnan black tea. "Well, did Simone Asher confess to the murder?"

"No," said Theodosia. "But she knew exactly why I was there."

"She knew Delaine sent you in to do reconnaissance at the enemy camp? To give her the third degree?"

"She sure did. Simone's not stupid."

"Neither are you," said Drayton. He placed the teapot on a silver tray, then added two silver-rimmed bone china teacups and a small plate of paper-thin lemon slices. "Did you pick up any vibes from her at all?"

"Only that Simone acted like she'd been poked with a hot wire when I mentioned cocaine."

"Meaning she denied knowing anything about it."

"Let me put it this way," said Theodosia. "If we'd been doing a scene at an improv class, Simone would have received a gold star."

"Huh," said Drayton.

"The weird thing is," said Theodosia, "I went to meet Simone just as a kind of pro forma favor to Delaine. Not really believing she had anything to do with Granville's death."

"Yes?"

"And now I'm not so sure about her. There's a sneaky, snarky side to Simone. The woman's a little . . . nasty."

"Wait just a minute," said Drayton. "You don't really think she could have murdered Granville, do you?"

"I don't know. But Simone certainly likes to push people's buttons."

Drayton snatched up his tray. "But does she also push drugs?"

Theodosia stood at the counter pondering this for a moment, until a friendly voice called out, "Hey, Theo."

Theodosia spun around. "Leigh!" she called out. Leigh Caroll owned the Cabbage Patch Gift Shop down the street. She was an African American woman with beautifully burnished skin, sepia-toned hair, and almond eyes that turned up slightly at the corners, giving her an upbeat mischievous look.

"I see you're busy as usual," said Leigh. "Why don't you send your customers down to my place when they're finished here?"

"Why don't you give me a stack of business cards and I will," said Theodosia, delighted to see her friend. "Can I offer you a scone and a cuppa? We could brew your favorite peach tea if you'd like."

Leigh gave an airy wave. "Just give me whatever's handy." She leaned across the counter. "Did I hear right? That you were at a wedding where some fellow got killed?"

"Delaine's wedding," said Theodosia. "Her fiancé."

Leigh clapped a hand to her chest. "No!"

"It was awful," said Theodosia.

"And you were some kind of witness?" asked Leigh, curious now.

"I was the one who discovered the victim."

"Poor Delaine," said Leigh. "She must be beside herself. And on her wedding day like that." Leigh's face crumpled and she shook her head sadly. "How could something like that happen?" she asked. "If you're not safe at your own *wedding*, then where are you safe?"

Just when Theodosia was delivering a plate of black currant scones and a pot of vanilla spice tea, the ghost hunters came charging into her shop. They spotted her, gave an enthusiastic wave, then trooped over to the same table they'd occupied yesterday.

A few minutes later, her customers all taken care of and

Drayton's watchful eyes surveying the shop, Theodosia went over and joined them.

"Okay," she said, as she slid into a chair. "I'm in."

"That's terrific," Jed enthused. "We were hoping you'd say yes."

"Wonderful," said Tim, grinning. "And we've obtained the full consent of the Rattlings. In the form of a written release, I might add."

Theodosia held up a hand. "Just a second. My yes comes with a rather large codicil. I had to run your request past Delaine Dish, of course."

"Mr. Granville's ex-bride," said Jed.

"Uh . . ." Theodosia hesitated. Was that the correct term? Ex-bride? Or was Delaine Granville's former bride? How *would* you describe Delaine's current status? Bride in mourning? Goodness, that sounded awful!

"You were saying?" said Tim.

"Yes," said Theodosia, plugging back into the conversation. "I ran your ghost-hunting expedition past Delaine and she basically approved. In fact, she expressed a strong desire to come along."

"She can come," said Jed. "In fact, her presence might be very helpful. If Mr. Granville's spirit is lingering, she's the one person who might be able to draw him out."

Or Delaine might freak out, thought Theodosia.

"So we're on for tonight," said Jed.

"When?" asked Theodosia. She felt tingly inside, like her adrenaline had started to pump. And there was a note of apprehension, too, as if she'd just agreed to participate in a bank heist. "What time?"

"After dark," said Tim. "Let's say we all meet at Ravencrest Inn at nine o'clock."

9

❧

"*I can't believe* you're really going to indulge this ghost-hunting fantasy," said Drayton. He'd been courteous to the two brothers but visibly relieved once they'd finally left.

"Hard to believe," said Theodosia, "but Delaine's all for it."

"She likes it in theory," said Drayton. "Your little rendezvous sounds quite spiritual and soothing to her, a last-chance opportunity to say good-bye to her dearly departed. But when you get Delaine back in that dingy little room and something goes bump in the night, she might just have herself a heart attack."

"Thanks for your upbeat take on things," said Theodosia.

Drayton smiled. "Always happy to oblige."

Theodosia skipped into the kitchen and grabbed a couple of Haley's ploughman's platters that had been special-ordered. She'd put together a tasty assortment of Gouda, Cheddar, and Stilton cheeses; rare roast beef; chopped pickled pears; dried apricots; and salted pecans. After delivering the platters and receiving oohs and aahs from the recipients, she dashed back into the kitchen. "What else is on the docket for today? Lunchwise, I mean."

"Some pretty good stuff," said Haley, as she sculpted a radish into a perfect rose. "We've got lobster salad in mini brioche rolls, triangles of Black Forest ham and Swiss cheese on rye, and chilled strawberry soup with cinnamon raisin biscuits."

"Superb," said Theodosia. "And what else besides our scone offerings?" She knew Haley had been baking like a fiend. Then again, she always did.

"That would be my zucchini bread and miniature chocolate cappuccino cakes."

"Drayton's favorite," said Theodosia. He'd once polished off six of the little cakes all by himself.

"That's right," said Haley, as she deftly carved another radish. "You know I live to please him."

"Don't tell him that," laughed Theodosia.

"Or he might start believing it!" said Haley, cackling.

The Indigo Tea Shop was enjoying a packed house this lunch hour. All their reservations had shown up on time, tourists had found their way in, and a few locals were perched at their favorite tables.

"Only one table left," observed Drayton, as he hastily dumped sugar cubes into a crystal bowl. "Who's going to be the lucky party?"

"Whoever's behind door number one," joked Theodosia, as a shadow played behind the curtains on the front door. She grabbed a pair of tea menus and smiled as the door began to swing open. "Welcome to . . ." ˉ

A bright light exploded directly in her face!

Temporarily blinded, Theodosia wondered for a brief moment if a pack of roving aliens hadn't just crash-landed their flying saucer on Church Street. Then she saw Bill Glass flash his smarmy grin from behind his offending camera.

"You!" she cried. "Why are you always in my face and annoying?"

"Relax, babe," said Glass. "You know you're happy to see me."

"Hardly," Theodosia said, her voice suddenly as stiff as her posture.

"Got a table?" asked Glass. "We need to talk."

"I doubt we have much to say to each other," said Theodosia, but she led him to her last table anyway.

Glass plunked himself down, then said, "Sit. Come on, we need to talk."

Theodosia sat down. "About what?"

Glass leaned forward. "You pick up any more poop on the Granville murder?"

"No," she said. "Not much out there. The police are being pretty tight-lipped." She hesitated. She hated to do it, but then she asked, "Have you?"

That was Glass's cue. "Have you ever heard of a guy by the name of Bobby St. Cloud?"

"No. Why? Who is he?"

Glass hunched forward. "Far as I can figure, he's some kind of wholesaler. But an off-the-books wholesaler, if you know what I mean."

"I'm not sure I do," said Theodosia.

"Look," said Glass, "I've been asking around here and there. And it looks like this Bobby St. Cloud guy might have been Granville's Cuban connection."

"You mean he sold him Cuban cigars?"

"Yeah, yeah," said Glass. "That's it."

"Wait a minute," said Theodosia. "Are you implying that this Bobby St. Cloud killed Granville?"

"I'm not saying that at all."

"Then what are you blathering about?"

"I'm just wondering if this Bobby St. Cloud knows anything," said Glass. He poked a finger at her. "You gotta ask
Delaine about him. See if he was on the guest list at the
wedding."

"What if he was?"

"Then we try to track him down," said Glass. "Pump
him for information."

"Shouldn't the police do that? And what if this Bobby
St. Cloud is the killer?"

"Why would he be?" said Glass. "He had a good deal
going. He was supplying Granville with his product."

"If we find Bobby St. Cloud, what's in this for you?"
asked Theodosia. She knew Glass always had an angle.

Glass spread his hands apart. "Probably a story. You know
me, always trying to get the latest gossip on these Charleston swells."

"Even though they all want their picture in your crappy
little tabloid," said Theodosia.

Glass grinned. "I get 'em coming and going. Ain't it
grand?"

Bill Glass never did order lunch. Or even tea. So Theodosia
eventually eased him out the door and gave the table to a
couple that really did want to eat. Theodosia took their
order, then ran it back to Haley while Drayton circulated
with a pot of tea in each hand. Because the day was getting
warmer and warmer, Drayton had also made a pitcher of
raspberry iced tea. Basically his red berry blend with a little
hibiscus and citrus thrown in.

"Whew," said Theodosia, brushing back a tangle of hair.
As the day had gotten progressively warmer, the humidity
had also built. And her auburn hair, always sensitive to
changes in the atmosphere (probably the barometric pressure), seemed to be poufing and expanding.

"Your hair looks great today," Haley told her.

"That's what you think," said Theodosia. "For me it's awful." She was always a little self-conscious about her mass of curly hair.

"Are you kidding?" said Haley. "How would you like to have stick-straight hair like me? I can layer on gobs of Dippity-do and crunch it in rollers for forty-eight hours straight. But two minutes after I take the rollers out, blech. It goes completely straight. So why bother? But you, on the other hand . . ."

"Have too much hair," said Theodosia.

"No," said Haley. "A woman can never have too much hair."

"Don't you have something in the oven?" asked Theodosia. Haley was hanging around the front counter, chatting like it was cocktail hour.

"My last batch of biscuits doesn't come out for twenty minutes yet," she said, checking her watch. "So I've got time." She glanced around the tea shop, her appraising, slightly closed eyes landing on a man who was sitting at a table in the corner. "Mmm," said Haley. "Who's the good-looking dude?"

Theodosia glanced over at the man. "No idea. He just wandered in off the street a few minutes ago. Drayton took his order for a pot of black plum tea."

"I kind of dig that alert German shepherd look," said Haley.

Theodosia stole another quick glance at their guest. Haley was right. The man was attractive. Short, almost brush-cut gray hair; aquiline nose; high cheekbones; piercing blue eyes.

"And he's skinny," said Haley. "With those ropy muscles that always look so good on skinny guys. Like he works out all the time. Kind of like, mmm . . . that actor, Daniel Craig."

"Then maybe he wants his tea shaken, not stirred," said Theodosia.

Haley craned her neck. "Is he wearing a wedding band?"

"No idea."

"Try to find out if he's single," said Haley.

"He's too old for you," Theodosia admonished. "That man is forty-five if he's a day."

"That's true," said Haley, with a sly smile. "But he's not too old for you."

"Haley!"

But when Theodosia approached the man's table with a friendly smile and his pot of tea, the man's casual demeanor changed immediately. He jumped from his chair and flipped open a small leather wallet that revealed a gold badge.

"Jack Alston," he told her. "ATF agent."

"Goodness," said Theodosia, completely taken aback. She'd figured the man for a tourist who was patiently waiting for his wife while she shopped at the Cabbage Patch.

"Can we talk?" asked Alston.

Theodosia took a step backward. "About what?"

"Please," Alston said, indicating the chair opposite him. "Sit down. I'm not going to bite."

"I have customers."

His cool blue eyes glided around the tea shop. "You're not that busy."

"All right," said Theodosia. "But only for a minute." She sat down, put her hands flat on the table, and said, "What is it you want?"

"I'd like to ask you a few questions about your neighbor," said Alston. "Dougan Granville."

"He died," said Theodosia. "In what looks to be a strange set of circumstances. So perhaps you should contact the Charleston Police Department for complete information. The chief investigator, Detective Burt Tidwell, heads their Robbery-Homicide Division. He can probably answer all of your questions and bring you up to speed." Theodosia gave a perfunctory smile and started to get up.

Alston held up his hand. "Please, I've already done that. Obviously. But I have a few questions for you."

Theodosia eased back down.

"Do you know how Dougan Granville was obtaining his cigars?"

Oh, crap, she thought. Instead, she said, "I don't know. Probably from some tobacco wholesaler?"

"I'm talking about his Cuban cigars," said Alston.

"No idea," said Theodosia. "I don't really know anything about cigars." *Should I mention the name Bobby St. Cloud? No, Glass could be way off base and I might just muddy the water. Better to keep my mouth shut.* "I thought Cuban cigars were illegal."

Alston offered a thin smile. "Hence my presence here."

"I don't mean to be rude," said Theodosia. "But wouldn't you have more luck snooping around Granville's cigar shop? This is, in case you hadn't noticed, a tea shop."

"And a very pleasant one at that," said Alston. "You were Granville's neighbor; perhaps you might have seen deliveries that came to his home?"

"What are you getting at?" asked Theodosia. "Are you implying I'm some kind of black market smuggler? Excuse me, but I sell tea. Tea from China, Japan, India, Ceylon, and a dozen other countries. But no tea from Cuba. And I have no knowledge of stinky, smuggled cigars. The fact is, I loathe cigars."

"You're a very attractive woman," said Alston. "Did you know that your face is extremely animated when you get angry?"

"Excuse me?" Now he was flirting with her? The nerve of this man!

Alston held up his hands in a gesture of appeal. "Okay, okay, apologies. I didn't mean to get fresh. It's just that, well, you *are* an attractive woman."

"Thank you," said Theodosia. "I think."

"In my line of work I so rarely meet someone like you."

"You're very good," said Theodosia. "When you flatter women like that, do they always cooperate? Do they always answer your questions?"

"Pretty much," said Alston.

"How lovely for you. You must be one of the most successful ATF agents on record."

"Did you just insult me?" he asked.

"Not at all," said Theodosia, with a gracious smile.

"Sure, you did," said Alston. "And here I was thinking I might want to ask you out for coffee."

"But not for tea."

"I figured you might like to change things up."

"Really," said Theodosia, "I should get back to my customers." She stretched out a hand. "Agent Alston, it was a pleasure to meet you."

Alston accepted her hand but held on. "I never knew a real live Theodosia before."

Theodosia stared at him, a blip of curiosity rising inside her.

"The only other Theodosia I know of was my great-great-grand aunt," said Alston.

"Oh, my goodness," said Theodosia, finally extricating her hand. "You're talking about Theodosia Alston?"

Alston nodded. "That's right. You've heard of her?"

Theodosia stared at him. "Of course, I have. I was *named* for her." Theodosia Alston had been the daughter of Aaron Burr and the wife of Joseph Alston, governor of South Carolina, back in the early 1800s. "In fact, my mother used to tell me stories about Theodosia Alston. About how she disappeared at sea aboard the schooner *Patriot* on her way to New York. Simply . . . vanished."

"Poof," said Jack Alston, picking up the story. "They never knew if her sailing ship foundered off the Outer

Banks in a raging storm or if a roving band of pirates captured her."

"Poor Theodosia," said Theodosia.

"Missing out on so much life," said Jack Alston as he
stared at her with obvious interest.

Theodosia couldn't wait to get to a phone and call Tidwell.

"Do you know an ATF agent by the name of Jack
Alston?" she asked, as soon as she had him on the line.

"And a good afternoon to you, too," said Tidwell. "Why?
Did Alston drop by to see you?"

"Yes, he did. Did you send him?"

"I might have mentioned your name," said Tidwell.

"Why. On. Earth?"

"Because he's trying to hunt down Granville's supplier,"
said Tidwell.

"I gathered that," said Theodosia. "And you thought
that maybe I've been importing Cuban cigars in my spare
time?"

"Not quite. But I did want the two of you to become
acquainted."

"Why is that?"

"Because I'm guessing there's a stash of Cuban cigars
floating around somewhere and that Granville's supplier
might be looking to get his merchandise back."

"You think this supplier hasn't been paid?"

"Actually, Miss Browning, let's call it what it really is.
Whoever supplied Granville with Cuban cigars is not a
supplier at all. He's a smuggler."

"Don't ever sic anybody like that on me again!" said
Theodosia. "Alston was completely rude and insensitive."
And very attractive, though I hate to admit it.

"His type of personality is standard government issue,"
said Tidwell.

"Listen," said Theodosia. "While I have you on the phone . . ."

"Yelling at me," said Tidwell.

Theodosia plowed ahead. "I wanted you to know that I dropped by Archangel this morning. Did you know that Simone has a collection of paperweights in her shop?"

"Or what's left of the collection she sold to the Rattlings," said Tidwell.

"You know about that?"

"Of course, I do."

"Don't you find it strange?" said Theodosia. "That Simone sold them the murder weapon?"

"We don't know that's what killed Granville at all," said Tidwell. "It could have been the butt of a gun; it could have been a candlestick."

"Colonel Mustard in the library with a candlestick?" said Theodosia. "Please."

"The point is," said Tidwell, "you're jumping to conclusions. Correction, you're leaping to them. So kindly stop."

"Okay, how about this little tidbit? Have you heard of a guy named Bobby St. Cloud? He's supposed to be Granville's cigar supplier."

"And where did you pick up that rumor?"

"From Bill Glass."

"Bill Glass dines out on rumors," said Tidwell.

"I realize that," said Theodosia. "But somebody should check it out."

"That someone being me?"

"Well . . . yes. I suppose so," said Theodosia. "And then if you could just . . ."

But Tidwell had already hung up.

"Get back to me," Theodosia said into dead air. She balanced the phone in her hand, thinking, then hung it back on the wall.

"Problems?" asked Drayton.

"Maybe," said Theodosia. "But nothing I can't handle." She untied her apron and hung it on a peg.

Drayton cocked an eye at her. "Good heavens, you're going out again?"

"Apologies," said Theodosia. "But I have to. I made a promise to Delaine."

"I imagine you're going to the funeral home?"

"I wish," said Theodosia. "Since it would probably be a lot more hospitable." When Drayton looked confused, she explained. "We're going to pay a visit to Granville and Grumley."

"Ah," said Drayton. "The law firm. Well, try to keep your wits about you, especially since you'll have Delaine in tow. Those lawyer fellows can be awfully cunning."

"That's what worries me," said Theodosia.

10

The offices of Granville and Grumley were located in a huge brick mansion just two blocks from Meeting and Broad Street, what was commonly known in Charleston as the Four Corners of Law.

As they approached the double doors, thick glass faced with curlicue wrought iron, Delaine reached out and squeezed Theodosia's hand.

"Thank you for doing this," said Delaine. "Thank you for coming along as moral support."

"You're welcome," said Theodosia.

"And by the way, you look very nice," said Delaine.

Theodosia had tossed a navy blue blazer over her khakis and white T-shirt. And, at the last minute, she had tied on a printed scarf to add a little dash. Delaine, of course, looked very glamorous and adult in her tomato-red skirt suit and sky-high white Manolos.

"Thank you, I . . ."

"Did you get a chance to talk to Simone?" Delaine interrupted.

"I stopped by her shop this morning."

"And?"

"Not much to tell," said Theodosia. "She claims to be very upset about Granville's passing."

"Huh," snorted Delaine. "What did you think of her shop? Of the vintage clothing? Pretty ratty stuff, right?" Delaine had recently added a few racks of vintage clothing in her Cotton Duck boutique, so she was understandably nervous.

"Actually, her shop looked very nice," said Theodosia. "But there was one thing . . ." She wondered if she should reveal her discovery of the paperweights to Delaine. Well, why not?

"Oh?" said Delaine. "What was that?"

"Simone had a couple of glass paperweights."

Delaine's eyes went huge. "Are you serious? You mean like the one that cracked poor Dougan's skull? Like that?"

"Similar to the one that *might* have dealt the fatal blow," said Theodosia.

"I hope you told Detective Tidwell about this!"

"As a matter of fact, I did."

"Is he going to arrest her?"

"I doubt it," said Theodosia. "In fact, he didn't seem particularly concerned."

Delaine was aghast. "Well, I never . . . !"

"Please don't be disheartened," said Theodosia. "We'll get to the bottom of Dougan's death yet."

Delaine worried her front teeth against her bottom lip. "What about the drugs? Did you ask Simone about the drugs?"

"She swore she had no knowledge of drug use."

"His or hers?" asked Delaine.

"Either."

"And you believed her?"

"I really don't know what to think," said Theodosia. And she didn't. The evidence in Granville's room had been fairly damning. And as far as Granville using drugs with Simone . . . well, that was in the past. So who knew?

"She's a druggie," Delaine said, and there was harsh conviction in her voice. "I mean, how else does the woman stay so gosh-darn skinny?"

"I can think of a few ways," said Theodosia.

Millie Grant greeted them with a nervous smile. "They're expecting you," she said in a quiet voice.

"Who is?" asked Theodosia. She wanted to know exactly what she was in for.

"Mr. Grumley and Mr. Horton," said Millie.

"Both of them?" said Theodosia.

Millie's head bobbed. "It looks that way."

"I was under the impression I was meeting only with Allan Grumley," said Delaine. She'd walked in under full steam; now her confidence seemed to be eroding.

Millie looked apologetic as she led them to a conference room. "It seems strange to me, too," she whispered.

"Millie," said Theodosia, "I know this question is way out of left field, but do you know anything about a shipment of cigars?"

Millie's brows knit together. "I know that Mr. Granville owned a cigar shop, but . . . why, is something missing?"

"We're not sure," said Theodosia.

Millie shook her head. "I don't really know much about the shop. He kept his different businesses fairly compartmentalized."

"Okay," said Theodosia. "But if you hear anything . . ."

"If I do, I'll be sure to let you know," Millie whispered. Then, in a louder voice, she said, "You can wait in here."

Theodosia glanced around the conference room. It basically screamed *law office*. The walls were burnished wood, the conference table an acre of polished mahogany. A dozen red leather chairs with hobnail studs were clustered around the table. Law books populated the floor-to-ceiling bookshelves at both ends of the room.

"Tailor made for billy goats," Theodosia remarked.

"Excuse me?" said Delaine.

"Billy goats," said Theodosia. "Men who posture and prance and try to intimidate."

Delaine smiled faintly. "Which describes this law firm to a T."

"That's right," said Theodosia. "So don't let these trappings fool you."

"Ladies!" Allan Grumley exclaimed loudly as he bustled in to greet them. Grumley was balding and portly and possessed the flat eyes of a rattlesnake. His suit was hand-tailored, his fingernails were buffed to a high gloss, and his watch was a vintage Cartier. He looked like old money with a side of trouble.

"Good day, Mr. Grumley," Delaine said demurely as she offered a hand. "I think you know my friend Theodosia Browning . . ."

"Indeed I do," said Grumley, smiling and showing a wide expanse of teeth.

Theodosia had met Allan Grumley for the briefest moment last Saturday at Ravencrest Inn, and he'd hardly been warm or even cordial to her. Really, not even tepid. But today Grumley was smiling, chattering away like crazy, and pulling out chairs for them. She figured he must be up to something.

"I understand Charles Horton wants to join us, too?" said Theodosia.

"Indeed, he does," said Grumley.

"Why would that be?" asked Theodosia.

Grumley was taken aback. "Why . . . because he's a relative."

"Not really," said Delaine.

"As I understand the situation," said Theodosia, "Miss Dish is here because she was named beneficiary in Mr. Granville's life insurance policy. Is that not so?"

"You're quite correct," said Grumley, steepling his fingers together and staring at her from across the table.

"Which makes this a private matter," said Theodosia.

Grumley looked momentarily stunned. "Fine," he said. "If you wish this meeting to remain completely private, Miss Dish, then that's what we shall do."

"Please," said Delaine. Delaine was a social gadabout, a world-class gossip, and a demon when it came to twisting people's arms and raising money for charitable causes, but right now she seemed more than a little shaken.

"So the life insurance," said Theodosia, trying to hasten things along.

"It's all fairly straightforward," said Grumley. "Miss Dish was the sole beneficiary and will receive the sum of half a million dollars."

"Goodness!" said Delaine. "I had no idea it was so much!"

"My partner was generous to a fault," said Grumley. "And, as you can see, he firmly believed in estate planning."

"About the estate," said Theodosia. Her confident smile let Allan Grumley know he wasn't the only friendly barracuda in the room.

Grumley raised his brows as if making a polite inquiry. "Yes?"

"Delaine was under the impression that she'd been named in Mr. Granville's will," said Theodosia.

Now Grumley drummed his fingers on the table. "Uh-huh."

"Since you are Mr. Granville's former law partner," said Theodosia, "I'm going to assume that you were the one who drew up his will."

More drumming of fingers. "Uh-huh," Grumley said again.

"Did you?" Theodosia pressed. Honestly, this was like pulling teeth.

Grumley's chuckle was harsh and forced. "I did indeed. But I'm afraid we're not able to move ahead with that piece of business."

"Why on earth not?" asked Delaine.

"Please explain," said Theodosia. And this time she wasn't smiling.

"Since there is a murder investigation under way," said Grumley, "the police have requested that the deceased's last will and testament not be released."

"That seems like an unusual request," said Theodosia. She decided she'd better check with Tidwell to verify that.

"These are unusual circumstances," said Grumley.

"And once the circumstances are resolved?" said Theodosia.

"Then the contents of the will shall be made known and will proceed through probate," said Grumley.

"And on to the heirs," said Delaine.

"Unless . . ." said Grumley. He held up an index finger. "Unless someone challenges the will or elects to make a claim."

"Who would do that?" asked Delaine.

"Family," said Grumley.

"Or extended family?" said Theodosia.

"Possibly," said Grumley.

"Like Charles Horton?" Delaine spat out.

Grumley just lifted a hand.

*   *   *

Two minutes later, out on the front sidewalk, Delaine turned to Theodosia and said, "That turned out to be a big nothing."

"On the contrary," said Theodosia.

Delaine's brows pinched together. "Did I miss something?"

Theodosia smiled. "We found out that you're getting Granville's life insurance, that you're undoubtedly mentioned in his will, and that Charles Horton is probably going to launch a claim against Granville's estate."

Delaine pressed her clutch purse close against her chest. "I did miss something."

"Don't worry about it. In your defense, you're probably still in shock."

"I am, aren't I?" said Delaine, looking a little dazed. "That probably explains it."

"Which is why you really don't have to go back to Ravencrest Inn tonight."

"But I want to go," said Delaine. "If there's a chance . . ." She snapped her mouth shut and said, "If there's a chance."

"I understand," said Theodosia, patting Delaine on the shoulder. "Just don't peg your expectations too high, okay?"

Delaine nodded, as they walked down the sidewalk.

Theodosia gestured at her Jeep, which was parked on the street at a meter. "I have to get back to the tea shop. But . . . well, let me ask you something that's kind of out there in left field. Do you know anything about Granville's cigar suppliers?"

Delaine shook her head. "Not really."

"Because an ATF agent stopped by the tea shop this morning and . . . oh, never mind. It's nothing you have to concern yourself with."

"Thank you," said Delaine. "I appreciate that."

Theodosia turned and headed for her car. Then she stopped and called back to Delaine, "Do you . . . have you ever heard of someone named Bobby St. Cloud?"

Delaine looked puzzled. "I *think* I might have."

"Was he at the wedding?"

Delaine shrugged. "No idea, really. But the name rings a bell. Maybe he's from Miami?" Then she waved a hand. "He *could* have been one of Dougan's cigar suppliers, but who knows. I never really got involved in his business."

Only four tables were occupied when Theodosia returned to the Indigo Tea Shop. Then again, the day was winding down and the kitchen was probably low on baked goods. Theodosia made a mental note to tell Haley to please go ahead and bake extra. For some reason, they were doing a land office business in take-out scones, tarts, bars, and slices of cake. So why not have a little extra on hand? Besides, she could always bring the leftovers home and give her backyard birds a treat.

Drayton had just brewed a pot of oolong tea and was standing at the front counter sipping a cup.

"Can I pour you a cuppa?" he asked. "This is the oolong from the Wuyi Mountains in Fujian that I told you about."

"I'd love some," said Theodosia.

"I can't believe you're going on a ghost hunt tonight," said Drayton, as he poured the tea.

"Believe it," said Theodosia. She glanced about the tea shop and saw that one of her handmade grapevine wreaths had sold while she was gone. Which meant it was time to whip up a couple more.

"I just hope Delaine can hold up to the stress of it," said Drayton.

"If she doesn't, we'll send her home." Theodosia took a sip of tea. "Mmm. Good."

"A toasty flavor, but also a little sweet," said Drayton. "I ordered two pounds of it."

Theodosia sipped her tea and let her mind ramble. The act of sipping a cup of tea always felt calming to her, and inhaling the lovely aroma (really a sort of aromatherapy!) always helped her sort things out in her mind.

"You know that ATF agent who was in here earlier today?" she asked.

"The one who found you so highly attractive?" said Drayton.

"I don't know about that. But I think I might know who he's looking for."

"Who might that be?"

"This sort of shadowy guy by the name of Bobby St. Cloud. Bill Glass mentioned him to me, and Delaine thinks she might have heard of him, too."

"What, pray tell, is a Bobby St. Cloud?" said Drayton.

"Delaine thought he might be one of Granville's suppliers. From Miami. And that he was possibly here for the wedding."

"So an out-of-towner here for the wedding," said Drayton. "Interesting. Do you know where he is now?"

"No," said Theodosia. "But I keep thinking, what if Bobby St. Cloud was the mysterious guy in room three-fourteen?"

"What if he was?"

"Maybe Granville and this St. Cloud fellow had a falling out?" proposed Theodosia.

"A falling out with a cigar supplier?" said Drayton. He sounded skeptical.

"Maybe they were also coke buddies who got into some sort of dispute?" said Theodosia. "Could have happened."

"If you really believe that," said Drayton, "then you have to tell Tidwell. Because your information might actually be a serious lead."

"I was afraid you'd say that."

"Maybe you should inform your ATF friend as well."

Theodosia grimaced. "He's not my friend." Then, "You think so?" She didn't care if there were ramifications for Glass, but she hated to drag Delaine in any more.

"Absolutely," said Drayton. "Besides, it'll give you another chance to flirt with Alston."

11

It *was a* perfect night for ghost hunting. Wisps of gray clouds scudded across a thin sliver of moon, revealing an occasional tangle of constellations in the blue-black sky. Wind sang softly through the leaves of live oak and crepe myrtle. And Ravencrest Inn, ground zero for the ghost hunt, was steeped in dark shadows and seemed practically deserted.

"It's the awful publicity," Frank Rattling told them with the mournful face of a funeral director.

"And the murder," said Sarah Rattling. "That murder is keeping guests away in droves."

Frank Rattling gave a miserable nod.

"Five cancellations," said his wife Sarah, shaking her fist. "And this is supposed to be our busy time!" She had her hair slicked back in a ponytail and wore not a speck of makeup. She couldn't have done less to make herself look plain.

They were all gathered in the lobby: Theodosia, Delaine,

Jed and Tim Beckman, and the very angry Frank and Sarah Rattling.

But even if the Rattlings hadn't been there to vent their wrath, the lobby still wouldn't have been any cheerier than the rest of the place. It was small and bare-bones. A large, scarred wooden registration desk dominated the room. Over by a bay window, four faded upholstered chairs of an undetermined peach or rose color were clustered around a round coffee table. Two torchieres cast light onto the dingy ceiling but left the corners of the lobby lost in shadows. The de rigueur postal box was stuffed full of brochures for low-country day trips, sport fishing, antiquing, sailing, and, yes, even literature on Charleston ghost tours.

Only, as Theodosia was quick to note, they had their own little ghost tour going tonight. No pesky route map to follow, no talky, overbearing guide to contend with. Just a traipse up the back stairway to room 313 . . . and who knows what?

"This is very kind of you to allow us back in here," said Delaine. She was wound up and jittery but exuded politeness.

"It doesn't matter to us," said Frank. "Not anymore."

"It's pretty much out of our hands," said Sarah Rattling, though no one seemed to know exactly what she meant by that.

"We'd like to begin in room three-thirteen," said Jed. "If that's okay with you."

Sarah Rattling gave a defeated shrug. "Go ahead, go on up."

"And if you don't mind, we might want to explore the basement, too," said Jed.

"Basements are often a hotbed of activity," said Tim.

"Sure," said Frank Rattling. "You need us for anything?"

"We can manage," said Jed, as he and Tim grappled with their equipment.

"You need anything, just scream," said Frank, trying for a joke and failing miserably.

Theodosia led the way up the back staircase. To the second-floor landing, where it was absolutely pitch-black. And then up to the third floor. Here, the hallways were dark, but with a few dim lights set high on the walls at distant intervals. As they traipsed along, going from one puddle of light to the next, they still hadn't seen or heard another soul.

"The Rattlings weren't kidding," said Tim. "This place really is deserted. Which works perfectly for us."

"That's right," said Jed. "No outside interference."

Theodosia knew he meant no interference in the airwaves, not a guest strolling down the hallway in his flannel bathrobe.

As they crept down the hallway toward room 313, Delaine hung back. Theodosia noticed this and quickly let Jed and Tim assume the lead.

"Are you okay?" she whispered to Delaine.

Delaine put on a brave face and forced a smile. Then she managed a strangled, "I think so."

"Like I said before, if you don't want to do this, you certainly don't have to," said Theodosia. "There's no hard-and-fast rule. I only want you to do what your head and heart tell you."

"That's the problem," said Delaine. "My head tells me this is probably a bunch of hooey, but my heart asks, 'What if I could talk to Dougan for one last time?'"

"Honey, I don't think you're going to be able to talk to him."

Delaine gulped hard. "Really? You don't think so?"

"I don't think it works that way," said Theodosia. "At best, we might hear a faint noise or feel some sort of presence."

"No talking?" said Delaine.

"Probably not."

Delaine seemed to debate this for a few moments as they

watched the Beckmans pull down the crime-scene tape that crisscrossed the doorway of room 313. Then she said, "Still, just feeling Dougan's presence would be better than nothing. It would be a kind of good-bye."

"It's your call," said Theodosia.

Room 313 remained dark even as Jed and Tim moved about quietly, setting up their equipment, plugging in cords, and turning on dials. A green screen glowed faintly as Jed waved around a small piece of matte-black equipment that was the size of a paperback novel.

"What's that?" asked Delaine. Her eyes were huge and she jumped at every little sound and movement.

"An EMF," said Jed, tilting it toward her so she could see. "An electromagnetic field detector."

"And it does what?" asked Delaine.

"Locates and tracks energy sources," said Tim. "But it also detects fluctuations in electromagnetic fields."

Delaine gulped. "What does it mean when an electro-magnetic field fluctuates?"

"It means there's a high probability of paranormal phe-nomena," said Tim.

Besides the EMF, the boys had also brought along a video camera, motion detector, and thermal scanner.

"Will you look at this?" said Jed, staring at the readout on a small device. "The thermal scanner is already indicat-ing a two-degree drop in temperature."

Delaine pounced on this, too. "What does that mean?"

"A rapid drop of eight to ten degrees is also clear indica-tion of paranormal activity," said Tim.

"Like a cold spot," said Theodosia.

"Exactly," said Tim.

"It's happening," said Delaine, giving a little shiver. "I can feel it. I'm getting cold already."

"Or else the Rattlings just cranked up the air conditioning," said Theodosia.

Once the Beckman brothers had all their equipment set up, there wasn't much to do except wait. They'd placed most of the equipment on the table in front of the fainting couch and were now seated on that same piece of furniture. Delaine perched tentatively on the edge of the bed, while Theodosia stood with her back to the windows. Interestingly enough, at least to Theodosia, the glass paperweights were all on their shelf except for one that still remained missing.

"I think I hear something," Delaine whispered. "Like . . . a creaking sound."

"Nothing registering here," said Tim, scanning his meters.

"It's probably Ravencrest Inn just settling on its haunches," said Theodosia. The building was old and arthritic, like a nonagenarian whose bones snapped and popped with each little exertion.

Then Jed put an index finger to his mouth and said, "Shhh."

They all sat quiet and motionless for a good thirty minutes. Wind sighed in the eaves, boards creaked, somewhere a faucet dripped. But no apparition filled the room with glowing light, no eerie noises emanated from within hollow walls.

Tim glanced at Jed. "You getting anything?"

Jed shook his head. "No. Not yet."

"What's the protocol for something like this?" asked Theodosia. "Do you guys just hang around all night?" *Hoping for the best?*

"Sometimes we do," said Jed. "And sometimes we try to make things happen. We try to prompt a spirit to manifest."

"How on earth do you do that?" asked Delaine. She'd had her initial five minutes of high anticipation but was now reaching the limit of her patience.

"We move around," said Jed. "Try to shake things up."

"You mean you move your equipment?" said Theodosia. "To another spot?"

"Sometimes we do that, yes," said Tim.

"Maybe worth a try?" asked Delaine. "I mean, it would be nice if *something* happened."

So they picked up all the equipment and moved downstairs to the basement.

The basement of Ravencrest Inn was just as dreary as the rest of the place. Two dim overhead lights cast faint illumination on a floor of packed earth. Rafters overhead were dusty with cobwebs. And a strange assortment of junk—a spinning wheel, an old tricycle, broken lamps, a coffee grinder—was piled alongside discarded and broken furniture. A small mountain of old steamer trunks was stacked against one wall, as if long-ago guests had checked in, unpacked their belongings, then mysteriously disappeared, leaving all their luggage behind.

"Cold down here," said Delaine, crossing her arms in front of her and shivering.

"That's good," said Jed. "Now maybe we can coax something to happen."

Theodosia really wondered if temperature was a key factor in determining whether a spirit might or might not appear. Somehow she doubted it. If spirits or ghosts really did dwell in some nether world and had the ability to manifest at will, she didn't think a few degrees either way was going to make much difference to them. And she certainly couldn't envision them checking the Weather Channel for favorable conditions.

Tim was staring intently at the miniature screen of his motion detector. "Something's moving," he said in a low voice.

"Already?" said Theodosia.

"Where?" asked Jed.

Tim flapped a hand toward a dark corner.

Delaine looked suddenly hopeful. "Dougan?" she said. "Is it Dougan?" She stumbled to her feet and said in a hoarse warble, "Is that you, sweetheart?"

Theodosia tiptoed across the dirt floor and positioned herself directly behind Tim. She leaned forward and stared over his shoulder. Yes, amazingly, shards of green zigzags were blooming and moving erratically across his screen. Indicating . . . what? The presence of an entity? Or something else?

Tim suddenly stood up and began to walk slowly toward that corner of the basement. "It's going crazy," he whispered excitedly.

Delaine put a hand to her chest. "It's happening, it's really happening. Oh, dear Lord, I feel faint!"

Everyone basically ignored her.

"Flashlight," Tim said, pointing at the corner. He snapped his fingers at Jed. "Do it now!"

Jed grabbed a large Coleman lantern and aimed twelve hundred lumens of light at the corner. Everyone strained to see what was there.

Liquid eyes appeared in the sudden burst of light!

"Holy smokes," Theodosia muttered as her heart gave a little hitch. Had the ghost hunters really found something? Were ghosts for real? Her heart thumped again, *wanting* this to be real. Hoping, for everyone's sake, that something was about to make contact.

Dust motes swirled around shining eyes. Then the eyes blinked and, just like that, a cat strolled out of the shadows! A large black feline with glinting green eyes.

"A cat!" cried Delaine. "It's a cat!"

"False alarm," said Tim. He sounded tremendously disappointed.

But Delaine wasn't one bit put off. "You realize, cats are very adept at detecting spirits. They have the innate ability to see things our human eyes cannot."

"Face it," said Theodosia, who was ready to call it quits. "We gave it a good try."

"Oh, we're not finished yet," said Jed. "Now we're going back upstairs to set up again."

Are you really? Theodosia thought to herself. *Why?*

Delaine was all for it, too. "I think that's a smart idea. I mean, we've been here for a while, so now the spirits realize we're serious. Maybe this time they'll manifest."

"That's the spirit," Jed told her. "No pun intended."

12

They trooped back through the lobby, which was completely deserted—no sign of the Rattlings at all—and climbed the back stairs again. Delaine, her energy suddenly renewed, chatted breathlessly with Tim.

"Do you think maybe I could hold the thermal scanner this time?" she asked.

"I don't see why not," said Tim, handing it to her.

"This whole process is really quite intriguing," said Delaine, as they rounded the second-floor landing and headed up the final flight of stairs. "I don't understand why . . ."

Up ahead of them, a step creaked. And then an enormous shape suddenly loomed up out of the darkness.

Delaine saw the amorphous shape rise up, unleashed a shrill, high-pitched scream, and teetered backward on her high heels, almost losing her balance.

"Watch out!" cried Tim, as he juggled equipment while trying to catch her.

"It's happening!" Delaine cried. "I just knew it! Something is manifesting!"

Jed struggled to raise his video camera and point it at the dark apparition before them.

All Theodosia could do was peer up the stairs as she murmured, "Dear Lord. What now?"

"What's going on?" a loud voice demanded.

Theodosia suddenly checked her surprise and did a double take. She knew that voice! It sounded very familiar.

"What are you people *doing* here?" said the voice.

"Tidwell?" Theodosia muttered. Had to be. Who else would be creepy-crawling this old place?

It suddenly dawned on Delaine, Tim, and Jed, too, that this was no supernatural being before them. It was a flesh-and-blood human. An *angry* flesh-and-blood human.

"It's Tidwell," Theodosia said from directly behind them.

"Of course, it's me," snarled Tidwell, stepping into the light. "Who were you expecting? The Green Hornet?"

"It's just that . . ." began Delaine. She fumbled for the right words. "We were trying to . . ."

Tidwell descended two steps. "What exactly *are* you people doing here?" he asked as the steps creaked again in protest to his weight.

They all shifted about nervously until Jed finally spoke up and said, "We're doing paranormal research."

"What?" said Tidwell, as if he was hard of hearing. "What's that you just said?"

"They're engaged in a form of ghost hunting," Theodosia said, trying to clarify things.

Tidwell rocked back on his heels and stared at them with dark eyes that were decidedly not amused. "How very strange," he said. And now an undercurrent of sarcasm colored his voice. "I had the distinct impression someone actually uttered the words *ghost hunting.*"

"That's right," said Delaine. "We came here to try to commune with Dougan."

"Did you indeed?" said Tidwell. "And whose harebrained idea was that exactly?"

Delaine, eager to deflect blame, suddenly pointed at Jed and Tim. "Theirs."

"But you're here, too," Tidwell chided her. Then his eyes slid over to Theodosia. "And you. I expected more from you."

"What can I tell you?" said Theodosia. "It was an experiment."

"More likely a cheap parlor trick," said Tidwell. He drew a wheezy breath and said, "Who tore down my crime-scene tape?"

When no one answered, he snorted, "A ghost hunt. How utterly preposterous."

"I'll have you know," said Jed, "that we're utilizing the very latest in ghost-hunting equipment. All our gear is completely field-tested."

"Good for you," said Tidwell. "Now kindly remove yourselves from *my* field."

That pretty much broke everyone's spirit. They trudged back downstairs, lugging gear, looking thoroughly chastised. Only Theodosia lagged behind so she could talk to Tidwell.

"Are you really still poking around here?" she asked him. She couldn't imagine what more he'd find in room 313. Or maybe he'd just dropped by to sniff the turf again. Maybe *he* was the one who was psychic.

"Isn't it obvious?" said Tidwell.

"We were just in room three-thirteen and I noticed there's still a paperweight missing from the collection."

"Yes," said Tidwell.

"Have you found it yet?"

He stared at her for a long moment, then said, "No." With that he turned around and disappeared into the dark.

Back downstairs, Delaine was dispirited. "It didn't work," she said. "I hoped I'd have a chance to say good-bye to Dougan, to commune with him, but I didn't."

"Better to say good-bye at the funeral tomorrow," said Theodosia. "Think of that as his final send-off."

"Yes," said Delaine, as if she'd forgotten all about the service. "The funeral. I better go home and figure out what to wear."

Time to pull out the grief garb, Theodosia thought. She herself had a sedate little black suit she'd earmarked as her funeral outfit. Although, with the weather warming up, she wondered if it would be more like a sauna suit. Maybe better to pull out a black cocktail dress and wrap a modest shawl around her shoulders. Maybe add a pair of black gloves and a hat. And then she'd look like . . .

Just like Morticia from the Addams Family. And I really don't want to do that.

It might be better, Theodosia decided, if she wore her navy dress.

"Hey," said Jed, extending a hand. "Thanks for all your help."

"You're welcome," said Theodosia, shaking hands and wondering just what help, if any, she'd dished up.

"See you later," said Tim. "We'll for sure try to drop by your tea shop again."

"Great," said Theodosia as Jed, Tim, and Delaine banged their way through the front door and out onto the street.

Theodosia stood there, glancing about the lobby, wondering again where the Rattlings were. Probably upstairs in some dark room, watching TV and feeling regretful about all the cancellations.

Or had they locked themselves in their owner's suite, still nervous about the killer who had prowled through here? Did the specter of Granville's murder keep them awake at night?

Theodosia whirled around when she heard Tidwell's heavy footsteps descending the staircase.

"Did you find anything new?" she asked.

He shook his head. "No, but I didn't expect to."

"I need to ask you something," she said.

Tidwell didn't say yes, but he did offer an inquisitive tilt of his head.

"Did you tell Allan Grumley not to release the contents of Granville's will?"

Tidwell stared at her. "Why would I do something like that?"

Theodosia stared back at him, stunned. "I don't know. But that's exactly what Grumley told Delaine and me this afternoon."

Tidwell crossed the lobby, moving swiftly for such a large man, and put a hand on the front door. "Perhaps he was simply mistaken."

"No," said Theodosia. "I think he was rather deliberate."

What was Grumley trying to hide? Theodosia wondered, as she lingered in the lobby. Or better yet, what information was he trying to delay? Had Delaine inherited the whole shooting match? Granville's home, his assets, and half of the law firm? Or was something else going on?

She wandered into the Fireplace Room where, three days ago, a plethora of guests had congregated for Delaine's wedding. Now it was silent and empty. No crackling fire, no pots of hot tea or crystal snifters filled with fine brandy. Metal folding chairs were stacked; vases of wilted flowers looked sad and droopy. And they exuded a distinctive past-their-peak aroma . . . almost like flowers in a funeral home.

Theodosia continued to ponder what had gone on here.

Had one of the guests conspired to murder Granville? Or had someone else sneaked in? She walked over to the fireplace, touched a hand to the mantel, and came away with dust on her fingers.

Another question that had been plaguing her was the missing murder weapon. If someone had clunked Granville on the head with a paperweight, then skipped down the back staircase to escape, would they have taken the murder weapon with them?

To her, the answer was a resounding no. If she'd been the killer, the paperweight would have been too much of a hot potato. She would have gotten rid of the darned thing as soon as possible.

But where?

Theodosia wandered back into the lobby and glanced around. Not very many hiding spots here. Then again, the murderer could have rolled the paperweight down the basement stairs to be lost forever among heaps of rubbish.

Sighing now, Theodosia wondered briefly if she should turn off the lights and lock the front door. Then she figured it really wasn't her call. The Rattlings would probably do a final check and take care of all of those things.

Theodosia slipped out the front door and headed for her car. Then, on a whim, she hooked a right turn and followed a narrow stone path, overgrown with grass and vines, around the side of Ravencrest Inn and into the backyard.

She saw at once that the backyard, in its former life, had been a classic Charleston garden. Once, when it had a gardener to care for and prune the plants, the place had been a walled oasis filled with magnolias, camellias, and jasmine. Moths had fluttered and frolicked here at night, perhaps even a magnificent giant luna moth.

Now the garden was completely overgrown. Flower beds were a tangle; trees and shrubs were unruly and untrimmed; a wall of ivy looked more like a jungle of kudzu. As she wandered in, wondering why the Rattlings had allowed the garden to fall into such disrepair, tendrils of Spanish moss swung low from the live oak, practically brushing the top of her head.

Theodosia shuddered as she skittered beneath it. Tourists always found Spanish moss so elegant and romantic. They didn't realize it was really a convenient nest for bugs!

Sitting down on a semicircular stone bench, Theodosia gazed upon an old marble statue. It was a woman wearing a Grecian toga and balancing an urn on her shoulder. But the piece was dirty and chipped and pitted with age. And the poor woman's facial features had pretty much melted away over time.

Five feet ahead of her was a small fish pond, similar to the one she had in her own backyard. She doubted the presence of any goldfish but could see a shiny purple water beetle, swimming and skimming its way across the surface.

Wind riffled nearby pond fronds, bringing a hint of salt air. And Theodosia wondered again why this lovely garden hadn't been cared for.

Maybe the Rattlings are just too busy. Maybe Ravencrest Inn is too much for them to handle. Then again, maybe they just don't care.

Spotting a penny on the ground, Theodosia leaned forward and picked it up. It was a wheat penny, one of the older ones. Figuring the Rattlings could use a smidgen of good luck, she stood up, moved forward a few feet, and tossed it into the pond. As the penny landed in the water with a little *plunk*, it set off a small circle of ripples.

And that was when Theodosia noticed the colored rock.

She leaned closer and gazed into the pond. And suddenly inhaled sharply.

Because the colored rock wasn't a colored rock at all.

It was a glass paperweight.

Theodosia stared at it for a few moments longer. Then,

anxiously, she dug into her bag for her cell phone. When she found her phone, she fumbled it twice before punching in the correct number.

Answer, answer, please answer.

Tidwell answered on the second ring with, "This better be good."

"It is," said Theodosia. "So please get back over here."

"What on earth for?" Tidwell chuckled. "Did you by chance locate a wayward spirit after all?"

Theodosia glanced down into the shimmer of water again. Yes, it was still there. She hadn't just seen a mirage. "Nothing that dramatic," she told him. "But I did find the missing paperweight."

13

Dougan Granville's funeral was held at St. Phillip's, just a block or so from the Indigo Tea Shop. St. Phillip's was an Episcopal church with neoclassical arches reminiscent of London's St. Martin's-in-the-Fields Church.

Theodosia arrived at the funeral purposefully late, slipping into a pew near the back of the church. She was only mildly surprised to find that the church was packed. Probably, she figured, many of Granville's current and former clients had shown up out of polite respect. Plus there were board members and volunteers from the various charities that Granville's serious sums of money had helped support. And, probably, some of his cigar-smoking buddies were here, too—businessmen who'd dropped by DG Stogies to grab a cigar and chew the fat with him while they bragged about mergers and dandy profit margins.

It was pretty clear that while Granville might not have been everyone's favorite in life, he'd become Mr. Popularity in death.

Edging to her right, peering through a sea of people, Theodosia saw that Delaine was seated in the very first row. Allan Grumley sat to her right, Charles Horton to her left. She wondered if Delaine had made peace with the two men or was just dependent on them for emotional support. Probably the latter.

Upstairs, in the choir loft, an organist began to pump out the opening notes of a sorrowful dirge by Mozart. The notes spiraled out and upward, hanging in the air and filling the church with their solemnity.

Way down front, just this side of the altar, Theodosia could see a sterling silver urn resting on a small wooden table.

Cremated, she thought to herself. *Granville's been cremated.*

So that was that. Ashes to ashes, dust to dust, just as the English *Book of Common Prayer*, adapted from Genesis 3:19, had professed.

Theodosia glanced around again. Max had promised to join her. Except he had a meeting at the museum. She scanned the crowd. Was he here already? Maybe he'd wiggled out of his meeting? Why was life always so filled with conflict?

Her eyes fell on Simone Asher, who was sitting four rows ahead of her. Simone had wound her long blond hair into a French twist and was wearing a black bouclé jacket. Theodosia craned her head forward, wondering if the jacket was vintage. Maybe Dior or Chanel? Hard to tell. Those particular couture houses had a way of making all their pieces look timeless.

As if she could actually feel Theodosia's eyes burning against the back of her head, Simone suddenly swiveled around. Her eyes skimmed the crowd, then landed on Theodosia. There was a flare of recognition and a sudden harshness in her expression. Then Simone touched a Kleenex to her nose and turned back toward the front of the church.

"Sorry I'm late," whispered Max. He slid in next to her, suddenly filling her little space with his being. He sat down heavily, shoulders and knees touching and bumping hers, a reassuring male presence.

"I was worried you wouldn't make it," Theodosia whispered.

Max rolled his eyes and grabbed her hand. "I had to do some artful dodging, but I'm here now." He glanced around. "How's Delaine holding up?"

"She called me this morning and asked if I thought it was okay for her to wear open-toe shoes," said Theodosia.

"So she's doing fine," said Max. "Delaine is being Delaine."

"But she's still a sad Delaine."

"Sure, she is," said Max, just as the organ music switched over to an even more somber rendition.

As if on cue, everyone stood up.

"Now what?" asked Max. He wasn't particularly religious, so he didn't attend church regularly. Theodosia thought she might have to do something about that.

"The service is starting," said Theodosia.

Reverend Jeremiah Blaise, who'd been at St. Phillip's for more than a dozen years and knew pretty much everyone in Charleston, began the service. He strode to the lectern, gripped it with both hands, and said, "This is a sad day for the city of Charleston." With his long snow-white hair and angular face and body, he looked the embodiment of a modern-day prophet.

Reverend Blaise went on to give a moving and very touching eulogy, recounting Dougan Granville's many civic contributions as well as his support of many local charities and arts organizations. Theodosia figured either Delaine or Allan Grumley had coached him heavily.

Then Allan Grumley took his turn at the lectern. He spoke of Granville as a smart, hardworking partner, as well as a lawyer who fought hard for the rights of the common man. Theodosia wondered how the common man would feel if he stepped into Granville's elegant mansion and saw the paintings, antiques, and Spode china.

Max, who was getting a little restless, leaned forward, gripped the pew in front of him, and scanned the row they were seated in.

"Who's that guy?" he whispered to Theodosia.

Theodosia tilted her head forward and glanced down the row. And immediately saw Jack Alston. In a dark suit and blue shirt that made his eyes look even bluer, he noticed her noticing and gave a small smile. "He's nobody," she told Max.

"Seems like he's been staring at you," said Max.

"I'll tell you about him later," said Theodosia.

"He's got eyes like a Samoyed. Piercing blue."

Yes, he does, thought Theodosia. *And I wish he'd get them off me.*

Charles Horton, Granville's stepson, delivered the final eulogy. Dressed in a light-colored linen jacket and khaki slacks, he looked like he was on his way to lunch at Charleston's Fox Ridge Country Club. For all Theodosia knew, maybe he was.

Horton, not exactly a world-class public speaker, droned on about reconnecting with family as the audience shuffled their feet and cleared their collective throats.

Until, suddenly, bizarrely, a cry rose from up front. It spiraled upward like the shriek of a wounded animal and spiked with an anguished gasp.

"Poor Delaine," whispered Max.

"That's not Delaine," said Theodosia. "That's her sister, Nadine."

"The poor woman must be emotionally overwrought."

Theodosia wanted to tell Max that Nadine got overwrought if her tea went cold. Or if her designer shoes pinched her big toe. Instead she said, "Perpetually."

*   *   *

When the service finally concluded, Theodosia and Max were among the first to leave the church. Max had to run back to the Gibbes Museum, but Theodosia hung around, specifically so she could talk to Tidwell. She hadn't spotted him in the crowd, but she knew the bulky detective had to be lurking somewhere.

She didn't have to wait long. As guests streamed out, Tidwell was easy to spot. He was the guy in the too-tight, oversized suit who cast wary glances at everyone.

Theodosia raised a hand and waved. "Detective!" she called out. "Tidwell!"

He saw her and wandered over to her. "What?" he asked, his eyes still scanning the crowd.

"The paperweight," said Theodosia, frustrated that she had to bring it up. That he wasn't offering her the latest news. "Anything?"

Tidwell shook his head. "Unfortunately, no. It was submerged far too long to get any meaningful prints off it."

"Rats," said Theodosia.

"Or Rattlings," Tidwell murmured as he quickly moved off.

Before Theodosia could run after Tidwell, she was hit with a strange surprise. Jed and Tim Beckman rushed to greet her. Jed carried a video camera, while Tim, with a battery pack strung around his waist, held their sound equipment and a boom microphone.

"Good heavens," said Theodosia. "Don't tell me you guys have been filming?"

"Didn't you see us up front?" said Tim.

"Miss Dish said it was okay," Jed assured her.

"She did, really?" said Theodosia.

"She's awfully nice," said Tim.

"She's awfully sad today," said Theodosia. "I hope you didn't impose on her too much."

"We wouldn't do that," said Jed, as he aimed the lens of his camera into the crowd.

"What are you going to use the footage for?" asked Theodosia.

Jed shrugged. "Not sure."

Theodosia gazed at the crowd that had congregated on the sidewalk and spotted Bill Glass. Just like Jed and Tim, he was busy recording the event, snapping photos like he was at a Hollywood red-carpet event.

Theodosia slithered through the crowd and tapped Glass on the shoulder. "What are you doing here?" she asked.

Glass never broke stride. "What does it look like I'm doing?" he said, as he clicked off another half-dozen shots. "This is great stuff. Bunch of swells at a funeral? You can't beat it."

"Glass," she said, suddenly getting an idea. "Can I take a look at the photos you shot the day of the wedding?"

Glass glanced at her. "You mean Delaine's nonwedding?"

"Whatever you want to call it," said Theodosia. "The thing is, can I see them?"

"Yeah, sure," said Glass. "But not until tomorrow, okay? I'm crazy busy today; we go to press tonight."

"Maybe you could stop by the tea shop?"

"Sure," said Glass. As he continued to shoot, Allan Grumley and Charles Horton walked by.

"Hey guys, look this way!" Glass called to them. "Gimme a big smile! Say *circumstantial evidence*!"

Annoyed, both men turned away.

But not before Theodosia had nabbed Grumley. "Grumley!" she called out, putting a note of authority in her voice. "I need to talk to you!"

Grumley didn't look happy, but he hesitated nonetheless. "What?" he asked.

"You told Delaine and me that Detective Tidwell wanted you to keep Granville's will under wraps."

"Yes," said Grumley.

"No," said Theodosia. "That's not what he said at all. You lied to us."

"You don't get it," said Grumley. "I'm protecting Delaine." He turned and moved away.

"Protecting?" Theodosia called after him. "Protecting her from what?"

But Grumley was gone.

"Bizarre," Theodosia muttered to herself. "Totally bizarre." Had Grumley already cleared up the matter of the will with Delaine? Perhaps he had. After all, they'd sat together through the service. Okay, then, she had to speak to Delaine.

Theodosia elbowed her way through the crowd, nodding and smiling to folks she knew, but heading toward the main entrance where she figured Delaine should be by now.

And she was right. Delaine stood in front of the double doors, clutching the silver urn in her hands. Millie Grant was next to her. And so were Hillary Retton and Marianne Petigru, the two women who owned Popple Hill, one of Charleston's premier interior decorating firms.

Delaine looked tense and tired, and Theodosia figured she'd probably hit her limit on accepting condolences. Now she was just on autopilot, poor dear.

A few more people shook Delaine's hand and administered air kisses before she spotted Theodosia waiting for her. She whispered something to Millie, handed her the silver urn, and quickly buttonholed Theodosia.

"We've got a huge problem," were Delaine's first words.

"What's wrong now?" asked Theodosia. Something about the will? The burial? Delaine's boutique?

"It's the Summer Garden Tour," said Delaine. "Dougan's house is on it."

Theodosia stared at her. "You're talking about the big Summer Garden Tour that starts day after tomorrow?"

"That's right."

"Well, that's a shame," said Theodosia. "Too bad Dougan's house can't be showcased on it anymore. Obviously the organizers will have to drop it at the last minute."

"Dougan's home is not being dropped," said Delaine.

"What are you talking about?"

"The thing is," said Delaine, "we can't just opt out. Dougan's house is listed in the printed program. It's already been *advertised* as one of six homes on the tour."

"Tell them to *un*advertise it." The answer seemed obvious to Theodosia.

Delaine shook her head. "It's too late. We'll just have to pull it together as best we can."

"You keep saying *we*," said Theodosia.

"Because you live right next door," Delaine reasoned. "It's only a hop, skip, and a jump from your cottage to Dougan's place. I figured you could help out."

"What!" Theodosia yelped. Delaine had just thrown her one heck of a curve ball. "Good Lord, Granville's home and gardens can't possibly be ready in two days' time!" She fought to get a grip as people around them suddenly stared with curiosity. "You can't make that happen! *I* can't make that happen!"

"Well, someone has to," said Delaine, rather irritably.

"Maybe you could hire someone," said Theodosia. "Or get Nadine to pitch in and help."

Delaine puckered her lips in distaste. "Are you serious? You saw my sister today. She's about as useless as a garden slug." Delaine shook her head. "No, Theo, it's up to us to make it happen. There's just no other option."

Theodosia was still stunned. "But I . . . um, what would I have to do?"

"First off," said Delaine, "I'll contact the gardener and cleaning staff and have them get everything ship-shape."

"Okaaay," said Theodosia, as she waited for the other shoe to drop. And she didn't have to wait long.

"And you can handle the refreshments," Delaine smiled. *Thud.*

"Me? Seriously?"

"Yes," said Delaine. "That's what you do, isn't it? You cater little gatherings?"

"But this wouldn't exactly be a little gathering. We're talking about the possibility of hundreds of people touring Granville's home and gardens. Maybe even a thousand people who'll need tea and desserts!"

"Theo," said Delaine, looking both serious and a little frightened, "I'm asking you as a friend. Out of *desperation.* I really need your help. Now are you *in* or not?"

"Okay, yes, I'll help," said Theodosia, feeling sufficiently browbeaten.

"Good," said Delaine. "I'm glad that's settled."

Theodosia shifted around. "Will we be going to the cemetery?"

Delaine shook her head. "No. Since Dougan was cremated, I've decided to take his ashes and have them made into a diamond."

"Excuse me?" Theodosia rasped. Had she heard Delaine correctly? No, she couldn't have. Delaine had muttered something about a diamond. The poor woman must be confused and mad with grief after all.

"It's a rather straightforward process," Delaine went on. "I found a company in Chicago that specializes in this type of thing. A place called Diamonds Forever."

"You're not serious," Theodosia stammered. Delaine couldn't be making this up, could she?

"Of course, I'm serious," said Delaine.

"Pray tell, what exactly does Diamonds Forever do with the ashes?" asked Theodosia. *I have to know. Wait a minute, do I really want to know?*

"They compress them," Delaine explained. "Diamonds are, after all, highly compressed carbon. Same as people.

We're carbon. So when you put a person's ashes under tre-
mendous pressure, you get a diamond."

"That's totally bizarre," said Theodosia. She'd never
heard of such a thing.

Delaine gave a sad smile. "I'm just hoping I have enough
ashes to get something that's at least three carats. That way,
Dougan's death will be far more meaningful." She lowered
her voice. "A gemstone as opposed to a headstone."

"Delaine," said Theodosia, "you never fail to amaze me."

"Why, thank you, Theo. I try very hard to be amazing. I
really do."

14

❦

Theodosia made it back to the Indigo Tea Shop just in time
for lunch. She found a few tables occupied, while others had
been readied with white linen tablecloths, flickering candles, and elegant place settings. She was happy to see that
Drayton had pulled out the Shelley chintz cups and saucers.
Their tiny, colorful print lit up the tables and lent a nice bit
of British cheer.

Drayton finished scooping tea leaves into a matching
Shelley teapot, then glanced up at her. "How was the
funeral?"

"Sad," she said. "And a little strange."

He glanced at his watch, an old Piaget that ran perpetually slow. "I must say you're back sooner than expected.
Didn't you all troop out to the cemetery?"

"No cemetery," said Theodosia. "Granville was cremated."

Haley stepped out from the back of the shop. "What's
Delaine planning to do?" she asked. "Keep his ashes in an
urn over her fireplace?"

"Noooo," said Theodosia. "Instead of having Granville's ashes interred in Magnolia Cemetery or some other peaceful resting spot, Delaine is opting to have them squished into a diamond."

"What?" Drayton and Haley cried in unison.

So Theodosia had to fill them in on Diamonds Forever's process of compressing carbon.

"That's totally whack!" said Haley.

"It's unorthodox," said Drayton. "But it's also very much in keeping with Delaine. A little bit cuckoo but a touch of practicality at the same time."

"That's right," said Theodosia. "Nothing gone to waste."

"Gack!" said Haley, making a face.

Theodosia and Drayton followed Haley back to the kitchen where she rattled pans and clattered knives, the better to demonstrate her indignation.

"Why don't we go over today's menu," Theodosia suggested. She knew this would calm Haley down. Haley could be moody, but she was also a perfectionist. She liked things to run smoothly, especially when lunchtime rolled around.

"It's a pretty straightforward menu," said Haley, grabbing a bowl filled with hummus.

"You always say that," said Drayton. "And then you tickle our imagination with all your wonderful offerings."

Haley slapped a dozen slices of whole-wheat bread onto the counter and began spreading them with hummus. "Well, for starters, we've got hummus with sliced tomatoes and olives on whole-wheat bread."

"Always a popular tea sandwich," said Drayton. "What else?"

"Curried chicken salad on croissants," said Haley. "As

well as a nice salad of tea-smoked chicken and grapefruit sections served on baby field greens."

"So that's it?" said Theodosia. It seemed to her like a slightly abbreviated menu.

"I'm also prepped for an egg-white omelet with spinach, asparagus, and Gruyère cheese," said Haley.

"For our health-conscious customers," said Drayton.

"What about our non-health-conscious customers?" said Theodosia.

Haley brightened at this. "Oh, we've got lemon chamomile custard, peanut butter scones, and chocolate cupcakes."

"The ones you call the blackout?" said Drayton. "The super chocolatey ones?"

"You got it," said Haley.

Hearing the da-ding of the bell over the front door, Theodosia and Drayton hurried out into the tea shop and found themselves suddenly dealing with an influx of customers. Theodosia greeted and seated guests, then took orders while Drayton busied himself behind the counter brewing pots of gunpowder green tea, Moroccan mint tea, and Ceylon black tea. Though he barely had time to draw a spare breath, he also brewed a pot of strawberry tea. When it was sufficiently cooled, he transferred it to a pitcher filled with ice.

"If I garnish this tea with fresh mint leaves, we can call it strawberry mint tea," he told Theodosia.

"And I had a request for a lemon sweet tea," said Theodosia.

"Not a problem," said Drayton, reaching overhead for another glass pitcher. "I'll brew some of our lemon verbena tea and stir in a little simple syrup."

At one fifteen, just when the crush seemed to be

abating, Tidwell sauntered in, glanced about, and nodded curtly at Theodosia. Then he casually seated himself at a small table by the window.

Two minutes later Theodosia was at his side. "I didn't think I'd see you again today," she told him.

He patted his protruding stomach. "The thought of one of your delicious tea luncheons proved irresistible."

Theodosia tapped her foot. The unpredictable detective was proving to be predictable. Particularly when it came to food. "Could I interest you in an egg-white omelet?" she asked, flashing a wicked grin.

Just as she knew he would, Tidwell looked shocked. "Surely you have something a tad more appealing. And . . . dare I say it, more substantial."

"Tea-smoked chicken salad?" Theodosia asked. When Tidwell hesitated, she said, "Or how about curried chicken salad on a croissant?"

"The curried chicken sounds lovely," said Tidwell. "And it's served on one of Haley's homemade croissants? The flaky, buttery kind?"

"That's right."

"And perchance a sweet?" asked Tidwell, feigning innocence. He knew they always offered three or four different sweet treats.

Theodosia sighed. She might as well lay the big guns on him. "Haley has a cupcake she calls a blackout. Dark chocolate with a chocolate pudding filling."

"That should serve my purpose," said Tidwell. He paused. "And perhaps you have a tea suggestion?"

"I'd recommend a pot of Pai Mu Tan tea," she said. "It's a delicate Chinese white tea with a peony flower flavor."

"You're the expert," said Tidwell.

Theodosia took another tea request from the table next to Tidwell, gave it all to Drayton, then ran into the kitchen and ordered Tidwell's croissant. By the time she delivered

Tidwell's lunch a few minutes later, she was once again mulling over the issue of the paperweight.

"Anything more on the glass paperweight?" she asked, as she placed his sandwich and teapot in front of him.

"Still no fingerprints," said Tidwell. "No whorls or friction ridges have magically appeared."

"Unfortunate," said Theodosia. She paused. "Do *you* think it's the murder weapon?"

Tidwell popped a bite of croissant into his mouth and chewed thoughtfully. Then he said, "I spoke to the Rattlings no more than an hour ago. And they're fairly sure it's the missing paperweight." He chewed some more. "But I'm going to stop by Simone Asher's shop and try to get her confirmation as well."

"Don't turn your back on her," Theodosia warned. "She's got more of those killer paperweights in her shop."

"Inventory doesn't make her a killer," said Tidwell.

"No, but I find Simone a bit . . . strange."

"That's because you have it in your head that she killed Granville," said Tidwell. "In law enforcement we call that a preconceived notion. Never particularly helpful in resolving a case."

"In the real world I call that a hunch," said Theodosia.

"You and your many hunches."

"I don't know for a fact that Simone was involved," said Theodosia. "But I do think she should be on your suspect list." She glanced around, then sat down in the chair opposite Tidwell. She lifted the lid on his teapot and found the tea to be perfectly steeped. So she poured out a cup for him.

"Thank you," said Tidwell. "How much do you know about the Rattlings?" He looked suddenly thoughtful.

His question caught Theodosia by surprise. "Not much at all," she said. She'd always viewed the Rattlings as having a walk-on role in this whole murder mystery mess. They were the kind of whiny supernumerary characters you'd see in a drawing room play. Not the main characters, just peripherals who added to the jumble of noise. "I don't know them at all," she added. "Aside from the fact that they're the proprietors of Ravencrest Inn."

"Ah," said Tidwell, suddenly looking pleased with himself. "Not anymore they're not." He took a quick sip of tea.

Theodosia stared at him. "What are you talking about? Of course, they are. I mean, you should have seen them last night, fretting and fussing about all their lost business. It's absolutely *killing* them."

Tidwell smiled his Cheshire cat smile. "As always, a smart investigation hinges on solid forensics." He held up his teacup. "By the way, this is excellent tea."

"What *are* you talking about?" Theodosia demanded. Once again, Tidwell was playing cat and mouse with her, talking in riddles. "Please stick to the subject!"

"I'm referring to financial forensics," said Tidwell. "After a routine investigation wherein one of my investigators tip-toed through their books and a number of court records, it turns out the Rattlings no longer hold the title to Ravencrest Inn."

This news hit Theodosia like a ton of bricks. "They're not the owners?"

Tidwell nodded his head, pleased.

"Then who is?" This wasn't making any sense to Theodosia. Surely Tidwell had his facts screwed up, right?

"For the past three years," said Tidwell, "a real estate company by the name of Gimmler Realty has held a contract for deed on the place."

"You said *has* held," said Theodosia, jumping on his words. "Are you telling me that Gimmler Realty sold the contract for deed to someone else?"

"Indeed they have," said Tidwell.

"Wow," said Theodosia. The Rattlings had certainly acted like concerned owners. They'd wrung their hands and clucked unhappily about the fortunes of Ravencrest Inn as though their life depended on it.

"Hang on to your tea cozy," said Tidwell. "Because there's more." He paused for dramatic effect. "With the help of a certain attorney, a certain Dougan Granville, Gimmler Realty actually *foreclosed* on Ravencrest Inn."

"What!" said Theodosia. "The Rattlings *don't* own Ravencrest Inn anymore and Dougan Granville spearheaded the foreclosure?" This was stranger than fiction. "What does it all mean?" Theodosia sputtered.

"Added complications, for one thing," said Tidwell. "Apparently, after the foreclosure, the contract for deed on Ravencrest Inn was sold to brand-*new* owners."

"Holy Toledo," said Theodosia. She was absolutely floored.

Tidwell took a quick sip of tea. "It seems the Rattlings were not the most hospitable of innkeepers. Nor were they prepared to sink time and money into marketing as well as making overall improvements."

"You're saying they failed to make a go of the place," said Theodosia. "And that they couldn't keep up on their payments."

Tidwell aimed a stubby index finger at her. "Bingo."

Theodosia's mind was in a whirl, thinking about the angry Rattlings and the rather smug Granville. "This is a game-changer!" she sputtered. "Maybe the Rattlings were angry and upset with Granville for helping to engineer the foreclosure. Maybe they were the ones who sneaked upstairs and murdered him!"

"That possibility certainly exists," said Tidwell.

Theodosia tried to think. "Maybe, on the day of the wedding, the Rattlings tried one last negotiation with Granville. Made one final appeal."

"Yes?"

"But something happened. They argued and it all went bad."

Tidwell didn't look convinced. But he was listening intently.

"Maybe Frank Rattling went to Granville's room to plead his case," said Theodosia. "And found Granville doing cocaine. Maybe that's when it all went bad."

"And Rattling clobbered Granville with the paperweight?"

"Maybe he didn't set out to," said Theodosia. "Maybe it was a crime of passion. Frank Rattling could have sort of blacked out and lost it. Boom! Or maybe there was an argument or a struggle and the paperweight got knocked off the shelf and struck Granville accidentally."

"An awful lot of maybes," said Tidwell.

"Yes, there are," Theodosia agreed. She sat there and stared at Tidwell as he finished the last of his croissant. "So what happens now?" she asked.

"From what I understand," said Tidwell, "the new owner plans to update Ravencrest Inn and turn it into a cozy B and B—try to make it more of a going concern."

"I mean with the Rattlings," said Theodosia.

"Oh," said Tidwell. "I suppose we haul them down to police headquarters and beat them silly with a rubber hose."

"You wouldn't really," said Theodosia.

"No, but they'll be questioned again. At length."

"Do you think they'll crack?" asked Theodosia.

"Only if they have something to confess."

"Meanwhile, the Rattlings are still there," said Theodosia. "At Ravencrest Inn."

"Only until the end of the month," said Tidwell.

"And then what?" said Theodosia. "Then they vacate the premises? They move away?"

"Possibly."

"If they really are guilty, that would make it harder to arrest them, right?" said Theodosia.

"Hopefully," said Tidwell, "this case will be resolved by then."

"Hopefully," echoed Theodosia.

Theodosia spent the next twenty minutes in a thoughtful daze. She ferried tea and scones to the various tables, smiled at customers, and made small talk with friends. But all the time her mind was swirling like an F-5 tornado. She wondered about the inept Rattlings. About the foreclosure that had hung over their heads like a sword of Damocles. And their dealings with Dougan Granville.

Had the negotiations between Granville and the Rattlings been filled with vitriol and hostility? Probably. Had the Rattlings insulted Granville, or had Granville demeaned them? Was that why Granville had been drawn to Ravencrest Inn as a wedding venue? Had he been thumbing his nose at the unlucky Rattlings? And then it all backfired on him?

Theodosia knew this was a thread she had to follow up on. And in order to unravel it, she had to talk to Delaine.

By three o'clock the tea shop was quiet, so Theodosia slipped into her office in back. Settling into her cushy office chair, she dialed Delaine's home phone number.

"Hello?" came a choked and tearful voice.

"Delaine?" Theodosia wondered if Delaine's poise had finally crumbled. If she'd broken down and was caught in the throes of hard grief.

There was a loud sniffle, then a honk. Someone blowing their nose. Then a faint voice said, "No, this is Nadine."

"Oh, Nadine, hello. How are you doing?"

"Terrible!" Nadine wailed. "This tragedy with Dougan has severely impacted the both of us."

"I'm sorry to hear that, Nadine. Can you put Delaine on?"

Another honk and then whispered voices. Finally Delaine came on and said, "Theo? Is that you?"

"It's me. Sounds like I might have interrupted something."

"Not really," said Delaine. "Nadine's just indulging herself in another round of hysterics." Her voice was suddenly harsh. "Which seem to occur like clockwork around here! Old Faithful, I'm starting to call her."

A background voice, presumably Nadine's, said, "You don't have to be so cruel!"

"And you don't have to have a nonstop case of the vapors!" came Delaine's sharp retort. Then she was back on the phone. "Anyway," said Delaine. "What can I do for you?"

"I've got a couple of questions," said Theodosia. "That pertain to my investigation."

"Yes," said Delaine eagerly. "What do you want to know?"

"Why did you choose Ravencrest Inn for your wedding?"

"Oh, gosh," said Delaine, and now she sounded a little drifty. "Mostly because Dougan suggested it. In a way, he came to the rescue after every place I called was already booked and I was pretty much ripping my hair out, trying to find a suitable venue."

"So Ravencrest Inn was really Dougan's idea?"

"I'd have to say so, yes." Delaine paused. "Really, Theo, do you think *I* would have chosen a rat trap like that? You know me. My taste in clothing and décor is impeccable."

"I have another question," said Theodosia. "I know I mentioned this to you yesterday, but do you know anything at all about Bobby St. Cloud? Now that you've had a chance to think about it, do you have any recollection at all?"

"Nooooo," said Delaine. "Why do you ask?"

"There's an ATF agent looking for him," said Theodosia. *And looking at me. Actually, more like flirting with me.*

"I don't know a thing about St. Cloud," said Delaine. "Sorry. Sorry I can't be more helpful."

"Okay, it was a shot in the dark. Maybe I'll stop by DG Stogies and see if anyone there knows anything."

"Listen, Theo," said Delaine. "Can you meet me at Dougan's tonight so we can go over our plans for the Garden Tour?"

"Ah . . . I suppose I could." Theodosia had planned to meet Max for a concert tonight at the Gibbes Museum, but she could probably change her plans.

"That would be wonderful, dear. I'll knock on your back door around sevenish, okay?"

"Okay, see you then," said Theodosia.

The minute she hung up on Delaine, Theodosia dialed Max's phone. He snatched it up on the first ring. "Hello?"

"Max, it's Theo."

"Hey, cutie. What's up?"

"Would you be real disappointed if I canceled tonight?"

"Not unless you're dumping me to go on a date with someone else."

"I would never do that," said Theodosia.

"Whew," said Max. "Glad we got that cleared up. So . . . yeah, if something else came up . . . something more important."

"Truth be told, I got roped into helping Delaine with the Summer Garden Tour."

"Delaine?" He sounded surprised. "Wait a minute, isn't she supposed to be in mourning? Isn't she supposed to be wearing a black veil and saying the rosary or something?"

"Not quite," said Theodosia.

"What's her involvement with this garden tour?"

Theodosia explained about Dougan Granville's place being one of six private homes in the lineup.

"Can't Delaine just mumble a polite excuse-me and get out of it?" asked Max. "I mean, the owner of the house is *dead*. That's a crackerjack excuse right there."

"You'd think so," said Theodosia. "But it turns out

Granville's home has already been advertised as being on the tour."

"Oh, sure," said Max, chuckling. "If it's been *advertised*, then it's carved in stone. Advertising being so essential to our well-being and way of life."

"Hey," said Theodosia. "I gave her the same talk."

"I'm also guessing," said Max, "that you're the convenient next-door neighbor."

"And the go-to caterer," said Theodosia.

"Ouch," said Max. "Okay, I'm convinced. I guess prepping for the Summer Garden Tour takes precedence over sitting next to me tonight and listening to a flute concerto by Carter."

"Mmm," said Theodosia. "Carter. I can't say he's one of my all-time favorite composers."

"Me neither," said Max. "But I work here, so what can I do?"

15

❧

"Knock, knock," came Drayton's voice.

Theodosia looked up from her desk. She'd been skimming through a tea catalog, debating between the merits of ordering the bumblebee mugs or the floral mugs. "Come on in," she told him, giving a casual wave.

Drayton sidled in and parked himself on a big, overstuffed chair, the one they'd dubbed the tuffet. "I was wondering if we could go over my summer tea blends," said Drayton. He put on his glasses and opened a small black leather notebook.

"Love to," said Theodosia. "But aren't you starting a little late this year?"

"What can I say," said Drayton. "It's a late summer." He gave a nervous smile as he fidgeted with his bow tie.

"But I'm sure our customers will love whatever you come up with." Case in point, she already had several requests for what customers referred to as "Drayton's summer teas that can be served hot or cold."

"My first blend," said Drayton, "is one I call Plantation Pekoe. Flowery orange pekoe with a little bit of lemongrass and blackberry."

"I love it," said Theodosia. "It's a kind of tribute to all the plantations out on Highway 61."

"Exactly."

Theodosia picked up a pen and tapped it against the catalog, suddenly deciding on the bumblebees. "What else?"

"Low-country Lapsang. Lapsang souchong blended with mango and hibiscus. Rich and deep with some sparkling notes."

"That one will fly off the shelves," said Theodosia. "Anything else?"

"One more," said Drayton, peering at her through tortoiseshell half-glasses and looking like a wise old owl. "Kiawah Island Cooler."

"So it's specifically an iced tea?"

"Yes. A black tea base with subtle hints of bergamot, orange, and lemon."

"Sounds delicious," said Theodosia. "Then again, your blends are always a huge hit. Which is why we usually have a tough time keeping them in stock."

"That's not a bad problem to have," said Drayton. "Considering these turbulent times."

"Agreed." Theodosia turned the page on her catalog, wondering in the back of her mind if she should also order some bamboo trivets.

Drayton stabbed the air with his Montblanc pen. "And we also have a tea party to plan."

Theodosia looked up and squinted at him. "Which one is that?"

"Our Scottish tea on Friday. For the Highlanders' Club." Drayton swiveled in his chair and called out, "Haley!"

Two seconds later, Haley popped into the office. "You rang, sir?"

"We still need to work out a menu for Friday's Scottish tea," Drayton told her.

"Yup, I'm on top of that," said Haley.

"Any initial thoughts?" asked Drayton. Like Haley, he was a stickler for nailing down details.

"Well," said Haley, "certainly not haggis. I don't think my culinary skills are up to something like that."

"How about the cock-a-leekie soup we talked about?" asked Drayton.

"The *what*?" said Theodosia. They'd just sprung a strange new dish on her.

"Cock-a-leekie," said Drayton. "It's a traditional Scottish soup made with chicken, leeks, potatoes, and celery."

"I can manage that okay," said Haley. "As long as you source a good recipe for me."

"Consider it done," said Drayton.

"So what else?" asked Theodosia.

Haley thought for a minute. "Smoked salmon tea sandwiches garnished with capers, cucumber slices, and crème fraîche."

"Love it," said Drayton. He was jotting all this down.

"Along with a Cheddar and chutney tea sandwich," said Haley.

"And shortbread," said Drayton. "We can't forget the shortbread."

"And maybe scones or oatcakes," said Haley.

"Either would be fine," said Drayton. He hesitated, as if wanting to add something more.

"What, Drayton?" asked Theodosia.

"What I'd really love to do," said Drayton, "is decorate cupcakes with tartan designs."

Haley considered the idea for a few moments, then nodded. "Yeah, we could do that. I'd just need to whip up a bunch of different-colored frostings. Then put 'em in my decorating pens and icing bags and layer them on." She squinted at Drayton. "Do you, by any chance, have a sample of the tartans you'd like me to do?"

"I'm so glad you asked," said Drayton. He reached into his jacket pocket and pulled out two small swatches of cloth. "Right now I'm favoring the Stewart tartan and the Black Watch tartan."

"These are very cool," said Haley, fingering the two fabrics. "But which is which?"

"The Stewart tartan is the red and green on a white background," said Drayton.

Haley studied it. "This should be simple enough to do with colored frosting. And this other one, the Black Watch . . . blue and green. Hmm."

"What's hmm?" asked Drayton. "Trickier?"

"In a way." Haley wiggled her hand left, then right. "But not impossible. I just have to figure out the warp and weft."

Drayton smiled broadly at Theodosia. "I knew our Haley could do this."

The late Dougan Granville's sideline business, DG Stogies, was located on Wentworth Street sandwiched in between a wine shop and a men's shoe store. It was a narrow, two-story shop with colorful neon signs in the front window, wooden shutters painted a British racing green, and an awning to match.

A CLOSED sign hung in the window, but the lights were still on and Theodosia thought she could see a shadow moving around in back. She rapped on the door sharply, feeling the window vibrate in its frame. When a man finally appeared at the front door, he shook his head, and mouthed, *We're closed.*

Theodosia shook her head back at him. "Open up," she mouthed back. "I need to talk to you about Granville's murder."

With a resigned look on his face now, the man unlatched the door and pulled it open.

"Thank you," said Theodosia. She stepped into a small shop where the aroma of cigars and cigar smoke practically overpowered her. "Goodness. It certainly is . . . aromatic in here."

The man was staring intently at her. "You're here because of Mr. Granville?" he asked. "Are you working with the police? Because I've already talked to them twice already." He was midfifties with an apologetic expression and watery blue eyes. He looked tired, sad, and wary, like an old bloodhound.

"I'm conducting a private investigation," said Theodosia. "On behalf of Miss Delaine Dish, Mr. Granville's fiancé."

"Terrible thing," said the man, and he looked like he meant it. "And on the day of their wedding."

"And you are . . . ?"

"Corky," said the man. "Corky Rhodes."

"You're the manager of DG Stogies?"

Corky bobbed his head. "Yup. Manager, sales consultant, stock boy, and anything else that needs doing around here."

"And you've been keeping the store open," said Theodosia. "Who told you to do that?"

"Mr. Granville's son," said Corky.

"Stepson," Theodosia corrected.

"I guess he wants this place to remain a going concern," said Corky. "At least until he can find a buyer for it."

Theodosia considered Corky's words. This was another thing Charles Horton had stuck his fat fingers into without being asked. And, again, she wondered who the legal owner of DG Stogies might be. Did DG Stogies now belong to Horton, or had Granville bequeathed it to Delaine? She'd have to get a look at that elusive will in order to know for sure.

"This is a very impressive shop," Theodosia said, making polite conversation. She scanned the bookcase-style humidors packed with cigars that had interesting names such as Gurkha, Macanuda, Arturo Fuente, and Davidoff. Then she noted the half circle of leather lounge chairs and the fifty-inch flat-screen TV that hung on the wall. This place had obviously been a cigar smoker's hangout.

"If you'd come a little earlier, I'd still have Turkish coffee to offer you," said Corky. "Of course, we always have brandy and wine."

"But you reserve that for your regular customers," said Theodosia. "Not just casual walk-ins."

"Correct," said Corky.

"Tell me about your imported cigars," said Theodosia.

"They're all imported," said Corky. "From Nicaragua, El Salvador . . ."

"What about Cuba?"

"Those are illegal," Corky said hastily. "Because of the trade embargo."

"I know that." Theodosia held up a hand. "Please, spare me the innocent routine. I happen to know for a fact that Dougan Granville had a seemingly endless supply of Cuban cigars. So what I'm wondering is, do you know who his supplier is?"

Corky gave a reasonable facsimile of looking puzzled. "Like I told the police, I have no idea."

"Does the name Bobby St. Cloud ring a bell?"

Corky's watery eyes slid sideways.

"I see that it does," said Theodosia.

Corky tried to remain cool. "Mr. Granville might have mentioned him once or twice."

"Really," said Theodosia. "And Jack Alston from the ATF asked about him, too?"

Corky shifted from one foot to the other. "He might have."

"Do you have any Cuban cigars on the premises right now?"

"Nope."

"But you were expecting some?" Theodosia made a wild guess. "There was another shipment coming in?"

Corky looked a little less sure of himself. "Supposedly. But Mr. Granville handled all that. I don't know anything about his connections or how he took receipt of the cigars or where they were delivered." Now there was a pleading note in his voice.

"The cigars never came here?" Theodosia asked.

"Only a handful at a time."

"No bulky packages wrapped in anonymous brown paper?"

Corky shook his head again. "No."

"I take it the police have been through your records?"

"Absolutely," said Corky. "We have nothing to hide."

"Except a shipment of Cuban cigars."

Corky ducked his head. "Well . . . maybe."

Theodosia was speeding down King Street, heading for home, when suddenly, on a whim, she cranked her steering wheel hard and sped around the block. She zigged and zagged through the Historic District, finally finding her way back to Ravencrest Inn.

As she sat in her Jeep, staring at the decrepit building, she wondered about the Cuban cigars and the mysterious Bobby St. Cloud. Obviously, Corky knew about him, though he claimed he didn't know how to contact him. Had Granville's murder been about Cuban cigars? Was it something that stupid?

Theodosia continued to ponder these questions as she walked around the side of Ravencrest Inn and stared at the ruined garden.

And what about the Rattlings? How did they fit into all

of this? Or did they even have a role? Were they just unlucky bystanders?

Theodosia climbed the two crumbling steps that led up to the back door and let herself in. She was in the hallway at the rear of the building now, where three bags of trash kept company with a broken desk chair and a stack of newspapers.

Voices floated back to her, and she cocked her head to listen. After about ten seconds she picked up the gist of the conversation. Amazingly, a couple was actually checking in, and Frank Rattling was giving them his innkeeper's welcome speech. She wondered how he felt about that. Did it make him sad that his tenure was almost at an end? Or was he happy to be rid of a white elephant that hadn't turned a profit?

Did it matter? Not to her, it didn't.

Quietly, Theodosia crept up the back stairs. For some reason she was curiously drawn to this place. Not that she thought she'd find another clue here. She just thought . . . what?

What do I think? That I can drink in the atmosphere and intuit what really happened here? No, I can't do that. Nobody can.

She settled for the realization that she was just naturally curious. And, of course, she'd promised Delaine that she'd look into things. So . . . this was looking into things. Sort of.

When Theodosia reached the third-floor landing, she stopped and glanced around. One dark hallway led straight toward the suite of rooms Delaine had occupied. The other went off to the right and led to where Granville's suite had been.

It was so dark up here that Theodosia figured none of these rooms were occupied. In fact, the only bit of real light came from the small window on the landing. She turned around and peered out that window. Craning her neck, she looked down and saw that she was just to the left of the little fish pond. The fish pond where she'd discovered the glass paperweight.

And she wondered—had someone killed Granville, then popped open this window and tossed the murder weapon into the pond? With the thunder booming and the lightning crackling, nobody would have heard it hit. You could have dropped a dozen bowling balls from this window and nobody would have heard them hit the ground. Or land in the pond.

Hmm. Interesting.

Theodosia glanced around again. And, for the first time, she wondered about the floor above her. The stairs continued up, although they were narrower again by half.

So what's up there? The attic?

There was only one way to find out.

Theodosia crept up the narrow stairs, mindful of the dust on the handrail, the creaking of each step. Arriving at a cramped landing, she found a small window and a narrow door. She tried the door immediately and found it locked tight.

It probably leads into the attic. Which is filled with more junk.

Losing interest now, she turned to the window and saw that it was dirty and smeared with dust. No wonder the Rattlings hadn't made a go of this place, she decided. Everything about Ravencrest Inn smacked of lackadaisical care. She touched an index finger to the window and rubbed. Her finger came away grimy. Shaking her head, Theodosia hunched forward to look out. Interestingly enough, she was now positioned directly over the small fish pond.

Her heart gave a little blip, like a trout flipping over lazily in a sun-dappled stream.

Could someone have dropped the paperweight from up here? More importantly, could someone have even opened this window? Or was it glued shut from years of grime and lack of use?

There was only one way to find out.

This was an old-fashioned kind of window, Theodosia noted. A two-parter. The top part remained fixed, while the lower part slid up. Flipping open the latch, Theodosia put her hands against the window sash and pushed.

It didn't budge an inch.

She drew a deep breath and tried again. This time there was slight movement, a shudder.

Third time's the charm.

She canted her body sideways and gave a mighty shove. As the window groaned upward, she pressed her hands tightly against the frame. And, just as the window yawned open, something sharp pricked her finger.

Ouch!

She pulled her hand back fast and saw that a small gray splinter had lodged in the tip of her index finger.

Nasty.

As she flicked out the sliver, her eyes sought out the offending window frame. Rain, humidity, heat, age, termites, whatever, had caused it to swell and buckle, then dry out and splinter.

And that was when she saw a tiny strand of thread caught on one of the splinters. As if someone had caught the sleeve of their sweater or jacket.

What on earth. Could this mean something? Could this be something?

Theodosia dug into her hobo bag and pulled out her iPhone. She held it close to the thread and snapped a photo. Then she stepped back and took another shot from a different angle.

She stood there staring at the thread. It wasn't coated with dust like everything else, so it must be fairly recent. She frowned, wondering who might have been up here and what they'd been doing that their jacket or sweater had gotten snagged.

Getting rid of damning evidence?

Like the proverbial lightbulb going off above her head, Theodosia suddenly remembered the light-colored linen jacket Charles Horton had worn to the funeral this morning.

Was it you, Chuckles?

Like a biologist who'd suddenly discovered a rare new species, Theodosia reached out and carefully pulled the thread from the splinter.

And wondered to herself, *Is this the clue that could finally crack the case?*

16

"What do you think?" Theodosia asked Earl Grey. "Should I call him?"

Theodosia was sitting in her kitchen, enjoying a quiet dinner with Earl Grey. While he'd gone facedown in a bowl of kibbles, she hadn't been any less enthusiastic with her crab chowder. Or in her conversation with her dog. As she shared her last triangle of toast with him, she related her adventure about finding the thread.

"The thing is, it could be an important clue."

Earl Grey's limpid brown eyes stared back at her. He was listening intently, lending his nonverbal agreement.

"You think so, too?" she said. "Then I really do have to call him."

Earl Grey lay down and rested his muzzle on his front paws. Now his eyes rolled up at her and his soft velvet brow wrinkled ever so slightly.

"Yes, I know he'll be upset. At first, anyway. But when I tell him what I found . . ."

Theodosia grabbed her phone and punched in numbers decisively. After getting the runaround and bullying her way through two different gatekeepers, she finally got Detective Tidwell on the phone.

"What now?" was his opening salvo.

"You'll never guess what I found when I went back to Ravencrest Inn," Theodosia burbled.

"A ghost?"

"No. Be serious, please. I found a piece of thread." When her news was greeted with dead silence, she continued. "I went up the back stairs to the fourth floor, the attic. And, believe it or not, there's a little window that sits directly above the fish pond. You know, where I found the glass paperweight?"

Tidwell's breathing was heavy in the phone.

"Anyway, I wondered if maybe someone had tossed the paperweight from up there, so I tried to open the window, got a sliver in my finger, and found the thread."

"Describe, please," said Tidwell.

"The sliver or the thread?"

"Don't play games."

"It's just a small thread, kind of light beige in color. Like maybe the sleeve of someone's blouse or jacket got snagged on the rough part of the windowsill."

"And where is it now?" asked Tidwell.

"I put it in an envelope that was in my purse," said Theodosia. "A bank deposit envelope."

"And you've told no one about this?"

"Of course not."

"Stay put. I'm going to send a squad car by to pick it up."

"Okay," said Theodosia. "Do you want me to relay my story to them, too?"

"No, I do not," said Tidwell. "Simply hand over the envelope and go about your business."

"I don't think I can do that anymore," said Theodosia. "I mean, this *is* my business. This murder investigation."

"No, it is not," said Tidwell. "Never, ever, think that it is." There was a loud *click* and then he was gone.

"You're wrong about that," Theodosia said to dead air, a crooked smile on her face.

Ten minutes later, the police cruiser showed up and Theodosia handed over the envelope to two eager-looking young officers. Five minutes after that, there was a loud knock at her back door.

"Delaine," she said, scurrying through her kitchen.

She pulled the door open. "Hey, come on in."

"You're awfully chipper tonight," observed Delaine. She was all business in a military-tailored black pantsuit as she stepped inside. Then she glanced around and finally cracked a smile when she saw Earl Grey.

"Oh, I'm just . . ." Theodosia hesitated. Should she tell Delaine about the clue? No, better to wait until they had a real live suspect in custody. Why cause her any more pain or aggravation than necessary? "I'm just eager to get going," Theodosia said.

"Glad to hear it," said Delaine. Earl Grey had come over and nudged his muzzle into Delaine's hand. Now he was getting gentle pets and a chuck under his chin. "Because this is going to be a big job."

Theodosia grabbed her handbag and handed Earl Grey a dog cookie. "Okay, let's go over there and get to it."

They exited the back door into fast-approaching twilight. Birds cheeped their evening songs from hiding places in the vines that curled on Theodosia's back wall. A breeze stirred tendrils of hosta and fiddle ferns that had been dug up at Aunt Libby's plantation and recently transplanted.

"I have a few ideas about the menu," said Delaine. Her high heels clacked on ragged patio stones.

"I figured you would," said Theodosia.

"Macaroons are so . . ." Delaine suddenly threw up an arm and let loose a bloodcurdling scream! "Aieee!" She spun frantically and bumped foreheads with Theodosia.

Seeing stars for a few seconds, Theodosia finally had the presence of mind to focus on the dark shape that was now sitting atop her back fence. As her eyes became more accustomed to the dark, she could make out a fuzzy outline, shiny eyes, and a black mask.

"Oh, no," Theodosia said in a disgusted tone. "It's a raccoon. Doggone it, he's back. Or at least one of his cousins."

Recovering quickly, Delaine turned and stared at the offending animal. "Oh." Then her voice softened. "Gosh, he's kind of cute." She smiled, extended a hand, and said, "You didn't mean to scare us, did you? You're really a good boy, aren't you? A nice boy."

"Please don't make friends with him," said Theodosia. "Unless you intend to take him home with you."

"Theo," said Delaine, and now there was a hectoring tone in her voice. "That little raccoon is a sentient being who has just as much right to live on this planet as we do."

"He can live anywhere on the planet that he chooses," said Theodosia. "Just not in my backyard, dining à la carte off my goldfish." She grabbed the grill off her barbecue and laid it across the top of her fish pond. Then, for security's sake, she weighted down the grill with a couple of rocks.

"Poor raccoon," Delaine cooed, as the raccoon slid off the wall and lumbered down the alley without so much as a good-bye or backward glance.

"Hang in there, guys," Theodosia told her fish. "That grill is going to have to do until I can get a trap and catch that darned raccoon."

The little fish seemed to gaze up at her with pleading looks.

"You're going to *trap* him?" said an outraged Delaine.

"With a live trap, yes," said Theodosia. "And then I'm going to relocate the little pest." She held up a hand. "And I don't want to hear one more word about it."

Unlike Theodosia's postage stamp–sized backyard, Granville's yard was enormous. It was a decorator-done showcase garden that was the perfect complement to his enormous mansion. A dazzling rectangular pool was surrounded by flower beds, shrubbery, and exotic statuary. In the two back corners, live oak trees stood like sentinels.

Closer to the house was a flagstone patio with a built-in barbecue and wood-fired pizza oven.

Theodosia surveyed the grounds, which were practically immaculate. "So you called the gardening service?"

"Yes, I did," said Delaine. "They promised to send a crew over first thing tomorrow morning and get everything shipshape."

"It doesn't look half bad now," said Theodosia. "A little judicious trimming and pruning and we'll be in business. Except we're going to need a lot more patio furniture. At least two dozen tables with plenty of chairs to go around."

"I already called my favorite party rental place," said Delaine. "They'll deliver Friday morning, and then all we have to do is arrange the tables and chairs."

"Excellent," said Theodosia. So far this had all been relatively painless. Maybe everything else would be, too. Fingers crossed and knock on wood.

Delaine pulled out a ring of keys as she led the way to Granville's back door.

"Are you okay?" Theodosia asked. Delaine seemed to be fumbling with the keys.

"I'm fine," said Delaine. The door swung open and they stepped into the back hallway. All in all, it was quite cozy and elegant. Wine-red walls, a black-and-white tiled floor, nice painting on the wall above a wooden bachelor's chest that held a bowl of coins and a brass lamp with a green shade. Delaine turned the light on, then stepped lightly to the left. Lights blazed on and she said, "And here's the kitchen. This is what you need to check out."

Theodosia stepped into what she decided was a dream kitchen. Eight-burner Wolff stove, double oven, lots of counter space, and plenty of storage. The décor was country French, and it was all strategically anchored by a granite island that featured two sinks.

"It must be incredible to cook in here," said Theodosia.

"Dougan never cooked," said Delaine. "Neither did I."

"Ever?" Theodosia was amazed. If she lived here, they'd have to use a crowbar to extricate her.

"You know me," said Delaine, giving a little shrug. "I never eat carbs, only protein. Plus I'm very big on doing takeout." She glanced around. "Dougan really only had this kitchen updated to add to the resale value. I don't know why, but some home buyers seem to like a large, well-furnished kitchen."

"That is strange, isn't it?" said Theodosia.

Delaine paused, her hands flat on the granite counter, staring across at Theodosia. "The thing is, will this work for you? For the catering part, I mean?"

"I can make it work." *Can I ever.*

Delaine pointed at the stove. "You can brew tea there?"

"Or at best heat the water," said Theodosia. "Yes, this will work just fine." *Better than fine.*

"Okay, then," said Delaine, dusting her hands in a gesture of finality. "Shall we continue?"

"Lead the way," said Theodosia.

Granville had lived the life of a plutocrat. His expansive

living room was hung with enormous oil paintings in Baroque frames. Two matching pale-green silk sofas sandwiched a square cocktail table lacquered in Chinese red. One wall was dominated by a Hepplewhite sideboard. Granville's home had been built on a grand scale, and he had furnished it with precious antiques, fine furniture, and silk Oriental carpets.

No wonder his home had been selected for the Summer Garden Tour, Theodosia decided. Guests would stream through the main floor, ogle the goods, then head into the backyard where they would visit the garden and be impressed all over again.

Except Granville wouldn't be here to enjoy it. Or collect the compliments.

"I had no idea it would feel so awful and empty in here," Delaine said in a quavering voice. "Everything seems so . . . lifeless."

That's because it is.

But Theodosia didn't say that. Instead she said, "Try to think of this upcoming event as something we can tinker with in the best possible way. To make this stop on the Summer Garden Tour a kind of memorial to Dougan."

Delaine fought back tears. "Why, Theo, I think that's a *lovely* idea. I like that. I like it very much."

Theodosia appraised the room. "What we're going to need in here are flowers," she said. "After all, it is a garden tour."

"Okay," said Delaine, sniffling.

"Maybe on the cocktail table, an enormous bouquet of pink peonies."

"What about green plants?" asked Delaine. "I think this place could use some."

"Excellent idea," said Theodosia. "You get on the horn tomorrow and have some delivered. But think large scale. Maybe a couple ficus trees or palm trees."

"Got it," said Delaine.

"You have the house cleaners coming, too?"

"Yes. Of course." Delaine seemed to be feeling some better now.

"Better call that party rental place back and have them bring plastic runners and some velvet ropes and stanchions," said Theodosia. "That way you can funnel everybody through here with a minimum of fuss."

"And get the gawkers outside," agreed Delaine.

"There are a lot of fine things in here, so maybe some security, too."

"Sure," said Delaine.

"As for refreshments," said Theodosia, "I think we should keep things fairly simple. Tea, lemonade, scones, and a couple different types of dessert bars. After all, we want people to have a nibble and then move on to the next home on the tour."

"Lingering is *verboten*," said Delaine.

Theodosia strolled across the room and into the dining room. This, too, was done in baronial splendor with an enormous Sheraton dining room table, chairs covered in peach silk, and a tall pecan credenza. Elegant silver teapots and serving dishes lined the top of the credenza.

"We're going to want to put this silver away," Theodosia called to Delaine. "Just to be safe." She picked up an ornate wine cooler, turned it over, and glanced at the maker's mark. It was sterling silver by Tiffany. "Gorgeous," she said under her breath.

Then, just out of curiosity and partly because she wondered if she might discover a stash of Cuban cigars, Theodosia pulled open the double doors on the lower part of the credenza. No cigars, but there was more silver. A treasure trove of it.

"Delaine, maybe you should think about moving this silver upstairs," said Theodosia, as she walked back into the living room. "Just to be safe." But her words echoed hollowly. Delaine seemed to have disappeared.

Theodosia walked to the foot of the curved stairway. Had she gone upstairs? "Delaine?" she called out. "Are you up there?"

No answer.

Theodosia hesitated for a few seconds, then climbed the stairs. The carpeting underfoot was whisper soft, unlike the practically threadbare Oriental runner on her own stairway. Oh, well. She was still on this earth and able to enjoy her cozy home, while Granville was not.

When she got to the top of the stairs, Theodosia called out again. "Delaine! Where are you?"

"I'm in here," came a faint voice.

Theodosia padded down the hallway. "Where?"

"Master bedroom," came Delaine's voice again.

Continuing down the hallway, pausing to admire a pair of antique ceramic Staffordshire dogs, Theodosia finally pushed open one of a set of double doors.

And found Delaine.

"What are you doing?" Theodosia asked.

Delaine spun around. The expression on her face conveyed deep sadness.

"Look at this place," said Delaine. "So empty." Her voice was a hoarse whisper.

It didn't look empty at all to Theodosia. The bedroom held a large barley-twist plantation bed covered in blue brocade, antique side tables, and a gleaming mahogany dresser. The windows were swagged with silk brocade draperies, and a white marble fireplace had a plump white velvet love seat facing it.

"We should go," Theodosia urged. "The longer we stay here the more upset you're going to be."

"Because I *am* upset!" was Delaine's abrupt reply.

Theodosia went over to Delaine and put an arm around

her. "I know you are; you have every right to be. You don't always have to act so brave."

"Do you think . . . ?" began Delaine. She stopped, licked her lips, and said, "Do you think it would be okay for me to take some kind of keepsake?"

"I think that would be lovely," said Theodosia. *As long as it's not a ninety-five-thousand-dollar oil painting.*

"There's a particular tie that I bought for Dougan. A yellow-and-blue Hermes tie."

"That sounds perfect," said Theodosia.

Delaine disappeared into Granville's walk-in closet. Theodosia waited for a few moments. Then the moments seemed to stretch into minutes.

"Did you find the tie?" Theodosia called. "Do you need any help?"

Delaine suddenly appeared in the doorway. Her face looked puckery and red; her hair was disheveled. She was clutching the door frame with both hands, looking decidedly unsteady.

"Are you okay?" asked Theodosia. Delaine looked like she'd just encountered a ghost. Then again, maybe she had.

"No, I'm not okay," Delaine croaked out. "I . . . I was looking for the darn tie and I . . . well, I discovered an entire rack of women's clothes!"

"What? Um . . . ?" Theodosia was suddenly at a loss for words.

Delaine jabbed a fist in the air. "And I can tell you with absolute certainty, they're *not* mine!"

"Are you sure about that?" asked Theodosia. "Take a good, hard look. Maybe you just forgot that you, ah, left a few things."

Delaine's bewilderment was turning to anger. "No, they're *definitely* not mine!"

Oops, thought Theodosia. Clearly, Granville had had something going on the side.

"Maybe it's time to leave," said Theodosia.

But Delaine was clinging to her anger like a rat terrier with a bone. "Those clothes must belong to that skank Simone Asher!"

"You think so?" Theodosia said in a small voice.

"That weasel must have been carrying on with her," she huffed. "He was two-timing me!"

"You're positive they're not your clothes?"

"Are you serious?" said Delaine. "They're so not my taste at all. Or even my *size*!"

"Okay," said Theodosia. She wondered what exactly had been going on in Granville's life. Obviously not a monogamous relationship!

Delaine placed her hands on either side of her head, as if she were having a brain aneurysm. "I have to get out of here!" she shrieked. "I can't think about this right now!"

"Calm down," said Theodosia. "I'm sure there's a reasonable explanation." *Is there really? No, but it might help if I say there is.*

But nothing she could say would calm Delaine down.

In a fit of rage, Delaine thrust the keys to Granville's house into Theodosia's hands. "Lock up, will you? I'm . . . I have to leave immediately." And with that she was gone.

"Yikes," Theodosia muttered. She thought about the clothes, decided she had to see for herself. *Not that I don't believe Delaine. But she is good at fabricating stories.*

Darting into the closet, Theodosia gazed at double racks of expensive European suits and bespoke shirts. Granville had been a bit of a clotheshorse. Then again, he could afford to be.

At the very back of the closet Theodosia found the offending clothes. A few skirts, blouses, a black cocktail dress, and a pale-pink peignoir set.

Maybe, she thought, the clothes really did belong to

Simone. Maybe they were clothes from a couple of years ago. Maybe Simone had just forgotten about them. Maybe she'd lost weight since she'd broken up with Granville. Or maybe Simone, upon opening her vintage shop, had dieted down to a smaller size and no longer needed or wanted these clothes.

Turning off the lights, Theodosia retreated downstairs. Suddenly, she was anxious to get out of there, too. The house did give off a dead and deserted vibe. One that felt more than a little oppressive.

Theodosia made a quick inspection of the first floor, checked the front door to make sure it was locked, and discovered a huge pile of mail in the front hallway. Making a snap decision, she swept up all the letters, bills, and junk inserts and shoved them into her bag. There could be something important among all these papers, something critical to Delaine. And, in the back of her mind, Theodosia was also thinking that she really didn't want Charles Horton to horn in on this, too.

Earl Grey greeted her with a woof and a wag.

"You want to go outside for a while?" Theodosia asked him. "Hang out in the backyard?"

Earl Grey lifted his head and aimed his nose at the doorknob.

"But, please, if you should run into a marauding raccoon, do not, I repeat, do *not* engage him in paw-to-paw combat. Okay?"

Theodosia opened the door and Earl Grey scooted out.

Okay then. What now? Maybe a nice cup of tea?

Grabbing her red enamel teakettle, made in the shape of a giant strawberry, she filled it with water and set it on the stove. Then she opened her cupboard and pulled out a tin of her favorite chamomile tea. Chamomile, of course, was the perfect evening tea. It imparted a restful feeling, so conducive to relaxation and sleep.

Theodosia grabbed a small blue-and-white teapot, measured two scoops of chamomile tea into it, and then stood there, waiting for her water to heat. As her eyes roved across the kitchen, they fell on her handbag. She'd haphazardly slung it onto her kitchen table, and it had fallen over and spilled out part of Granville's mail. She wandered over to the table, idly picked up an insert for Patio Pizza, and then, out of sheer curiosity, pawed through the rest of the mail. There were umpteen bills. From SCE&G, Amoco, Bud's Lawn Service, and Comcast. What looked like invitations from the Charleston Opera Society and the Library Association. And Granville's American Express bill.

Theodosia picked this last envelope up, wondering if it might contain any clues as to Granville's recent activities. And then, because the envelope was just sitting there in her hot little hand and the teakettle was steaming like mad, it was just that easy to wave the envelope through a swirl of steam. As if by magic, the flap unglued itself and popped open.

Open sesame. But what now?

Theodosia tipped the envelope and the statement slid out.

Now I take a look at it. And, no, it's probably not exactly kosher, but we're investigating a murder here, folks.

Scanning Granville's recent charges, Theodosia was struck by how much money the man spent. There were hefty charges for at least two dozen different high-end restaurants, Butterfly Garden Florist, McDougal's Haberdashery, Popple Hill Decorators, Schaefer's Rare Books, Metropolitan Barbers, Lightning Delivery Service, numerous gas stations and convenience stores, and one jewelry shop, Heart's Desire, which happened to be owned by Brooke Carter Crockett, a dear friend of hers.

What wasn't on the bill were the rooms at Ravencrest Inn. Although Theodosia figured those might not come through until the next billing cycle. And, probably, Tidwell had already checked with the Rattlings about the rooms. Had figured out who had paid for Delaine's room, the bridesmaids' room, and Granville's room.

Which started her thinking again about that other mysterious room. Room 314. Who had occupied that room? The mysterious cigar broker? The ex-girlfriend, Simone? Or someone entirely different? Someone she hadn't figured out yet?

A high-pitched whistle suddenly jarred her from her thoughts. Her teakettle was seething away. Theodosia grabbed it from the burner and poured hot water into her teapot. And as she watched the tea leaves twist and turn, she wondered what twists and turns might be in store for her.

17

Thursday dawned gray and overcast. As Theodosia hustled
about the tea room, putting out cups and saucers, lighting
candles, and wiping an errant spot or two from the silver, she
fretted about the weather. Tomorrow night and Saturday
night, guests would be trooping through Granville's home,
enjoying the Spring Garden Tour's block-to-block ramble.

But what if it rained? Then what would happen? Obviously the tour wouldn't be canceled. If Granville's murder
hadn't been a good enough reason to call it quits, then rain
wouldn't be, either.

So then what?

At the front counter, Theodosia poured yellow puddles
of lemon curd into tiny glass bowls.

*Then I'll have to serve tea and treats inside. And won't that be
a mess?*

"Theo," said Drayton. "What would you say to me brewing a pot of Doomni Estate Assam?"

Drayton's words snapped her back to the here and now.

That particular Assam, grown in the Assam Valley in northeast India, was strong, full-flavored, and sweetly dry. "If you think our guests would go for it, sure," she told him. "But it's a bit of an acquired taste. We might want to suggest that people use a touch of milk to smooth it out."

Drayton's nose wrinkled. Born in China to missionary parents, he was, and would forever be, a tea purist. Drayton had earned his tea chops working at Croft & Squire Tea Ltd. in London and had attended many of the major whole-sale tea auctions in Amsterdam.

Haley came buzzing out, saw Drayton at the counter, and careened to a stop. "Why is your face all puckered up like that?" she demanded of him.

"I suggested a splash of milk for the Assam," said Theodosia.

"Gotcha," said Haley. "So Drayton's on one of his strong tea binges again, huh?"

"Something like that," said Theodosia.

"It's not a binge," said Drayton. "It's tradition."

"I think it's the weather that's got him all stirred up," said Haley. "With everything all overcast and cloudy, it does make you want to sip a heartier brew."

"See?" said Drayton. "Even Haley agrees with me."

"Haley," said Theodosia. "Talk to me about scones for our morning guests."

"Two kinds," said Haley. "Butterscotch walnut scones and cinnamon raisin scones."

"Black or golden raisins?" asked Drayton.

"Please. Dude." Haley drawled her best Valley Girl impression. "Golden. Don't you know me better than that?"

"And for lunch today?" asked Theodosia.

"It's a pretty cool menu," said Haley. "Lentil soup, fennel and apple salad, chicken and asparagus quiche, chicken pâté on French bread, and vegetable terrine tea sandwiches."

"Remember," Theodosia told Drayton, "we've got a tea

club coming in for lunch. A party of eight. And they're planning to do a teacup exchange."

"Right," said Haley. "So we'll serve the scones first, whichever kind they prefer, then I'll arrange all the sweets and savories on a couple of our three-tiered serving trays."

"Excellent," said Drayton. He frowned and said, "I wonder if *they'd* care to taste my special Assam?"

"When they called their reservation in," said Theodosia, "they specifically requested a pot of Moroccan mint and a pot of decaf Darjeeling."

"Well, it doesn't hurt to *ask*," said Drayton.

Midmorning brought the return of the ghost hunters. Theodosia seated Jed, Tim, and their assorted equipment at a table, then was surprised when Drayton came scurrying over.

"Just the two men I was hoping to see," was Drayton's ebullient greeting.

Theodosia raised an eyebrow. What was he up to now, she wondered?

"I want you to taste one of my favorite teas," said Drayton. He hurriedly poured out steaming cups of the Assam for both brothers. "Just take a sip and tell me what you think."

They both took a sip.

"Good," said Jed.

"Bracing," said Tim.

"A-ha," said Drayton, beaming.

Theodosia chuckled to herself. Looked like the two sides had finally won each other over.

"We've got some exciting news," Jed told them. "We're going to be filming at Barrow Hall!"

"Goodness," said Drayton. "I haven't heard anyone mention that old place in years."

"You know about it?" asked Tim.

"Indeed, I do," said Drayton. "There's a good deal of history attached to Barrow Hall. Of course, it's undoubtedly a tumbledown wreck now, but it started out as a thriving plantation." He closed his eyes as if in deep thought. "Probably built in the early eighteen hundreds."

"What was grown there?" asked Tim.

"Oh, it was a rice plantation to be sure," said Drayton. "What else could it be, located out there on the banks of the Dixfield River? Back in the day, when fine Carolina gold was grown and exported to hundreds of overseas markets, Barrow Hall was a force to be reckoned with."

"But then Barrow Hall experienced darker days," prompted Jed.

"Unfortunately, yes," said Drayton. "Following the War between the States, it fell on very hard times."

"We heard the place was deserted for a while," said Tim.

"Probably was," said Drayton.

"Until Barrow Hall was bought by the state and turned into a mental institution," said Jed, consulting his notes.

"Was it really?" said Theodosia. She hadn't known about that.

"Yes," said Drayton. "Back in the dark days of psychiatric medicine. They added on to the original homestead and built an enormous institution." He drew a deep breath. "But that was all a long time ago and probably best forgotten. I'll wager that Barrow Hall has been empty for almost fifty years and is practically falling down by now."

"No," said Jed. "We took a trip out there first thing this morning. The place didn't look half bad."

"Are you serious?" said Drayton.

"Here," said Tim, sliding his digital camera across the table. "See for yourself. I took a few still shots."

Drayton slipped on his tortoiseshell half-glasses and peered at the photos. "You're right. The old place is still standing."

"And ready to be explored," said Jed.

"Goodness," said Drayton, "you're not going to go inside, are you?" He slid the camera toward Theodosia.

"We see it as prime real estate," said Jed. "For ghost hunting, anyway."

Theodosia studied the photos and threw in her two cents' worth. "Don't you think the place must be infested with rodents?"

"We'll soon find out," said Tim. "We plan to explore Barrow Hall on Saturday night."

"Now there's a bad idea," said Drayton.

"Why would you say that?" asked Jed.

"You don't want to put that old place in your TV show," said Drayton. "It just reminds people of the fact that mental institutions used to be sad, overcrowded institutions with primitive conditions."

Actually," said Tim, "that's exactly *why* we want to feature Barrow Hall."

"The other thing we were wondering," said Jed, directing his question at Theodosia, "is if we could do some location shooting in Mr. Granville's home?"

"Tell you what," said Theodosia. "If you buy a ticket and drop by his home tomorrow night, you can look around all you want."

"How's that?" Tim asked.

"As it turns out," said Theodosia, "Granville's home is on the Summer Garden Tour."

"So the house will be wide open?" asked Jed.

"The first floor, anyway," said Theodosia. "As well as the back garden."

"Hot dang!" said Jed. "That would be pretty much perfect!"

At twelve noon on the dot, the Leaf Lovers Tea Club arrived. Eight women, all wearing hats and gloves and carrying brightly wrapped packages. They were also bubbling over with excitement.

So, of course, Drayton did the honors.

"Ladies," he said, greeting them with a deep bow. "Welcome to the Indigo Tea Shop. I have a special table all prepared for you." He escorted them to their table and pulled out chairs, all the while doling out charm and compliments.

"He's in his element," Haley whispered to Theodosia. They were at the counter, watching the whole thing unfold.

"Drayton's a true Southern gentleman," said Theodosia.

Haley sighed. "Now there's a dying breed."

"You think?" said Theodosia. She knew a few gentlemen, for sure.

"Well, there aren't many true gents among the guys *I* date," Haley giggled.

Theodosia gave her a friendly nudge. "That's because you always go for the motorcycle guys. Tough guys in leather."

"Aw," said Haley, "they only look tough. They're really pussycats."

Theodosia gazed at Drayton, posed ramrod stiff, rattling off a list of teas. "Face it," she said. "Guys like him are the real tough guys. When it comes to character and moral fiber, our Drayton never wavers."

"Gosh," said Haley, "I never thought of it that way."

Theodosia was in a whirl then, serving scones, pouring tea, answering questions, then pulling out her Tea Totalers drink menu for one customer who apologetically said she really didn't care for tea.

"What you might enjoy," she explained, "is one of our tisanes or infusions."

"But they're not really teas?" asked the women.

"Not a hint of *Camellia sinensis* in them, if that's what you mean," said Theodosia. "But our Orange Blossom Tisane does contain orange peel, apple pieces, and hibiscus blossoms. And our Rose Hips Tisane has rose hips, red clover, and star anise."

"They both sound delicious!" said the woman.

"Believe me, they are," said Theodosia.

"But what's the very best one? Which one's your favorite?"

Theodosia thought for a moment. "How about I bring you a pot of Mango Tango, a tisane with a lovely blend of passion fruit, mango, and blueberries?"

"Sounds great!" said the woman.

Theodosia brewed her tisane, delivered it, then scurried into the kitchen to help Haley with her tea trays.

"What can I do?"

Haley was slicing sandwiches into triangles and placing them carefully on the trays. "Just grab that tray of edible flowers," she said. "And sort of scatter them among the sandwiches and bars."

"No problem," said Theodosia. Two years ago, when the economy seemed to be tanking, Theodosia had suggested that they skip the edible flowers for the time being. But Haley wouldn't hear of it. To her, a tea tray wasn't complete unless it was a feast for the eyes as well as the stomach.

"Okay," said Haley, placing the last sandwich and taking a step back. "How do they look?"

"Gorgeous, as always," said Theodosia.

"Then let's deliver them," said Haley. She grabbed one three-tiered tray while Theodosia grabbed the other. Slowly, carefully, they made their way out into the tea room.

Drayton saw them coming. "Ladies," he announced to the table of eight in his melodic baritone. "May I present your luncheon tea trays." There was a spatter of applause and then he was quickly pointing out the quiche and elaborating on the sandwiches and chocolate bars.

Theodosia, meanwhile, had spotted Bill Glass standing at the front door. She swept over to him and said, slightly out of breath, "You came."

"I told you I'd drop by," said Glass. He waved a stack of flimsy newspapers in her face. "Brought you a few copies of *Shooting Star*, too. I figured you might like to pass them out to your customers."

It was the last thing Theodosia wanted to do, but she accepted the tabloids, thanked Glass profusely, and then stuck them behind the counter.

"And I brought my camera," said Glass, indicating the Nikon he had slung around his neck. "So you can look at my wedding snaps. Well, prewedding, anyway."

"Great," said Theodosia. She was frantically busy and didn't have time to drop everything and take a look this instant. So she said, "How about you sit down and have some lunch first?"

Glass narrowed his eyes. "You really mean it? Usually you're trying to give me the bum's rush."

"I don't do that," said Theodosia. She grabbed his arm and steered him over to a vacant table in the corner, where she hoped he wouldn't be too intrusive. "You relax here and I'll be back with some scones and sandwiches."

"Jeez, thanks," said Glass.

"Haley," said Theodosia, as she squirted around the doorway and into the kitchen, "I need a quick plate for Bill Glass."

"What?" said Haley. "What's that jerk doing here?"

"He took photos the day of Delaine's wedding," said Theodosia. "He's going to let me look at them."

"Oh."

"Just throw a scone and a couple of sandwiches on a plate; that'll be good enough."

"Hold everything," said Haley. "If we're going to do this, we have to do it properly." She mounded a citrus salad on a plate, then added a scone, two sandwich wedges, and a brownie bite.

"Perfect," said Theodosia.

"Wait," said Haley, as Theodosia snatched it up. "What about a cup of Devonshire cream, too?"

"No. We don't want to make him feel *that* welcome."

While Glass was munching away, Theodosia poured refills for the tea club. They were busily exchanging their gifts with each other and tearing them open. Mildly curious, she hovered at their table to see what kind of teacups the ladies had found. Theodosia always prided herself on being able to source vintage teacups and teapots at various antique stores, tag sales, and yard sales. But lately, everyone seemed to be having the same idea. So it was getting tougher and tougher to find unique pieces.

"Oh, my!" exclaimed a woman named Jenny who was a frequent visitor to the tea shop. "Look at this!" She held up a floral decorated cup.

"Haviland," said Theodosia. "Their tulip-and-garland pattern."

"Is it old?" asked Jenny.

"From the forties," said Theodosia. "So old enough."

Another woman held her teacup up. "What do you know about this one?" The teacup featured multicolored floral bouquets on a white background and had a jaunty handle and a scalloped saucer.

"That's H&G Bavaria," said Theodosia. She gazed at another teacup set. "And that one's a Shelley. I think it's called Dainty Pink Polka Dots."

"Because of the polka dots, no doubt," said Drayton. He held up his teapot. "Refills anyone?"

"Pretty tasty stuff," said Bill Glass, when Theodosia sat down across from him. "I guess you really do make a living selling these little dinky sandwiches."

"I guess I do," said Theodosia.

"Did you catch the front page of my tabloid?"

"Of course." The headline blared, MURDER AT THE ALTAR! BIGWIG ATTORNEY BLUDGEONED TO DEATH. "Very pithy. Right to the point."

Glass narrowed his eyes at her. "You think it's too sensational."

Theodosia shrugged. "It's what you do. It's your specialty, isn't it?"

Glass grabbed a brownie bite from his plate and popped it into his mouth. "I'll tell you something," he said, as he chewed noisily. "These guest photos I took are nothing special. All those self-proclaimed socialites turned out to be a bunch of stiffs."

"Let me take a look," said Theodosia.

Passing his camera to her, Glass showed her which button to push to advance the shots. "I took maybe thirty or forty shots of the guests, then I got another dozen or so shots of the dead guy before the cops kicked me out."

"Nice work." What Theodosia was most interested in were the guests, of course. She had the guest list with everyone's name, but she wanted to see what they were wearing. She wanted to know if someone's outfit might account for that beige fiber she'd found stuck to the window frame.

"See anything interesting?" Glass asked, as she clicked through the photos.

"Not yet," said Theodosia. Looking at the photos this way was difficult at best. They were small and Glass was too close for comfort, breathing hotly down her neck. She wished she could upload the photos to her computer and peruse them when she was alone. Still, she persisted.

"Pretty good, huh?" said Glass. "I mean my composition and framing." He seemed to delight in bugging her. On the other hand, he was always annoying and overly chatty. That was his normal state of being.

"Everything's wonderful," Theodosia muttered. Glass had taken shots of the guests milling around, as well as the floral arrangements and tea table. There were also close-ups of the more prominent guests—a state senator and a board member from the Charleston Opera.

It wasn't until about the thirtieth shot that Theodosia came across Allan Grumley. He was chatting with two other guests that Theodosia didn't know and had been caught while talking. His mouth was skewed wide open, his eyes were rolled sideways and the angle made him look positively manic. But it was Grumley's clothing that stopped Theodosia dead in her tracks. Although the photo wasn't flattering, she could still see that Grumley was wearing dark checked slacks and a light-beige sport coat.

18

Theodosia studied the shot intently.

Allan Grumley is wearing a beige jacket. Almost the same color as the thread I found. Could Grumley have murdered his law partner?

Theodosia figured the odds were three to one that he had. There was something hostile about Grumley, something strange. Plus, he was acting stiff and almost disrespectful to Delaine. So, even if he'd been only a tertiary suspect before, he'd certainly been elevated to prime suspect now.

Theodosia clicked on with resolve. Eight shots later she came across Delaine's nemesis, Simone Asher.

Hello, there, Simone. Fancy seeing you here.

Simone was posing for the camera, standing sideways with her head cocked over her shoulder in a classic fashion model stance. She was wearing a skirt suit with a tightly fitted jacket and a super short skirt. And both pieces were tailored from a light-beige linen.

Theodosia considered this. She hadn't expected to find a real link to the fiber, and here she'd already found two. Correction, make that three. Because Charles Horton, though not in any of these shots, also had a light-colored blazer. So what did all this mean? That it was all a strange coincidence? Or that one of the people close to Granville was the murderer? She pondered this idea for a few moments, then said to Glass, "Can you do me a favor?"

Glass stuffed a last bit of scone into his mouth, then gazed at her with dark-eyed suspicion. "It depends."

"I'm wondering if you could e-mail your photos to Detective Tidwell. Because, well, he hasn't seen these yet, right?"

"Not yet. I don't even think he knows about them."

"I think it might be helpful if he took a look," said Theodosia.

"Because of the murder investigation?"

"That's right."

Bill Glass's hand snaked across the table and his index finger came to rest on top of his camera. "I'm guessing you think there's an important clue in one of these photographs?"

Theodosia wasn't about to tell Glass any more than she had to. "There could be."

"And that's why you think Detective Tidwell would want to see these?"

"Something like that."

Glass studied her for a moment, then said, "All right. I'll e-mail them to Tidwell. But I'm going to want first crack if any kind of story or arrest comes out of this."

"I'm sure Detective Tidwell would agree to that," said Theodosia. *Yeah, right.*

"Okay," said Glass. "I'll send them as soon as I get back to my office."

"Thank you," said Theodosia. "I really appreciate it."

Glass pointed a finger at her. "You owe me. You know that, don't you?"

"Okay," said Theodosia. "And you know I'm good for it." *At least I think I am.*

"I can't believe you were civil to that scoundrel," said Drayton, once Bill Glass had left. Drayton never called anyone a jerk or a sap or even a scumbag. He was too polite for that. Instead, he called them a scoundrel. It was an old-fashioned term, but generally spot on.

"I pretty much had to be nice to Glass," said Theodosia. "Because I wanted something from him."

"You were looking at his photos?"

"The ones he took at Delaine's wedding," said Theodosia.

"Did you find anything interesting?"

"Maybe," said Theodosia. And then, because Drayton had always been her closest confidant, she spilled the beans about going back to Ravencrest Inn and finding the beige fiber stuck in the window frame. And then she told him about Allan Grumley and Simone Asher both wearing clothes made from beige linen. And then she tossed the stepson, Horton, into the mix, too.

Drayton gave a low whistle. "Which leads you to believe the killer could be any one of them?"

"It's possible," said Theodosia. "Of course, it could be someone else entirely."

"Still," said Drayton, "you came up with some very interesting evidence. The problem I see is, how do you go about obtaining conclusive proof? Aside from breaking into their homes and ransacking their closets."

"I asked Bill Glass to e-mail the photos to Detective Tidwell. That way he can get a court order to go into their homes and ransack their closets."

"That's smart thinking," said Drayton. "If that's how the law really works."

"We can only hope," said Theodosia.

"Excuse me," said Haley. "I hate to interrupt, but we just received an awfully strange delivery at our back door."

Theodosia and Drayton exchanged glances. A *what now* kind of glance.

"Oh," said Theodosia, suddenly remembering the call she'd made earlier. "I think I know what it is. And it's definitely for me."

"Really?" said Haley, scrunching up her face. "Because it's very unusual."

"I think I need to see this mysterious item for myself," said Drayton. "Whatever it is."

They all trooped past the kitchen and through Theodosia's office. When they pushed their way out the back door, it would barely open because of the large metal trap blocking it.

Haley squeezed outside and kicked the trap with her toe. "Are you gonna rent a boat and drop that thing in the water? Are we that hard up for fresh seafood?"

"That's not a lobster trap," said Theodosia. "It's a live trap for raccoons."

"You're going to trap raccoons?" she said.

"I'm going to try," said Theodosia. "One's been hanging around my backyard, trying to mess with my goldfish."

"Not again," said Drayton. "I thought you drove that poor beast off."

"I did, but he's back for another go-round," said Theodosia. "Or at least one of his kin is."

"I've got an idea," said Haley. "When you catch him, maybe I could bake a raccoon pie."

Drayton's eyes practically crossed. "Surely, you're not serious!"

"But I am," said Haley. "You've lived in the South for long

enough, Drayton. Haven't you ever eaten squirrel?" There was a funny light twirling in her eyes now. "Or 'possum?"

"Gracious, no!" said Drayton.

"Well, those varmints are awfully good eatin'," said Haley. "So I'm thinking, why stop there? Why not expand our culinary horizons to include raccoon?"

"No, definitely no," said Drayton. "I put my foot down at that."

Haley was grinning now. "Come on, Drayton, live a little."

Exasperated, Drayton shook his head and said, "You know I don't appreciate your bizarre brand of humor one bit."

"But I had you going," said Haley. "Right? I had you going?"

"If that's what you choose to believe, fine," said Drayton.

By three o'clock, business at the Indigo Tea Shop was winding down. Two tables remained. Drayton was putting away his tins of tea, probably organizing them first according to country of origin and then tea-growing region; and Haley was singing a slightly off-key rendition of Katy Perry's "Last Friday Night" in the kitchen.

Still thinking about the thread (a shred of evidence?) and the charge that had been on Granville's American Express bill, Theodosia bid a hasty good-bye to them and strode down Church Street to Heart's Desire.

"Hey, Brooke," she called out as she let herself into the shop and a tiny bell tinkled overhead.

Brooke Carter Crockett looked up from her workbench behind the counter where she was polishing a white agate, recognized Theodosia immediately, and grinned. Brooke was a spry fifty-something woman with a cap of white hair cut into a perfect-for-her pixie. She specialized in high-end estate jewelry and was also a skilled jewelry designer. Brooke had created a series of sterling silver turtle pendants to help raise money for the preservation of the local logger-heads. And she crafted the most exquisite Charleston charm bracelets. Some of her charms included tiny sweetgrass baskets, palmetto trees, crayfish, church steeples, wrought-iron benches, bags of rice, and models of Fort Sumter.

"I've got something you might be interested in," Brooke said as she jumped up to greet Theodosia.

"What's that?" Theodosia asked. There was always some tasty jeweled tidbit in Brooke's shop that tickled her fancy. Problem was, it wasn't always in line with her budget.

"I was in New York last week," said Brooke. "At the Caravel Jewel and Gem Show. And I managed to pick up a few choice estate pieces, one of which reminded me of you." She unrolled a thick piece of black velvet, then reached down, slid open her glass case, and pulled out a cameo pin. She set the pin on the velvet, where it gleamed enticingly.

"That's gorgeous," said Theodosia. "And it's hand-painted?"

"Right," said Brooke. "We're used to seeing carved cameos, but during the Victorian era many cameo images were painted by hand. This one was done on Limoge porcelain."

Theodosia gazed at the tiny, elegant cameo. It depicted a French noblewoman with high color in her cheeks and a low-cut bodice. Her auburn hair was tumbled into a messy pompadour and she wore a single strand of pearls. For some reason, it *did* remind Theodosia of herself—if she'd been born into an earlier era and had her portrait captured on a delicate brooch.

"I really love this," said Theodosia.

"See?" said Brooke. "I knew it the minute I laid eyes on it. You don't wear a lot of jewelry, but when you do, you tend to gravitate toward unusual, one-of-a-kind pieces."

"This piece is certainly unique. Dare I ask how much?"

"Three hundred dollars and the painted lady goes home with you," said Brooke.

"Can the lady reside here for another week?" Theodosia asked. "Until I sort through my finances?"

"Absolutely. In fact, I'll tuck her in my desk drawer for safekeeping."

"These other estate pieces are gorgeous, too," said Theodosia. Nested on a black velvet tray were a large amethyst ring, a string of pistachio-colored Baroque pearls, and a silver bracelet that looked like it might be an early Tiffany design.

"A lot of people are selling their jewelry these days because they're hard up for cash," said Brooke. "I heard from a couple of Florida dealers that, right after the Bernie Madoff fiasco, women in Palm Beach were selling their family jewels for a song."

"That's kind of sad," said Theodosia.

"Isn't it?" said Brooke. "I can understand selling your grandmother's ring if it's clearly not your taste. But to sell because you're desperate for cash? Kind of tragic, really."

"Brooke," said Theodosia, "have you ever run into a woman by the name of Simone Asher? She has a shop called Archangel over on King Street. She specializes in vintage clothing, but she carries some jewelry, too."

Brooke shook her head. "No. She must be fairly new. Is the place worth visiting?"

Theodosia shrugged. "Maybe. But I think her stash of jewelry is less high-end estate and more vintage."

"You mean like Bakelite bangles and colored glass brooches?"

"Right," said Theodosia. She paused. It was always awkward to ask a shopkeeper about a customer. "I've got kind of a tricky question to ask you."

"Ask away," said Brooke.

"If you can't tell me, I'll certainly understand."

"Now you've amped up my curiosity," said Brooke.

"The thing is, I've been looking into things for Delaine," said Theodosia.

"Because of her fiancé's murder," said Brooke. "Yes, what a terrible tragedy. And for it to happen right here in the Historic District . . . it makes one feel rather unsettled."

"I know what you mean."

"And it's kind of you to help Delaine out," said Brooke. "I mean, the police don't have any conclusive answers yet, do they?"

"Not really."

Brooke cocked her head. "But I bet you're onto something. In fact, I know you are. I can tell by the intensity in your face."

"*Maybe* I'm onto something," said Theodosia.

"So what's your question?"

"I happened to take a look at Dougan Granville's most recent American Express bill . . ."

"Yes?"

"And one of the charges listed on it was for Heart's Desire."

Brooke nodded. "I don't think I'd be revealing any deep, dark secrets if I told you what it was for." She paused. "I did some custom engraving on a couple of sterling silver key chains."

"Really," said Theodosia.

"Probably for his contingent of groomsmen."

Theodosia considered this. "I don't think so," she said slowly. "As far as I know, there was only a best man. His stepson, Charles Horton."

Brooke shrugged. "Still, the sentiments were pretty garden-variety stuff, as I recall."

"What do you recall?" said Theodosia. "I mean, do you remember what you engraved?"

Brooke looked thoughtful. "I've got the paperwork around here somewhere. Want me to try to find it?"

"Well . . . sure."

Brooke rummaged around her back counter, poking and prodding in cubbyholes, until she finally pulled out a yellow sheet of paper. "Okay. One of the key chains was engraved with *CHH*."

"For Charles Horton," said Theodosia. "And the other ones?"

Brooke scanned her paper. "There were only two."

"What did the other key chain say?"

"It was engraved with the word *Forever.*"

"That's it?" said Theodosia.

"That's it," said Brooke.

"Kind of strange," said Theodosia.

"Maybe the second key chain was for a friend or business acquaintance. A client, perhaps?"

"Would an attorney give a client a key chain that says *Forever?*" Theodosia wondered.

"Maybe if it was a longtime client?" said Brooke.

"Possibly," said Theodosia. But to her, the sentiment sounded more heartfelt. Like something you'd present to a lover.

Once she was back at the tea shop, Theodosia put in a quick call to Tidwell.

"Did you receive the photos from Glass?" she asked. "Did he e-mail them to you?"

"Yes," said Tidwell. "And I was a little surprised. I had no idea they even existed."

"You can thank me later," said Theodosia. "But for now, tell me, what did you think?"

"About . . . ?" said Tidwell.

"You must have noticed what Grumley and Simone Asher were wearing. Do you think the thread I found might match up with the fabric from one of their jackets?

"I suppose it's possible."

"Oh, and by the way, Horton's got a light-colored jacket, too."

"How very observant of you."

Theodosia rolled her eyes. This was like pulling teeth, like extracting molars. "Are you going to check this out? I mean, I see this as a definite lead!"

"We have several leads that we're following," said Tidwell.

"Oh, really?" said Theodosia. "Well, guess what, I've got another one for you." She quickly told him about the two engraved key chains. When she was met with more silence, she said, "Don't you find that interesting? The key chain engraved with *Forever.* Don't you wonder who it was intended for?"

"I'd find it far more interesting," said Tidwell, "if I could locate Bobby St. Cloud."

19

❧

Earl Grey sniffed the live trap warily. Then his eyes rolled up at Theodosia and he backed away slowly.

"This has nothing to do with you, sweetheart," Theodosia told him. "It's for the raccoon that tried to stage a raid here the other night. I'm going to trap the little rascal."

But Earl Grey was still nervous. He decided that retreating behind a large azalea bush was the smartest thing to do.

"Peanut butter," said Theodosia, unscrewing the lid on the jar. "I'm going to stick a big glob of peanut butter inside that trap and hope it tickles his fancy." She glanced at Earl Grey. "But don't *you* go sticking your head in there!"

Earl Grey edged back a little farther.

Satisfied that her trap was baited, set, and ready, Theodosia went back inside with Earl Grey. They'd spent a relaxing evening together—a quick run down to White Point Gardens, a dash up Gateway Walk, and then home for a late supper. Kibbles for Earl Grey, a croque monsieur for Theodosia.

Now, tucked into an easy chair in her upstairs turret room, Theodosia settled in to read a mystery about a crime-solving feline. But her mind kept returning to the real murder mystery at hand—and worrying that a killer was still on the loose.

The fabric shred she'd discovered at Ravencrest Inn seemed to point to Grumley, Simone, or Charles Horton. But Theodosia wasn't letting Frank and Sarah Rattling off the hook, either. Any one of them could have dealt a death blow to Granville. Because any one of them might have a serious grudge against him.

The question was—who among them was the most desperate? In Theodosia's experience, desperate people often committed desperate acts. So . . . which one was it?

She closed her book, set it on the little table beside her chair, and tried to focus. She grabbed a silk pillow stuffed with jasmine tea leaves and put it behind her neck. Then, leaning forward, she stuck one leg out and toed a kilim-covered footstool toward her.

There. She felt better having her tootsies up. Wiggling her toes, she decided this relaxed pose was definitely conducive to letting the mind ruminate over the events of the past few days.

Her eyes fluttered shut and she was suddenly carried back to the long, dark corridors at Ravencrest Inn. Someone had quietly, surreptitiously, slipped down one of those corridors, gained admittance to Granville's room, and murdered him. And they'd done so under cover of gloom and a terrible downpour on the day of his wedding.

Someone who didn't want Granville to get married?

Maybe. Or someone who just wanted him out of the way and knew that would be the perfect moment to catch him alone and unguarded.

Theodosia slipped a hand behind her head and massaged the base of her neck. That was where the tension gathered, where the fizzing nerves seemed to be located. She kneaded slowly and shifted her thoughts to the Summer Garden Tour that kicked off tomorrow. Tomorrow, at this time, she'd be brewing tea and serving scones and running around like a crazy woman. Probably ticking down the seconds until the night was over.

Her eyes opened and she stared across the tall, shared hedge toward Granville's palatial home. It was dark outside and, with her lamp reflecting in the window, she could barely see the outline of the place. But tomorrow it would be lit up like a Christmas tree with . . .

She blinked, not exactly sure what she was seeing, and stared harder.

Whoa. How come there's a light bobbing around in the second-floor window?

Could it be Delaine pussyfooting around? No, if paranoid Delaine was over there, she would have turned on every light in the place. So it had to be . . .

A burglar? Someone's burglarizing the place?

Theodosia jumped to her feet and flew into her bedroom. Grabbing the bedside phone, she punched in 911. Once the dispatcher came on the line, she hastily babbled her suspicions along with Granville's street address and implored him to send a police cruiser as soon as possible!

Then Theodosia went back to her upstairs window to watch and wait.

But now she didn't see any light.

Are they gone? Maybe they're gone. Maybe it was a reflection and I made a terrible mistake!

No, there was a sudden flash of light in the downstairs window now! Theodosia knew firsthand that Granville's place was filled with priceless oil paintings, antiques, and silver. Certainly that was what must have attracted this burglar. And Lord knows how long he'd been in there rummaging around. Filling his sack or pillowcase chock-full of Granville's treasures, chuckling over his spoils.

As Theodosia waited with bated breath, she recalled how she'd once heard about a horrible, cunning thief who'd kept his eye on the obituaries. Then, when the bereaved family was least expecting it, he'd swoop in and rob them blind.

Feeling jittery and unsettled, Theodosia wondered when the police would arrive. Had they sent out a squad car yet? If so, what was taking so long? Should she call again?

Tossing a black sweater around her shoulders, she hurried downstairs and roused Earl Grey.

"C'mon, boy, I need you. We've got a problem!"

Slowly, quietly, Theodosia pushed open her back door and the two of them eased their way onto the back patio. She figured this would be a fairly decent observation point. They could remain undetected and safe and still keep an eye on things. Taking care, Theodosia stepped up onto a stone bench where she had an unobstructed view of Granville's back door.

But what if the intruder is gone? What if he dashed out the front door?

A small click made Theodosia perk up her ears.

Something going on?

She gazed into the darkness that shrouded Granville's back portico.

Then, like a ninja stealing through the night, a shadowy figure eased his way out the back door.

Oh, no! He's leaving! He's going to get away!

What could she do? Follow him? Call 911 again? Or were the police just seconds away?

The back door *snicked* shut and the shadowy figure moved stealthily along a brick pathway, heading for the back alley.

There's no time to think! I just have to . . . do something!

Theodosia grabbed Earl Grey by the collar and carefully eased out her back gate into the alley. Maybe she could nonchalantly run into the burglar. Pretend she was out walking her dog and just give a friendly nod. If she played it cool enough, maybe she could get a look at his face. Get a decent description.

No way was her plan going to work. Because when the burglar eased through Granville's back gate, he quickly spun in the opposite direction.

Now what? Think fast!

Taking a step forward, Theodosia called out, in what she hoped was a friendly tone, "Excuse me, but I think you dropped something."

Her ruse didn't work. Like a shot, the intruder took off running down the alley.

Acting on pure instinct, Theodosia released Earl Grey's collar and yelled, "Go!" And then her dog was bounding down the alley, barking loudly and scrambling after the burglar in hot pursuit. She kicked it into high gear, too, and ran down the alley, clattering over cobblestones, praying the intruder would stumble, drop his bag of stolen goods, or get bitten in the seat of the pants by Earl Grey. But when she reached the spot where the alley took a dog-leg turn behind the Winfield Mansion, Earl Grey was huffing heavily and pacing back and forth. And there was no one in sight.

"He's gone?" she said. "Just like that?"

Earl Grey looked up sheepishly, as if he knew he'd blown his secret mission.

Theodosia patted his head. "That's okay, I didn't expect you to single-handedly capture a robber, handcuff him, and read him his rights. You did your best. We both did our best."

They'd almost returned to her back gate when a

black-and-white squad car roared up to them and rocked to a stop.

Two officers jumped out.

"Ma'am?" said one. "Are you the one who called in the disturbance?"

"It wasn't a disturbance," said Theodosia. "It was a burglary." She pointed at Granville's home. "Someone was sneaking around inside and then I saw them come out the back door." She pointed again. "I live right here. I'm the neighbor."

The second officer was taking notes. "After you saw the intruder exit the back door, what happened?"

"I sent my dog after him," said Theodosia.

Both officers stared at Earl Grey, who suddenly looked nervous at being the center of attention.

"And then what?" asked the first officer. He was gazing at Earl Grey and seemed to be addressing the question to him.

"I chased him, too," said Theodosia. "But we lost him. He got away."

"Did you get a description?" asked the first officer.

"No," said Theodosia. "Sorry. It was too dark."

The officers hitched up their utility belts and headed for Granville's back door, with Theodosia and Earl Grey following in their wake.

"It's been pried," said the first officer. He moved his flashlight up and across the door frame. "You see the marks?"

"Unless the guy's got a dog," said the second officer. Which made them both turn and look at Earl Grey again.

"No dog and nobody home," Theodosia explained. "This house belongs to Dougan Granville, the man who . . ."

"The murder victim?" said the first officer. He frowned and his mouth worked soundlessly, as though he were processing the information. "Aw, jeez, I gotta call this in. There's something fishy going on."

"You think?" said Theodosia.

Twenty minutes later, Detective Burt Tidwell was on the scene, dressed in billowing khaki slacks and a College of Charleston sweatshirt. This was one of the few times Theodosia had seen him not looking all buttoned up for business. Somehow, dressed in casual clothes, Tidwell looked a little more human. A little more . . . normal.

Unfortunately, Tidwell was peevish at being roused.

"I was deep into the third chapter of *Walden,*" he rasped at Theodosia accusingly.

She held up her hands, palms out. "*I'm* not the one who pried open my neighbor's back door. *I'm* not the one who creepy-crawled around inside his home with a flashlight."

"But you called it in," he said accusingly.

"Excuse me," she said, getting a little steamed. "You don't want me to be a conscientious citizen?"

Tidwell sighed heavily, then left her standing in the backyard while he walked through Granville's house. Ten minutes later, he reappeared.

"Anything missing?" she asked.

"Afraid so," said Tidwell. "Looks like a few small paintings have been appropriated, some silver might be missing, and the place has obviously been ransacked."

"Ransacked how?" asked Theodosia.

"Drawers have been pulled open and overturned," said Tidwell. "Things are generally somewhat messy."

Theodosia was beginning to get the picture. "So an art heist and more."

"We'll need to obtain some sort of inventory list," said Tidwell. "Probably from the insurance company."

"Besides grabbing a bunch of tasty valuables, it seems like the intruder had a kind of agenda," said Theodosia. "As if he were also searching for something specific. So a burglary and a kind of . . . reconnaissance mission."

Tidwell stared at her.

"I have to call Delaine," said Theodosia. "Right now." She spun on her heels and darted back toward her house. Tidwell followed close after her, trying to catch up.

"I don't think that's a good idea," Tidwell huffed.

"Yes, it is. There's a very real possibility Delaine's the new owner of that house," said Theodosia as she pulled open her back door. "She has to be informed."

Tidwell had intruded his way into her kitchen now, his bulk almost filling the space between her sink and her stove. "Why don't you let me handle this? In a way, this might be the answer we've been looking for. Now I'm free to bring in a team and search the house from top to bottom."

Theodosia considered this. "But you'll still notify Delaine?"

"Yes, of course," said Tidwell. "First thing tomorrow."

Theodosia decided this would work. Probably, Delaine didn't need to be roused for an emergency just when she was getting ready for bed.

"Okay," said Theodosia. "Just as long as you keep her in the loop."

Tidwell glanced around Theodosia's kitchen, taking in her collection of teapots, her antique canisters, her small teak breakfast table. "This is nice in here. Cozy."

"It needs some work," said Theodosia. It was late and she was tired, probably not the best time to get into a discussion about woodwork and planned renovations to her kitchen cabinets. And she certainly wasn't going to offer him any sort of refreshment, if that was what he was angling for.

Earl Grey flopped on his dog bed and splayed out his front legs possessively, as if daring Tidwell to make any kind of move.

"What's this?" asked Tidwell. He swooped a hand toward the stack of mail that still sat on Theodosia's kitchen table.

"Um, Granville's mail."

"And why do you have it?" he asked.

"I picked it up last night when Delaine and I were over there getting the place ready for the Spring Garden Tour."

"The what?" he said sharply.

"Spring Garden Tour," Theodosia said again. "The one that's happening this weekend. Friday and Saturday night. Granville's home is on the tour."

"No, it's not," said Tidwell. His furry eyebrows rose and his jowls sloshed sideways as he shook his head vigorously.

Theodosia snatched up a brochure and thrust it into his hands. "Yes, it is. *You* try telling those garden club ladies to drop it from the program!"

Tidwell made a big show of reading the proffered program. "You've already tried to unlist it?"

"Yes, of course, I've tried," said Theodosia. "So did Delaine. But our arguments fell on deaf ears."

"So hordes of people will be tromping through my crime scene tomorrow night." Tidwell gazed at Theodosia as if it were all her fault.

"I guess . . . yes," said Theodosia. "Which means you're going to have to work fast."

Tidwell was about to say something, then changed his mind. "I'll speak to Miss Dish tomorrow. Ask her to take a look and also help determine what she thinks might be missing."

"Okay," said Theodosia. "Whatever." Now she was anxious for Tidwell to leave. It had been a long day and she was aching to crawl into bed and turn out the light. "Just latch the gate on your way out, okay?"

Tidwell gave a mumble as he stepped out her back door. He took a few steps, and then his heels seemed to drag on the flagstones as he hesitated.

No, no, no, Theodosia thought to herself.

Tidwell's voice floated back to her. "Ho-ho, what have we got here?" He sounded almost amused.

Theodosia leaned out the back door. "Now what?"

"I'd say you caught something in your trap," said Tidwell.

"What?" Theodosia flew across the patio and peered into the boxy wire trap. Two bright eyes peered back at her! "Oh my gosh! I got him! I caught the little demon." She couldn't believe it. Mr. Raccoon had come a-calling and been caught in her trap!

"The creature doesn't look particularly happy with his situation," Tidwell observed.

But Theodosia was elated. "This will teach him not to feast on my defenseless little goldfish!"

The raccoon gave her an accusing look, as if to say, *But I was hungry.*

"I don't know why you can't just pry open a garbage can or two," Theodosia told the raccoon. "Like any other self-respecting raccoon."

The raccoon grasped the metal grate with his small paws and gave her a baleful look.

"Now what?" said Tidwell.

"Maybe . . ." Theodosia had been so focused on trapping him, she hadn't really thought about the disposal aspect. "Could *you* do something with him?" she asked Tidwell.

Tidwell was taken aback. "You're asking *me* to dispose of this animal?"

"Well, I don't want you to take it out and shoot it or anything. Just . . . I don't know . . . fingerprint it, give it a stiff talking-to, and then release it in a nearby park. Preferably a park that's several miles from here."

"And if the little bandit finds its way back to you?" said Tidwell.

Theodosia shrugged. "Then I suppose we'll have to get it into the witness protection program."

20

"And then what happened?" asked Drayton. It was Friday morning at the Indigo Tea Shop and Drayton and Haley were hanging anxiously on Theodosia's every word.

"Then the intruder ran down the alley and I sent Earl Grey cannonballing after him," said Theodosia.

"Woo-hoo!" cried Haley. "Did Earl Grey catch the guy?"

"No," said Theodosia. "But he gave it his best shot and I think put a good scare into him."

"Then he won't be back," said Haley.

Drayton measured out scoops of Keemun tea as he processed Theodosia's words. "Excuse me, you're telling us that someone broke into Granville's home last night, stole a bunch of valuables, then pawed through the drawers?"

"That's what Tidwell seemed to imply," said Theodosia. He hadn't let her go inside with him, even though she'd asked.

"That does sound strange," said Haley. "If it had been me, I would have helped myself to a few more paintings."

"But maybe the intruder wasn't out to solely steal art," said Drayton. "Maybe he was after something else, too."

Theodosia pounced on Drayton's words. "Yes! That's exactly what I've been thinking."

"So what was he after?" asked Haley. "Money? Was there cash stashed around the place?"

"Somehow I don't think so," said Theodosia.

Haley put her hands on her slim hips. "Then what?"

Theodosia grabbed a small tin of lemon verbena tea and unsnapped the lid. "This is going to sound kind of strange, but what if the intruder was looking for information?"

"That seems odd," said Haley.

"Does it really?" Theodosia mused. She didn't think so. More and more she was inclined to believe the intruder was after a specific item.

"What if the intruder was trying to find that missing shipment of cigars you told us about?" said Haley.

"I suppose we can't rule that out," said Theodosia.

"And you said Tidwell's going to search the place again this morning?" said Drayton.

Theodosia nodded. "He's probably there right now. Or his team is. Doing a super thorough search."

"Maybe they'll find those cigars," said Haley. She wrinkled her nose and said, "Do you think that's why Granville was murdered? Over a bunch of lousy cigars?"

"I don't think so," said Theodosia. "It feels like there's something larger and more sinister going on."

"But what?" asked Drayton. "Was he involved in some other contraband or illegal deal?"

"I don't know," said Theodosia. "But *something* odd is going on."

"Hmm," said Drayton.

The three of them got busy then. Drayton lined up his teapots on the counter like some sort of Greek chorus. Haley rushed back into her kitchen so she could tend to her baking and prepare for a busy morning and luncheon service. And Theodosia moved through the tea room, making sure candles were lit, sugar bowls were filled, silver was polished, and each place was perfectly set.

When the place sparkled enticingly, with warm morning sun streaming in through the leaded-glass windows and the pegged wooden floors gleaming, she turned her attention to her displays. Somehow, the DuBose Bees Honey jars had been shuffled around, so she stacked those into a single, neat display. Then she fluffed up her display of chintz and print tea cozies and hung one of her handmade grapevine wreaths. This was a sort of freestyle, oblong wreath with a dozen miniature teacups tied in with pink silk ribbon.

Everything was perfect, Theodosia decided. Except for . . . her teacup jewelry. She untangled the chains for her teacup pendants and, once again, smiled at the shards of vintage teacups and saucers that Brooke had outlined with silver and crafted into pins and charm bracelets.

Now, Theodosia decided. Now everything was perfect. At which point Haley came scooting out and yelled, "Hey gang, we got another delivery!"

Drayton looked up from the counter where he'd been fussing. "Not another one of those awful traps, I hope."

"It's something for you," Haley told him.

Drayton was suddenly alert. "My floral arrangement. I was hoping it would arrive before the start of business."

"What did you order?" Theodosia asked. But before she could get her words out, Drayton had disappeared. "Something from Floradora?" she asked Haley.

Haley threw up her hands. "I suppose."

"Will you look at this!" exclaimed Drayton. He bustled back into the tea room holding aloft a large bouquet of pale pink bell-shaped blossoms.

"Pretty flowers," said Haley. "But what are they?"

"Heather," said Drayton, looking pleased. "And they're technically not flowers, they're from a flowering shrub."

"As in heather from the Scottish moors?" asked Haley.

Drayton nodded. "That's it exactly."

"For our Scottish tea," said Theodosia, smiling. "What a perfect touch."

"You're a stickler for details, aren't you?" said Haley.

"No more than you," replied Drayton.

"And you're all dressed up, too," said Haley. She twiddled a finger at her collar. "With your tartan bow tie and all."

"Naturally," said Drayton, heading for the front counter. "We're hosting a special event today."

Haley glanced at Theodosia. "Don't you think Drayton looks like he stepped right out of the pages of a magazine? *Southern Living* or something like that?"

"That's our Drayton," said Theodosia. "Picture perfect."

Midmorning found Theodosia practically breathless. The tea shop buzzed with activity, customers poured in, and Theodosia poured cup after cup of tea.

"I'm having trouble keeping up," she told Drayton, as she grabbed a pot of spiced plum tea.

He gave an abrupt nod. "Just wait until lunchtime. We'll have them packed in like sardines."

"Oh joy," said Theodosia.

Still they managed to brew and serve pots of Golden Monkey, English breakfast, and French linden tree tea, as well as deliver fresh-baked scones, almond croissants, and banana bread.

Eleven fifteen brought a break in the action, the calm before the storm.

"Did you get a gander at our tartan cupcakes yet?" asked Drayton.

"No," said Theodosia. She pushed a stray tendril of hair out of her face. "Should I? Did Haley outdo herself again?"

Drayton crooked a finger and she followed on his heels into the kitchen, where a dozen frosted cupcakes sat on a two-tiered milk glass serving tray.

"See?" said Drayton. "Stewart and Black Watch tartan, just as we discussed."

"What are you two goggling at now?" asked Haley, glancing up from the stove.

"The word is *ogling*," said Drayton. "Not *goggling*. And if you must know, we're admiring our fabulous cupcakes."

"*Our* cupcakes?" said Haley. "Excuse me, but I'm the one who whipped up the batter, did the baking, and figured out the frosting patterns."

"As a result of my conceptual thinking," said Drayton. "You have to give me that."

"Okay, okay," mumbled Haley. She picked up a wickedly sharp knife and deftly sliced a piece of Scottish salmon. Then she placed it on a triangle of dark bread spread with crème fraîche. "How are we doing out there? Still so busy?"

"There's a lull," said Theodosia. "Thankfully."

"So for your Highlanders' Club," said Haley, glancing at the menu she'd tacked on the wall, next to dozens of recipes and food photos, "we'll have the cock-a-leekie soup, a salad, and two types of tea sandwiches. Along with shortbread and marmalade."

"Excellent," said Drayton. "And I'll brew a pot of Scottish heather tea that I special ordered. It's basically a blend of Assam and Kenyan teas with a taste of heather."

"You're really going all out for this," remarked Theodosia.

"Absolutely," said Drayton. "I'll set the table with my Royal Stafford Robertson series cups and saucers."

"The bone china with the crest and tartan ribbon?" asked Haley.

"That's right," said Drayton. His collection of teapots and teacups was even larger than Theodosia's collection.

"Oh, yeah," said Haley. "Those are way cool."

"So which baked treat did you finally decide on?" Drayton asked. "Are we serving oatcakes or scones?"

Haley grinned. "For you, Drayton, I melded the best of both worlds. I baked a batch of oatmeal scones with butterscotch chips."

"That sounds wonderful," said Drayton, his enthusiasm positively brimming over. "You know, I have a feeling this luncheon is going to be one of the best themed teas we've ever done."

"What about our chocolate tea?" Haley asked.

"Or our Victorian tea?" said Theodosia.

"Those were excellent, too," said Drayton. "But I predict this will be even better." He zipped back out to the café, humming as he went.

Haley gazed at Theodosia. "I haven't seen Drayton this whipped up since his bonsai won best of show last year."

"He's a man on fire," Theodosia agreed.

"So are you," said Haley. "Except you're burning the candle at both ends. Between ghost hunting, searching for clues, and helping Delaine with the Garden Tour, you're gonna wear yourself out."

"You're still working on the menu for tonight, aren't you?" Theodosia asked quickly.

Haley nodded. "Oh, yeah, you know I've got your back. But I still think it kind of stinks that Delaine stuck you with so much responsibility."

"She thinks because I live next door that it's no trouble at all. All I have to do is saunter across the back lawn and set up for tea."

"So *she* can greet the guests and play Lady Bountiful," said Haley.

Theodosia shrugged. "I suppose you're right."

*   *   *

At precisely twelve noon, the Charleston Highlanders' Club arrived for lunch. Six men bustled into the tea shop, were greeted somewhat formally by Drayton, and were shown to their seats at the round table in the center of the room. If they realized they were men in a practically female-dominated tea shop, they paid no notice. Rather, they commented favorably on the bouquet of heather, the tartan plaid placemats and napkins, and the Robertson cups and saucers from Drayton's private collection.

Theodosia was pleased that they were pleased. She knew that tea was not solely a woman's domain and wished she could convince more men of that. Fact was, in most of the world, both genders eagerly embraced tea drinking, whether it was in centuries-old tea shops in China, busy offices in India, or shops and bazaars in the Middle East where they drank their tea from small, delicate glasses. Next to water, tea was the second most popular drink in the world. And perhaps even more beloved!

As Drayton served their first course of oat scones and Devonshire cream, Theodosia skittered into the kitchen to pick up two orders.

"How's it going out there?" Haley asked.

"Controlled chaos," said Theodosia.

"I'll wager Drayton's in his element."

"You should see him," said Theodosia. "He's in full major-domo mode. I'm surprised he's not wearing tie and tails."

"I'd expect nothing less from our Drayton," said Haley. She quickly mounded salad and slid the plates across the counter to Theodosia. "Here you go. It's back into the fray for you."

Theodosia delivered her luncheon entrées, seated some newly arrived customers, and made the rounds with two pots of freshly brewed tea.

Once she'd taken care of all her customers, Theodosia noticed that Drayton's group had already enjoyed their cock-a-leekie soup and tea sandwiches. Taking a deep breath, having a few spare minutes, she wandered over to the Highlanders' Club and introduced herself.

Ten seconds into the introductions, Theodosia realized that she knew most of the group, or was at least familiar with them. She'd met two of the men at Heritage Society events. Three were local business owners. And Stanton McDougal, who seemed to be the group's ringleader, owned McDougal's Haberdashery, one of several fine men's shops located over on King Street.

For some reason, maybe because her name had been mentioned in the newspaper along with Granville's passing, McDougal immediately brought up the murder. Then everyone seemed to chime in with either a condolence-laced remark or a theory on what really happened.

"If you ask me," said Ewan Wallace, who was a longtime board member at the Heritage Society, "it was a business deal gone bad."

"Could have been," said Theodosia. The missing shipment of Cuban cigars was still on her mind.

"Any way you cut it," put in McDougal, "Granville's death was a real tragedy. Charleston is out a darned fine attorney."

"I take it you knew Granville fairly well?" said Theodosia.

"Oh, sure," said McDougal. "Granville was forever ordering custom-made shirts from my shop." McDougal allowed himself a chuckle. "And, as his girth steadily increased, so did his orders for *more* shirts."

"Granville must have been a good customer," said Theodosia. She knew Granville had grown portly in the last six months of his life. Whether that was due to his overindulgences or Delaine's dragging him to trendy new restaurants every night, she wasn't sure.

"Granville was one of my best customers," McDougal told her. "He always wanted to look sharp in court, you know. Plus, everyone at the shop thought Granville was such an interesting, gregarious guy. He was constantly going on about his investments to whoever would listen."

"You mean investments in the stock market?" asked Theodosia.

"No," McDougal said slowly. "He never mentioned that. But Granville was very effusive about his cigar store and his various real estate holdings."

"He was big into real estate?" This was news to Theodosia. She'd never heard a peep about real estate and wondered why Delaine had never mentioned it. Then again, maybe she didn't know. Maybe Delaine had just been too focused on their whirlwind courtship and impending wedding.

"Oh, yeah," McDougal continued. "Granville was crazy over real estate. It was his passion. He owned dozens of apartment buildings and a couple other properties he jokingly referred to as his white elephants."

How interesting, Theodosia thought to herself, as Drayton brought out the tartan-frosted cupcakes and everyone exclaimed over them. Granville's real estate was another thing she'd have to quiz Delaine about. Or maybe ask his partner, Allan Grumley. If the curmudgeon Grumley would ever deign to talk to her.

21

With lunch well under way, Theodosia and Haley were buzzing about the menu for tonight's Summer Garden Tour.

"What I was thinking about," said Haley, "was an assortment that included lemon bars, almond espresso cookies, and some sort of cake."

"That's more than I thought we'd serve," said Theodosia. "I was thinking just along the line of tea and cookies."

"But on last year's tour, the folks at the Wilmington House served biscotti and double fudge brownies," said Haley.

"And I'm guessing you want to outdo them?"

Haley gave a toss of her head and a snarky smile.

"It really isn't necessary," said Theodosia. "Especially since we're putting this together at the last minute."

"Come on," Haley wheedled. "Just let me do what I do best." She poked her blond hair behind her ears and said, "Turn me loose."

"Okay," Theodosia agreed. "But please don't kill yourself

over this. Because there's a chance it'll all whoosh right over Delaine's head. These days, she's not exactly big on doling out compliments or thank-yous."

"Whatever," said Haley.

"So what have you got in mind for the cakes?" asked Theodosia. "You mean like mocha cakes?" Haley whipped up the best mocha cakes she'd ever tasted. Tasty little morsels with vanilla frosting and rolled in chopped walnuts.

"Mmm, not those exactly," said Haley. "But something like them."

"You're being evasive," said Theodosia.

"Probably because I'd like to keep it a surprise," said Haley.

"Okay," said Theodosia. "You win."

Lunch came and went. And by midafternoon Theodosia had popped into the kitchen again to see how Haley was doing.

"Don't look, don't look!" cried Haley.

"Okay," said Theodosia. "Sorry.

Then Drayton suddenly appeared in the doorway. "How are we set for scones?" he asked.

"We've got a couple left," said Haley.

He hooked a thumb in the direction of the tea room. "Delaine's sister, Nadine, showed up a few minutes ago." He lowered his voice. "Accompanied by a gentleman."

"Really?" Theodosia and Haley said in unison.

"No one I've ever seen before," said Drayton, still in a slightly hushed tone.

"Must be a new boyfriend," said Haley.

"I didn't even know she was dating anyone," said Theodosia. "I mean, did she bring someone to the wedding?"

"No idea," said Drayton.

"I suppose she could have had a date stashed somewhere,"

said Haley. "Because I remember she showed up late and seemed awfully discombobulated."

"Maybe she'll be the sister who gets married first after all," said Drayton.

"I just hope she has better luck than Delaine," said Haley.

"Shhh," warned Drayton. He held a finger to his lips. "Keep your voices down!"

"Well, I'm going to go out and say hello," said Theodosia. "Haley, put two of those oat scones on a plate along with a couple of slices of banana bread. Nadine will like that. She has a real sweet tooth."

Nadine was giggling and simpering when Theodosia brought the desserts to her table, hanging on the arm of a man who was sitting so close their shoulders touched. He was good looking, with ginger-colored hair, bright brown eyes, a square chin, and high cheekbones.

"Theo-*do*-sia!" Nadine squealed when she saw her. "How lovely to see you!"

"Hello, Nadine," said Theodosia. "We've been crazy busy all day, but I managed to find some scones and banana bread to go along with your afternoon tea." She didn't want to point out that it was thirty minutes to closing on a Friday afternoon.

"Your hospitality is greatly appreciated," said Nadine. She grinned and giggled at her gentleman friend but still didn't bother to introduce him.

Theodosia picked up their teapot and carefully refilled their cups. Then she set the teapot on a tea warmer. "Well, enjoy."

"Thank you," said Nadine.

Theodosia hesitated. "Have you by any chance talked to your sister today?" She wondered how Delaine had reacted to the call from Tidwell about last night's break-in.

Nadine didn't bother to look up. "Not really," she said, biting into her scone.

"Who's the fellow?" Drayton whispered, when Theodosia came back to the front counter.

"No idea," said Theodosia. "She never introduced us."

"That's rude," said Drayton.

"That's Nadine," said Theodosia. "Always playing weird little mind games. Listen, I'm going back to my office to call Delaine. Try to get any news I can direct from the horse's mouth."

"Or some other choice part of the anatomy," Drayton mumbled.

"Drayton!" said Theodosia. But she smiled as she said it.

Theodosia kicked a carton of straw hats out of her way and slid into her desk chair. She called Delaine's cell and had her on the line within seconds.

"I take it Detective Tidwell got hold of you this morning?" said Theodosia. She felt bad that she'd been so busy she hadn't been able to call Delaine sooner.

"Yes, he did," said Delaine.

"And he told you all about the break-in?"

"Such unsettling news," cooed Delaine. "As if I needed one more thing to worry about."

"Same here," said Theodosia. "It caused a bit of a stir for me, too, you know."

"Sorry about that," said Delaine.

"So what's the story on getting Granville's place straightened up for tonight? Tidwell seemed to imply there was a bit of a mess. He said several drawers had been overturned and some cupboards were ransacked?"

"It's all taken care of," said Delaine. "I'm at the house now and everything looks perfect."

"What about the deliveries?" Theodosia asked. "I hope

those weren't derailed. The tables and chairs for the patio? The velvet ropes and stanchions?"

"Everything's being brought in right now," said Delaine. "So the only piece of the puzzle I have to worry about is *you*."

"Are you serious?" said Theodosia. "Excuse me, but Haley and I have the tea and treats completely under control. They'll be served exactly as promised."

"I must say that's a huge weight off my mind," said Delaine.

"Delaine," said Theodosia, feeling slightly miffed. "It shouldn't be an issue at all. You know I wouldn't drop the ball."

"Unlike my sister," Delaine sighed. "Big help she is."

"Nadine's here right now," said Theodosia. "She showed up maybe fifteen minutes ago. With a guest. A nice-looking man."

"Bully for her," said Delaine.

"What?" said Theodosia. "You don't approve of this fellow she's dating?"

"Even if I did," said Delaine, "Nadine wouldn't care two shakes. She pays no attention to anything I say. Besides, she's old enough to make her own mistakes."

Whatever that means, Theodosia thought to herself. "One more thing, Delaine. Did you set up a meeting with Allan Grumley like we discussed?"

"Oh, that. Yes. On your advice I retained my own attorney, and we're scheduled to meet at Grumley's office tomorrow morning."

"Good," said Theodosia. "Maybe now you can get all this will and insurance business straightened out." *And I don't have to get caught in the middle.*

"Theo," Delaine said in a singsong voice. "What are you wearing tonight?"

"Um, a T-shirt, slacks, and my long Parisian waiter's apron?"

"No," said Delaine.

Theodosia winced. Her wardrobe, curated for comfort, was always a bone of contention between them.

"You have to look *upscale* tonight," said Delaine. "So I want you to stop by Cotton Duck and pick something up."

"Delaine," said Theodosia. "I'm a little short on time. I have to prep and pack all the food, in case you forgot."

"There's always time for a proper wardrobe," Delaine said smoothly. "So what I'll do is call Janine at the shop and have her pull some summer silks for you."

"Well . . . maybe," said Theodosia.

"I promise, you're going to adore them!"

Doubtful.

Delaine heard the silence spin out and said, "Theo, don't you trust my fashion sense?" Now she sounded hurt.

"Sure, Delaine, whatever you think will work." Theodosia hung up the phone, bent forward, and dropped her head against her desk. *Clunk.*

"It can't be *that* bad, can it?" said Drayton. He was standing in the doorway, looking concerned.

"Delaine is driving me crazy," said Theodosia.

"Of course, she is," said Drayton.

"First she was paralyzed about going to a meeting at Granville and Grumley to talk about the insurance policy and the will. Now she's changed her tune and hired an attorney to oversee everything."

"And what else?" Drayton dropped into the chair across from her desk.

"She acts like I'm scheming to purposely let her down tonight. With the food and tea, I mean."

"Which you never would," said Drayton. "So why are you letting all this get under your skin?"

"I don't know," said Theodosia. "I shouldn't. I know in my heart that Delaine is just . . . I don't know, still in shock."

"Grief can often bring out the worst in people. They can act horrid even when they don't mean to be."

Theodosia put her hands flat on her desk and stared at Drayton. "You're right. I should just blow it off, huh?"

"That would be my sage advice."

"Are you coming tonight?" Theodosia asked.

"I thought I might drop by, yes. Take a gander at the Marisoll Hall gardens down the street, then ankle down to Granville's place." He raised his eyebrows. "Or is it Delaine's place now?"

"Who knows?" said Theodosia. "Everything's still up in the air."

Luck was with Theodosia and she managed to find a parking space just two doors down from Cotton Duck. She jumped from her car, raced down the street, and, outside the shop, ran smack-dab into Jack Alston.

"You shop here," he said, by way of a greeting.

"So what?" she said, wondering why he always adopted such a confrontational attitude.

He gestured toward Cotton Duck. "I find your choice of retail shops interesting."

"What's so interesting about it?" asked Theodosia. She found Alston impudent, annoying, and just this side of attractive.

"It's out of character for you. You don't seem like the social butterfly type."

"I'm not," she said. "I'm just picking up something for a special occasion."

His eyes twinkled an iridescent shade of blue. "Care to tell me what occasion that might be? A date, perhaps? Or . . . ?"

"That's right," Theodosia said as she brushed past him. "I have a date."

Please don't follow me, she thought to herself, as she pushed through the front door of Cotton Duck. *Please don't follow me*. But when she glanced back over her shoulder, Alston was nowhere in sight. And, much to her surprise, she felt just the faintest twinge of disappointment.

Janine, Delaine's perpetually overworked assistant, looked up from behind the counter and said, "Delaine called. She said you were having a fashion crisis?"

"Not me," said Theodosia.

Janine nodded knowingly. "Let me guess. You're helping out at the Summer Garden Tour tonight and Delaine wants to play dress-up with you?"

"Something like that, yes," said Theodosia. She glanced around the interior of Cotton Duck. Racks of long gowns hung next to circular racks of silky tops with matching pajama pants. Elegant peek-a-boo camisoles nestled in silk-lined boxes on antique highboys. Strands of opera pearls hung down and mingled with an array of charm bracelets, chain necklaces, and diaphanous scarves. Glass shelves displayed handbags of supple leather, gleaming reptile, and whisper-soft suede. A display of shoes offered teetering high heels by Louboutin and Jimmy Choo. There were also racks of elegant, airy cotton clothing perfectly suited to Charleston's high heat and humidity, as well as swishy skirts and even a few racks of vintage clothes. And Delaine's latest addition included several high-end lingerie lines, including La Perla, Cosabella, and Guia La Bruna from Italy.

"Delaine specified something silky," said Janine, as she grabbed a midnight-blue tunic top with matching tapered slacks. "I thought . . . maybe this?" She held it out to Theodosia. "It's by a Miami designer. Stephano Millar."

The drapey silk felt whisper-soft between Theodosia's fingers. "This is actually . . . tasteful. For Delaine, I mean." She'd been expecting a one-shoulder number with spangles.

Like a pageant dress or something from the old *Dynasty* TV show.

"Delaine is prone to glitz and glam," Janine agreed. "But this is lovely."

"So I should try it on," said Theodosia. The more she gazed at the outfit, the more she liked it. A nice change from her silk T-shirts, khaki slacks, and flats. "But could I still wear flats with this? I'm going to be on my feet all night."

"Slip it on, dear," said Janine. "Let's see what we're working with."

Theodosia took the outfit and was about to flit off to the dressing room when she turned and asked, "Did a man come in here a few minutes earlier? A fellow by the name of Jack Alston?"

"No," said Janine. "Not that I know of. And I've been here all afternoon."

"Okay, thanks." Theodosia pushed aside the dressing room curtain and kicked off her shoes. She wondered what Jack Alston was doing hanging around Cotton Duck. Had he been looking for Delaine? Waiting for her? If so, why? Was he planning to follow her? Did he think she might lead him somewhere? Somewhere where he might find a cache of contraband cigars?

Theodosia pondered this as she tried on the silk outfit. She didn't want to believe that Delaine had inside information she hadn't divulged. On the other hand, Delaine hadn't been thinking straight for the past five days. So maybe . . . maybe she held a small piece of the puzzle and didn't even realize it.

22

Teakettles hissed and shrieked as Theodosia and Haley flew around Dougan Granville's enormous kitchen like a pair of crazed wraiths. It was six forty-five at night. Seven was the witching hour when Summer Garden Tour guests would begin to arrive in droves.

"Now we have to watch the steeping times!" Theodosia warned. White teas required only one to two minutes, and black teas between two and three minutes, while herbal teas could steep for three to six minutes.

"I'm trying to stay right on the money," said Haley, grabbing teapots right and left. "But this is tricky! I mean . . . jeez, where's Drayton when we need him?" She touched the back of her hand to her forehead and said, "Did I really just say that? I was so sure we could handle this ourselves."

"We can," said Theodosia. She snatched a teakettle off the stove and placed it on a metal trivet. "If we keep our wits about us and stay focused."

"I don't know how you guys do it every day," said Haley. "Brewing tea is tricky business."

"Drayton and I think *you're* the one who's always in the hot seat," said Theodosia. "Between baking scones and quick breads and whipping up soups and tea sandwiches."

Haley gave an airy wave of her hand. "Naw, that's just my brand of fun. But this . . . I'm a little out of my element. Maybe I should have paid closer attention to Drayton when he gave all those tea lectures."

"Once we set up our tea table in the garden outside, we'll be able to ease up a little," said Theodosia. She had brought along three tea samovars, and the plan was to let everyone help themselves.

"Hey," said Haley. "I like that silky outfit you've got on. Did you get it at Cotton Duck?"

"Where else?" said Theodosia. "For whatever reason, Delaine wanted me to be all duded up."

"Say what you want about Delaine," said Haley. "But the lady does have style and beaucoup good taste. Um, do you want me to start setting out the desserts?"

"Please," said Theodosia. She knew Haley was anxious to be relieved of any and all tea-brewing duties.

"Wait until you see what I made," said Haley, looking impish and excited as she dug into the multiple baskets and boxes she'd carried in. "Wait! Don't look yet! Let me get everything all set up."

Theodosia went back to focusing solely on tea.

Haley worked busily for a few minutes, then whirled around to face Theodosia. "Ta-da!" She threw her hands up in the air.

Theodosia stared at what was one of the most innovative and delicious-looking food displays she'd ever seen, and couldn't help but smile. Haley had created a veritable ocean of espresso cookies, lemon bars, and . . . wait a minute. Were those really cake pops?

"You made cake pops?"

Haley nodded happily. Cake pops were a hot new trend: delicious little rounds of cake that were dipped in frosting, decorated, and then served on a stick.

Theodosia plucked one from the colorful display and said, "How on earth did you find the time?"

Haley shrugged. "Sandwiched in between everything else. I whipped up a triple batch of cake batter and baked them a batch at a time, using a set of special little cake pop baking molds. Then I stuck 'em on little wooden sticks and added my frosting."

"You also rolled some in powdered sugar and crushed pecans," said Theodosia. She was amazed by the artistry in Haley's work.

"And look, some also have buttercream frosting with bits of maraschino cherries," said Haley, taking pride in ownership. "And some of the chocolate ones are rolled in sea salt."

"Haley, they're gorgeous! You worked like a dog on this!"

Haley ducked her head. "No. Well . . . yeah. Maybe."

"You did," said Theodosia.

"The champagne buttercream frosting was a little tricky," Haley admitted. "And the milk chocolate cake pops were putsy. But, hey, I just wanted everything to be super nice."

"You're the one who's super nice. Working at the tea shop all day and then whipping these up like it was nothing at all."

"It's the least I could do," said Haley. "You shouldn't be stuck with honchoing this whole event."

"I probably should have just called in a caterer and sent the bill to Delaine," said Theodosia.

Haley clapped a hand to her chest as if she'd just taken a bullet. "A rival caterer! Ah, Theo, you'd never do that, would you?"

"Not if it's going to give you a case of apoplexy."

"Well, it would," said Haley. "I really think it would."

"Theo!" called a voice. "Theo! I need you, dear!"

"Delaine," said Haley, just as Delaine rushed into the kitchen. Her hair was swirled atop her head, her heart-shaped face was perfectly made up, and she wore a floor-length white gown that looked like something a Grecian goddess would have worn to a fancy party on Mt. Olympus.

"Wow," said Theodosia. "Look at you. All glammed up."

"If I'm going to play hostess it's the least I can do," said Delaine.

"That's funny," muttered Haley, "I thought *we* were the hostesses."

Delaine spun on her and her eyes glinted. "Well, you are, of course. You're my two dessert hostesses. But I'm the official meeter and greeter."

"That's quite a dress," said Theodosia, trying to steer the conversation into more neutral territory.

"Vintage," Delaine confided. "Halston couture."

"It's not from Simone's shop, is it?" asked Theodosia.

Delaine looked horrified. "Definitely not! Besides, you know I carry my own rack of vintage clothing at Cotton Duck. Vintage is one of the hottest things going, kind of a fashion insider's secret. I'm sure you've noticed a few big-name Hollywood stars wearing vintage gowns on the red carpet? In fact, ever since I expanded my shop, I've made a conscious effort to increase my vintage collection."

"Where on earth do you find all your pieces?" asked Theodosia. Was there a time warp somewhere she didn't know about? A tear in the fabric of the universe where all the vintage dresses were stored?

"Here and there," said Delaine, looking both mysterious and evasive. "I have a couple of contacts in Miami Beach, a pair of darling ladies in Beverly Hills, and a stylist in New York City."

"Sounds like you've developed quite a network," said Haley.

"Obviously," said Delaine.

"What do you think of Haley's cake pops?" asked Theodosia, gesturing at the rather grand display.

Delaine gave a cursory glance. "Lovely. Now shouldn't the two of you be transporting everything outside to the serving table? We're minutes away from throwing open the front door, and we wouldn't want to keep our guests waiting."

"We were just about to do that when you came dashing in," said Theodosia.

"I'm sure it's going to be a lovely dessert table." Delaine smiled at Haley. "What do you call your little pastries, dear? Cake plops?"

"Cake *pops*," said Haley.

Once the candles were lit, the tea samovars filled, and the dessert trays set on the large serving table in the back garden, Theodosia was able to relax. White linen tablecloths covered the tables that were scattered about the patio. Moody, low-level lights lit the stone paths that wove through the gardens. The harpist Delaine had hired was plucking away.

"This is gorgeous," said Haley. "We do good work."

"We do," said Theodosia. "Even though Delaine was in charge of the cleaning, gardening, and party rental crews."

"Well, it all looks positively grand," said Haley, as guests began filtering into the backyard. "And look, people are actually helping themselves to tea and desserts."

"And strolling through the garden," said Theodosia. They'd experienced a few hairy moments along the way, but everything seemed to have worked out nicely.

"And look who just showed up."

"Angie!" said Theodosia, as Angie Congdon, cute, petite,

with strawberry blond hair, strolled toward her on the arm of a tall, good-looking man. "I haven't seen you . . ."

"In ages," finished Angie. She was the proprietor of the Featherbed House B and B, located a few blocks from the Indigo Tea Shop.

"Or at least a few weeks," said Theodosia.

"It's our busy time, don't you know?" said Angie. "We've only just recovered from the Spoleto Festival and now we're into peak tourist season, so our rooms are rented to the rafters." She paused and said, "Theo, Haley, I'd like you to meet a dear friend of mine. This is Harold Affolter."

"Nice to meet you," said Theodosia, shaking his hand.

"Pleased," said Haley, nodding.

"Harold and I are . . . seeing each other," said Angie. She grinned widely and blushed.

"That's wonderful," said Theodosia.

"Cool," said Haley. Angie's first husband, Mark, had been killed a few years ago, and it had taken her a long time to finally begin dating again.

"I take it you two ladies are responsible for all this?" said Harold, gazing out over the patio and gardens.

"Just the tea and treats," said Theodosia.

"Still," said Angie. "I imagine it was a formidable task."

"But oh, so delicious," said Theodosia. "So please help yourself." She'd just spotted Allan Grumley out of the corner of her eye. "Please enjoy yourselves and hopefully we'll get a chance to chat later." She moved off hastily, wanting to buttonhole Grumley before Delaine did.

Speeding across the patio, Theodosia hooked Grumley's arm and said, in no uncertain terms, "A word, please?"

Grumley stared at her. "What do you want now?"

"I want you to start extending some professional courtesy to Delaine. I know she has another meeting scheduled with you tomorrow and I'm hoping this one will go better than the last one."

"She's hired an attorney," said Grumley.

"Yes, she did. On my advice."

"You didn't think you were a skillful enough advocate?"

"Advocate, yes. But I'm not schooled in the letter of the law. And Delaine needs to have some important questions answered."

"We'll take care of all that," said Grumley.

"I certainly hope so."

Grumley cocked his head and gazed out across the garden, where leaves rustled and flowers bobbed in the evening breeze. "This is such a magnificent property."

"It is lovely," Theodosia responded. She glanced sideways at him. "Are you interested in buying it?"

Grumley dodged her question. "I've always loved this place. As you well know, my partner possessed impeccable style and taste."

"That's what Delaine always says," said Theodosia. "About herself."

"Then the two of them were well suited for each other, weren't they?"

"*Were* being the operative word," said Theodosia.

Grumley lifted his teacup to his mouth and took a sip. "Excellent tea."

"You enjoy tea?"

"Depends on the occasion," said Grumley.

Theodosia gazed at Grumley and thought to herself, *You're a real slicko, aren't you?* And, for a brief moment, she wondered if Allan Grumley might have been the one pawing through Granville's house last night. Pulling open drawers, looking for . . . whatever.

Or, wild card candidate, had it been Delaine after all? But no, Delaine would never sneak in like that. It wasn't her style. She would have gone barreling in, flipped on all the lights, and searched top to bottom, very methodically. And when it came to fleeing the scene, Delaine wasn't any kind of runner. She was more of a . . . Theodosia racked her brain, trying to figure out what exercise Delaine enjoyed. Pilates. That was it. She was more into Pilates.

An hour into the event, just when Theodosia was beginning to think they'd pulled off a major coup, Delaine came flying into the kitchen.

"Theo!" she cried. "That hag Simone Asher just showed up! She's wandering around the living room as if she's the empress of China!"

This was the last thing Theodosia needed—a hysterical, crying Delaine on her hands. Hoping to defuse the situation, Theodosia said, "China doesn't have an emperor or empress anymore, remember? That all ended with Mao and company."

Delaine ground her teeth together and her eyes blazed demonically. "Theo. If you're any kind of friend to me, you'll shoo that woman out of this house!"

"We can't just toss her out on her ear," Theodosia reasoned. "Simone obviously purchased a ticket for the tour."

"I don't care if she holds a season pass!" said Delaine. "I don't care if she's got an engraved invitation from the grand poobah of the garden club. Just get rid of her! Please!"

Theodosia put her hands on Delaine's shoulders and attempted to steer her out the back door. "You be a good girl and go outside, okay? Promise me you won't make a scene and I'll see what I can do."

"Really?"

"Yes, really."

But when Theodosia went back inside, there was no sign of Simone anywhere. Theodosia thought Simone might have decided she didn't want to mix it up with Delaine so she just up and left. But, somehow, a quick hit-and-run didn't seem in keeping with Simone's personality. Simone was a lot more aggressive than that. Pit bull aggressive. So that meant . . .

Theodosia glanced around the living room, where people were filtering through on their way to the backyard garden. And suddenly she wondered if Simone hadn't maybe taken a detour upstairs. But why? To upset the apple cart and annoy Delaine even more? Or just have a last nostalgic look around?

Easy enough to find out.

Theodosia raced up the stairs, taking them two at a time. When she reached the second-floor landing, she stopped. No sign of anyone here. But that didn't mean Simone wasn't snooping around where she wasn't welcome.

Walking purposely down the hallway to the master bedroom, Theodosia pushed open one of the double doors. And found . . .

"Simone!"

Simone whirled around to face her, a mixture of surprise and shock on her face.

"What are you doing here?" Theodosia demanded.

"Nothing," Simone said in an airy tone. "I'm just . . . looking around."

Dressed in a tailored white pantsuit with snappy navy trim, Simone looked cool and calculating. Theodosia decided Simone might even be enjoying this impromptu confrontation.

"Were you looking for something in particular?" Theodosia asked. Did Simone, like Delaine, want something of Granville's to remember him by? Some sort of touchstone or link to him?

"Really, Theodosia," said Simone. "You're just brimming with curiosity, aren't you?"

"Not as much as you are," said Theodosia. She wondered if Simone had wandered up to see if her clothes were still safely tucked away in Granville's closet. "Did you come to retrieve your clothes?"

Simone gave a surprised look. "I don't have any clothes here."

"Those aren't your clothes hanging in the closet?" asked Theodosia.

"Really," said Simone. She let loose a haughty sniff and brushed past her. "I have no idea what you're talking about." And then she was out the door and gone.

Still not convinced, Theodosia ducked into the walk-in closet to take another look at the small assortment of women's clothing. There were maybe ten things on hangers, all crushed together at the back of the closet. Did they belong to Simone, even though she denied it? Or were they the property of some other lady friend?

Ready to chalk up Simone's visit to pure curiosity, Theodosia turned to leave. As she did, her eyes caught sight of a linen jacket. A beige linen jacket with nubby, almost fringed edges on the collar and sleeves.

She paused, stared at it, and thought, *Could the thread I found at Ravencrest Inn have come from this jacket?*

She pulled her iPhone from her pocket and scrolled to the picture she'd snapped of the thread in the window frame. Then she held her phone next to the jacket. Could the thread have come from this same jacket? Stranger yet, was this the jacket Simone had worn to the wedding? Maybe. Possibly.

But if it was the same jacket, what on earth was it doing back here?

23

❧

"*Where did you* disappear to?" Haley asked when Theodosia returned to the kitchen.

"Just checking on a few things," said Theodosia.

"Drayton's here," said Haley. "Looking all spiffy and debonair in his seersucker suit. In fact, he was just looking for you."

"Where is he now? Out back in the garden?"

Haley nodded. "Taking tea, I presume. Gosh, I hope he likes what we did."

"Haley," said Theodosia. "You know he will."

Theodosia pushed her way through the butler's pantry, past cans of soup and sacks of flour and sugar that, with Granville's passing, would probably be donated to a local food shelf now, and exited the side door. Then she walked around the house, following a bumpy cobblestone path. With the yard lights on; the lawn trimmed so short it looked like a putting green; beds of coneflowers, candytufts, and roses in full bloom; and dogwoods perfectly pruned, the garden looked absolutely amazing. At the last minute, Delaine had placed small candles along all the paths and around the pool, so the effect was pure magic. It was just too bad Granville wasn't here to enjoy the admiring gazes and soak up all the compliments.

Just before she got to the tea table, Theodosia ran into Delaine and Millie Grant.

"Is she gone?" Delaine hissed. "I ran into Millie here and was just telling her about Simone Asher. What colossal nerve that woman has!"

Millie nodded. "I can see it made for an aggravating situation."

"Simone's gone," said Theodosia. "She's out of our hair."

"Really?" said Delaine. "There were no problems? No major confrontation?"

"None whatsoever," Theodosia said in a reassuring tone, smiling inwardly at her little white lie. "In fact, she left rather quietly."

"Okay, then," said Delaine. She sounded a little disappointed. "That's good. A happy ending, I suppose."

Theodosia smiled at Millie. "It's nice to see you again." The harpist had just begun a rendition of "Bridge over Troubled Water."

"I wanted to come and show my support for Delaine," said Millie. "She was very game to take on this project at the very last minute. Plus, she's got her big meeting tomorrow." She smiled at Delaine and touched her hand shyly. "The office was all abuzz today."

"I'm sure everything will work out just fine," said Theodosia.

"I've got my fingers crossed," said Millie. And to Delaine, "You know I'm here for you."

"That's more than I can say about Nadine," said Delaine. "My sister didn't even bother to show up tonight."

"Maybe she'll come tomorrow night," said Millie.

"Huh," said Delaine. "Maybe."

They all grabbed a cup of tea and a couple of cake pops, then looked around for a place to sit. That was when Theodosia spotted Drayton, already seated at one of the black wrought-iron tables. And, lo and behold, who was sitting with him but the Beckman boys, Charleston's resident ghost hunters! Or at least they were for the rest of the week.

"Here we go," said Theodosia, leading the way. "We can sit with Drayton and the boys." They all clustered around the table, then dropped into chairs while Drayton hastily introduced Millie to Jed and Tim Beckman.

"Ghost hunting," said Millie, giving Jed a look of mingled amusement and awe. "I've watched some of those TV shows where they creep through old houses, but I've never met any real-life ghost hunters before." She gave a mock shiver. "It's kind of fun."

"Drayton was just telling us about some of the ghosts that reside in Charleston," said Jed.

Delaine's brows pinched together, and she shot Drayton a quick look. "I thought you didn't believe in ghosts."

"I don't, really," said Drayton. "But the legends and lore are highly entertaining."

"Such as?" said Millie.

"Well," said Drayton, leaning back in his chair, "you all know about Gateway Walk, don't you? About the orbs and the poor woman who's been heard singing lullabies to her dead baby?"

Heads nodded slowly.

"Awful," muttered Delaine.

"And then there are the boo hags," said Drayton. "Flaxen-haired vampires that have been mythologized all over the low country. Of course, those creatures only come out at night."

"Sure they do," said Theodosia.

"Where have people reported seeing the most manifestations?" asked Jed.

"Probably the Battery Carriage House," said Drayton. "Dozens of guests have been frightened out of their wits there. Apparently a headless torso roams the halls at night."

"What about the Provost Dungeon?" said Theodosia. "People who tour that old place often report feeling an intense burning sensation. Because of the awful fire that took place."

"And they've heard chains rattling, too," said Delaine. She seemed to be slowly getting into the spirit of their discussion, too.

"I think one of the neatest things about Charleston and pretty much the whole South," put in Tim, "are the old legends."

"Like Blackbeard," said Theodosia.

"And the ghost of Edgar Allan Poe," said Drayton. "Walking the lonely beaches."

"What about the legend of Madame Margot?" said Millie. "That's a strange one."

"But what's the most frightening tale of all?" asked Jed, really enjoying himself now. "What's the one story that scares the poop out of you and really raises your hackles?"

"Oh," said Drayton, giving his question careful consideration. "No doubt about it, it has to be the legend of the Screaming Lula."

"What's *that*?" asked Delaine. "I've lived here all my life and never heard that one."

"The Screaming Lula dates back to just after the War between the States," said Drayton. "A poor woman by the name of Lula Marsden lost everything to the war—her husband, her two sons, even her home. In fact, she was so destitute, she had to find work as a scullery maid at a boardinghouse over on Calhoun Street. One night, poor Lula was so down and desperate that she set fire to the building. As dozens of occupants fled the blaze, Lula stayed behind, ranting wildly and dashing from room to room. When her long skirts finally caught fire, she ran screaming from the building!"

"No!" said Millie.

Drayton nodded and continued his story. "Down Calhoun Street she tore, her skirt blazing and her burning hair streaming out behind her. Lula was in such a crazed state that she careened directly onto the railroad tracks, right in front of an oncoming train." He paused. "It's said the cowcatcher on the front of the train lifted her up and carried her along for several blocks, and that she screamed and cackled the entire way."

"Wow," said Tim. "Cool."

Delaine heaved a sigh and said, "Goodness, Drayton. That's an *awful* story!"

"Terrifying," said Millie. "Absolutely terrifying." But she still looked intrigued. "Tell me, how on earth did you come to learn all these strange tales?"

Drayton gave a mousy smile. "Let's just say I'm a true connoisseur of Southern legends."

An hour later, it was all over. Theodosia and Haley washed and stacked teacups, packaged up the leftover cake pops—only a dozen or so remained—and wiped the counters.

"Just think," said Haley, "tomorrow night we get to do this all over again."

"Just like at the Indigo Tea Shop," said Theodosia.

"I guess so," said Haley. She twirled a chocolate cake pop that she was nibbling on.

"Go home," said Theodosia. "I'll finish up here."

"You sure?"

"Absolutely. You've done enough. More than enough."

"Okay then," said Haley. She gulped the last bite of her cake pop and gave a wave. "I'll see you tomorrow."

Theodosia fussed around the kitchen, grabbing tea towels and packing them into a wicker basket. She decided that, rather than firing up Granville's washing machine and dryer, it would be easier to take the towels home with her. Toss a load into her own washing machine tonight.

She was rinsing off the last of the three-tiered serving trays when she spotted the note on the counter. It was half tucked behind a stack of blue-and-white gingham napkins.

What on earth? Something Haley left behind?

She picked it up and saw loopy handwriting scrawled across a square of thick parchment.

A note.

And even more strange, the note was addressed to her. It said, *Theodosia. Kindly meet me behind the Gibbes Museum at ten o'clock tonight.* It wasn't signed.

Theodosia whirled about suddenly, a little nervous, a lot perplexed. Who on earth could have written that note?

Had Max dropped by while she was sitting in the garden with Drayton and company? Had he left the note?

Could Haley be a co-conspirator in this? Was there some sort of surprise waiting for her? Wait a minute, was that even Max's handwriting?

Theodosia studied the note again but wasn't completely sure. Tapping her toe for a few seconds, she realized that the sound echoed hollowly in the empty house. And that made her jittery, too. Figuring she had to do something, had to sleuth this out somehow, Theodosia grabbed her phone and dialed Max's number. She knew he was supposed to be at a museum event tonight, but maybe he'd gotten out early. Or skipped out early.

To see me? That would be nice.

But, no, Max wasn't picking up. She was flipped over to his voice mail where she heard his voice, sounding friendly and familiar, encouraging her to leave a message.

"Max," she said. "Did you slip in here and leave me a note? Are you the person I'm supposed to meet behind the Gibbes Museum tonight? Um, is this your idea of romance? Because I find it a little spooky. Call me, okay?"

She hung up and thought, *Now what do I do?*

Should she go there? Or just go home? She touched the piece of parchment again with the tips of her fingers, as if she could intuit who had written it and what their intentions could be.

In the end she swallowed her nerves and went.

Gateway Walk was a hidden, four-block walk that rambled through lush gardens, an ancient cemetery, and a famous pair of wrought-iron gates. It stretched from the sixteenth-century graveyard that stood behind St. Phillip's Episcopal Church, past the Circular Congregational Church, the Gibbes Museum, and the Charleston Library Association, ending at Archdale Street. This historic walkway was quiet, contemplative, and abundant with flora and fauna. It was also reputed to be haunted.

Drayton had made mention of it tonight, and old legends spoke of hair that had turned to Spanish moss and now beckoned spookily to unsuspecting visitors. Countless folks had claimed to see the headless torso of a Confederate solider wandering aimlessly through Gateway Walk's serene gardens and secret cul-de-sacs. Glowing blue orbs had been photographed but never explained.

All of that spun through Theodosia's brain right now as she walked hastily down the path next to the Gibbes Museum. She'd parked her car on Meeting Street and found the museum, an elegant Greek revival building with four heroic columns, to be totally dark. No concert had just let out; there were no patrons in formal dress still milling around.

All that greeted her were a few tendrils of fog that had crept in from the Atlantic and, with it, the nip of sea air.

Reaching the back courtyard, the place where she and Max usually met, Theodosia hesitated. The place was dark and deserted.

Now what?

She crossed the patio, her footsteps echoing on the polished slate, and crept past looming statuary that, in the dim light, looked like strange, hunched figures. Maybe Max was still inside? But, no, the entire museum was shrouded in darkness.

So what am I supposed to do? Wait for him?

What else was there to do?

She found it hard to believe that this was Max's idea of a romantic rendezvous. On the other hand, he might be setting up something very special. Perhaps she'd slip around a feathery hedge into a dark, leafy corner where she'd find Max grinning with a proffered bottle of champagne and a big bouquet of roses.

If so, that would be extremely cool. And quite romantic. If not, this whole thing was getting just a little too spooky for words.

"So which is it?" she asked aloud. "What's it going to be?"

As if in answer, a sound, like the scrape of a footstep on gravel, sounded farther down the pathway.

Huh? Somebody there?

"Max?" she called out.

There was no answer save the sigh of wind in the trees.

Theodosia decided that two could play at this game. Slowly, quietly, she tiptoed down the narrow pathway. Flowering dogwoods brushed her shoulders; a nearby fountain pattered softly while a dove cooed mournfully from its hidden nest.

When she reached the wrought-iron Governor Aiken gates, she hesitated. A faint sliver of moon illuminated a metal plaque that read:

> *Through hand wrought gates, alluring paths*
> *Lead on to pleasant places*
> *Where ghosts of long forgotten things*
> *Have left elusive traces.*

"Ghosts," said Theodosia. "Maybe they're all that's here tonight. Just the sad, lingering souls of people who've been buried here. Maybe Max isn't going to show up. Maybe someone's playing a trick on me and enjoying a nasty chuckle."

She wondered if Simone Asher's fine hand had orchestrated this little no-show? It was possible. Maybe Simone had been so angry and distraught at being asked to leave Granville's home tonight that she'd concocted what was an elaborate hoax.

Of course, Theodosia reasoned, it could just as easily be Charles Horton or Allan Grumley. Neither of them had been particularly pleasant to her ever since she'd started looking into the murder of Dougan Granville. But would they take petty pleasure in sending her on a wild-goose chase? Hmm. Yes, they probably would.

Theodosia took a few more tentative steps and was suddenly overwhelmed by the scent of jasmine. Letting her guard down just a bit, she breathed in the intoxicating scent. There were so many flowers and shrubs here that you were basically ensconced in a cornucopia of aromatherapy.

Theodosia stared into the darkness and sniffed again. There was something else here, too. Something besides the sea breezes and the heavy floral essences that hung in the warm, humid air.

But what was it?

She inhaled again and was able to distinguish a toasty, pungent, almost sweet scent. And this time the limbic part of her brain, the primitive, reactionary reptile part, picked up on it.

Cigar smoke!

Theodosia spun on her heels and fled, running back down the walk and past the museum as though her life depended on it. Was she in danger? By the intense thudding in her chest and her fight-or-flight reaction, her body and mind were signaling yes. A resounding yes.

24

Saturday was their short day at the Indigo Tea Shop. That is, they were only open from nine to one. So, much like their hours, their menu was abbreviated, too.

Standing at the counter, wearing a yellow Lady Gaga T-shirt and a long, pale-blue diaphanous skirt, Haley looked cute and boho-chic as she ticked off her menu.

"Cream scones," she told Theodosia and Drayton. "And cranberry walnut bread. For lunch, I'm doing two tea sandwiches, chicken salad on cinnamon raisin bread and roast beef on whole wheat, along with cream of mushroom soup."

"Excellent," said Drayton.

"How are you holding up?" Theodosia asked.

Haley yawned. "Okay. I'm looking forward to some downtime, though."

Drayton adjusted his bow tie, a red polka-dot tie that contrasted nicely with his navy jacket and gray slacks. "Pity you two have to work again tonight."

"You could always drop by and help us," said Haley. There was a note of hope in her voice.

"Me?" Drayton looked aghast.

"We'll be fine. After last night we've got the drill down cold," Theodosia told them both. What she didn't tell them about was her foray into Gateway Walk. As well as the mysterious note and the scent of a sweet cigar riding on the wind. She was still disturbed that someone had tried to lure her there. To do what? Probably nothing nice.

Drayton reached up and grabbed a tin of Ming-Hung tea. "I believe I'll brew a pot of Fukien red tea today. Be a trifle daring with my selection."

"That's our Drayton," said Haley. "Ever daring."

"Haley," said Theodosia. "Could you help me move some boxes in my office? I'm trying to unearth a carton of strainers and tea timers."

"Sure," said Haley. "No problem."

The two of them trooped into Theodosia's office, where space was always at a premium.

"Whoa," said Haley, looking around at the clutter and stacks of boxes. "I see the problem. You're plum out of space."

"I've been out of space for the last three years," said Theodosia. "But that doesn't seem to stop me from ordering more teapots, mugs, and wooden tea chests."

"Good point," said Haley. She grabbed two boxes off the top of the stack, let loose a little grunt as she hoisted them, and shifted them onto Theodosia's desk. "Now, if we clear those other three boxes you'll at least have a fair shot."

"That's all I'm asking," said Theodosia. After they'd dug out the boxes, she remained in her office, putzing around, unearthing more tea ware, and finding a stack of tea magazines that had been delivered heaven knows when. "These have to go on display, too," she said to herself. "Before *next* month's issues show up."

But when she came flying into the tea room, arms over-flowing, she was in for a big surprise. Drayton was seated at one of the tables, along with Jed and Tim Beckman.

"You're back," she said to the two ghost hunters.

"We can't seem to stay away," said Jed.

"You and Drayton have turned us into confirmed tea lovers," said Tim.

Drayton caught Theodosia's eye and said, "I just received a rather interesting invitation."

"What's that?" said Theodosia.

Drayton smiled. "Jed and Tim have asked me to accompany them tonight on their mission to Barrow Hall."

Theodosia's eyes went wide with surprise. "And you're going to do it?" Somehow it seemed out of character for Drayton. Although, truth be told, he'd certainly dazzled everyone last night with his ghostly tidbits and crazy stories.

"I don't see why I shouldn't," said Drayton.

"Drayton's our resident historian," Jed said with a knowing grin.

"That's right," said Tim. "Drayton knows all the legends."

"About Barrow Hall?" said Theodosia. She didn't think there were any legends. Just a few details about its sad, almost sordid history as a mental institution.

"I think Barrow Hall might be an amusing foray," Drayton told her.

"A hoot," said Jed.

"It'll be a hoot all right," said Theodosia. "Just try not to pitch headfirst down a slippery stairwell. Or get lost in a warren of inmate rooms."

"Aren't you a bundle of optimism," said Drayton.

Lunch was busy with scads of tourists finding their way to the Indigo Tea Shop. A couple of months ago, Theodosia had printed colorful postcards that featured a photo of the exterior of her tea shop on one side and her menu and address on the reverse. She'd walked the postcards around to four dozen bed-and-breakfasts, inns, and hotels in the area. And her efforts had paid off almost immediately. Now they were bombarded with weekend traffic, and the shelves and cupboards in the tea room needed almost constant restocking. It seemed that between tours to the tea plantation on Wadmalaw Island, the B and Bs serving afternoon tea to guests, and the popularity of the Indigo Tea Shop, strategically located as it was in the Historic District, tea was on everyone's mind!

"Theo," said Haley, as the two of them fussed in the kitchen, "you think I should bake a couple more batches of cake pops?"

"You mean more than you have already, or more than you did for last night?" said Theodosia.

"More than last night."

Theodosia thought for a couple of seconds. "Yes. I'm guessing tonight's going to be the big push, the evening when the Summer Garden Tour gets the most visitors. So we should probably be armed and ready."

"Yup," said Haley. "That's what I've been thinking, too."

"You want me to help with the frosting and decorating?"

"Mmm, maybe."

Drayton suddenly stuck his head in the doorway. "Theo. Phone call."

"Is it Max?" She'd put a call in to him first thing and was waiting for him to call back.

"No," said Drayton. "I think it's Delaine."

Theodosia ducked into her office and grabbed the phone. "Hi. Is your meeting over with already? How'd it go?"

There was a peal of laughter and Delaine said, "It really couldn't have gone any better. That lawyer you recommended was terrific."

"Glad to hear it," said Theodosia. The small wire of worry that had been stretched tightly around her heart suddenly eased. Now maybe Delaine wouldn't feel so distraught or act so compulsive. "So, what happened? Obviously there was a reading of the will. I'm assuming you received a piece of the inheritance? Did Charles Horton get anything?"

"All was revealed," said Delaine.

"And?" After all the fuss and hysterics and drama, Theodosia wanted to be privy to all the juicy details. She'd *earned* the right, for gosh sake.

"But I think I'll wait and tell you all about it tonight," said Delaine.

"Delaine! Please don't be coy." Coy was annoying. Coy showed lack of trust.

"Tonight," said Delaine. "I promise I'll tell you everything tonight."

Two o'clock came and went, guests came and went, and still Theodosia remained at the tea shop. Drayton, whom Haley had suddenly taken to calling Mr. Sci-Fi Channel Reality Show, had left some fifteen minutes ago. Theodosia figured he'd gone home to lay out his wardrobe for tonight. A khaki jacket and slacks, maybe boots, some sort of cap. And maybe his black leather notebook, just in case he wanted to take notes or jot down the makings of a new legend.

Haley was in the kitchen, rattling pans and beating her frosting into a swirl. She wore a determined look, a look that clearly said *Do not disturb*.

Well, okay, Theodosia decided. She wouldn't disturb her. She'd already made it known that she was available to help decorate cake pops if help was needed. In the meantime, Theodosia was up to her ears in wreath-making paraphernalia and was busily assembling two new teacup wreaths.

Starting with a wild grapevine that she'd cut, dried, and shaped herself, she loosely threaded a piece of peach-colored satin organza ribbon through the wreath. Once that was done, the fun stuff happened. Theodosia wired in small teacups that she'd found at tag sales, added a couple of bunches of silk flowers, then wired in a bunch of frosted grapes.

Just as Theodosia was debating between dried star flowers versus tiny blue silk flowers, her cell phone rang.

"Max!" she said.

"You left me a couple of phone messages," said Max. "Last night and then again this morning. Something about a note?"

"You didn't leave me a note, did you?" said Theodosia. "At Granville's house last night."

"I was at a fund-raiser last night." Max sounded puzzled. "Until around eleven."

"Okay, I was just checking on something."

"Problem?"

"Not really," said Theodosia. She thought about telling him about last night, then hastily changed the subject. Why worry him? "Are you going to be able to stop by Granville's home tonight? I'd really love to see you . . ."

"I'm going to try," said Max. "But I can't promise anything."

"I have to warn you, Haley's really knocking herself out."

Max chuckled. "Are we talking chocolate desserts?" Max was a dedicated chocoholic.

"You got it."

"I'm really gonna try," said Max.

"Try hard," said Theodosia.

*   *   *

By midafternoon Haley decided that Theodosia could indeed help decorate the cake pops. So, robed in a long white apron, wearing plastic gloves, Theodosia dipped chocolate-frosted cake pops into various saucers filled with crushed pecans, flaky coconut, and tiny colorful nonpareils.

"This is fun," said Theodosia. Her hands were a sticky, chocolatey mess and nonpareils crunched underfoot, but their assembly line was running smoothly as they dipped and swayed, singing along to "Moves Like Jagger" on the radio and dancing in place.

"In about two seconds I'm gonna switch to butterscotch frosting," said Haley. She scanned the finished cake pops that were lined up like a bunch of tasty, edible Weebles. "Yup, about sixty percent are frosted with chocolate."

"You're working on a sixty-forty ratio?" asked Theodosia.

"I like things mathematical," said Haley. She grinned. "Even my cake pops."

Thump thump.

"Jeez," said Haley. "What the heck was that?"

"Somebody at the back door?" said Theodosia. She pulled off her gloves and grabbed a damp rag so she could wipe blobs of sticky frosting from her wrists and arms. "I'll go take a look."

"Tell whoever it is that we're closed."

Theodosia hurried through her office. Probably, she decided, it was one of the neighbors from the garden apartments across the brick alley. Sometimes they popped over unexpectedly to grab leftover scones or croissants or slices of quiche.

But when Theodosia looked out the window, she saw it was Tidwell.

Surprised, she pulled open the door and said, "What are you doing back here?"

"I knocked on the front door; didn't you hear me?"

"No. Sorry. We were working in the kitchen and had the radio turned up full blast." She opened the door wider. "Come on in. What's up?"

Tidwell cast a cautious glance at her as he eased his bulk through the doorway. "I was hoping you could tell me."

Theodosia was suddenly confused. "Tell you what?" Had she said or done something to ruffle his feathers yet again?

Tidwell made a seesawing gesture with both hands. "About the murder? About your cuckoo friend Delaine?"

"No, I haven't solved the murder," said Theodosia. "In fact, I distinctly remember you telling me to mind my own business. As far as Delaine is concerned, she's not cuckoo. She's merely stressed. She was just in a meeting at Granville and Grumley. Something about the reading of the will?"

"Exactly," Tidwell growled.

"I don't know anything about that, either. Delaine called but was playing her cards fairly close to the vest. She told me I had to wait until tonight to hear her all her big news." Theodosia put her hands on her hips in a slightly confrontational manner. "So . . . what have *you* been up to? Hopefully still spearheading an in-depth murder investigation that is deserving of our tax dollars?"

"What on earth smells so devilishly good in here?" asked Tidwell.

Theodosia sighed. Honestly, the man was so predictable. "We're making cake pops for the Summer Garden Tour tonight. And, no, they're not ready yet."

"Yes, they are," Haley called from the kitchen. "He can have a couple if he wants."

"I don't think he wants any," Theodosia called back.

Haley stuck her head in the office and registered innocent surprise. "He doesn't?"

"Pay no attention to your curmudgeon employer," said

Tidwell. "I would love nothing better than to partake of your excellent desserts."

"I can stick a few cake pops in one of our take-out cartons," said Haley. She held up a finger. "Give me a sec."

"Bless you, child," said Tidwell.

"You ought to be ashamed of yourself," Theodosia scolded. "Taking advantage of Haley's sweet and giving nature. You know she's bursting with pride over her baked goods and can never refuse samples to anyone."

"That's precisely what I was counting on," said Tidwell. He lurched toward the chair opposite Theodosia's desk. "May I sit down?"

"Why not?"

"I'm afraid I'm in a pickle," said Tidwell, facing her.

"Really," said Theodosia. This was a first. Tidwell rarely let down his guard like this.

"We finally located the mysterious Mr. Chapin of room three-fourteen."

"And?"

"He's merely a traveling salesman," said Tidwell. "And not a very successful one at that. The net result is he's not even remotely connected to Granville."

"So you're back to square one," said Theodosia. She could feel his disappointment. Heck, *she* was disappointed, too.

"That's right. We have suspects, yes. But no clear-cut motives."

"The suspects being . . . ?"

Allan Grumley for one," said Tidwell. "Except that the man is already quite wealthy and had a buy-sell partnership agreement firmly in place."

"Meaning?"

"Meaning that if Grumley and Granville had decided they didn't want to work together anymore, there was a hammered-out provision for divvying up the law firm."

"In other words," said Theodosia, "they could have called it quits amicably. One wouldn't have to kill the other."

"I'd say that's a fair assessment," said Tidwell.

"Have you looked at past cases that Granville handled? Maybe he sent someone to prison who was recently released and wanted to exact their revenge."

"He's not that kind of lawyer," said Tidwell.

Theodosia thought for a few moments. "My mind keeps circling back to Simone Asher."

Tidwell shrugged. "Old girlfriend, shop owner, pretty girl. I interviewed her. She didn't seem particularly malicious."

"You don't know what's in her heart," said Theodosia. She thought back to last night. "You know, Simone showed up at Granville's home last night."

"Did she?"

Theodosia told Tidwell about finding Simone upstairs in Granville's bedroom, taking a last look around. And then she told him about the beige linen jacket hanging in the closet.

"And you think the thread matches?" asked Tidwell. He was starting to look interested.

"I have no idea. But . . . I have to admit it's kind of a spooky coincidence."

"I'm not a big believer in coincidences."

"You should still stop by and grab a snippet of fabric. Take it to your lab and see if it matches the thread."

"I can get in the house right now?"

"I'm pretty sure you can," said Theodosia. "I think Delaine brought in another cleaning crew to spiff the place up."

"You said Simone Asher was taking what you termed 'a last look.' Does that seem at all peculiar to you?" said Tidwell.

"Maybe. But I can see Delaine doing the exact same thing if she'd been the ex-girlfriend."

"A lot of women might," said Tidwell.

"No," said Theodosia. "Not a lot of women. Just the ones who aren't terribly realistic."

25

Theodosia was right about having their routine down cold. As she heated water and measured out tea, Haley quickly unpacked her Charleston cookies, lemon bars, espresso cookies, and cake pops. On this second and final night of the Summer Garden Tour, with the temperature hovering in the low eighties, an even greater number of visitors were expected.

"It's hard to believe Drayton went off ghost hunting," said Haley as she arranged her desserts on a large tray. "It seems so out of character for him."

"I actually can believe it," said Theodosia. "If you mention anything that's remotely Southern Gothic, Drayton's antennae automatically perk up."

"But he's a nonbeliever," said Haley. "I mean concerning the spirit world."

"Doesn't matter," said Theodosia. "The minute you start talking legends and lore, our Drayton can't help being intrigued. The history buff in him just comes alive."

"Barrow Hall sounds like a creepy place. I hope he'll be okay out there."

"No reason for him not to be," said Theodosia.

"Hey," Haley said to Delaine as she breezed into the kitchen. "You look great." Delaine was wearing a long, black one-shouldered dress and sky-high silver sandals.

"So tell us," said Theodosia, pouncing. "How did your meeting turn out?" She was dying to know.

"The wait is finally over," Delaine trilled. "We went over everything with a fine-toothed comb and it's all mine!"

"*All* of it?" said Haley. "Are you serious? Wow!"

"What exactly is all yours?" asked Theodosia. Since Delaine tended to exaggerate, she wanted specifics. "You mean this house?"

"No, silly," said Delaine. "Not the house. But almost everything else. I'm set to receive the proceeds from Dougan's life insurance policy as well as a tidy amount of money, some blue-chip stocks, and a number of mutual funds."

"You're going to be rich!" said Haley. "Correction . . . you *are* rich!"

"Almost," said Delaine.

"Well, congrats, lady!" said Haley.

"I'm happy for you," said Theodosia. "Well . . . pleased, anyway. Of course, I know you'd give it all up if you could just have Dougan back."

Delaine managed a small sniffle. "I would. I really would."

"I'm curious," said Theodosia. "Who does own this house now?"

Delaine made an unhappy face. "It belongs to Allan Grumley. Apparently, this place was purchased through a subsidiary corporation of the law firm, so he was already a fifty percent owner."

"That's awfully convenient," said Theodosia. "For him, anyway." No wonder Grumley had been so circumspect last night concerning ownership of the house. "And what about the stepson, Charles Horton? Did he launch any sort of claim? Did he inherit anything?"

"Thank goodness, he did not launch a claim," said Delaine. "But he will inherit Dougan's Porsche 911 as well as DG Stogies and a tidy sum of money." She whipped out a hanky and daubed at her eyes, taking care not to smear her eye makeup. "But not as much as I will."

"Good for you," said Theodosia. Besides Delaine enjoying a little one-upmanship with Horton, she'd been a mere twenty minutes away from becoming Mrs. Dougan Granville. So she was practically the next of kin.

"I feel like an enormous weight has been lifted from my shoulders," said Delaine. She grabbed a Charleston cookie, munched a bite thoughtfully, then popped the rest into her mouth. "I feel so much more relaxed and unstressed. You know . . ." She shook an index finger at Theodosia and Haley. "I think this is going to be a truly memorable evening. I'm even feeling . . . very good vibes." And with that she flounced out of the kitchen.

"Get a load of her," said Haley. "Delaine's all happy and chipper over the reading of the will, but Granville's murder still hasn't been solved."

"And Tidwell doesn't seem to be one bit closer," said Theodosia.

Haley straightened out a row of cookies, then glanced at her. "What about you? Are you any closer?"

Theodosia shrugged. "Not really. And Delaine's interest has definitely waned. She's no longer pressing me to explore different angles."

"Doesn't matter," said Haley. "Because Delaine's always been flighty. The big question is, will you continue to pursue this?"

"I'd like to see justice served if at all possible."

"That's because you're a law-and-order kind of gal," said Haley.

"I never thought of it that way. But . . . yes . . . maybe I am." Theodosia's father had been a prominent Charleston attorney. And, early on, she'd toyed with the idea of following in his footsteps. Then she'd gotten interested in advertising and marketing, and an account executive position had sort of been dropped into her lap. That experience had been fun for a while, but it was a hustle-bustle, go-go experience at best. When she finally transitioned to the Indigo Tea Shop, life was better. She got out of it exactly what she put in. For every cause, an effect. For every action, a reaction. And, of course, all the tea she cared to drink!

Haley continued to peer at her. "What about Charles Horton? He was blipping like crazy on your radar screen just a few days ago."

"As a murder suspect, he doesn't feel right anymore," said Theodosia. "I think he really is a stepson who wanted to reconnect with his stepfather."

"And get a piece of the action at the law firm?" said Haley.

"I suppose you can't fault him for being a go-getter. Or wanting to be a junior partner."

"What about Allan Grumley?" Haley asked.

"I still think he's a possible suspect." Theodosia reminded herself that Grumley, smooth talker that he was, could have easily urged Granville to indulge in a little prewedding cocaine. And then had somehow overpowered him. Plus, Grumley had been wearing a light-colored jacket the day of the wedding. The thread she found could have belonged to him.

"But you're not sure."

"The *police* aren't sure," said Theodosia.

"Maybe they missed something. Or you missed something."

"I probably did. But I don't know what. And I don't know what to look at next."

"I'll bet you'll figure it out," said Haley. "You're pretty good at solving mysteries and things."

"I don't know . . . maybe. At least I hope so. But right now, if we don't kick it into high gear, we're going to disappoint our guests."

They got busy then, Theodosia brewing tea while Haley worked on her desserts. Still, Theodosia continued to ponder the murder. And the strange invitation she'd found last night. And the significance, if any, of the cigar smoke. She turned everything over and over in her mind as if working a string of worry beads. She was well aware that greed, jealousy, and anger were all powerful drivers. Any one of them could compel a person to commit murder. The question was, which motivator had driven which person over the edge?

"Our table looks good, huh?" said Haley.

They were outside on the back patio. Pitchers of sweet tea sat on the table and the tea samovars were filled and ready to dispense cups of Russian Caravan and black spice tea. Haley's assortment of bars, cookies, and cake pops were beautifully arranged, making it look as if the Sugar Plum Fairy had swept in and waved her magic wand. And once again, the patio and gardens looked elegant and amazing. Delaine had asked the gardeners to change out the bulbs in the lights flanking the patio, taking out the white bulbs and replacing them with soft pink bulbs. So now the patio was bathed in a dreamy light. Very conducive to romance and reverie.

Suddenly, the back door clattered open and high-pitched laughter punctuated the night.

"Somebody's here," said Haley. She glanced at her watch. "And they're a good ten minutes early."

"I thought Delaine told the security people to hold everyone at the front door until seven," said Theodosia.

In a fast-moving blur of hot pink, Nadine, Delaine's sister, suddenly appeared on the arm of a tall, good-looking man. The same man who'd accompanied her to the tea shop this afternoon.

"Who's the guy?" Haley asked under her breath.

"No idea," said Theodosia. "He was at the tea shop earlier today and, for some reason, Nadine chose not to introduce us."

Haley nudged her with an elbow. "I'll bet five bucks you can finagle your way around that."

Theodosia grinned and decided it might be fun to try.

"Good evening, Nadine," she called. "Looks like you and your friend are the first ones to arrive."

Nadine tossed her head, her crystal earrings flashing and reflecting the color of her hot-pink dress. "Not quite," she said. "We just spoke with Delaine as we came through. Along with a few of the organizers and the ushers or security people or whoever those rather large gentlemen are."

"Then let's just say you two are the first to tour the garden area tonight," said Theodosia. "And enjoy our tea and treats." She sidled closer to Nadine's date and offered what she hoped was a winning smile. "Hello, I'm Theodosia Browning. You were in my tea shop this afternoon? I'm not sure we were ever properly introduced."

"This is my fella," Nadine blurted hastily. Even though she was draped possessively on the man's arm, she snuggled even closer. "He's quite the catch if I do say so myself."

Theodosia continued to smile at Nadine's date as she said, "How about if I pour you a cup of tea, er . . . ?" She gave an inquisitive cock of her head, a visual prompt for him to fill in his name.

But he never did. Or at least he never had a chance to.

"We'd *adore* some tea!" Nadine squealed. "And something to eat, too. We've been so busy running around that we pretty much breezed past dinner. Never did stop to eat."

"Okay, then," said Theodosia, giving up. "On second thought, maybe you should just help yourself."

The evening unfolded rather magically. Guests drifted in, exclaiming over the house, the tea table, and, finally, the elegant gardens. Mostly, Theodosia hung out in the kitchen, ready to restock desserts or hustle outside with more tea.

"I think we might be running low on that spice tea," said Haley, as she eased her way in through the butler's pantry.

"Good thing I've got two more pots brewing," said Theodosia.

"You know, it really is a madhouse out back. Tons of people are milling around and wandering through the garden."

"I guess that's why they call it a garden tour," said Theodosia.

"Yeah . . . whatever," said Haley. She began to unpack another basket stacked with plastic containers. "Oh, and that guy Allan Grumley is outside. He was looking for you."

"Interesting," said Theodosia. She grabbed her two pots of tea. "I'll have to go see what he wants."

Outside, Theodosia refilled the samovar and glanced around, on the lookout for Grumley.

She didn't have to look far. He was standing on the patio some ten feet away from her talking to, of all people, Frank and Sarah Rattling. Not wanting to intrude but curious as to what they were talking about, Theodosia busied herself with straightening out one of the dessert trays while she cocked an ear toward their conversation.

"This really is a great house," said Frank Rattling. "And in a far better location than we have now."

What you had, Theodosia thought to herself. *You don't own Ravencrest Inn anymore. The owner foreclosed on you. With a little help from Dougan Granville, of course.*

"And I took a peek in the kitchen!" Sarah Rattling

rhapsodized. "So modern and spacious! What I couldn't do in there. This place could be much more than just an inn, it could be an ultra luxe bed-and-breakfast."

What? The Rattlings are talking to Allan Grumley about buying this place? Oh my goodness! Please no!

Theodosia hurried over to insinuate herself into the conversation.

"Excuse me. I didn't mean to listen in," she said to Frank Rattling. "But, am I right? You and your wife are thinking about *buying* this place?"

Rattling turned to her, an earnest look on his hawkish face. "It would be a dream come true. We're head over heels in love with this house."

"I didn't think it was for sale," said Theodosia. She focused her gaze on Grumley, who gave an offhand shrug.

"Never say never," said Grumley.

"That's right," said Frank Rattling. "For the right price . . ."

Theodosia was amazed at Rattling's bravado. He and his wife had been foreclosed on for not making monthly payments on Ravencrest Inn. Now they were talking about buying an even more expensive piece of property? Was this just big talk, or was it some kind of weird payback against Granville? Even though the man was dead.

Grumley aimed a finger at Frank Rattling. "Toss out a number," he said, as he moved away. "You never know."

"Are you two serious?" said Theodosia. Her heart was fluttering and she was on the verge of panic.

"Absolutely," said Frank. "I get a feeling that, for the right price, Grumley really might be amenable to selling."

And then you'd be my next-door neighbor, Theodosia thought to herself. *Wouldn't that be a funhouse chock-full of monkeys?*

Theodosia forced herself to calm down. "I suppose it never hurts to float him a number."

"We're going to do just that," said Sarah.

"Good luck," Theodosia said without much enthusiasm.

She knew in her heart that if the Rattlings put in a serious offer, she was going to have to consider moving. No way did she want them as neighbors. No way could she tolerate them as neighbors.

When she returned to the kitchen, Nadine and her boyfriend were fussing about, talking to Haley.

"All I need," said Nadine, "is a scissors. I have this teensy little thread on the hem of my dress that's driving me crazy. Tickles every time I move."

Haley had pulled open a couple of cupboard drawers and was pawing through them. "I thought I saw a scissors here somewhere. Sorry. I'm just not used to this kitchen. I'm afraid I don't know my way around here."

"You really don't, do you," said Nadine.

Nadine's boyfriend tugged at her arm. "Come on, I think there's one in the drawer of that pine chest in the dining room."

"Thank goodness, somebody who knows *something*," said Nadine, as they hurried out.

"What's the problem?" asked Theodosia. She was still distracted by the Rattlings' big talk.

"Nothing," said Haley. "Just Nadine drama. Kind of like Delaine drama only with a touch more sarcasm."

"Nadine's a real character."

"Her guy seems nice enough, though," said Haley. "Nicer than she is, anyway."

"Nadine still hasn't introduced him," said Theodosia. "Somehow I find that strange."

"I just chalk it up to bad manners," said Haley.

Theodosia grabbed a cookie. "You're probably right."

"So did you find Grumley?"

"Yes, and he was talking to the Rattlings, who were tossing out innuendos about buying this place."

"No way!" said Haley.

"I don't think there would be a way," said Theodosia.

"Not with a conventional bank loan, anyway. If they couldn't make the payments on Ravencrest Inn, I don't see how they could get bank financing and trade up to this place."

Haley digested this bit of information for a few moments, then said in a quiet voice, "Not unless they had a partner."

Haley's remark caught Theodosia completely off balance, causing her to practically choke on her cookie. "What do you mean?" she stammered. "What are you talking about?"

26

"Sorry," said Haley. "I didn't mean to get you all upset."

"You didn't," said Theodosia. "Now tell me what you're talking about."

"You know," said Haley. "Like a silent partner. That's a fairly common business practice, wouldn't you say?"

"Yes, I suppose it can be," said Theodosia. "But I honestly don't know who in their right mind would trust the Rattlings at this point, given their rather sour track record."

"You never know," Haley said with a sharp bark. "Maybe Allan Grumley would give them a deal in exchange for a piece of the action."

"Haley!" Once again Theodosia was stunned. "You mean as an investor? Do you know something I don't?"

Now it was Haley's turn to look surprised. "No, of course not. I'm just saying . . ."

But like a grain of sand implanted in an unsuspecting oyster, Theodosia was suddenly turning this notion over and over in her mind. "What would be Grumley's reason?" she asked.

Haley waved a hand. "No idea. It's not based on anything concrete, I just kind of blurted it out."

"Okay."

"Mostly because of what you said about Frank and Sarah Rattling. How they sounded . . . kind of serious."

Theodosia was still alarmed. "You really haven't heard any gossip about this?"

"No, of course not," said Haley. "If I had, you know I would've told you." She gave Theodosia a look of concern, then said, "No offense, but I think you're being a little paranoid."

"I know I am."

"Is it the prospect of having the Rattlings as your next-door neighbors?"

"In part," said Theodosia. "But mostly because I trust Allan Grumley about as far as I can throw him."

"He's one of those cagey lawyers who's slippery when dry," said Haley. "Hey, did you ever think that Grumley might have plans to turn this place into some kind of fancy B and B by himself and that he's just using the Rattlings? You know, pumping them for information and ideas. Do you think he'd do that?"

"I don't think he'd hesitate to do that," said Theodosia.

"Huh," said Haley, snapping the lid off a plastic container. "I guess it takes all kinds." Then, "Theo, I'm going to put out these sugar cookies. Do we have any more large trays?"

"Um . . . sure. If you need one, I can probably grab something from the dining room."

"I need one."

"Hang on, then," said Theodosia. She pushed her way through the swinging door, still thinking about how Allan Grumley was now the owner of this house.

Gosh, I hope he doesn't decide to move in here. That's all I need. An idiot neighbor like him. And I don't think Earl Grey would take kindly to him, either.

When Theodosia hit the living room, she was momentarily stunned. There were so many people queued up in line that she didn't know how they'd ever accommodate them all. Still, she understood this was what the Summer Garden Tour was all about. Throwing open the doors to six of Charleston's finest homes and inviting tourists and the local populace in for a look-see. And considering that the proceeds from ticket sales went to charity . . . well, it probably was a wonderful, worthwhile event.

Theodosia also saw that the two security guys were doing a masterful job. They were polite yet firm as they answered questions and kept the line moving. Even Delaine was doing her part, chatting with guests, shaking hands, and administering elaborate air kisses to a select few.

When Delaine saw Theodosia paused in the doorway, she hurried over to talk.

"This evening is a huge success!" Delaine chirped. "Hillary and Marianne just told me that we're well on our way to having the largest attendance ever!"

"That's great," said Theodosia. She hesitated. "But do you think there's also a curiosity factor involved? Owing to the fact that, you know, Granville was recently murdered?"

Delaine looked pained. "Well, it didn't happen *here*! And, no, I absolutely do not believe that's a factor. I think we're a success because we did our jobs smashingly well. Really, Theo, you can be such a pessimist."

"That's funny, most people think I'm a realist."

They wandered through the dining room together over to the pecan credenza.

"Haley wants to put out some more desserts, so we need another tray," said Theodosia. She knelt down and pulled open the bottom cupboard. "I guess there's a reason she made quadruple batches of everything."

"Use whatever you want," said Delaine. "I have a feeling some of this is going to end up being mine."

As Theodosia slid out a heavy silver tray, she happened to glance downward. And her eye caught the flash of something gold. A strip of something curled up on the plush carpet, halfway under the cabinet.

She frowned. What was it? Something the cleaning crew had missed? Or something recently dropped or discarded?

"I don't know if it's worth keeping *all* this silver," Delaine prattled on. "Although I thought there was more . . . still, silver's at an all-time high right now."

Balancing her tray on one edge, tuning out Delaine, Theodosia reached down and let her fingertips brush the object. It was a scrap of paper. Gold metallic paper. She scooped it up and stared at it carefully as her heart gave a sudden thump. It was a cigar band. She could just make out the word *Alejandro.*

What? Who was smoking a cigar in here?

Better yet, who had been rummaging around in the dining room, outside the boundaries of the cordoned-off area?

The answer clicked into her mind almost immediately.

Nadine and her boyfriend.

"Excuse me," she said to Delaine, as she raced back into the kitchen.

"Oh, good," said Haley, reaching a hand out. "You found a tray."

"Haley," said Theodosia, "when Nadine and her boyfriend were in here a couple of minutes ago, what were they doing?"

Haley, who'd grabbed the tray and was already arranging cookies and bars, didn't look up. "Nothing much. Looking for a scissors. Gosh, these lemon bars turned out great if I do say so myself. There's a reason all the top chefs use Meyer lemons."

"That's it?"

"Yeah, well, I never found a scissors, but Nadine's boyfriend said there was probably one in that chest in the dining room. In one of the drawers."

Theodosia stiffened. "Really." How strange was that? Theodosia thought to herself. Nadine's boyfriend knew exactly where to find a scissors. In a drawer. Yet, to her knowledge, the man had never set foot inside this house before tonight.

Or had he?

Theodosia fingered the cigar band and reread it. *Alejandro*. And underneath in smaller script, *Primo Cubano*. So, a Cuban cigar. She wondered if Nadine's boyfriend had dropped this? She wondered if he knew his way around this house? And if so, how had he come by that knowledge?

Theodosia stood stock-still for a few moments, practically holding her breath. Was Nadine's boyfriend the burglar from the other night? Could he be the same guy she'd chased down the alley?

At that exact moment, Delaine breezed into the kitchen. "Excuse me, ladies, but we need . . ." Delaine stopped midsentence and stared at Theodosia. "What on earth is wrong now, Theo? You look like you've just seen a ghost."

Theodosia rolled the gold paper in the palm of her hand. "Do you know if Nadine's boyfriend is a cigar smoker?"

Delaine leaned in and peered at her so closely her eyes practically crossed. "Why, yes," she said finally. "Now that you mention it, I believe he is."

Theodosia was faced with a dilemma. Should she spell out for Delaine the possibility that Nadine's boyfriend might have ransacked this house two nights ago? Or should she stay mum? She could be completely mistaken, of course.

In which case Delaine would probably stomp off in a snit and never speak to her again.

Theodosia quickly made up her mind, deciding on a more oblique approach.

"Delaine, I know this is going to sound strange, but there's a very real possibility your sister might be in danger."

Delaine looked perplexed. "Whatever do you mean?"

"Do you know how Nadine met her boyfriend?"

Delaine shrugged. "Just . . . through mutual acquaintances. Friends."

"Good friends?"

"Really, Theo, I don't recall. And truth be told, you're starting to scare me. Always being such an alarmist."

"And you're being evasive."

Delaine reared back. "I don't mean to be."

"You know what?" said Theodosia. "I need to speak to Nadine. Right this minute."

"Must you really?" huffed Delaine.

Theodosia slipped past her. "You'll thank me later, Delaine!"

Rushing outside, Theodosia came up against a wall of people. The tea table was mobbed, every table and chair was occupied, the patio was filled with a jostle of guests, and the night was alive with the sound of laughter, conversation, the clink of teacups against china saucers, and the sweet swell of harp music.

So where was Nadine?

Theodosia's eyes swept the patio, searching for Nadine in her hot-pink dress. And didn't see her. Determined now, she dodged through the crowd, smiling brightly but inwardly feeling her tension ratchet up. She was still trying to figure out what role Nadine's boyfriend might have played this past week. Had he been at the wedding? Had he ransacked

Granville's house? Was he the one who'd sent the note? If so, had this boyfriend, for whatever reason, murdered Dougan Granville?

In a panic now, Theodosia backed down one of the garden paths, hoping to get a more panoramic view of the gaggle of visitors. She scanned the crowd again, hoping to see Nadine. But, no, the woman was nowhere in sight.

Could Nadine have left? Could her boyfriend have lured her away from the group, cutting her out of the safety of the crowd like a wolf separating a lamb from the flock?

Her stomach a bundle of nerves, Theodosia drew breath sharply. And that was when she smelled a hint of cigar smoke wafting in the night air.

Then she heard Nadine's high-pitched giggle, sounding so much like Delaine's.

Theodosia turned and scanned the garden behind her.

There they were! They were standing close together next to a pattering fountain, talking and whispering in a lovey-dovey conspiratorial way.

But how could she get Nadine away from him? Because— and this was a big *what if*—what if he was the killer?

At that moment Nadine's boyfriend put his hand up to Nadine's face and gently caressed her cheek.

All set to run up to them and pull Nadine away, Theodosia checked herself. Hold everything. What was the plan here? What exactly was she going to do? Rush up to Nadine and start screaming like a madwoman? Or whisper to Nadine that she might be in danger?

If the guy turned out to be harmless, she'd look like an idiot in front of a few hundred of Charleston's finest citizens. In fact, she'd never live it down.

Spinning about, Theodosia was ready to beat a hasty retreat. She needed a better plan. She needed a moment to think. She needed something a little more definitive to go on.

Her hand reached out and touched a stalk of jessamine that vined around a lamppost. The aroma from the yellow flowers was fragrant and calming. Almost the way chamomile tea worked to soothe jangled nerves.

Tea. That was what she needed. Theodosia decided she'd get a cup of tea and let her thoughts about Nadine's boyfriend percolate in her brain. Because maybe he was perfectly harmless. Maybe he was just . . . intuitive.

Making her way to the tea table, she grabbed a teacup and held it under a spigot. And just as she lifted the handle, just as hot, fragrant liquid cascaded into her teacup, there was a ripple of voices raised in surprise at the back of the crowd. And then, like a seismic wave, a murmur of surprise and outrage came crashing toward her.

What on earth? Theodosia wondered. Holding her teacup steady with both hands, she turned and saw a line of blue uniforms filing out onto the patio.

And then a loud voice called out, "Police! Don't anybody move!"

Jack Alston, the ATF agent Theodosia had encountered earlier, charged onto the patio, looking like some kind of gung-ho cop in a Bruce Willis movie. He was followed by a flying wedge of police officers with Detective Burt Tidwell bringing up the rear. The officers spread out around the edges of the patio, slowly pushing guests toward the center as if they were herding longhorn cattle.

"What's the meaning of this?" shouted Delaine. She was nipping at their heels like a rabid Schnauzer, screaming and launching a barrage of angry protests.

Of course, the police paid no attention to her.

Delaine continued to shove and shoulder her way through the crowd until she came face-to-face with Theodosia. "Please, Theo!" she implored. "Talk to that detective friend of yours! Find out what on earth is going on!"

Sizzling with curiosity herself, Theodosia wormed her way through the crowd until she was within a few feet of Tidwell.

"What are you people doing here?" she demanded. She, too, was dismayed that they'd come storming into a social event and caused such a blatant disruption.

"Please don't interfere," said Tidwell, holding up a chubby hand.

Now Delaine was at Theodosia's elbow. "Stop it!" she yapped at Tidwell. "You're ruining my event!"

Tidwell waved a hand again. "Shush," he told them. Then pointed toward Jack Alston, who'd loped into the far garden and planted himself directly in front of Nadine's date.

"You're *arresting* him?" said Theodosia. She was as shocked as Delaine. But, truth be told, a little relieved, too. She grabbed Tidwell's sleeve and said, "What for? What's he done?" Had the murder just been solved? Had she been on the right track after all?

"Remember the elusive Bobby St. Cloud?" said Tidwell.

"I do," said Theodosia. But what did that have to do with this bizarre scene?

Tidwell hooked a thumb and aimed it at Nadine's date. "That's Bobby St. Cloud," he said.

27

❧

"What?" said Theodosia. "Are you serious?" She turned to Delaine. "Did you know who he was?" she asked.

"Um . . . what?" said Delaine, suddenly looking flustered.

"You *did* know!" said Theodosia. "Oh, no, Delaine, are you kidding me? You knew the police were looking for Bobby St. Cloud and you didn't *say* anything? What's wrong with you!"

Delaine's voice dripped ice. "Bobby didn't *do* anything," she said. "He was Dougan's *vendor*."

"A vendor that an ATF agent has been hunting for," said Theodosia, lashing out with cold fury. "As well as the entire Charleston Police Department."

"Oh, please," said Delaine.

"They're probably going to arrest him," said Theodosia. *And maybe even charge him with murder.*

"But Bobby didn't *do* anything!" Delaine said through clenched teeth. "Except cheer up my sister." Seething with anger, she stormed off.

*   *   *

Theodosia turned to Tidwell. "Bobby St. Cloud is under arrest for Granville's murder?"

Tidwell did a double take that might have been comical in any other situation. "Well . . . no. Not for murder. We're looking at him for smuggling. And we don't exactly have a stockpile of conclusive evidence on that, so what we really want to do is question him."

"You mean make him sweat bullets," said Theodosia. "Hence, this overwhelming show of force."

"Something like that," said Tidwell.

"But you don't think he murdered Granville?"

"I didn't say that," said Tidwell, tap-dancing now. "St. Cloud certainly could have. The two of them could have had some sort of falling out."

"But there's no hard evidence," said Theodosia.

"And no apparent motive," said Tidwell. He pursed his lips and said, "In actuality, Granville was a good customer. You don't generally bump off a good customer."

Theodosia contemplated Tidwell's logic for a few moments then said, "But if Granville's conveniently out of the way, you might just break into his home and try to get your goods back."

Tidwell nodded. "There is a distinct possibility that St. Cloud was the Thursday-night burglar."

Theodosia felt a jolt of pride that she and Tidwell had been on the same suspicious wavelength.

"And you believe the cigars are still here?" asked Theodosia. "Hidden somewhere in this house?"

Tidwell shook his head. "There's no way they can be. Yesterday morning we tore through this place from top to bottom. We even brought along a sniffer dog but came up with squat."

"So where are the missing Cuban cigars?" Theodosia

wondered. Not that she cared all that much. She was much more interested in finding the killer.

Tidwell glanced across the yard at Jack Alston, who was waving his hands at St. Cloud, who was gesturing back just as wildly. "We don't know."

"But St. Cloud could be the killer."

"We have to assume that possibility exists," said Tidwell.

"What about Simone Asher?" said Theodosia. "Did you take a thread from the jacket upstairs and test it against the one I found?"

"Of course," said Tidwell.

"And?"

"They don't match."

"Oh." Feeling a little disappointed, Theodosia watched the heated argument that continued to rage between Jack Alston and Bobby St. Cloud. Nadine stayed mostly on the periphery but darted in once in a while to get her digs in.

"Cigars," said Tidwell. He sounded disgusted.

"Call me crazy," Theodosia said, "but I don't think Granville was murdered over cigars. There's just not that much money involved."

"People have committed murder for less than five dollars," Tidwell reminded her.

"But not in Granville's universe," said Theodosia. "If he was dealing cocaine, okay. But the small amount of drugs he had seemed more recreational."

They stood there for a while, watching the guests get bored and leave, all the while keeping an eye on the heated conversation between Alston and St. Cloud.

Finally, Jack Alston pulled himself away from St. Cloud and came over to talk to Tidwell.

"He's giving up nothing," said Alston.

"Can you arrest him?" Theodosia asked the two of them.

"It would be tenuous," said Tidwell.

"Can you take him in for questioning?" said Theodosia.

"We're going to do that," said Alston. "But we can't hold him for very long."

"Obviously not for Granville's murder," said Theodosia. "Since there isn't any real evidence. But what about for the break-in? I mean . . . it seems almost certain that he was the burglar."

"The one you chased down the alley," said Tidwell.

Alston's mouth pulled into a grin. "Wait a minute. You chased him down an alley?"

"Technically my dog did," said Theodosia.

Alston's flashing blue eyes met hers. "You're a pistol, you know that?"

"Please," said Tidwell. "Could we get back to the issue at hand?"

"We'll take St. Cloud in," said Alston. "Pepper him with questions, try to shake him up."

"I don't think he scares all that easily," said Theodosia.

From across the garden, St. Cloud flapped his arms and called to them, "Seriously, folks, I don't *have* any Cuban cigars!" He pulled one jacket sleeve up in a display of bravado. "See? Nothin' up my sleeve."

"We'll see about that," Alston called back.

"If you can't find your stupid Cuban cigars, then maybe they don't exist!" St. Cloud shouted.

"Oh, they exist, all right," said Alston.

Theodosia was impressed by St. Cloud's audacity. He certainly wasn't going down without a fight.

"Work on him, will you?" said Theodosia. "If for some reason he really did kill Granville, maybe he'll let something slip."

"We'll work on it," said Tidwell. "Trust me."

"At least you have him on smuggling charges," said Theodosia.

"Weak as those charges are," said Tidwell.

Theodosia gazed at Alston. "You're sure he's a smuggler?"

"Ninety-nine percent sure," said Alston.

"Ninety percent," said Tidwell.

Across the garden, St. Cloud made an elaborate show of pulling out his cell phone. "Excuse me while I call my lawyer."

Tidwell jerked away angrily. "Probably has him on speed dial."

An hour later, Granville's house had emptied out. The guests had departed, the police had finally gone, and Delaine and Nadine had stalked out in cold silence.

"Well, this is nice," said Haley. "The Keystone Cops have left, the Twisted Sisters have taken their leave, and so has everyone else. We can clean up amid relative peace and quiet."

"What a night," said Theodosia. Leaning against a kitchen cupboard, she felt drained. She was tired, her feet hurt, and the beginning of a headache poked at the outer fringes of her frontal cortex.

"You can say that again," said Haley. "Imagine my surprise when a flying wedge of cops swooped through the kitchen." She glanced around. "Don't quote me on this, but I think a couple of those boys in blue helped themselves to some cake pops."

"I'm not surprised," said Theodosia, rubbing her temple gingerly. "Nothing surprises me anymore."

"And you say that Delaine knew all along that her sister was dating Bobby St. Cloud?"

"That's about the size of it."

Haley considered this. "Then Delaine can't possibly think that St. Cloud had anything to do with Granville's murder. If she even had an inkling, Delaine would have crooked her little finger and had him arrested."

"This whole thing is a hot mess," said Theodosia. "One that I no longer have any interest in sorting out."

"You're saying this is one for the professionals?" said Haley.

Theodosia gathered up a tea towel and folded it. "Exactly." She longed to go home. To experience soothing music or a relaxing bubble bath. She wanted to put her arms around Earl Grey and tell him what a sweet boy he was.

"Probably best that you leave it to Tidwell, then." Haley turned on the water, tested it, and used the spray attachment to rinse a plastic tray filled with teacups. "This is the last of the china. Soon as I dry these off, I'm gonna pack 'em up nice and careful-like. Then I'll load all the boxes into the back of your Jeep, okay?"

"Sure," said Theodosia.

"You won't forget, will you, and drive down some bumpy road and bust everything to smithereens?"

"If it'll make you feel any better," said Theodosia, "I'll run everything over to the tea shop first thing tomorrow morning."

"That *would* make me feel better," said Haley. "Because I feel like some of these teacups are priceless."

"Not priceless," said Theodosia. "But certainly collectible."

While Haley finished up, Theodosia walked into the living room. The plastic runner was still stretched down the center of the Aubusson carpet; the silver stanchions that held the velvet ropes were still in place. The room had the air of a movie premiere or fancy party that had hosted throngs of people but was now deserted. Even the potted palms that Delaine had rented looked worn out. Hopefully they'd receive a little TLC once they were picked up. Hopefully they wouldn't be ferried off to yet another event.

"Okay," said Haley, sauntering into the living room. "Everything's loaded." She looked around, sighed, and dusted

her hands together. "This puppy's over and done with, so
I'm gonna take off."

"Thank you so much for all your hard work," said Theodosia. "I can't tell you how much I appreciate it."

Haley glanced around the living room. "This house is
really something, isn't it? All the artwork and antique furniture give it that old Charleston, turn-of-the-century feel.
As if ladies in long gowns and carriages drawn by matching
teams of horses could magically appear." She paused.
"Those Rattling people aren't really gonna buy this place,
are they?"

"I sure hope not," said Theodosia. Maybe she could have
a little chat with Allan Grumley. Suggest, and none too
subtly, either, that the Rattlings would not be a great addition to the neighborhood. "Don't mind me." She waved a
hand. "I'm just . . . I don't know . . . jumpy and tired."

"Then you'd better go home and jump into bed," said
Haley.

"I guess."

"Okay, this time I really am taking off. Hey, I left a
thermos of sweet tea on the kitchen counter for you. Just in
case you're in need of something cool and refreshing."

"Thanks," said Theodosia. "Lock the back door behind you?"

"Yup. But don't stay too long, okay? I worry about you,
Theo."

"I'll be out of here in two minutes."

But she wasn't. Two minutes came and went and still Theodosia remained in the house. Now, with just her padding
around, the place felt deserted and dreary. Almost as bad
as . . . Ravencrest Inn.

She was still unnerved by the notion of the Rattlings
and Allan Grumley partnering up. But that would never

happen, would it? She didn't think so. Grumley was a hot-shot attorney who fancied himself in the inner circle of Charleston society, while the Rattlings were failed inn-keepers. The Rattlings might *hope* that Grumley would jump on board as a willing investor, but, pardon the pun, it was close but no cigar.

Cigars. Where did they end up? And was Granville's death really related to them?

Even though Theodosia had told Haley she was going to leave the investigating to the professionals, she couldn't help but contemplate all the players, all the clues, all the loose ends.

Which made her think of threads. Like the thread Tidwell had taken from the jacket upstairs. The thread that didn't match the one she'd found stuck to the window frame at Ravencrest Inn.

But what if the thread had been snipped from the wrong part of the jacket? What if the jacket was a blend of cotton and linen, or silk and wool? And the snipped sample was an incorrect random thread?

Could happen. Sure it could.

Without really meaning to, Theodosia found herself venturing upstairs again. She flipped on the hall light and sauntered down the hallway into Granville's bedroom with more bravado than she really felt.

I'm just going to take another look, she told herself. *Or maybe another sample.*

Snapping the closet light on, Theodosia went inside. This time the space smelled musty and unused, as if old discarded clothes had been hanging there for a while.

She supposed all these fine jackets, slacks, suits, and bespoke shirts would be donated to charity. And wasn't that a strange twist of fate? That a man who'd seemingly had it all . . . a palatial home, a collection of fine art, ele-gant silver, antique furnishings, an eager fiancée . . . would have his clothes passed on to men who might even be homeless.

Theodosia thought this might even be an object lesson of sorts. The lesson being . . . what? Don't get too attached to your possessions? Even the mighty can fall? Life is a crapshoot?

She shook her head, located the small cache of women's clothing, and pulled the jacket off the hanger. She decided she was just going to take the whole thing. After all, Granville's murder was far from being solved. And if a stash of cigars could disappear, so could a jacket. You never know.

Theodosia closed the closet door and glanced around the room. Delaine obviously hadn't put the house cleaners to work up here because the bedside tables and dresser were coated with a fine film of dust. She wondered briefly if Allan Grumley would move in here. If so, would everything remain the way it was? The furniture, the silver, the artwork? Would Grumley jettison the clothes in Granville's closet but sleep in the rather grand four-poster bed?

Theodosia thought if he did, it might be an uneasy sleep.

She folded the jacket over one arm and looked around. Somehow, the place looked a little more austere than it had the other night, the walls slightly less crowded. As she gazed at the paintings, one of the smaller ones caught her eye. An oil painting with an elaborate gilt-edged frame that tilted slightly on the wall. It was a portrait, almost Northern European—looking in origin, of an old man smoking a pipe. With its dark, moody atmosphere, the painting looked almost like a piece that might have been done by one of the Old Masters. Except she didn't think Granville had the kind of money that could afford a Rembrandt or a Hans Holbein.

Theodosia dropped the jacket on a nearby chair and walked over to the painting. She put her hands on either side of the frame and straightened it. Stepping back, she studied it closely. Interestingly enough, the subject of the painting looked almost like an aged Granville, right down to the sharp-edged nose, but without a beard. Really quite a curiosity.

She wondered if the likeness had initially drawn Granville to the painting. Or if he just fancied the subject matter, an old man obviously relishing a draw on his clay pipe.

Unfortunately, the painting had been framed poorly, because even though Theodosia had carefully straightened it, the darned thing was already listing to one side. She took a step forward and fixed it again. Then, on a whim, she lifted the painting off the wall so she could adjust the wire on back.

As she turned the painting over, Theodosia saw a piece of flimsy yellow paper tucked into the back edge of the wooden frame.

What's this? A bill from the framer? Or something else?

Slowly, Theodosia unfolded the paper.

It wasn't a bill from a local framer, but, rather, a copy of an invoice from something called Lightning Delivery Service.

Hmm?

Something pinged in the deep recess of Theodosia's brain. The name somehow carried a familiar ring.

Theodosia shook her head, unable to shake the answer loose. She frowned and stuck the paper back in the frame. Then she thought, *Wait a minute.*

Because, just like that, her brain dredged up the memory of perusing Granville's American Express bill. And seeing a charge for Lightning Delivery Service!

Fumbling with the paper again, unfolding it all the way, Theodosia wondered what it was for and why it was stuck back here? She scanned the page and read a handwritten note that read, *Four cases.*

Four cases of what?

What came in a case? Beer? Bottles of wine? As Theodosia slowly pondered this, the answer leaped out at her.

Could this have something to do with smuggled cigars? The contraband that Granville had purchased and that Jack Alston had been looking for? The Cuban cigars that Bobby St. Cloud had sold to Granville and—she thought—had possibly tried to steal back?

Or was this piece of paper the thing Simone Asher had been hunting for last night? When she'd come up here on the pretense of having a last look around?

Maybe.

So where had the four cases of—supposedly—cigars been delivered to?

Theodosia scanned the faint type. And there, at the very bottom, written in an almost illegible scrawl, were the words Barrow Hall.

Theodosia's eyes widened and her mouth formed a perfect O. Then she said, in a strangled voice, even though no one was around to hear her, "But that's where Drayton and the Beckman brothers are right now!"

28

Theodosia drove one-handed while attempting to dial her phone. Shards of moonlight spattered down on her windshield as she gunned her way down Logan, cut over to Coming Street, and hit Calhoun. A few minutes more and she was speeding across the Ashley River Bridge.

When Theodosia finally forced her fingers to punch in the correct digits, all she got was Tidwell's voice mail. After screeching a garbled plea for help, she hung up and dialed 911. This time she tried to explain her problem, as calmly and succinctly as possible, begging the dispatcher to get hold of Detective Tidwell.

"Stay on the line," the dispatcher instructed in a crisp, even voice.

Theodosia tromped down harder on the accelerator as she steamed down the highway.

"He's not answering," came the dispatcher's voice. "But if you'd—"

"Please keep trying!" Theodosia implored. "It's really important!"

"I need you to stay on the—"

Theodosia punched the Off button and tossed her phone onto the passenger seat next to her thermos of tea. "Not good enough," she murmured. Then, because her brain was suddenly cognizant of barreling right through a red light and missing the front fender of a little blue car by inches, she shakily eased off her speed.

Her heart thudding loudly, she willed herself to drive at a reasonably sane rate and try to focus. Hard to do, though, when Drayton, Jed, and Tim might have walked into some sort of trap.

Or had they? Was she just overreacting?

Theodosia didn't think so. She thought that all the clues were finally pointing in one direction. That direction being Barrow Hall.

As she drove, she tried to sort through her disparate thoughts. A, someone had murdered Granville. B, the killer had done it out of passion, on the spur of the moment, and probably for a valid (or so they thought) reason. And C, someone, maybe Bobby St. Cloud, maybe Simone Asher, maybe a wild-card someone else, was actively hunting for those cigars. Her gut told her all these things were integrally connected. How the pieces and parts fit together exactly, she didn't know. What she did know was that her nerves were strumming a warning and her gut was churning. And if she didn't get out to Barrow Hall to warn her friends, she feared something dreadful might happen.

Cranking her steering wheel into a hard turn, Theodosia sped down Highway 61. This was the road that led into the heart of plantation country. To Magnolia Plantation and Middletown Place and a few more historic estates. And this same road, once they'd passed by all the nice, picturesque plantations, would eventually lead to Barrow Hall.

She bounced along as a kaleidoscope of images flew by. Long tunnels of live oaks, kudzu-covered barns, brackish swamps where water glistened like dark coal.

How far out was Barrow Hall? Theodosia wondered. She hadn't been out this way in years. Now, as minute after minute dragged by, it seemed like a strange, improbable journey that was taking far too long. She grabbed her cell phone again, punched in Tidwell's number, but once again got his voice mail. Too late now to call for backup. She'd have to wing it.

The turnoff to Magnolia Plantation flew by. During the day, the place was thronged with tourists eager to tour the historic manse, wander through acres of gardens, and enjoy the boat tour or nature train. Now the place looked as deserted as the road ahead.

Just how much farther was Barrow Hall? Theodosia racked her brain. Maybe another three miles? Five miles? She edged her speed upward, figuring she wouldn't encounter pedestrians or many cars out in this neck of the woods.

And she didn't. There were just stands of cypress and tupelo, old rice dikes, and overgrown fields. She was so busy snatching glimpses of these ancient signposts that she almost missed the turn for Barrow Hall.

The stone pillars and dilapidated wrought-iron sign were practically obscured by an overgrowth of trees and shrubs. But Theodosia caught sight of the pile of stones that passed for the gate out of the corner of her eye. She slammed on the brakes, her Jeep slewing from side to side. When she finally rocked to a stop, she hastily slammed into reverse and backed up. Then, rolling down her front window, she gazed down the long drive into the darkness.

As the moon drifted out from behind a bank of gray clouds, she could just make out the faint outline of Barrow Hall. To her eyes the place looked enormous and foreboding, like an ancient crumbling castle. Two tall towers anchored each end of the large stone building, their peaked Victorian caps lending a sinister look. The center of the building was lost in shadows.

But if there aren't any lights, maybe that's good, Theodosia decided. Maybe it meant Drayton and the Beckman boys were out here all alone, just poking around with flashlights and magnetometers and cameras and having themselves a fun little creepy-crawl.

Theodosia crunched slowly down the driveway. Thirty yards in she saw a small red car parked off to the side, half hidden among a copse of trees. As if someone had run it into the bushes on purpose.

Whose car? she wondered. And on the heels of that she thought, *That's not a promising sign.*

Turning off her headlights, Theodosia drove another fifty yards, bumping along the narrow, overgrown driveway as branches *tick-ticked* at her windows like skeleton fingers.

A blue-and-white van was pulled up close to the front of the old building. So her friends were here, all right. But were they safe? Were they okay?

Theodosia had no clue. But she knew the safest thing, the smartest thing to do, would be to alert them and pull them out of Barrow Hall immediately.

She glanced around the interior of her car. She'd basically rushed out here totally unprepared, wearing a silk outfit suitable only for a garden party. The least she could have done was grab some sort of weapon. A knife, a garden hoe, anything. But she was basically empty handed except for . . . her thermos bottle. She grabbed the metal cylinder and hefted it. If push came to shove, maybe she could use it as a kind of club? Maybe.

Easing out of her car, Theodosia squared her shoulders and walked toward the building. Its monolithic presence was physically imposing, and she could almost sense the building leaning toward her. Tall, narrow windows covered with bars and metal grates seemed to peer down at her. The smooth stone stairs yawned widely.

Slowly, Theodosia climbed the worn stairs. She wondered if, in days gone by, inmates had climbed these same steps with an insurmountable feeling of dread in their heart. Poor souls. She could almost sense their lingering spirits.

The front door, one of a set of gigantic wooden double doors, stood partially open. So Theodosia pushed her way in. The smell of mold, mildew, and rot assaulted her nose, almost causing her to sneeze.

She stood for a moment, rubbing a finger under her nose, feeling sick and a little bit overwhelmed. Then she drew breath and struggled to gather her wits about her. She had unfinished business here. She had to find Drayton and the Beckman boys.

But where to begin looking?

The entry hall was cavernous, with a vaulted ceiling and double stairways that wound upward on either side of it. Would they have gone upstairs? Somehow she sensed they wouldn't. Having already been on one ghost hunt with the Beckman brothers, Theodosia figured they'd probably gravitate in the other direction. They'd go downstairs, searching for areas that were a bit unorthodox. Treatment rooms, underground passages, the boiler room, the morgue.

She sighed. Going down into the basement wasn't something she exactly relished. Crossing the floor, she stepped across fallen plaster, mounds of moldering papers, and what looked like rotting rags. At the back of the entry hall, she located a set of swinging doors.

Tucking her thermos under one arm, Theodosia reached into her shoulder bag and pulled out her trusty Mag-Lite. Two seconds later, dust motes twirled slowly in the thin beam of yellow light.

Okay. Ready as I'll ever be.

Gingerly, Theodosia extended her hand and pushed

open one of the doors. And there, yawning into the depths of Barrow Hall, was a long, cement ramp.

A ramp? Why a ramp?

But she knew why. Easier to transport food down to the kitchen and dirty sheets to the laundry. Easier to roll gurneys down to the morgue.

The ramp felt damp and almost slick as she descended. Theodosia wondered if it was just condensation from this dank interior or if mildew had grown so thick it was like walking on a kind of nasty carpet. She decided she wouldn't dwell on the answer.

Flashing her light against the walls, she saw peeling institutional green paint and, in a few places, spray-painted graffiti. She wondered what other explorers had braved Barrow Hall to poke around in here. Then she decided they were probably of the same ilk as the Beckman boys. And Drayton. Was he still part of their merry band? Or had he begged off at the last minute? She'd find out soon enough.

Reaching the bottom of the ramp, Theodosia paused. She could hear the slow, steady drip of water somewhere. And, farther off, a low whooshing sound. Wind through a tunnel? Machinery running? Something else?

She stood absolutely still and called out, in what she hoped was a clear, controlled voice. "Drayton."

Her cry echoed hollowly back at her.

"Drayton," she called again. "It's Theodosia."

There was no reply, no other sound, except the same incessant *drip drip drip.*

Theodosia flashed her light one way and then the other. From where she stood, two corridors branched off in opposite directions. Her small light couldn't pierce the gloom at the far ends of the corridors, but she saw that there were multiple doorways on each side. Walking carefully, mindful not to trip or step in something awful, Theodosia walked fifteen feet down the left-hand corridor. When she came to the first doorway, she shone her light inside.

It wasn't good.

The room must have served as some sort of holding room for disturbed patients. What looked like tufts of cotton batting stuck out from the grimy walls, and leather straps hung down from the ceiling.

The words *padded cell* formed in her brain, but she was too overcome with revulsion to let the thought travel any further.

Theodosia continued down the corridor, sweeping her light to and fro, stopping every ten feet or so. Here was also a pharmacy, what had been a small infirmary, and a room piled to the ceiling with rusted metal wheelchairs and old office furniture. She could hear soft scuttling and figured there must be rodents.

As she ducked back out into the corridor, something caught her eye.

Huh?

She'd picked up—or thought she had—a quick flash of light.

Were they down here? Were they filming? There was only one way to find out.

Doggedly, Theodosia continued down the corridor. She walked slowly and silently. If they were here, she didn't want to freak them out. On the other hand, she'd have to make her presence known sooner or later.

When she finally came to a set of doors with small windows covered in metal screening, she felt sure she'd arrived at the morgue.

Oh joy. Just where I really don't want to be.

But she was fairly confident that was where the flash of light had come from.

Were the three of them on the other side of this door

right now, nerves fizzing, wondering who was out there? Had they detected her presence with their magnetometer or temperature gauge and figured she might even be a ghost?

Just as Theodosia put out a hand to push open the door, it began to creak inward on its own. Rusty hinges moaned and the door swung open into darkness.

Then a frightened, quavering voice—Theodosia thought it might be Jed—called out, "Who's there?"

Theodosia's heart leaped. "It's me, Theodosia!" she called back.

Three anxious-looking faces suddenly appeared in her flashlight beam.

"Theodosia?" said Drayton. He seemed absolutely shocked. "What are *you* doing here?"

She didn't waste any time. "I'm here to pull you guys out," she told them. "There's a good chance those Cuban cigars are hidden out here and that somebody might show up to claim them."

"Cuban cigars?" said Jed. He had no idea what she was talking about.

"Never mind," said Theodosia. "I'll explain later."

But Drayton pounced on her words. "Claim them? Who would do that?"

"I don't know," said Theodosia. "But the thing is, there's a red car stashed out front in the bushes. Does it belong to either of you guys?" She looked pointedly at Jed and Tim.

"We all came in our van," said Jed.

"Okay," said Theodosia. "That means somebody else is pussyfooting around this place. You have to pack up all your gear and get out of here pronto."

"You really think we're in danger?" asked Tim. He seemed reluctant to leave.

"There's a reasonable chance of it, yes," said Theodosia.

"It could just be other urban explorers," said Jed.

"Really, guys," said Theodosia. "Do you think I drove all

the way out here in the middle of the night just for the fun of it? Now come on, let's get a move on!"

"Theodosia has good instincts for this sort of thing," said Drayton. "If she thinks we're in danger, then it's time to clear out."

They packed up their gear and humped it down the hallway, Theodosia leading the way. As she approached the ramp, she stopped and waited for everyone to catch up.

"What an amazing place," said Jed. He had gear slung across him and was clutching his camera with both hands, practically walking backward. "You can almost feel the presence of ghosts."

"You can almost *hear* them," said Tim. He paused. "Wait a minute, what was that?"

"Water dripping," said Drayton. "I heard it earlier when we came through here."

"Must be leaky pipes," said Tim.

"Or an underground stream," said Drayton.

But Theodosia, who'd been listening intently, had picked up on something else. A strange, whirring sound. Almost a metallic *click-clack*.

Jed heard it, too. "That sounds more like . . . machinery?"

"But nothing's working here," said Drayton. His head spun around nervously. "Is it?"

Theodosia glanced up and caught a faint flicker of light on the ramp's upper walls.

"Maybe somebody's using some sort of equipment," said Tim.

Theodosia's eyes were still glued to the walls above them. Shadows of light and dark suddenly played against it, like some weird psychedelic light show. Even as she wondered what might be causing this strange phenomenon, her ears picked up a louder, more repetitive clacking sound.

"Gotta be machinery," said Jed, glancing backward again.

That was when Theodosia saw it. Like an apparition from a Freddy Krueger movie, an old metal gurney was suddenly rocking and roaring its way down the ramp directly toward them! And whatever had been piled on top of it—old newspapers, rags doused in kerosene, whatever—had been set on fire!

"Holy crap!" said Tim, in an almost reverent voice. "It's . . . it's . . ."

Theodosia stared in disbelief as the flaming gurney hurtled toward them, clacking and swaying madly, flames shooting high into the air. Above their heads, a strange chuckle rose up.

"Dear Lord!" cried Drayton, as the strange contraption roared toward them, streaming flames and belching noxious smoke. "It's a Screaming Lula!"

29

❧

"The thing's headed right for us!" Jed shouted. He seemed mesmerized, rooted to the ground.

The demonic gurney careened directly toward them. It was twenty feet away and still gaining speed. Then fifteen feet. Just as it was about to crash headlong into them and mow them down in a fiery storm, Theodosia popped the top off her thermos and flung it at the conflagration! Sweet tea spilled and spattered everywhere, landing on the fire, causing it to hiss like a dozen demon cats, then sputter into a swirl of white smoke.

They all jumped out of the way as the gurney flew by and crashed headlong into the opposite wall in a dreadful fusion of smoke, sparks, and screaming metal.

"What. On. Earth?" said Tim.

"Cigars," said Theodosia. "Somebody set those dang Cuban cigars on fire and tried to kill us!" Anger sank its talons into Theodosia, and she suddenly lurched forward as if a starting gun had been fired. Waiting for no one, she raced headlong up the cement ramp.

"Theo! Don't!" Drayton called after her, but there was no stopping her.

Theodosia pounded her way up, intent on catching whoever had meant to harm them. Reaching the top of the ramp, she glanced around fast and saw a slender figure pause in the far doorway.

"Who is that?" she cried in a throaty, angry growl. It looked to her like a woman.

"Simone, is that you!" Theodosia screamed out. "I see you! You're not getting away from me!" She spun across the entry hall, kicking up plaster, shards of glass, and dust in her wake. Down the steps she pounded, slowly gaining on the fleeing woman.

The woman had a head start, but Theodosia was fast, angry, and determined. She pounded her way across the gravel, her legs driving like pistons, toned and tuned from her daily sprints with Earl Grey.

Just as she was twenty feet from the woman and closing in, a black-and-white cruiser roared into the parking lot. Its siren whooped madly while its light bar pulsed red and blue. Two seconds later, the driver's-side spotlight flashed brightly.

The woman, whoever she was, was suddenly silhouetted in the brilliant glare!

"Tidwell!" Theodosia cried out. Thank goodness he'd gotten her message and commandeered a cruiser! Thank goodness he'd responded!

But the fleeing woman, backlit in a haze of driveway dust and light from the spotlight, suddenly panicked, changed course, and dashed left.

The black-and-white's passenger door popped open and suddenly Tidwell was out and sprawled across the hood of the car, revolver in hand.

"Get down!" Tidwell shouted.

Theodosia barely comprehended his warning. As the woman jogged left, she'd darted after her, angry and determined to chase her down!

"No! No! No!" were Tidwell's frantic words as the two of them disappeared from sight around the side of the building.

Theodosia heard the woman's footsteps as she sprinted through the weedy, rubbish-strewn side yard. But she couldn't actually see her.

Still she cried out, "Simone! I see you!"

Upon hearing Theodosia's words, the woman made a sudden misstep and crashed heavily into a wooden gate. Disoriented for a split second, she spun around, stumbled, then rallied and continued her frantic pace.

Theodosia picked her way after her. It was pitch-black behind Barrow Hall, the moon having once again vanished behind a tangle of clouds. And it was dangerous going. Theodosia rushed pell-mell past old farm implements, rusty but still dangerous, as well as heaps of refuse that were scattered everywhere. She just prayed there wasn't an old well or cistern whose gaping hole had been pried open.

Easing back on her pace slightly, Theodosia felt the terrain shift beneath her feet. What had been gravel or sand with head-high weeds had now turned into a soggy mess. Where was she? Heading into a swamp? Old farm fields?

A quick glance around held the answer. An assortment of crumbling tombs, wooden crosses, and tilting stone tablets met her eyes.

Cemetery.

She was running through Barrow Hall's old cemetery.

Theodosia shivered. This was where the poor unfortunates who'd resided here had ended up. In this spooky, dank place that had basically been abandoned for decades. And just who was this woman she was giving chase to? This woman was strong. And fast!

Maybe too fast for me?

Gonna get her. Gonna run her down, Theodosia vowed to herself.

Even though her breath was coming in short wheezes and grunts, Theodosia redoubled her efforts. She dropped her head, balled her fists, and kept going. But when she lifted her head a few moments later, the woman was gone! Vanished!

What? Where? Where'd she disappear to?

Theodosia decided the woman had to be hunkered down behind one of the tombs or tilting headstones. But which one?

Cautiously, Theodosia slowed to a stop and surveyed the overgrown cemetery. Without a caretaker or inmates to tend the grounds, trees, scrub brush, and buckthorn had sprouted everywhere. Kudzu had also run rampant and turned some of the trees into leafy green shrouds. Mosses and lichens had encroached on ancient tablets and gravestones, giving them a strange hunchback look.

Feeling suddenly uneasy, Theodosia pondered what to do next, how to handle this bizarre situation. Try to flush this person out of her hidey-hole? Drive her back to the front of the building where Tidwell waited? It seemed reasonable. But just how was she supposed to accomplish this?

Theodosia bent down and scooped up a handful of sharp rocks. Jiggling them in her hand, she clawed her way through the dense bushes and foliage. Then she eased her way down the sloping hillside, where it seemed to dead-end in a swampy morass. When she was finally on the far edge of the cemetery, fairly sure the woman was somewhere between her and Barrow Hall, she let fly a few rocks. They banged loudly off gravestones and rolled harmlessly away.

Try again.

Theodosia tossed another couple of rocks into the center of the cemetery. This time she was rewarded with a slight scrabbling sound. Had her rock found its target? She hoped so.

She wound up and pitched a few more rocks. This time she detected a distinctive "Oof." Something told her she'd found her mark.

That was all Theodosia needed. Snatching up a splintered hunk of wood, pretty sure it had once been the crosspiece in a crucifix, she rushed toward the center of the graveyard.

Like a jackrabbit startled from its hiding place, the woman suddenly leaped to her feet and took off in a flash. Theodosia pounded after her. Now she was the one in charge! Driving the woman back up the hill toward Barrow Hall!

"Tidwell!" Theodosia screamed. "We're coming right at you!" She hoped he could hear her. Hoped he'd be ready!

Dodging between graves, taking care not to twist an ankle, Theodosia stayed in hot pursuit. The woman wasn't more than fifteen feet in front of her and she could hear her ragged breathing. Now if she could just see her face!

"Tidwell!" Theodosia cried out again. Her hip slammed into a metal post, causing her to wince in pain and miss a step, allowing the woman to gain a little ground.

I'm gonna lose her.

Gamely, Theodosia galloped on. Now she was the one who was gasping for air, limping a little, and losing momentum with every stride.

Gotta . . . try.

Suddenly, the woman stopped dead in her tracks. Then Theodosia saw her bend down and grab something off the ground.

The woman hefted a metal rod over her shoulder and

turned back toward her. "Come on," the woman snarled in a low voice. "Come and get me."

Theodosia hesitated. Was this what she wanted? A slugfest behind an abandoned asylum? No, this was pure craziness!

The woman moved a step toward her and waved the rod in a threatening gesture. "Try me," she said, in a throaty, defiant growl.

Footsteps sounded up on the hill. For a few seconds, the woman didn't bother to turn and look. Then the moon slid out from behind the clouds, icing everything in dark silver, and the woman's curiosity got the better of her.

Tidwell stood at the top of the rise, feet planted wide apart in a classic police shooting stance.

"Put down your weapon!" Tidwell shouted. "Or I'll shoot!"

Like a cornered animal, the woman leaped directly toward Theodosia. As she did so, a tangled cry rose in the back of her throat, a cry of rage and supreme frustration.

"Stop right now!" Tidwell screamed again.

The woman didn't stop. She raised her metal rod at the same moment Theodosia lifted her piece of wood. They came together in a cataclysmic collision, like two medieval knights in a joust to the death. Parrying and thrusting, Theodosia was spun dizzily around in a complete circle.

"Oh, no!" Theodosia rasped out. Now that she was finally within a hair's breadth of the woman, she recognized her face!

"Out of the way!" Tidwell screamed. "Get down, get down *now*!"

Suddenly cognizant of Tidwell's barked orders, Theodosia's brain sorted out his words and she leaped sideways and hit the ground like a base runner sliding into home plate. Shards of gravel sliced her palms and knees, the taste of rotting earth filled her mouth and throat, and she was aware of three tremendously loud bursts.

BAM! BAM! BAM!

She was also acutely sure she felt the searing hot trajectory of Tidwell's bullets as they passed just inches above her head.

And then she heard . . . an ungodly scream!

30

Millie Grant, Dougan Granville's former secretary, screamed like a dying banshee. Hissing and spitting and writhing in stinking mud, she clutched her shoulder frantically and yelled, "I'm hit! I'm hurt!"

Mouth hanging open, stunned beyond belief, all Theodosia could do was lift her head and stare blankly.

"Are you okay?" Tidwell screamed at her. "Are you hit?"

"I'm hit, I'm hit!" shrieked Millie.

"Miss Browning!" Tidwell thundered. "Answer me!"

"I'm okay," Theodosia gasped. She was shaking and suddenly ice cold, barely able to muster a shred of energy. "I'm . . . fine."

Well, not really.

Struggling mightily, Theodosia finally managed to pull herself to her feet. Then she tottered over to Millie and said, in a quavering voice, "It was you all along!"

"Help me!" Millie pleaded. She tried to pluck at Theodosia's slacks with her fingers. "Call an ambulance. I'm hurt baaad."

Theodosia stared down at her. "Did you kill him?" she asked, putting some harshness into her voice. "Did you?"

Millie's face twisted into a grimace. "Stupid, two-timing jerk. He *deserved* to die. He loved me, not that stuck-up, prissy friend of yours. It was me! *Me!*"

Theodosia was distantly aware of Tidwell hovering nearby, and she saw that the uniformed officer he'd brought along was having a terrible time keeping Drayton, Jed, and Tim away from them.

Theodosia felt totally drained as she pointed a finger at Millie. "She killed Granville. You all heard her."

Tidwell peered into Theodosia's face and saw a strange mix of exhaustion coupled with relief. Then his gaze shifted to Millie. "The secretary?" he said, frowning down at her. He sounded positively gobsmacked. "From the law firm?"

"Millie Grant," Theodosia spat out. "She was in love with Granville, but she killed him anyway."

"Help meeee!" Millie moaned piteously. Clutching her bleeding shoulder, she rocked back and forth, drumming her heels on the ground.

Now Drayton pushed forward anxiously. "But why?" was his only question. And this was directed at Theodosia. "Why would she kill him?"

"Jealousy," said Theodosia. "Rage. Because she didn't want Delaine to have him." Her lip curled and her voice dripped with disdain. She put a hand up to pat her hair and saw that her fingers were caked with mud. She looked down and saw that her silk outfit, so cute and festive earlier, was mud-spattered and shredded at the knees.

"Goodness," said Drayton. He gaped at Millie as the uniformed officer knelt down and hastily pressed a compress to Millie's wounded shoulder.

"Goodness had nothing to do with it," said Theodosia. "Millie Grant is pure evil. She seduced Granville with cocaine and made a final, impassioned plea to him, hoping he'd change his mind about marrying Delaine. When that didn't work, she killed him."

"Just like that," said Tidwell.

"And she knew about the cigars, too," said Theodosia. "Knew they'd been delivered out here. Knew that Granville owned this place. That it was one of his real estate white elephants."

"Does he own it?" asked Drayton.

Theodosia shrugged. "Probably. Millie probably knew all of Granville's little business secrets."

"And she knew we were coming here," said Drayton. Now he sounded accusatory. "She sat with us last night, listening to stories, knowing Jed and Tim planned to explore Barrow Hall."

"I guess she didn't want you guys intruding and finding her little stash," said Theodosia. "I'll wager there's more than contraband cigars hidden out here. I wouldn't be surprised if she siphoned off artwork and other valuables."

"Wow," said Jed. He was cradling his camera in one arm as he listened to Theodosia's explanation. "I'm impressed. That's some story you pieced together, lady."

"That's our Theo," said Drayton, pride coloring his voice. "Quite the amateur detective."

"Maybe we should do a reality show on *her*," said Tim. He made a motion to Jed, who lifted his camera just as the high-pitched *whoop-whoop* of an ambulance siren pierced the night. It was probably three minutes out, speedballing toward them.

Jed aimed his camera at Theodosia, who stared point-blank into the lens. Then he shifted his camera toward a growling, grimacing Millie and said, "This *would* make a great story. Do you think I could shoot her?"

"No need," said Theodosia. A hint of a smile played at her mouth as she ducked her head and looked sideways, exchanging a meaningful glance with Burt Tidwell. "Detective Tidwell seems to have beaten you to it."

Killer Sweet Tea
(They say revenge is a dish best served cold. So is this sweet tea!)

3 cups water
3 tea bags
¾ cup sugar
6 cups cold water
1 tray ice cubes

BRING 3 cups of water to a boil in a saucepan. Add the tea bags. Simmer for 2 minutes, then remove from the heat. Cover and let steep for 10 minutes. Remove the tea bags and add the sugar, stirring until dissolved. Pour into a 1-gallon jar or pitcher, then add 6 cups of water and the ice. Enjoy!

Peach Scones

2 cups all-purpose flour
½ tsp. salt

¼ cup sugar
1 tsp. ground nutmeg
1 Tbsp. baking powder
6 Tbsp. butter
2 eggs
⅓ cup sour cream
½ tsp. almond extract
1 cup fresh or canned peaches, diced

PREHEAT the oven to 375 degrees F. In a large bowl, whisk together the flour, salt, sugar, nutmeg, and baking powder. Cut in the butter using a fork or pastry blender. In a separate bowl, whisk together the eggs, sour cream, and almond extract. Stir this mixture into the dry mixture until well combined. Add the peaches and stir until combined. Drop about ¼ cup of dough onto a greased baking sheet or into each cup of a greased muffin tin. Bake until golden brown, about 16 minutes on a baking sheet or 18 minutes in a muffin tin.

Dandy Devonshire Cream

8 oz. heavy whipping cream
1 Tbsp. sour cream
1 tsp. powdered sugar

BEAT the whipping cream for 2 to 3 minutes, until stiff. Mix in the sour cream and powdered sugar. Serve as a topping for your favorite scones.

Tea–Simmered Chicken

2 tsp. cooking oil
2 garlic cloves, chopped
1 cup water
½ cup soy sauce
4 chicken breasts
2 tea bags, black tea or flavored

HEAT the oil in a medium frying pan and add the chopped garlic. Sizzle for about 3 minutes. Add the water and soy sauce and simmer for 5 minutes. Add the chicken and simmer for 5 minutes. Add the tea bags and simmer for an additional 30 minutes. Serve hot with rice.

Tomato Cream Cheese Tea Sandwiches

1 can (14 oz.) chopped tomatoes, drained
8 oz. cream cheese, softened
1 cup Cheddar cheese, shredded
½ cup butter, softened
1 small onion, finely chopped
½ tsp. salt

MIX the ingredients together until well combined. Spread onto whole-wheat bread, top with another slice, cut off the crusts, and cut into triangles.

Easy-Bake Scottish Shortbread

2 cups butter
1 cup brown sugar, packed
4½ cups all-purpose flour

PREHEAT the oven to 325 degrees F. Cream together the butter and brown sugar. Then add 3¾ cups of the flour and mix well. Sprinkle the remaining ¾ cup of the flour on a smooth surface. Knead the dough on top of it for about 5 minutes, allowing some flour to incorporate. When the dough is soft and pliable, roll it out about ½ inch thick and cut into 1-by-3-inch strips. Use a fork to prick the strips, then place them on ungreased baking sheets. Bake for approximately 20 minutes or until golden.

Drayton's Cock-a-Leekie Soup

2 lb. chicken pieces, bone in, skin removed
5 cups water
⅓ cup onion, chopped
2 medium potatoes, cubed
1 can (10.5 oz.) condensed chicken broth
3 leeks, sliced
1 stalk celery, sliced
½ Tbsp. fresh parsley, chopped
½ tsp. salt
¼ tsp. black pepper

PLACE the chicken, water, onion, and potatoes in a large pot. Bring to a boil, then reduce heat to low and simmer for 1 hour. Remove the chicken, pull the meat from the bones, and chop into bite-size pieces. Add the chicken meat back to the pot. Now add the chicken broth, leeks, celery, parsley, salt, and pepper. Simmer for another 45 minutes to 1 hour. Serves 6.

Brie and Pear Crostini

1 baguette
Brie cheese, softened
1 pear, thinly sliced
Honey

SLICE the baguette into thin slices and lightly toast. Spread the toast with Brie cheese, top with thin slices of pear, and drizzle with honey. Enjoy!

Peanut Butter Scones

1 cup all-purpose flour
½ cup light brown sugar
1¾ tsp. baking powder
⅓ cup butter
½ cup peanut butter
¼ cup milk
1 egg
1 tsp. vanilla extract

PREHEAT the oven to 375 degrees F. Mix together flour, brown sugar, and baking powder. Melt the butter and stir it into the flour mixture until crumbly. In a separate bowl, stir together the peanut butter, milk, egg, and vanilla. Add the mixtures together and combine well to make the dough. Drop 8 large tablespoons of dough onto a greased cookie sheet. Bake for approximately 15 minutes or until golden brown.

Summer Tea Sparkler

Jasmine, raspberry, or rose hips tea
Ginger ale

BREW a small pot of jasmine, raspberry, or rose hips tea. Allow to cool, then pour over a glass of crushed ice until half full. Now add ginger ale and stir. Garnish with lemon slices.

Cinnamon Raisin Biscuits

BISCUITS

2 cups all-purpose flour
1 Tbsp. baking powder
1 Tbsp. sugar
1 tsp. ground cinnamon
½ tsp. salt
½ cup butter

⅔ cup milk
⅓ cup raisins

ICING

1 cup confectioner's sugar
1½ Tbsp. milk
½ tsp. vanilla extract

PREHEAT the oven to 450 degrees F. In a large bowl, combine the flour, baking powder, sugar, cinnamon, and salt. Cut in the butter until the mixture is coarse and crumbly. Add the milk and raisins and stir until combined. Place the dough on a floured surface and knead until smooth. Roll out ½ inch thick and cut out biscuits using a 2½-inch round cutter. Place the biscuits on a baking sheet and bake for 12 to 15 minutes or until golden brown. For the icing, combine all ingredients until smooth and drizzle over the biscuits.

Haley's Espresso Bars

BARS

¼ cup butter, softened
1 cup brown sugar, packed
½ cup brewed espresso
1 egg
1½ cups self-rising flour
½ tsp. ground cinnamon
¾ cup chopped slivered almonds

GLAZE

1½ cups confectioner's sugar
3 Tbsp. water
¾ tsp. almond extract

PREHEAT the oven to 350 degrees F. In a large bowl, cream the butter, brown sugar, and espresso until blended. Beat in the egg. In a separate bowl, combine the flour and cinnamon. Gradually add the flour mixture to the creamed mixture and mix well. Stir in the almonds. Spread the batter into a greased 10-by-15-inch baking pan and bake for approximately 20 minutes or until lightly browned.

FOR the glaze, in a small bowl, combine the confectioner's sugar, water, and almond extract until smooth. Then spread the glaze over the warm bars.

TEA TIME TIPS FROM
Laura Childs

Retro Tea

Pull out your retro tea ware, plates, and mugs and have a retro tea party. Still have a lava lamp left over? Or a lime-green ice bucket or tablecloth strewn with red cherries? So much the better. Go retro in your tea sandwiches, too, with roast beef and Cheddar cheese or chicken salad garnished with sliced strawberries. Surely you've got a Jetsons-style pitcher you can use for good old-fashioned iced tea. For hot tea it's got to be Lipton's Tea bags, of course.

Moss Garden Tea

The Japanese are extremely fond of moss gardens, and creating your own moss garden can make for an elegant centerpiece. Using a large, flat ceramic tray, arrange a few pieces of moss with a few interesting rocks and a bit of white sand. If you have a small bonsai to add to your arrangement, so much the better. Serve tea-smoked chicken, steaming white rice, miso soup, a green salad, and Japanese green tea. And if you've never tasted green tea ice cream (which makes a wonderful dessert) or Japanese black bean cookies, you're in for a treat!

Country Table Tea

Spread out a red-and-white checkered tablecloth, grab a few metal trivets, and put your teapots right on the table. A large crock brimming with fresh flowers makes a great centerpiece, and mugs can take the place of delicate teacups at this tea. Serve cornbread with honey, maraschino cherry scones, and chive egg salad on marble swirl bread. A hearty black tea or even chai would be perfect.

Front Porch Tea

When butterflies and dragonflies are flitting about, why not serve a luncheon tea on your front porch? Think floral print tablecloths, delicate china, small votive candles, and fresh flowers from your garden. Start with cream scones and Devonshire cream, then enjoy tea sandwiches of chicken salad or cream cheese and cucumber. Sugar cookies and brownie bites make for a sweet dessert. A vanilla spice or black plum tea would be elegant with this menu.

A Royal Tea

The queen takes tea every afternoon, so why shouldn't you? Go traditionally British with English breakfast tea or Earl Grey served in fine china (Shelley chintz if you have it!). Serve ginger scones with Devonshire cream or cream scones with lemon curd. Serve a medley of tea sandwiches such as ham, cream cheese, and English chutney, or shrimp salad sandwiches. Place cards for your guests could be tiny cut-outs of the royal family!

Bridal Shower Tea

Why not plan a formal tea party for the bride-to-be in your life? Make your table elegant with a white linen or lace tablecloth, lots of silver, and gleaming crystal. And for this event, you'll want tall tapers and perhaps an orchid or two for the centerpiece. The menu might include white chocolate scones, lobster salad tea sandwiches, and banana bread with cream cheese. Serve a honey hibiscus tea or perhaps a Moroccan mint. Guest favors might include lace handkerchiefs, teacups, or demitasse spoons.

TEA RESOURCES

TEA PUBLICATIONS

TEA Magazine—Quarterly magazine about tea as a beverage and its cultural significance in the arts and society. (www.teamag.com)

Tea Poetry—Book compiled and published by Pearl Dexter.

TeaTime—Luscious magazine profiling tea and tea lore. Filled with glossy photos and wonderful recipes. (www.teatimemag azine.com)

Southern Lady—From the publishers of *TeaTime* with a focus on people and places in the South as well as wonderful tea time recipes. (www.southernladymagazine.com)

The Tea House Times—Dozens of links to tea shops, purveyors of tea, gift shops, and tea events. (www.teahousetimes.com)

Victoria—Articles and pictorials on homes, home design, gardens, and tea. (www.victoriamag.com)

The Gilded Lily—Publication from the Ladies Tea Guild. (www .glily.com)

Tea in Texas—Highlighting Texas tea rooms and tea events. (www.teaintexas.com)

Tea Talk Magazine—Covers tea news and tea shops in Britain. (www.teatalkmagazine.co.uk)

Fresh Cup Magazine—For tea and coffee professionals. (www .freshcup.com)

Bruce Richardson—This noted tea authority has written several definitive books on tea. (www.elmwoodinn.com/books)

Jane Pettigrew—This author has written thirteen books on the varied aspects of tea and its history and culture. (www.janepet tigrew.com/books)

A *Tea Reader*—An anthology of tea stories and reflections by Katrina Avila Munichiello.

AMERICAN TEA PLANTATIONS

Charleston Tea Plantation—The oldest and largest tea plantation in the United States. Order their fine black tea or schedule a visit. (www.bigelowtea.com)

Fairhope Tea Plantation—Tea produced in Fairhope, Alabama, can be purchased through the Church Mouse gift shop. (www.thechurchmouse.com)

Sakuma Brothers Farm—This tea garden just outside Burlington, Washington, has been growing white and green tea for more than a dozen years. (www.sakumamarket.com)

Big Island Tea—Organic artisan tea from Hawaii. (www.bigislandtea.com)

Mauna Kea Tea—Organic green and oolong tea from Hawaii's Big Island. (www.maunakeatea.com)

Onomea Tea—Nine-acre tea estate near Hilo, Hawaii. (www.onomeatea.com)

TEA WEBSITES AND INTERESTING BLOGS

Teamap.com—Directory of hundreds of tea shops in the United States and Canada.

GreatTearoomsofAmerica.com—Excellent tea shop guide.

Cookingwithideas.typepad.com—Recipes and book reviews for the bibliochef.

Cuppatea4sheri.blogspot.com—Amazing recipes.

Seedrack.com—Order *Camellia sinensis* seeds and grow your own tea!

Friendshiptea.net—Tea shop reviews, recipes, and more.

Theladiestea.com—Networking platform for women.

Jennybakes.com—Fabulous recipes from a real make-it-from-scratch baker.

Allteapots.com—Teapots from around the world.

Fireflyvodka.com—South Carolina purveyors of Sweet Tea Vodka, Raspberry Tea Vodka, Peach Tea Vodka, and more. Just visiting this website is a trip in itself!

Teasquared.blogspot.com—Fun, well-written blog about tea, tea shops, and tea musings.

Bernideensteatimeblog.blogspot.com—Tea, baking, decorations, and gardening.

Tealoversroom.com—California tea rooms, Teacasts, links.

Teapages.blogspot.com—All things tea.

Possibili-teas.net—Tea consultants with a terrific monthly newsletter.

Baking.about.com—Carroll Pellegrinelli writes a terrific baking blog complete with recipes and step-by-step photo instructions.

Teawithfriends.blogspot.com—Lovely blog on tea, friendship, and tea accoutrements.

Sharonsgardenofbookreviews.blogspot.com—Terrific book reviews by an entertainment journalist.

Teaescapade.wordpress.com—Enjoyable tea blog.

Bellaonline.com/site/tea—Features and forums on tea.

Lattesandlife.com—Witty musings on life.

Napkinfoldingguide.com—Photo illustrations of twenty-seven different (and sometimes elaborate) napkin folds.

worldteaexpo.com—World Tea Expo, a premier business-to-business trade show, features more than three hundred tea suppliers, vendors, and tea innovators.

Sweetgrassbaskets.net—One of several websites where you can buy sweetgrass baskets direct from South Carolina artists.

Goldendelighthoney.com—Carolina honey to sweeten your tea.

FatCatScones.com—Frozen ready-to-bake scones.

KingArthurFlour.com—One of the best flours for baking. This is what many professional pastry chefs use.

Tvbakepops.com—Order your own cake pops kit.

Thedippshop.com—Order ready-made cake pops.

Teagw.com—Visit this website and click on Products to find dreamy tea pillows filled with jasmine, rose, lavender, and green tea.

Californiateahouse.com—Order Machu's Blend, a special herbal tea for dogs that promotes healthy skin, lowers stress, and aids digestion.

PURVEYORS OF FINE TEA
Adagio.com
Harney.com
Stashtea.com
Republicoftea.com
Teazaanti.com
Bigelowtea.com
Teasource.com
Celestialseasonings.com
Goldenmoontea.com
Uptontea.com

VISITING CHARLESTON
Charleston.com—Travel and hotel guide.

Charlestoncvb.com—The official Charleston convention and visitor bureau.

Charlestontour.wordpress.com—Private tours of homes and gardens, some including lunch or tea.

Charlestonplace.com—Charleston Place Hotel serves an excellent afternoon tea, Thursday, Friday, and Saturday afternoons, 1 to 3.

Culinarytoursofcharleston.com—Sample specialties from Charleston's local eateries, markets, and bakeries.

Poogansporch.com—This restored Victorian house serves traditional low-country cuisine. Be sure to ask about Poogan!

Preservationsociety.org—Hosts Charleston's annual Fall Candlelight Tour.

Palmettocarriage.com—Horse-drawn carriage rides.

Charlestonharbortours.com—Boat tours and harbor cruises.

Ghostwalk.net—Stroll into Charleston's haunted history. Ask them about the "original" Theodosia!

CharlestonTours.net—Ghost tours plus tours of plantations and historic homes.

TURN THE PAGE FOR A PREVIEW OF
LAURA CHILDS'S
NEXT SCRAPBOOKING MYSTERY . . .

Gilt Trip

COMING SOON IN HARDCOVER FROM
BERKLEY PRIME CRIME!

It was your typical New Orleans Garden District party. Wealthy, careless men sloshing down too much bourbon, tucked and lifted socialites flaunting their latest fashions, and twenty-something women looking sleek as alley cats as they prowled for rich husbands. And every dang one of them on their best baddest behavior as they shrieked, shimmied, danced, and drank while the Bayou Breezers cranked out a string of raucous zydeco tunes.

"And then there's us," said Carmela Bertrand. She gave a rueful smile as butlers in white tie and tails glided through the crowd serving tiny canapés of duck liver, baked oysters, and Beluga caviar.

"Nothing wrong with sniffing the rarified air and seeing how the other half lives," said her friend Ava Gruiex.

"I'd say it's all very posh and predictable," said Carmela. Her tone was flat, but her blue eyes danced with mirth as she ruffled a hand through short, choppy blond hair that was, as Ava so delightfully phrased it, chunked and skunked.

Blessed with a radiant complexion and relatively calm demeanor (by New Orleans standards, that is), Carmela also possessed a nimble mind and burning curiosity. Which, on more than one occasion, had sent her rushing in where pro-verbial angels feared to tread.

"Watch this," said Ava, grabbing a champagne glass and tipping it toward an enormous ice sculpture. "Tell me this isn't cool."

A slosh of excellent French champagne gushed down a steep tunnel of ice, foamed slightly as it navigated a quick series of S-turns, and emptied into Ava's crystal flute with a satisfying fizz.

"Isn't that too much!" exclaimed Ava.

"Service with a flourish," said the smiling bartender.

Carmela decided maybe she needed a hit of bubbly, too. "What do you call this ice carving thing?"

"A champagne luge," said the waiter. "Guaranteed to deliver a super-chilled serving of champagne."

Ava, who was Carmela's BFF, shopping cohort, and French Quarter neighbor, gave Carmela a nudge. "C'mon, you do it." She smiled coyly at the bartender. "Ready, baby?"

Nodding, the bartender hefted a magnum of cham-pagne, poured a judicious serving into the delicately carved ice slot at the top of the sculpture, then stood back and smiled.

"Isn't that the darndest thing you've ever laid eyes on?" said Ava as she watched the froth of champagne wend its circuitous route to Carmela's glass. The ice luge, carved from a solid block of ice, was almost five feet high and fea-tured, besides the zig-zagging slide, three enormous stars topped by a crescent moon.

"Only the best for Margo," said Carmela.

"And Jerry Earl," said Ava. She pushed a mass of dark curly hair off her cheek, angled out one curvaceous hip, and struck a red carpet–worthy pose. "This is some super welcome home party for him." Margo's husband, Jerry Earl Leland, had just been released from the Dixon Correctional Institute, and Margo was throwing what she called a Get Out Of Jail Free Party.

"Jerry Earl's a lucky man," said Carmela. And she meant that in more ways than one. He'd been Margo's ex-husband, then the two had remarried in a red hot flurry right before Jerry Earl had been carted off to the slammer. And now he'd been released from prison early.

"Champagne, caviar, and a spattering of eligible men," said Ava, glancing about with predatory eyes. "How'd we manage to wrangle this invitation again?"

"We're here out of pure politeness," said Carmela. "I got roped into designing the invitations for this fais-do-do, and Margo went *bonkers* when she saw them. Told me I just had to attend. A command performance was what she called it." Carmela's scrapbooking shop, Memory Mine, carried all the latest papers and albums and was the go-to spot for having cards, announcements, and invitations designed. Besides being the French Quarter's resident scrapbook maven, Carmela was also a skilled graphic artist.

"I gotta say," said Ava, helping herself to a toast point loaded with glistening caviar, "the lady has style. As well as a pot full of money. I mean, did you get a gander at that gilded fireplace? And all that fancy artwork? And the silk upholstery on her cabriolet sofa? The word 'opulent' does come to mind."

Carmela nodded in agreement. But, truth be told, she wasn't all that impressed. It hadn't been too many years since she'd resided in this part of town herself. In a white elephant of a house that was currently on the market for two point three million. Of course, her tenure in the Garden District stretched back to the bad old days when she'd been married to Shamus Allan Meechum, heretofore known as The Rat. Shamus, who possessed silky charm, a dazzling smile, and a wandering eye, hailed from the same rich-as-Croesus, crazy-ass family as the Crescent City Bank Meechums. Thus, he'd always felt above it all and not bound by ordinary convention.

Carmela nudged Ava. "There's Margo now."

Margo Leland looked like she'd been hung by her heels and dipped in gold. Her dress was an explosion of gold sequins, her fingernails shimmered, her cantilevered beehive hairdo was spackled with threads of pink and gold, and the chains that clanked around her neck and chubby wrists were real-deal twenty-four-karat gold. Though pushing sixty, she still dressed like she was trotting off to Studio 54.

"Holy Coupe deVille," Ava whispered. "Margo's a walking Fort Knox."

Margo immediately noticed them noticing. A wide grin split her flushed face, her eyes lit up, and she immediately tottered over on sky-high gold silk heels to greet them.

"Carmela!" Margo cried exuberantly, throwing her arms wide and losing half of her drink in the process. "You came! *Vous êtes arrivé!*"

"How could we not?" said Carmela. She tried to ratchet up her enthusiasm, feeling a little fake and knowing in her heart that she'd rather be cozied up in her garden apartment, wearing jammies and reading a good mystery. Spending time with her two dogs Boo and Poobah. She sighed. "And you remember Ava."

"Ava!" Margo shrilled. "You gorgeous thing, you!" Then she turned to Carmela and slurred, "Oh, to be thirty again."

"Twenty-nine," said Ava, somewhat crisply.

"And so pretty and model thin," Margo enthused.

"And look at you," Ava drawled back, ever the good sport. "All drippy in gems and jewelry."

Margo wiggled her ample hips, giddy that they'd noticed. Then she fingered a chunky necklace that encircled her neck. "Vintage," she chirped. "Twenty-five carats of Sri Lankan amethyst set in pure gold. Designed and signed by Louis Comfort Tiffany himself."

Carmela, whose jewelry consisted of a gold bangle and small diamond stud earrings, smiled politely. She didn't much care that Margo had decked herself out in the crown jewels. But she was starting to sincerely regret that she and Ava had dropped by this lavish party. It was all a trifle too ostentatious, the gaiety a little too . . . forced.

But the second act was yet to come.

Margo snatched a glass of champagne from a passing waiter's tray and said in a conspiratorial whisper, "I'm going to offer a congratulatory toast to Jerry Earl."

"I guess it isn't every day your hubby gets sprung from the joint," said Ava.

Carmela had to stifle a giggle. Ava didn't have much of a filter.

But Margo wasn't one bit bothered. "Thank *heavens* we were able to apply some judicious pressure to the judicial system," she said, giving an elaborate wink-wink. "And it certainly helps to know the right people."

"I'll bet," said Carmela. While her roots were English, Cajun, and a smatter of French, Margo Leland could trace her ancestry all the way back to the Vicomte François Pierre-Marie. That distant nobleman had fled France for New Orleans in 1815 following the exile of Napoleon, and had spawned an entire lineage of prominent New Orleanians. Which Margo never let anyone forget.

Margo took a quick slug of champagne and said, "Time to kick this party into high gear!" She grabbed Carmela's wrist and pulled her over to the band. Standing on tiptoe, she waved airily to the group's front man, a bearded and mulleted redhead. The musicians immediately ceased playing and a microphone was passed to Margo.

There was a momentary high-pitched squeal, then

Margo shouted out, "Everyone! Everyone! I want to thank you *so* much for coming tonight to celebrate what is truly the most splendid day of my life. And now, I'd like you all to join me in a toast. A toast to the man who puffs me with pride, the husband who still curls my toes!" She hoisted her champagne glass high in the air and paused dramatically. "To Jerry Earl!"

Jerry Earl Leland, who Carmela thought had the rather unfortunate countenance of a Galápagos turtle, was ensconced in a Louis XVI chair and deep in conversation with local businessman Buddy Pelletier. He barely looked up during Margo's heartfelt tribute. And when he finally did, aimed a perfunctory, knowing nod in the direction of the revelers. Then Jerry Earl turned back to resume his conversation.

Fueled by too much champagne, bourbon, and rich food, the tony crowd didn't seem to mind his dismissiveness. "To Jerry Earl!" they roared. Glasses clinked and laughter echoed as one hundred of New Orleans's most prominent socialites poured even more liquor down their gullets.

"You'd think Jerry Earl would be a bit more humbled," observed Ava. "On account of his being incarcerated and all."

"Doubtful," said Carmela. She didn't believe that Jerry Earl was one bit concerned, embarrassed, or mollified. She had no doubt that he'd be back doing whatever he'd been sent to prison for in less than forty-eight hours.

As if reading her mind, Ava asked, "What was he in prison for?"

"That would be your white-collar crime," said Carmela.

Ava cocked her head. "Which means . . . ?"

"Basically something fraudulent," said Carmela. She wasn't sure if Jerry Earl had engineered a phony land deal or cooked the books on a mythical corporation. And she didn't really want to know, since it was a moot point. Jerry Earl was a free man now and back in business, even though his dealings were probably nefarious.

"And Jerry Earl only did eighteen months?" Surprise colored Ava's voice.

"On a five-year sentence," said Carmela.

"Wow. I guess he got serious time off for good behavior."

"Most likely it was time off because someone was paid off."

"Ohhhh," said Ava, her eyes going wide. "Now I understand. We're talking good old-fashioned Louisiana law, politics, and cronyism."

"Which are all pretty much one and the same," said Carmela. She paused for a few moments and decided the air had gone out of the evening for her. "You know what? It's probably time to go."

"Go?" said Ava. "I thought we were just getting warmed up." She swiped a hand across her tummy. "Besides, I'm starving. And I happen to know there's an enormous dessert buffet set up in the solarium. Wouldn't you like a sugar hit to get your heart a-pumping? Maybe a slice of bread pudding soaked in brandy and dripping with ooey gooey caramel sauce?"

"Ten more minutes," said Carmela. "Then we call it a night, okay?"

"Got it," said Ava. "Besides, there are some good-looking guys here that I'd like to say how-do to. Beats scouting for a date on craigslist."

"Ten minutes," said Carmela, as they pushed through the crowd.

Like everything else in Margo's home, the dessert bar was over the top. Silver chafing dishes overflowed with bananas Foster, bread pudding, and cherries jubilee. There were plates of killer brownies, carrot cake, and pecan pie. Pastel-colored French *macarons* were stacked like poker chips.

Carmela and Ava piled up their plates, hooked up with a

couple of people they knew, then strolled out to the back patio and sat down. It was a balmy April evening with a light wind that made the humidity more than tolerable. Intoxicating jasmine blossoms and bougainvillea perfumed the air, and a giant green-winged luna moth fluttered leisurely through the dusk.

Just as Ava held a spoonful of cherries jubilee to her mouth, it dribbled down onto her silk blouse. "Oh no!" she cried, making a motion to jump up.

Carmela held out a hand. "No, stay put. If you stand up, it'll only blob down and make things worse. I'll run get a towel or something." She hurried back inside and tiptoed down a back hallway, figuring it would lead to a butler's pantry or the kitchen. When she saw a waiter bustling toward her, she made a small helpless gesture and said, "We've had a spill. Is there soda water? A towel?" But the waiter merely hooked a finger over his shoulder and continued on his way.

"Huh," said Carmela, slightly miffed. "I guess I'll have to find it myself."

But the first door she opened led to an office. Carmela poked her head in and glanced around. A cypress-paneled wall held dozens of oil paintings and awards in ornate frames. Another wall was covered in floor-to-ceiling bookshelves and crammed with shimmering geodes, fossils, gold coins set in black velvet, what looked like an Egyptian gold necklace, and glass tubes filled with gold nuggets. An enormous desk sat smack dab in the center of a black and persimmon-colored silk Aubusson carpet.

Jerry Earl's office, Carmela decided. She'd stumbled upon it from the back entrance, the servant's entrance.

Curiosity suddenly amped, Carmela took a step in and decided it was quite an amazing place. What had to be a mastodon tusk was mounted on a base of white marble. A large gold mask on a black metal stand, a gold skull of some primitive cat-like creature, and sparkling gold coins were displayed on Jerry Earl's desk, making it look for all the world like the office of some museum curator.

Amazing, Carmela thought to herself. An incredible collection of fossils and gold antiquities. Just as she was about to turn and leave, a slight breeze fluttered the curtains.

Carmela hesitated. *Someone there?*

A noise sounded just beyond the green velvet curtains. A kind of scrape, like boot heels on cement. Then a dull clunk, like something metallic.

Was someone outside? Peeking in at her? Or doing . . . what? Had someone been attracted by all this loot?

"Hello?" she called out. "Jerry Earl? Is that you?"

There was nothing save a warm breeze stirring the curtains.

Realizing she shouldn't be in here, feeling guilty and a little discombobulated, Carmela ducked back out and pulled the door closed behind her. She paused for a moment, then took another few steps down the hallway. Placing her hand on a second doorknob, she was about to pull it open when she heard a muffled thump on the other side of the door.

Oh no, what now?

A woman's voice, low and urgent, murmured, "Just one more, please? Just one eensy little line?"

A man's voice, husky and slightly taunting, said, "You sure about that, baby?"

Oh great. Carmela moved away quickly. She had a pretty good idea what the woman was asking for. She also had a fairly good idea what her boyfriend Edgar Babcock would say about that. And just to be clear, he was *Detective* Edgar Babcock of the New Orleans Police Department. Her own personal Dudley Do-Right snuggle bunny.

"He'd tell me to hustle my sweet patootie out of here," Carmela muttered to herself. "Before I got involved in some kind of drug incident."

And just as she was about to do exactly that, she heard another thump. Only this was the tell-tale thump thump thump of a clothes dryer tossing its contents to and fro.

Breathing a sigh of relief, for her errand had somehow turned into a mission, Carmela hurried to the end of the hallway and pushed open a louvered door.

A sizzle of bright fluorescents revealed a tidy, compact laundry room. It was warm, steamy, and noisy, as laundry rooms generally are when there's a load in the washer and one in the dryer.

Probably a bunch of bar towels, Carmela surmised. Or the caterer had thrown in a load of dish towels. But that wasn't quite right, was it? Because the top-loading washing machine was standing open and silent. Casting a quick glance at the loudly thumping dryer, Carmela casually wondered what they'd tossed in that was making such an awful racket.

Her eyes had almost pulled away, ready to grab a clean white towel, when she saw what looked like a leather shoe momentarily flash past the dryer's window.

What. On. Earth? Who would toss shoes in a dryer?

Feeling slightly apprehensive, Carmela took two robotic steps forward. And then, like a warning shot fired across the bow of a ship, something deep in the limbic portion of her brain spit out a cautionary note.

Something's wrong here. Something's really wrong.

Don't be silly, she told herself. There's nothing to be nervous about.

Except . . . there was that shoe.

Carmela's nose tickled. Her temples throbbed. She was suddenly aware that the air around her was redolent with a strange scent. A sweet, sickening, unnerving scent that was definitely not Downy or Febreze.

Mesmerized, moving as if she were in a trance, Carmela

stepped forward, curled her fingers around the handle of the dryer, and yanked open the door.

As the dryer groaned to a sudden halt, Carmela jumped back just in time to see a limp hand flop out. And then watched in horror as the bloody, battered body of Jerry Earl Leland spilled out onto the tiled white floor.

WATCH FOR THE NEXT
TEA SHOP MYSTERY

Steeped in Evil

What began as an elegant black-tie event at the museum spirals into a bizarre murder. Who is the killer with a taste for blood and an impeccable taste in art? Can Theodosia find him before she becomes a target, too?

AND ALSO THE NEXT
CACKLEBERRY CLUB MYSTERY
BY LAURA CHILDS

Eggs in a Casket

When Suzanne and Toni deliver flowers to a local cemetery, they discover an open grave and the crumpled body of one of Kindred's most prominent citizens. There wasn't a funeral, there aren't any mourners—so it must be murder!

This is a cozy café series everyone will enjoy—three crazy ladies on the high side of forty who serve eggs in the morning, tea in the afternoon, and murder on the side!

Living a Tea Shop Life

Drinking Tea, Finding Balance,
and Reclaiming Your Creative Spirit.

A nonfiction book that applies life lessons learned from tea shops and tea masters to everyday life. Learn how to de-stress, amp up your creativity, tap your inner entrepreneur, and develop your own personal "you" brand. Also included are more than a hundred recipes and tea time tips.